✔ KU-662-099

Lisa
Scottoline
Dirty Blonde

PAN BOOKS

First published 2006 by HarperCollins Publishers Inc, New York

First published in Great Britain in paperback 2007 by Pan Books
an imprint of Pan Macmillan Ltd
Pan Macmillan, 20 New Wharf Road, London N1 9RR
Basingstoke and Oxford
Associated companies throughout the world
www.panmacmillan.com

ISBN 978-0-330-51656-3

FT Pbk

Copyright © Lisa Scottoline 2006

The right of Lisa Scottoline to be identified as the
author of this work has been asserted by her in accordance
with the Copyright, Designs and Patents Act 1988.

All rights reserved. No part of this publication may be
reproduced, stored in or introduced into a retrieval system, or
transmitted, in any form, or by any means (electronic, mechanical,
photocopying, recording or otherwise) without the prior written
permission of the publisher. Any person who does any unauthorized
act in relation to this publication may be liable to criminal
prosecution and civil claims for damages.

9 8 7 6 5 4 3 2 1

A CIP catalogue record for this book is available from
the British Library.

Printed and bound in the UK by
CPI Mackays, Chatham ME5 8TD

This book is sold subject to the condition that it shall not,
by way of trade or otherwise, be lent, re-sold, hired out,
or otherwise circulated without the publisher's prior consent
in any form of binding or cover other than that in which
it is published and without a similar condition including this
condition being imposed on the subsequent purchaser.

FOR LAURA

My girlfriends are the sisters I picked out for myself.

—*Mary-Margaret Martinez*

Justice is but truth in action.

—*Justice Louis Brandeis, Supreme Court of the United States*

Dirty Blonde

Cate Fante was the guest of honor at this celebration, which was drawing to a liquefied close. She raised a final snifter of cognac, joining the judges toasting her appointment to the district court. Tomorrow would be a slow day on the bench. The wheels of justice weren't lubricated by Remy Martin.

"To Judge Cate Fante, our new colleague!" Chief Judge Sherman shouted, and the judges clinked glasses with a costly chime. Wrinkled cheeks draped their tipsy smiles, and their bifocals reflected the flickering candlelight. Their average age was sixty-two, and an appointment to the federal bench was for life. At thirty-nine, Cate felt like she was joining the world's most exclusive retirement village.

"Speech, speech!" the judges called out, their encouragement echoing in the private room. Golden light glowed from brass sconces, and coffee cooled next to scalloped half-moons of crème brûlée and bread pudding veined with cinnamon. "Speech, Judge Fante!"

"Order in the court, you crazy kids," Cate called back, rising with her glass and only apparent bravado. She managed a smile that masked her panic about what to say. She couldn't tell the truth: namely, that she was secretly intimidated by a job described in the Constitution of the United States. Or that she only looked the part, in a Chanel suit of butterscotch tweed, donned like overpriced armor.

"Keep it short, Cate." Judge William Sasso formed a megaphone with his hands. "It's past my bedtime."

Judge Gloria Sullivan chuckled. "Give her a break, Bill. We listen to you, and God knows what a trial that can be."

"No, he's right." Cate gathered her nerve. "Thank you for this lovely dinner, everyone. You said a lot of nice things about me tonight, and I just want you to know—I *deserve* every single word."

"At last, an honest judge!" Chief Judge Sherman burst into laughter, as did the others. The young waiter smiled, hovering by the wall. The judges clapped, shouting, "Way to go!" "Well done!"

"Thank you and good night." Cate mock-bowed and caught the waiter's eye, then looked away. She accepted the congratulations and good-byes as the judges rose to leave, collecting their briefcases and bags. She grabbed her purse and they all walked to the door, filing out of the Four Seasons restaurant. On the way out, Cate felt a soft touch on her arm and turned to see Chief Judge Sherman, tall and stooped at her shoulder, his sterling silver hair slightly frizzy.

"Don't look so happy, kiddo. You're taking a major pay cut."

Cate laughed. "Chief, you give fixed income a good name."

Chief Judge Sherman laughed, as did Judge Jonathan Meriden, who fell into stride. Meriden was fifty-something, conventionally handsome, with sandy hair going to gray and a fit, if short, stature. Cate had legal history with Meriden. When they were both in practice, he'd tried a securities case against her and ended up losing the jury verdict and the client. Tonight he'd acted as if all was forgotten, so he'd sucked it up or warmed to her, with Glenlivet's help. They walked out of the lobby into the humid summer night, and Cate played the good hostess, waiting, until everyone had dispersed, to grab the last cab.

Inside, she leaned against the black vinyl as the cab lurched into light traffic. Its tires rumbled on the gritty streets, wet from an earlier thunderstorm. The air conditioning blew only faintly, and Cate eyed the rain-slick buildings like a stranger to the city. She'd lived in Philadelphia since law school, but her heart wasn't in the city. She'd grown up in the mountains, in a small town erased from the map. Cate still felt a twinge at the thought, even though she knew she wasn't supposed to care about her hometown anymore. She was pretty sure the official cutoff was fourth grade.

Cate's head began to ache. Today she'd presided over opening arguments in her first major trial, a construction contract case with damages of fifty million dollars. Fleets of pricey lawyers from New York had filed special appearances, and the witness lists contained more PhDs than most colleges. It was a bench trial, with no jury to make the decision, but at least it was a civil case. Cate had already sentenced four men to federal prison, which was four too many.

The cab was stifling, and Cate lowered the window. A breeze blew in, too sticky to offer any relief, and she unbuttoned the top of her silk blouse. She felt the weight of her pearls like a noose. The night sky was black and starless, and the full moon a spotlight. She leaned back against the seat but her chignon got in the way, so she loosened it with her fingers.

She looked idly out the window. Couples walked together, their arms wrapped around each other, their hips bumping. A handsome man in a white oxford shirt dashed across the street, his tie flying. The cab turned onto one of the skinny backstreets that scored Center City, no more than an alley with rusted blue Dumpsters lining the curb. Cate caught a whiff of the rotting smell. "The scenic route, huh?"

"It's faster than South," the driver said, and the cab slowed to a stop sign, waiting for someone to cross the street.

Cate eyed a rundown tavern on the corner. DEL & ROY's flickered a failing neon sign, and graffiti blanketed its brick. Its side window was covered with plywood, though an amber glow emanated from yellow Plexiglas in the front door, which was the only indication the bar wasn't abandoned.

It's Miller time, Cate thought. The line from an old TV commercial. Her mother used to drink Miller. *The champagne of bottled beer.*

"I'll get out here," she said suddenly, digging in her purse for the fare.

"Here?" The driver twisted around on his side of the smudged plastic divider. "Lady, this ain't the best block. I thought we were going to Society Hill."

"Change of plans." Cate slid a twenty from her wallet and handed it to him. Ten minutes later, she was perched on a wobbly bar stool behind a glass of Miller. Lipstick stained the rim of her glass, a sticky red kiss slashed with lines, like vanity's own fingerprint. It wasn't her color, but she drank anyway.

The bar reeked of stale draft and Marlboros, and dusty liquor bottles cluttered its back underneath a cardboard cutout of Donovan McNabb, set askew. The bar area doubled as a hallway to a closed dining room, its darkened doorway marked by an old-fashioned sign that read LADIES' ENTRANCE. Cate looked away.

The bar was half-empty, and a man with dark hair hunched over a beer two seats from her, smoking a cigarette. He wore a white T-shirt that said C&C TOWING, stretching in block letters across a muscular back. Three men sat beyond him, silently watching the baseball game, the Phillies playing San Francisco, on a TV mounted above the bar. They watched with their heads tilted back, their bald spots an ellipsis.

Cate crossed her legs, bare in her brown pumps, and took a sip of warm beer. She hated herself for being here, and at the same time, wondered how long it would take. It wasn't that she wanted to get home to sleep. She could function on almost none, from a childhood interrupted by nighttime alarms. She'd be pulled from bed and dressed in a winter coat with an embroidered penguin, worn over a thin nightgown. The coat was turquoise and the penguin of raised black fuzz, she remembered now, for some reason. She had loved that coat.

"Hey," said a voice beside her, and Cate looked over. It was the man in the T-shirt, with his beer and Marlboro. Up close, he had bloodshot blue eyes, heavy stubble, and hair that shone in greasy strands. He smiled drunkenly and asked, "How're you, beautiful?"

Cate turned to him and smiled. "Evidently, beautiful."

The man chuckled and set his beer on the bar, his cigarette trailing a snake of smoke. "I think I know you from somewhere," he said, putting his hand on Cate's bare knee. "Whas' your name again?"

"Karen," Cate told him, then moved his hand up onto her thigh.

Feeling thrilled and miserable, both at once.

CHAPTER 1

Six months later, Cate sat in her high-backed chair atop the dais, waiting to start the day's session. The courtroom was packed, and she hid her anticipation behind a professional mask, which was turning out to be a job requirement. The jury trial had taken all last week, but today was the only day that counted, like the final two minutes in a basketball game.

Sixers-Hornets. It was on at the bar last night. Wonder who won.

Cate shifted behind the slippery wall of stacked pleadings in front of her. She hadn't slept well last night and was relying on her concealer, but was otherwise in full costume: synthetic black robes, dark blond hair in a judicial chignon, a swipe of pink gloss on her lips, and neutral makeup on largish, blue eyes. Finally the courtroom deputy flashed Cate a wink.

Showtime. Cate gestured to plaintiff's counsel. "Mr. Temin, let's begin. I assume that plaintiff continues his testimony this morning."

"Yes, Your Honor." Nathan Temin was a roly-poly lawyer with the paunch of a much older man and a dark suit that begged to be ironed, worn with equally unruly black hair. Still, Cate knew better than to judge a trial lawyer by his cover. She had dressed down for court many times. Prada didn't win jury verdicts.

"Excellent." Cate nodded. "Fire when ready."

"Thank you, Your Honor." Temin hustled to the podium with a Bic pen and a legal pad, then pressed down his suit with a pudgy hand. He greeted the jury and turned to his client, already rising from counsel table. "Mr. Marz, please take the stand."

Richard Marz walked to the witness stand, and necks craned from the gallery. Reporters scribbled away, and sketch artists switched to their flesh-toned chalk. The Eastern District of Pennsylvania didn't allow cameras in the courtroom, for which Cate thanked God and Chief Judge Sherman.

"Good morning, Your Honor," Marz said in his soft-spoken way, sitting down after he was sworn in. He was barely thirty years old, and his baby-blue eyes showed litigation strain. He smiled tightly, his lips taut as a rubber band, and he ran a finger rake through muddy-brown curls that sprouted from under a crocheted yarmulke. A dark suit jacket popped open over his white shirt, and his striped tie hung unevenly. Everybody knew that people looked like their dogs, but Cate thought they looked like their lawyers.

"Good morning, Mr. Marz." She smiled at Marz in a professional way, feeling subterranean sympathy for his position. He was claiming that a powerful TV producer had stolen his idea for a series about Philadelphia lawyers and developed it into the cable blockbuster *Attorneys@Law*. In this battle between David and Goliath, Marz held the slingshot.

At the lectern, Temin tugged the black bud of a microphone down to his height. "Now, Mr. Marz, you testified last week that you had two meetings with Mr. Simone, leading up to the critical meeting. Please remind the jury of what took place at the first meeting, on June 10."

"Objection, Your Honor," said George Hartford, defense counsel. Hartford had gray eyes behind slightly tinted bifocals and was prematurely bald. He had to be about fifty, and stood tall and fit in a slim Italian suit with a yellow silk tie. "Asked and answered. Plaintiff's counsel is wasting the jury's time."

Temin said, "Your Honor, it's appropriate to review this proof because the weekend intervened."

"Overruled." Cate shot both lawyers her sternest look. "Let's not let the objections get out of hand today, boys. Play nice."

"Thank you, Your Honor." Temin nodded, but a cranky Hartford eased back in his chair next to his client, producer Art Simone. Even seated, Simone looked tall and trim, in his prime at a prosperous forty-something. His reddish hair had been shorn fashionably close to his scalp, and his tortoiseshell glasses paired with a caramel-colored silk tie and tan houndstooth suit. If Marz and Temin were the mutts in this dogfight, Simone and Hartford were purebred afghans.

"Mr. Marz," Temin began again, "tell us briefly what happened at the June meeting with Mr. Simone."

"Well, my background is from the DA's office, handling cases concerning computer fraud and Internet crime. I always liked computers." Marz sounded almost apologetic. "But I wanted to be a writer, so I started writing a screenplay for a TV show about four lawyers and how they use computer skills to solve murders. I called it *Hard Drive*. It was my wife who said, 'Why don't you do something about it?'" Marz smiled at his wife in the front row of the gallery, a sweet-faced brunette wearing a long skirt and sensible shoes. "So I called Art—Mr. Simone—and told him what I was doing and asked if he would meet with me about it, and he agreed to fly out to Philly to take the meeting." Marz turned to the jury in an earnest way. "That's what they call it in L.A., 'taking a meeting.' When they say no, they call it 'taking a hard pass.' A 'soft pass' is a maybe. I thought a soft pass was about sex, but what do I know?"

The jurors chuckled with evident warmth. Nobody loved underdogs like Philly.

Temin asked, "Had you known Mr. Simone, prior?"

"Yes, I knew him from summer camp from when I was, like, ten years old. Camp Willowbark, Unit A. He was my senior counselor, and I looked up to him like a big brother. I heard he was doing TV in Hollywood, so I hoped he'd help me out."

"And what happened at the meeting, briefly?"

"We met at Le Bec Fin and I told him all the details about my idea and asked him would he consider it for his production company. The lead lawyer in my series is a former detective, an Italian guy from South Philly who dresses great and is, like, a tie freak—"

"You needn't repeat the details," Temin interjected, preempting Hartford's objection.

"Okay, right, sorry. All that's important is that the four lawyers I told Mr. Simone about ended up being exactly like the four lawyers on *Attorneys@Law.*"

"Objection, opinion!" Hartford said, and Cate waved him off.

"Overruled. The jury knows it's his opinion."

Temin paused. "By the way, Mr. Marz, were you surprised that Mr. Simone flew here to see you, as opposed to you flying out to California to see him?"

"I was, but he said he wanted to visit his mom anyway. She lives in a nursing home in Jersey." Marz's expression darkened. "Now I think he said to meet in Philly because Pennsylvania law is tougher than California law on—"

"Objection!" Hartford shouted, next to a stiffening client, and Cate raised a hand.

"Granted. That's enough opinion, Mr. Marz. Don't make me sorry."

The jury smiled, and Temin asked, "Did Mr. Simone take notes during this meeting?"

"No."

"Now, Mr. Marz, let's jump to the second meeting on September 15 and 16, also in Philadelphia. Who was present?"

"Myself, Detective Russo, and Mr. Simone and his assistant, Micah Gilbert."

"Is that Ms. Gilbert, seated in the gallery behind Mr. Simone?"

"Yes." Marz gestured to a pretty young woman in the front row. Micah Gilbert had attended the trial since day one, sitting next to an attractive jury consultant whose chin-length hair was an optimistic shade of red.

"What happened at that meeting?"

"Mr. Simone came to Philly to meet with me and a friend from the Homicide Division, Detective Frank Russo. Russo was the role model for the main character in my show, the South Philly guy. On the first day, we met at Liberties in Northern Liberties. I picked the place because real detectives hang there."

The jurors' eyes had lit up with recognition. The restaurant in *Attorneys@Law* was also called Liberties, and most of them had seen the show. It was impossible to find anyone in America who hadn't, despite Hartford's best efforts. The defense lawyer had used his three preemptory strikes to eliminate as many viewers as possible, with the help of his redheaded jury consultant. Cate never used a consultant. Picking a jury was Trial Lawyer 101.

"Now, what took place at Liberties?"

"Detective Russo and I told Mr. Simone about our characters and storylines. Also, I gave him some info on computers." Marz's gaze slid sideways to Simone. "Because he doesn't know anything about them."

"Did Mr. Simone or Ms. Gilbert take notes while you were talking?"

"No."

"Did you think that was strange?"

"I didn't then but now I think he didn't want a record of—"

"Objection! That's speculation again, Your Honor. Move that the irrelevant evidence be stricken." Hartford rose, but Cate waved him into his seat.

"Granted." Cate turned to Marz, on the stand. "Please refrain from editorializing."

Temin continued, "And what happened after lunch at Liberties?"

"Detective Russo and I took Mr. Simone and Ms. Gilbert to the Roundhouse, the police administration building, and we told him how things really work in Homicide. We showed him some details about the squad room, like how the detectives prop the door open with an old trash can and they never notice that the trash can stinks, only visitors do." Marz turned again to the jury. "The trash can matters, because it tells you about the characters. How they get so used to bad stuff, like the ugliness they see every day on the job."

Several of the jurors nodded soberly and one cast a cold eye at defense table. If the jury got the case now, they'd vote for Marz and his symbolic trash can.

"And what did you do the second day?"

"Detective Russo and I drove Mr. Simone and Ms. Gilbert around the neighborhoods where the stories took place. It's called 'scouting locations.'"

Temin turned a page on his legal pad. "Finally, we come to your critical meeting with Mr. Simone, on November 9, also at Le Bec Fin. Who was present at the meeting?"

"Me and Mr. Simone."

"And what took place at this lunch meeting?"

"Mr. Simone said we were celebrating. He ordered champagne, two bottles, even though I'm not a big drinker." Marz shot a resentful glance at defense table. "Anyway I told him I had the treatment ready ahead of schedule and I gave it to him."

"Please explain to the jury what a treatment is."

"A treatment is a detailed outline of who the characters are and what the storylines would be. I had told Mr. Simone I'd get the treatment done by August, but I couldn't do it and my job at the DA's office, so I quit my job."

"Your Honor, may I approach?" Temin asked, and Cate nodded. He took from counsel table three thick black binders labeled HARD DRIVE and gave one to Hartford, one to the court clerk, and walked to the witness stand, handing the third to Marz. "Mr. Marz, is this the treatment that you wrote and gave to Mr. Simone?"

"Yes," Marz answered, examining the notebook, which was admitted into evidence. Temin turned again to his witness.

"Did Mr. Simone take notes at the luncheon?"

"No."

Temin let the implication sink in. "And then what happened?"

"Then Mr. Simone said—"

"Objection, hearsay," Hartford called out, his shiny Mont Blanc poised in midair, and Temin stiffened.

"It's not hearsay, Your Honor."

"Overruled." Cate turned to Marz. "Please. Go ahead."

"He said he was going to get the show ready to be produced and when he got it together, he'd call me. He was very excited, and we made a deal."

"Objection to the characterization, Your Honor!" Hartford called out louder, rising. "There was no deal in this matter!"

"Yes, there was!" Temin matched him decibel for decibel, and Cate raised her hand, like a stop sign.

"Gentlemen, enough. The objection is overruled. Mr. Hartford, the plaintiff can give his side of the story in his testimony, and your client can give his side. It has a nice symmetry, yes?" Cate gestured at Temin. "Proceed."

"Mr. Marz, what was the deal between you and Mr. Simone?"

"The deal was that he would produce my idea as a TV series, and he said, 'If I make money, you'll make money.'"

"He said those words?" Temin asked, and back at defense table, Hartford shook his head in mute frustration. Simone remained stoic.

Marz answered, "Verbatim."

"Is it possible that you misheard him? You testified that you had been drinking champagne. Maybe he said, 'Pass the salt?'"

"No, I heard him perfectly. Plus he already had the salt."

The jury laughed, and so did the gallery. Temin was trying to take the sting out of the cross-examination to come, but Cate didn't think it would do any good. She disguised her concern, resting her chin on her fist.

"Mr. Marz, seriously, how can you be so sure?"

"Because I had been wondering about when we were going to discuss money. My wife kept wanting me to ask him, but it was never the right time." Marz reddened, and his wife looked down. "So when he said that, I knew we had a real deal."

"Did you and Mr. Simone put this deal into writing?"

"We didn't need to, at least I didn't *think* we needed to." Marz scowled. "We're friends, *were* friends. He was my senior counselor. I trusted him to take care of me." Marz pursed his lips, and his disillusionment hung in the air between him and the jurors.

On the bench, Cate was about to burst, but instead wrote on her pad, DIDN'T LAW SCHOOL CURE YOU OF TRUSTING OTHERS?

Temin said, "Mr. Marz, some jurors might not understand that you, as a lawyer, would go so far without a written contract. What would you say to that?"

"I'd say they were right, but lawyers are people, too." Marz turned again to the jury. "I admit, I got carried away with the whole Hollywood thing. He has a jet. A limo. He knows all these famous people. I felt cool for the first time in my life. I may have been naïve, but that doesn't change the fact that Art Simone stole my show."

"No further questions," Temin said, but Hartford was already on his feet.

"I have cross-examination, Your Honor."

Cate nodded, and Hartford strode to the lectern vacated by Temin.

He began in a clipped tone, "Mr. Marz, just a few quick questions about this alleged deal. You admit it was never put in writing?"

"It was an oral agreement. Oral agreements are made every day. It's called an 'if-come' deal, standard in California."

Cate picked up her pen. PLEASE, GOD, HELP THIS BOY. CAN'T YOU SEE HIS YARMULKE?

Hartford bore down. "Mr. Marz, I repeat, this deal wasn't written, was it? Yes or no."

"No, it wasn't."

"Now, you and Mr. Simone didn't discuss any specific terms of this deal, did you?"

"As I testified, he said, 'If I make money, you'll make money.'"

"Perhaps you misunderstood me." Hartford squared his padded shoulders. "I meant, you and Mr. Simone did not discuss a specific price for your idea, did you?"

"I gave him the treatment for *Hard Drive*, too," Marz added.

"I'll amend my question. You and Mr. Simone didn't discuss a specific price for your idea and your treatment, did you?"

"No."

"You didn't discuss when, where, or how any payment would be made, did you?"

"No."

"You didn't discuss who would pay you, whether it would be Mr. Simone or his production company, did you?"

"No."

"So you discussed no specifics of this supposed deal at your luncheon meeting, did you?"

"No."

"How about in any of the phone calls or the e-mails between the two of you, about which you testified last week?"

"No, as I said, because—"

"Yes or no."

"No," Marz answered reluctantly. His mouth snapped back into its rubber band, and the jurors eyed him, a sympathetic furrowing of their collective brow. They'd not only hold Simone liable for damages, they'd have him drawn and quartered.

"No further questions," Hartford said, finishing his cross more quickly than anyone except Cate had anticipated.

"Mr. Temin, any redirect?" she asked.

"Yes, Your Honor." Temin returned to the lectern and embarked upon a series of questions that rehashed old ground, and Cate sustained two of Hartford's objections for good measure. But the testimony didn't change anything, and by its conclusion, she adjourned court for lunch, grabbing her legal pad as she rose.

On it, she had written: IS THE ONLY JUSTICE ON TV?

CHAPTER 2

Cate understood on sight why Detective Frank Russo could be a fictional character. His craggy skin served as a rough canvas for dark eyes, a prominent forehead, and heavy, sensuous lips. His shiny hair, a suspicious shade of black, matched a pair of longish sideburns. He wasn't tall, about five nine, but powerful shoulders stretched his dark jacket across a broad back, and a flashy tie of red silk proclaimed him the aforementioned "tie freak." He sat forward in the witness stand, leaning to the black bud of a microphone.

"Going back to that two-day meeting, who asked you to come, Detective?" Temin asked, getting to the point.

"Mr. Marz."

"Did he say why?"

"Yes."

"What did he say?"

"He wanted me to help Mr. Simone with research."

"Where did you meet?"

"Liberties."

Up on the dais, Cate hid her smile. Russo's testimony was to the point, typical for law enforcement personnel. Detectives appeared in court so frequently they answered only the question asked and never

volunteered a word. Cate sympathized with poor Temin, struggling
to pull teeth from even his own witness.

"And by 'help Mr. Simone out with his research,' what do you
mean, specifically?"

"Give him the standard operating procedures in the Homicide Division. Tell him how we handle murder cases, work with the ADA,
and whatnot."

"Did you do anything after Liberties that day?"

"Yes."

"And what did you do? And please, explain as fully as possible."

Russo arched an offended eyebrow, like Italian kabuki. "Mr. Marz
asked myself to give Mr. Simone and his assistant a tour of the Roundhouse, which I did. I showed him the squad room, I let him see the
interview rooms. I introduced him to the guys, too. I was real popular that day." Russo chuckled, and so did everyone else.

"Detective, did Mr. Simone ask you any questions that day?"

"He asked about our slang. He said he wanted to make the character talk like a real detective."

"What did you tell him?"

"We speak English."

The gallery laughed again, as did the jury and the deputy, loving
every minute.

"Detective Russo, did Mr. Simone take notes on what you said at
the meeting?"

"No."

"Was his assistant with him?"

"Yes."

"Did she take notes?"

"No."

"Tell me, did you think that was strange?"

"I think everything about Hollywood people is strange," Russo answered deadpan, and the gallery laughed. So did Cate, caught off-guard.

Temin waited a beat. "Detective Russo, what happened the second day of your meeting with Mr. Simone?"

"Mr. Marz and myself drove Mr. Simone and his assistant down Delaware Avenue and other neighborhoods, not-so-nice ones in North Philly."

"And what took place during this drive?"

"Mr. Marz told them where the characters in the show would live, where their law office would be, and where they'd each lunch and whatnot. He also told about his experiences as an ADA. Rich is young, but before he started with the computer crimes, he tried a murder case and major felonies."

"Did you provide information during the drive, too?"

"No."

Temin blinked. "What did you do?"

"Drove."

"Then why were you there?"

"Protection."

The jury and the gallery laughed. Cate looked down, behind her fist.

Detective Russo added, "For the record, I used my vacation days to do this. The city didn't foot the bill."

Temin cleared his throat. "Detective Russo, did Mr. Marz ever discuss with you the terms of his deal with Mr. Simone?"

"Objection, irrelevant and calls for hearsay!" Hartford said, rising, but Temin shook his head.

"Your Honor, as you have said, relevance is broadly defined and it's coming in only for the fact that it was said."

"Overruled." On the dais, Cate turned to the witness. "You may answer, Detective."

"Yes, Mr. Marz discussed the deal with me," Russo said.

"And what did he say?"

"Continuing objection," Hartford said, and Cate nodded.

"Noted, Counsel. Detective Russo, you may answer the question."

"Mr. Marz told me that he made a deal with Mr. Simone and that Simone was gonna pay him when he got paid, like a contingency fee."

"When did Mr. Marz tell you this, Detective?"

"Right after his lunch with Simone. He called me on his cell, walking down Walnut Street, all excited. He thought we were gonna be players." Russo smiled in a benevolent way. "Rich gets like that, carried away, like he said. He's like a little kid."

Temin paused, letting it register. "Let's switch gears, Detective. Did you make a deal with Mr. Marz to be compensated for your time and services?"

"With Rich? Yes."

"What was your deal with Mr. Marz?"

"Objection, relevance!" Hartford rose.

"Overruled. Relevance is broadly defined in the Federal Rules, Mr. Hartford, and this is certainly within its definition." Cate turned again to Russo. "Go ahead and answer, Detective."

"Thank you, Your Honor." Russo faced Temin. "Mr. Marz and I had an agreement that we'd be equal partners when Mr. Simone produced the show. That I wouldn't get any upfront money but when the show got made, I'd make whatever he made."

"Did you consider that generous?"

"Yes and no." Russo raised a large, cautionary hand. "Don't get me wrong. Mr. Marz is an all right kid, but him and myself, we spent a lotta time developing the ideas for the series. Working at night, making up the four characters and their histories. The lead was gonna be me, the good-lookin' one."

Again, smiles all around, but for Cate, who knew the ending to this episode.

"Detective, was it your intention to quit your job after the show was produced?"

"Yeah, but this woulda been like winning the lottery. Marz quit his job to work on it full-time." Russo shot Simone a hard look. "Glad I kept mine, the way it turned out."

"Detective Russo, was your agreement with Mr. Marz ever written down?"

"We shook on it, and that was good enough for us." Russo eyed the jury, who got the message, rapt, to a member.

"No further questions," Temin said, obviously pleased, and took his seat.

Cate faced defense counsel. "Any cross, Mr. Hartford?"

"Thank you, Your Honor," he answered, standing up and approaching the lectern. "Mr. Russo, to the best of your knowledge, was the alleged agreement between Mr. Simone and Mr. Marz ever reduced to a written contract?"

"No."

"Thank you, Detective Russo." Hartford looked at the dais. "No further questions, Your Honor."

Temin stood up. "No redirect, Your Honor, and plaintiff rests its case-in-chief. We would like to reserve rebuttal."

"Of course, and thank you, Mr. Temin." Cate excused Detective Russo from the stand and looked expectantly at defense table.

Hartford stood tall. "I would like to call Arthur Simone to the stand, if I may."

"You may," Cate answered, shifting forward in her chair. She wanted to hear from this character.

CHAPTER 3

From the lectern, Hartford asked, "Mr. Simone, could you tell the jury a little bit about yourself?"

"Sure. I'm from Reno and went to UNLV, in Vegas. Graduated an English major. You know what that means, job-wise." Simone smiled crookedly. "'Hello, my name is Art and I'll be your waiter tonight.'"

A chuckle ran though the gallery, especially from the redheaded jury consultant and Simone's assistant, Micah Gilbert. Gilbert, who looked to be in her early thirties, sat with her legs crossed in tight pants, and her long, dark hair flowed to her shoulders in a sexy curl. She took almost constant notes, and Cate couldn't help wondering if her dedication to her boss was more than professional.

"I went to law school at Hastings, but as much as I loved reading cases, I got bored. I don't know how law school manages to make winning and losing, life and death, justice and injustice so deadly dull." Simone scoffed, and his fine hands rested on the edge of the polished wood, showing a thick gold wedding band. "I always loved TV, so I moved to L.A. and got into the business as a gofer, then moved up to producing my own true-crime shows and selling them to cable markets. Then I started writing and producing *Attorneys@Law*."

Hartford flipped a page of his legal pad. "Mr. Simone, you heard

Mr. Marz testify that he gave you the idea for the series that eventually became *Attorneys@Law*, didn't you?"

"Yes, I did hear him say that."

"Is that true?"

"No." Simone's good humor faded. "No. Absolutely not."

Cate saw Marz lean forward in his chair at counsel table.

"Mr. Simone, what gave you the idea for *Attorneys@Law*?"

"My imagination. One day in the shower, I realized that none of the current lawyer shows showed the inside view. The way lawyers really work, in court and out. So I said, if I want to see it, I guess I have to write it, and that was that."

"Did you copy the idea from anyone or anywhere?"

"Of course not. Let me state the obvious. The idea of a lawyer show isn't copyrightable, and it isn't even new, and there were four main lawyers in *L.A. Law*, *Ally McBeal*, and *Boston Legal*. Marz didn't invent it, and neither did I. It started as far back as Perry Mason, and I live in the same world as anybody else." Simone shifted forward, warming to the discussion, though Hartford's confused expression suggested that his client was veering from their script. "By that I mean, I'm influenced by reality, by my own life. I'm being sued in this ridiculous lawsuit, and on the bench sits an attractive woman judge, with real star power." Simone turned suddenly toward the dais. "Do you mind if I suck up, Judge Fante?"

Cate flushed, caught off-balance. "Is this relevant?"

"Yes, of course. I'm trying to explain that my ideas often come from my life. For example, I could turn this very lawsuit into a TV series. Write a spin-off from *Attorneys@Law*, and call it *Judges@Court*. And it could star a blond female judge who's a lot like you, Judge Fante. Charismatic, attention-getting. The most alive person in the room. What do you think?"

Cate stiffened at the flattery, but the jurors and gallery held their breath, waiting for her reaction. Most federal judges would have admonished him, but that wouldn't defuse anything. She answered, "Great idea. Get Charlize Theron, for me."

"Done!" Simone laughed, and so did everyone else.

Hartford cleared his throat. "Now, Mr. Simone, were you ever friends with Mr. Marz?"

"No, not at all. He was one of my campers, that's it. Long story short, we barely stayed in touch over the years. We were never close."

At counsel table, Marz scowled, and his wife looked equally unhappy.

Hartford asked, "Were you sitting in this courtroom when Mr. Marz testified that he met with you on three occasions?"

"Yes, I did hear Mr. Marz testify, but what took place at them wasn't what Mr. Marz said. At the June meeting, Mr. Marz told me he had an idea for a TV series, and I gave him my time because he was a nice kid and he was in dire straits. Things weren't working out for him at the DA's office and—"

"Objection," Temin interrupted.

"Overruled." Cate shook her head, and Simone continued before she directed to do so.

"Mr. Marz said he wanted a new career. I thought I'd do him a favor and listen to him talk. But that's it, and that's all. I promised him nothing, I offered nothing." Simone turned to the jury, his tone newly agitated. "His idea isn't what became *Attorneys@Law*. I was already working on the scripts for *Attorneys @Law* when we met and I set it in Philly because I'm from here, too. It's pure coincidence that both shows are about lawyers. What show isn't about lawyers and crime these days? *Law & Order. Monk. The Sopranos. CSI.* They're all the same hook."

The jurors looked disapproving, obviously disbelieving Simone in this credibility contest. Even the courtroom deputy looked down, examining his nails, his fingers curled like a grappling hook.

"Mr. Simone, skip ahead to the final meeting at Le Bec Fin. You heard Mr. Marz testify that you and he made a deal at this meeting, and you allegedly said to him, 'If I make money, you'll make money.' Did you hear him testify to that effect?"

"Yes, I heard that, but it's absolutely not true. We had no agreement or deal. I never intended to buy his idea or his treatment, and I never, ever said I would. And I certainly *never* said, 'If I make money, you make money.'"

At counsel table, Marz gasped, and Temin touched his arm to silence him.

Hartford asked, "Did you discuss a price term? That is, how much you would pay Mr. Marz for his idea?"

"No, not at all. He'd quit his job at the DA's office to work on his treatment, and I listened to him talk and nodded a lot, which is all I did to encourage him. I wanted to cheer him up."

"Did he cheer up?"

"After a few bottles of Dom, everybody cheers up."

The jurors didn't laugh, and Cate knew they didn't get the Dom reference. She wouldn't have, either, but for her legal education.

Mr. Hartford made a note. "Let me ask you a question. If you didn't want to buy his ideas, why did you accept his notebooks?"

"I couldn't not. He kept insisting, so I took them. As soon as I left the restaurant, I threw them in a trash can."

At plaintiff's table, Marz stirred, and so did his wife, behind him.

"Now, to finish up, did there come a time when you heard from Mr. Marz again?"

"Yes, he attempted to contact me a few times after that, but I didn't respond. I was busy, and he asked me if I read his treatment, which I hadn't, as I said. Then when *Attorneys@Law* became a hit, Mr. Marz wrote to me, alleging that I stole his idea. Then he filed this lawsuit against me and my production company." Resentment edged Simone's voice. "You know the saying, 'No good deed goes unpunished.'"

"Thank you, Mr. Simone." Hartford flipped the pad closed and looked up at Cate. "Your Honor, I have no further questions."

"I have cross, Your Honor." Temin shot to his feet.

"Go ahead, Counsel," Cate said, and the plaintiff's lawyer began an earnest cross-examination of Simone that didn't change anyone's view, least of all hers.

Hartford rose to his feet. "Your Honor, at this time, the defendant moves for a judgment as a matter of law under Rule 50."

Temin argued, "Your Honor, plaintiff opposes any such motion."

Cate banged the gavel. *Crak*! "Arguments at eight o'clock tomorrow morning, gentlemen."

She left the bench, checking her watch on the fly: 5:05. She had to get going.

She had a standing date.

CHAPTER 4

"Honey, I'm home!" Cate called out, and from the kitchen came a laugh. She let herself into the town house and shut the front door against the cold night.

The living room was dark, but light and music emanated from the kitchen. At this hour, her best friend, Gina Katsakis, would be washing leftover dishes and playing Mozart on the Bose. Of necessity, this household ran on a rigid schedule and listened 24-7 to *The Magic Flute*. And Gina, the biggest disco fan in their law school class, had adapted to that change in her life, and many others.

Cate set her purse and an aromatic brown bag on an end table, then slid out of her sheepskin coat, shook off the winter chill, and turned on a table lamp. The light illuminated a living room littered with toys, but it was no ordinary kiddie clutter. An orange Fisher Price sliding board had been upended, color flashcards and activity books had been strewn among dry Cheerios, and a Minute Maid juice box spilled over a denim beanbag chair. Cate picked up the juice box, then collected the flashcards and stowed them in the Reebok shoe box.

"Fante, stop cleaning!" Gina called from the kitchen.

"In a minute!" Cate picked up an activity book, lying open to a page titled ALL ABOUT ME, updated with a new photo. An adorable little boy with round brown eyes and shiny brown-black hair, whose bangs had been scissored off in a raggedy homemade cut, posed in front of a landscape found only in Wal-Mart's photo department. A closer look at the picture revealed that the child's gaze focused to the right of the camera, and his smile curved off-kilter. Cate reshelved the book, picked up a BabyGap sweatshirt, and set it on the couch.

"Stop now!"

"Gimme a minute!" Cate brushed the Cheerios back into an over-turned Dixie cup and stood up, having improved the room only because it was so small, a far cry from Gina's predivorce Tudor in suburban Villanova.

"Don't make me yell!"

Cate grabbed the trash and brown bag and went into the kitchen, where Gina stood at the sink in an oversized pink cable knit, and mom jeans that couldn't hide a killer body. She was emptying a large pot of boiling water into the basin, steaming up the window and filling the tiny kitchen with starchy fog. Spaghetti was on the menu to-night; it was the only thing Warren ate.

"I hate when you clean." Gina turned from the sink, frowning in mock offense. Even ersatz emotion animated large brown eyes that flashed darkly, thick eyebrows like bold slashes, and a strong nose that fit full cheekbones and generous lips, easily coaxed into too-loud laughter. Gina Katsakis was Maria Callas with a JD.

"Hey, girl." Cate threw out the trash and set the brown bag on the kitchen table, next to Warren. The three-year-old sat in his blue-padded high chair, taking no notice of her, his gaze focused on the steam blanketing the window. Cate knew he needed time to get used to her being here, so she didn't greet him. Instead, she said, "Dinner is served."

Gina scuffed to the table in tan Uggs and peeked in the brown bag. "What'd you bring me?"

"What I always bring. Crack cocaine."

"Chicken curry!" Gina reached an eager hand inside the bag. "And it's still hot!" She pulled out a white Chinese food carton and held it up with a broad smile. "You know what I love about this?"

"That it's free?"

"No, the carton." Gina pointed to the red letters on the white waxed pint. "The politically incorrect Asian font. Only a Chinese restaurant can get away with that. 'We love our customers.' How great is that? They *love* us!"

"How could they not?" Cate asked, but she didn't have to say anything. She knew that her friend needed to talk, pent up from the day. It struck her that this was Gina's Miller time.

"It's like my dry cleaners." Gina set the container down and unpacked the other one, then pint-sized rice boxes and tinfoil trays of egg rolls, with plastic tops. "The paper on the hanger says, 'We heart our customers.' I love that, too. I need more love in my business relationships. Don't you?"

"I don't even need love in my *love* relationships," Cate answered, then caught herself, but Gina barely heard.

"You just missed a great Dr. Phil."

"What about? People who love Dr. Phil too much?"

"No, fault-finders, like Mike. Remember he was like that? He found fault with everything. Marks on the walls, laundry on the floor. That's the whole problem, nobody's kind anymore." Gina went to the drawer, retrieved silverware, and grabbed two prefolded napkins on the way back. "We got a new speech therapist today, and she's horrible. Not anywhere near as dedicated as Lisa. The new one's just mean. Cold."

"That's too bad." Cate opened a cabinet and slid two dinner plates out of the stack, on autopilot. They set the table the same way, every time she came to babysit on Monday nights, moving around each other like an old couple. Their friendship had lasted almost fifteen years, spanning a marriage and divorce for each. They had even been each other's maid of honor, and if they'd just married each other, they'd still be together.

Gina was saying, "You can't have three different speech therapists in six months, not for a kid like him. How can he make progress, with that kind of turnover?"

"They probably don't pay them enough." Cate set the plates at their chairs, each catty-corner to Warren. She glanced at him, but he was still gazing at the cloudy window. "So you had some fussing in the living room today, huh?"

"Just a little. How're you?" Gina lined up their silverware beside the napkins, and a wiry black curl fell onto her cheek. Her hair was growing in again, and she tucked the shiny strand into its stubby ponytail. "How's the big trial?"

"Fine. " Cate went to the refrigerator and grabbed two cold Diet Cokes from the door. The white wire racks held only a few green peppers, a dozen eggs, a head of romaine, and a row of strawberry Yoplait. "You need food, honey."

"They really dumb down the trial coverage and they don't even mention you on the news. They just call you 'the judge.' They don't even say 'Judge Fante.' They give Simone all the attention, and his preppy lawyer, who I want to smack. Every day, he's holding press conferences."

Cate returned with the Cokes. "I should've gagged him. It would've been my first gag order. Isn't that sweet?"

"A girl never forgets her first." Gina sat down behind her plate and opened a container.

"And how's the baby?" Cate walked around the table to Warren, who still stared out the window. There was nothing there but bare trees obscured by vanishing steam. Cate lowered herself into the child's field of vision before she spoke to him, as she'd been taught. "Hello, Warren."

Warren didn't respond. At about eighteen months old, this happy, bright, and communicative boy simply withdrew, growing quieter and more still, slipping bit by bit from everyone. He used to call Cate for a big hug and cling to her with a kitten's tenacity, but that had stopped after a time and he'd gradually lost all speech. Cate believed he was in there, behind his eyes. "Warren? Hello, Warren."

"He's still got that ear infection. He's not feeling so good."

"Warren, hello," Cate repeated, modulating her voice, because he was soothed by singsong phrases. He loved classical music, too, which was why the Mozart. She checked his plate, covered with cooling spaghetti. "He isn't eating much."

"He will." Gina ate a forkful of chicken, dripping mustardy curry. "He had a hard day. After the bitchy speech therapist, we had to go to CVS to refill his Amox scrip. I wish they delivered."

"Hello, Warren." Cate knew he heard her. She ignored the constriction in her chest. "I'm very happy to see you."

"It's okay, let it go. Come and eat."

"Warren, it's you and me, after dinner." Cate went to the table, pulled out a chair, and picked up the small container. White rice fell out in a solid block, reminding her of the sand molds she used to make down the shore with Warren. They'd pack dark, wet sand in a blue plastic castle and turn it over. He'd been creeped out by the filmy-shelled sand crabs that would burrow away, and frankly, so was Cate. It seemed so long ago, but it was only last year.

"I'm wondering if I should go tonight." Gina broke up her rice with the side of her fork, eyeing Warren.

"Go to the Acme, my godchild needs food. Should I work with him or let it go tonight?"

"Work with him with the mirror, but just a little." Gina shook her head. "I hate to give up even one night, or he'll fall further behind."

"Go and don't worry about it."

"Thanks." Gina brightened and dug in for another forkful. "Hey, I might even take a shower before I leave. Lately, even the produce is looking at me funny. Also I could crash my cart into somebody single."

Cate smiled. "So what happened today? Why'd he have a tantrum?"

"I tried to do floor time after the doc." Gina popped open her Diet Coke and poured it into her glass, where it fizzed against the ice. "We were working on All About Me in the activity book."

"That's where you went wrong." Cate scooped goopy yellow curry onto her rice. "You shoulda stuck with Faces and Places."

"I know, right? I love Faces and Places!"

"All About Me is a ballbuster."

"Only thing worse is You and Me."

"You and Me will *kill* you."

Gina burst into laughter. "If I were better at You and Me, I wouldn't be divorced."

They both laughed again, though it wasn't true. Not every marriage survives a child with autism. When the doctors finally diagnosed Warren, Gina quit her job as an insurance lawyer and dedicated herself to finding the best early intervention programs. Her husband, Mike, had edged away and finally opted out of the marriage, though he sent support checks big enough to cover most expenses. Cate had set up a trust fund for Warren, contributing yearly. She'd tell Gina about it someday, if the girl ever stopped talking.

"So what's going on in the outside world, Cate? How was your weekend? Did you do anything?"

"No. Just worked."

"Hear anything from the old firm?"

"No, they don't call. It would be inappropriate."

"So who do you play with?"

"You."

Gina didn't smile. "What about that stockbroker, Graham What's-his-name? Is he still calling?"

"I see him tomorrow night."

"Yay!" Gina clapped, then stopped abruptly, her brown eyes wide. "Wait, is this the third date? It's time for third-date sex! Woohooo!"

"Slow down, girl." Cate hid her discomfort. She'd never admit to Gina what she did on the side. She barely admitted it to herself.

"You know the rules. You have to." Gina leaned over her plate, her dinner forgotten. "How'm I gonna live vicariously if you have such a boring life? You're a judge, not a nun. Maybe you got confused? The black robes are too matchy?"

Cate smiled. *Everybody should have at least one girlfriend who can make her laugh.* "Enough about me. Tell me about the bitchy speech therapist," she said, because she knew Gina needed to talk, and they were off.

Later, while Gina was upstairs getting ready to go, Cate sat at the kitchen chair next to Warren and a watery Diet Coke, its ice melted to slivers. The kitchen lights were dimmed, and Mozart played in the background. Warren remained focused on the window, and Cate followed his gaze, confounded.

Outside, under the security light, the branches of a bare tree moved in the wind, in a stiff, jittery way. Kids with autism saw details and patterns that people without it couldn't see, so she squinted and tried to see them the way Warren did. Spidery black lines coated with yellow light moved back and forth, then the black lines disappeared into complete darkness. Autistic brains saw everything, but normal brains didn't see things if they didn't expect to see them, in a phenomenon called inattentive blindness. There'd even been an experiment where airplane pilots had failed to see a jet on the runway, because they didn't expect it to be there.

He's got to come back to us. To his mother. To me.

Cate picked up a medium-sized round mirror rimmed with cheery red felt and tilted it at Warren so that it captured his face. "Warren. You're Warren," she said. In the reflection, the child's mouth tilted down at the one corner, though his gaze stayed at the window. She pointed to his reflection anyway. "Warren." Then she tilted the mirror to herself, so he could see her reflection. She pointed to her face in the mirror. "Karen."

What?

"Cate." Cate blinked and pointed again. She must be tired. *Carol. Sandra. Emily. Halley.* "*Cate.*" Then she tilted the mirror to the boy and pointed again. "Warren."

Warren stirred in the high chair and began to move his head, side to side.

"It's okay," Cate said in a calm voice. What was bothering him? Maybe too much pointing. Autistic kids don't point, and he was just learning how to point in school. She set the mirror down gently. Sudden noises wouldn't help. "We won't do this anymore, if you don't want to."

Warren shook his head, side to side.

"Warren, it's okay, we'll stop now, it's okay," Cate soothed, but sing-song wasn't working. She wanted to kick herself. "It's okay, Warren," she said, but he started shaking his head faster, then swinging his small arms, jostling the high chair. The chair banged against the kitchen table, and Cate's glass tipped over with a loud *clunk*, spilling Diet Coke and sending ice skidding across the table.

"Ahhh!" Warren burst into screaming, shaking his head back and forth so violently that he rocked the high chair, almost toppling it. Cate leapt up and grabbed him under his arms so he didn't fall, but he was strapped into the high chair and went ballistic. Cate managed to unlatch him and scoop him shrieking into her arms, kicking his feet, writhing back and forth. Cate tried to remember her training. Kids with autism are calmed by tight squeezing. She hugged him tightly, and he kicked against her stomach with his baby sneakers but she didn't let go.

"Cate!" Gina rushed into the kitchen in a towel, her expression stricken and her wet hair plastered to her shoulders. "Do you need—"

"No, I got it, it's okay, Warren, it's okay, it's Cate and it's okay," Cate said over and over, squeezing him. Gina stood at their side, her hand covering her mouth, her tears silent. The child stopped screaming and his kicking finally lessened, then ceased as his tense body loosened in her arms. "It's all right, Warren, it's gone now, I love you, Warren," Cate kept repeating, and Warren went finally limp in her arms.

Gina signaled in time that he had fallen asleep, but Cate didn't let him go. He felt so good in her arms, permitting her embrace only in slumber, and Gina understood, because she nodded to Cate to go upstairs to put him down. And when they were finished, Cate picked up her purse, slipped back into her sheepskin, and closed the town house door.

Grateful, and heartbroken, to leave.

Afterwards Cate found herself driving the long way home, knowing she was in some vague state of denial. She piloted the white Mercedes through Roxborough, a working-class neighborhood on the way home, a brick labyrinth of row houses with green plastic awnings, heaped now with crusty snow and trimmed with sooty icicles. She felt oddly comfortable here; it was a lot like her hometown, and she kept seeing her own past.

She drove by an old Catholic grade school, its windows covered with construction-paper snowflakes. She had gone to an elementary school like that, St. Ignatius, and remembered making snowflakes, folding the paper into thick eighths, cutting the corners with useless safety scissors, then unfolding the creation in a schoolgirl's suspense. She'd been either disappointed to discover cut holes that were bigger than they were supposed to be, or happily surprised when a humongous star burst at the center of the snowflake. She didn't know why she remembered it, now.

She drove past a small church with an attached rectory, then a large stone funeral home that was, ironically, the nicest building on the block. It was always that way in neighborhoods; it had been in hers, too. She cruised ahead, listening to the thrumming of the Mercedes engine and passing old Fords and minivans whitewashed with road salt and grime. She slowed when she came, inevitably, to a corner bar.

PADDY'S, read the neon sign, a glowing green cliché with a sideways shamrock.

Cate eyed the place as the car idled at the stop sign. Its brick facade needed repair and its one window, in the side of the building, was of old-fashioned block glass, almost stop-time. A broken concrete stoop led to a wooden front door, so close to the street that Cate could hear laughter from within. She felt a familiar tingle of arousal and fear.

HONK! HONK!

Cate started and checked the rearview just as a pickup flashed its high beams. She hit the gas and cruised forward, half-looking for a parking space, half-driving home. She checked the digital clock on the car's tan dashboard, illuminated with a ghostly white: 11:13. Then the temperature: 18 degrees.

Cate lapped the block once, then twice. Thinking, and not thinking. She flashed on Warren, sleeping spent in her arms. Then Marz, for some reason, which reminded her. She still had work to do tonight. Tomorrow would bring a big decision. The motion she had to rule on would prevent the case from ever going to the jury. They'd never get to decide who was telling the truth, and Marz would be dead in the water.

Cate took a left onto Ridge Avenue, heading home.

CHAPTER 5

"Good morning, gentlemen." Cate shook hands all around and gestured Temin and Hartford into the mismatched chairs across from her desk in chambers. The lawyers greeted her nervously, undoubtedly taken aback by her surprise request to meet with them, and as they sat down, they stole glances around the office. Cate still hadn't decorated the place, and for a second, saw it through their eyes.

Her leftover desk—medium-sized, GAO-issue, of brown mahogany-like laminate—would impress no one, and her desk chair was covered with brown pleather. Briefs and pleadings lay stacked on the conference table across the room, but at least the papers hid the water rings. Bookshelves lined the walls, but they remained empty except for unpacked boxes she'd brought from her old firm. There was, however, a floor-to-ceiling window with a spectacular view: gray clouds made a dreamy canopy over the blue Benjamin Franklin Bridge, which spanned the Delaware River and connected the snow-covered row houses of colonial Philadelphia to the renewed waterfront of Camden.

Cate asked, "Great view, huh?"

"Sure is," Temin answered, falsely cheery. His curly hair looked damp, and white conditioner plugged one ear. He wore his trademark wrinkly brown suit. "You can see forever. Or, at least, Jersey."

"It's lovely," Hartford agreed, tugging up his pants leg. He wore gray pinstripes, newly squeegeed glasses, and a tight smile.

"Thanks for coming, both of you," Cate said. "I called you in because I'm troubled by this case. As you know, I inherited this matter, so I wasn't involved in any settlement discussions. The way I see it, this is a garden-variety contract case, if we strip away the Hollywood glamour. Why hasn't it been settled?"

Temin sighed. "Plaintiff did try to settle, Your Honor, but defendant was unwilling."

Cate turned to Hartford. "How unwilling?"

"Completely," he answered firmly, but Cate wasn't hearing the firmly part. She turned back to Temin.

"What was your demand?"

"Your Honor, our financial expert examined what the *Attorneys@ Law* franchise has grossed to date, not counting future DVD sales, domestic and worldwide, and he tells us we're talking $760 million, gross."

Cate almost laughed. "As I said, what was your demand?"

"We started at twenty million, then went down to fifteen, then ten, then eight, then two." Temin shifted his girth. "Right now we're at $925,000."

It's a start. "Sounds like movement to me. What about you, George?"

"Your Honor, the rub isn't me, but my client. He refuses to pay a penny. Not a penny. He doesn't want to set a precedent, and successful producers become major targets if they pay. Besides, it's a principle with Mr. Simone."

Yeah, right. "He must have a number."

"He has no number. He believes that his reputation is on the line."

"His reputation is taking a pounding in the press." Cate hadn't been reading the articles, but her clerks memorized them. "*Enter-*

tainment Weekly, Variety, People magazine, they're all on Marz's side. The consensus is your client stole Mr. Marz's idea."

Hartford shook his head. "They just want to bring a successful man down, and Mr. Simone thinks long-term. He expects to be vindicated and change the public's mind. In any event, he says that all press is good press, and the ratings are up."

"The *ratings*?" Cate repeated, appalled. "Is that what's going on here? That as long as this case stays alive, your client is getting better ratings?"

"No, no, no!" Hartford rushed to say, holding up a conciliatory hand. "It's about the principle, I assure you, and the precedent."

Yeah right. Cate changed tack and faced Temin. "Let's close this deal, Counsel. Will your client take half the amount he's currently asking, let's say $500,000?"

"I believe he would. Confidentially, he's still out of a job."

"There is no number." Hartford shook his head, and Temin turned to him in appeal.

"George, what about 250 grand? That would make my guy whole for the time he was out of work and cover at least some of my fees."

"I can't help you out, Nate."

Cate folded her arms, bowing out for a minute.

Temin said, "Come on, you gotta be kidding. Your guy makes more dough than God."

"That's not the point."

"Would you recommend it to him, at least?"

"Honestly, no."

"Why not?"

"He wants vindication."

"He wants *blood*!" Temin shot back, and Cate stepped in.

"Mr. Temin, please, that won't help."

"But, Your Honor, what does he want?" Temin threw up his pudgy hands. "He took my guy's show, he took his livelihood, and my guy's got nothin'. I'll give up my fee, Judge." Temin turned to Hartford again. "George, he's a good kid. He made a mistake. How can you take advantage of that kid and sleep at night?"

"I'm not—"

"A *hundred* grand, then!" Temin said, raising his voice again. "No fee for me. Two years of salary for my guy. How about it?"

"No."

"A year then. The guy has two kids and a mother he supports. She lives in the duplex upstairs."

"Not for fifty grand or even twenty-five. It's not going to happen. Your client started this, and we're going to finish it."

Cate raised her hand, and Temin bit his tongue. Her only hope was convincing Hartford that there was a risk if he didn't settle. "Mr. Hartford, you act as if a verdict is guaranteed your client, but have you been watching? The jury favors Mr. Marz."

Hartford smiled without warmth. "With respect, we feel confident we will prevail. If not before you this morning, then in the Third Circuit. And if not there, I am authorized to take it all the way up."

"To the Supremes?" Temin interrupted, incredulous. "What? That's *burning* money! An appeal that far will cost a hundred grand. He can settle it right now for a song."

Hartford set his jaw. "I cannot settle this case. Even if I recommend it, he will not take it."

Cate had to let it go. Judges were permitted to aid settlements, not muggings. "Mr. Hartford, go and take the final demand to Mr. Simone. If you won't recommend it to him, tell him that I do. Tell him I strongly recommend that he do the right thing, the smart thing, and settle."

"But, Your Honor—"

"Go, Mr. Hartford," Cate repeated firmly, then rose, which cued the lawyers that the meeting was over. "You have an hour before we're in session. Tell the bailiff if you need more time."

"Your Honor—"

"Go and do. *Now*."

Ten minutes later, Cate was sitting at her desk across from Emily Carroll, she of the nose ring, eyebrow bar-pierce, and weird earlobe-stretcher-circle thing. The girl dressed in heavy Goth, with black eyeliner around her dark eyes, a maroon cardigan that picked up her purple fingernail polish, and black pants that fit too snugly under a wide belt dotted with silver studs. But if there was a case that would save Marz, Emily would find it. Hardware aside.

"Tell me something good," Cate said, leaning over her second cup of coffee. Temin and Marz were still in discussions. They had fifteen minutes until court started.

"Nothing, Judge. There are no cases."

"There have to be."

"There aren't." Emily shook her head and something metallic jingled. Cate didn't want to know what.

"Did you check all jurisdictions?"

"Yes."

Cate had researched the question herself online last night, with the same result. "Can you think of any new theory?"

"No. Sorry, I tried. The law is clear. You have to grant this motion. It's a slam dunk." Emily tilted her head, or maybe her eyebrow ring was weighing it down. "You feelin' this guy, Judge?"

"Marz?" Cate hadn't thought about it. "Yeah, I guess I am."

"But he's so lame. He should've known better."

"It still doesn't excuse intentional wrongdoing." Cate understood Marz, for the first time. "He's a guy with a dream, that's all. Everybody's entitled to their dream, aren't they?"

"My dream is to pay off my student loans. I have trailer-trash dreams."

"Don't say that about yourself."

"Whatev." Emily shrugged her soft shoulders. "Anyway, Marz had to know he'd lose in court. He's a lawyer."

"He figured there was at least a chance that I'd let it go to the jury. It's his dream, and he wasn't going down without a fight. Actually, I admire that."

Suddenly there was a rustling at her office door, and they both looked up. It was Jonathan Meriden, who shared the floor. Val must have let him past, or maybe he'd ignored her, which was his style. He leaned into the doorway in his dark suit, gripping the threshold.

"Cate, I understand you've got a motion today."

"Yes."

"Praise be." Meriden rolled his eyes. "I can't abide these Hollywood people. They were blocking the hallway all day yesterday, and my parties before me couldn't get to my door. Today's motion will finally end this circus, eh?"

"If they don't settle."

"Would you?" Meriden raised a skeptical eyebrow. "From what I hear, they've got that kid over a barrel."

"I like to think I'd settle. I could get it for a song, and it's fair."

"Fairness? Ah, youth!" Meriden said dismissively, which annoyed Cate.

"I'm not *that* young."

"You'll always be a rookie to me," Meriden shot back, then his head popped from the doorway as quickly as it had appeared.

Jerk.

"What an ass!" Emily wrinkled her perforated nose. "His clerks are asses, too. Everybody hates them, and everybody wishes they were working for you. You're the fun judge."

Great. "That's me, class clown of the Eastern District."

Emily smiled. "We're the *cool* chambers."

"Totally."

They both laughed, but Cate was wondering if Marz and Temin had a settlement yet.

CHAPTER 6

Cate strode to the dais, her robes billowing theatrically, making her feel like an actress playing a role. Someday she'd feel like she belonged in this costume, but today wasn't that day. The negotiations had failed, and Simone had refused to settle, even when the demand decreased to ten grand. It made no sense. The attorneys' fees for today alone would be that much. Hartford didn't sneeze for less than twenty grand.

"All rise!" the deputy boomed, his voice echoing in the crowded courtroom.

At the bar of court, Temin and Marz stood in matching wrinkles and brave smiles. Hartford and Simone, both tall, gym-toned, and Armani-clad, didn't bother to smile. The gallery of reporters, sketch artists, and spectators rose, setting aside newspapers and notepads. Detective Russo anchored the first row next to Marz's wife, and occupying the seat beside the redhaired consultant and Micah Gilbert was a woman reporter whom Cate recognized from Fox. She'd evidently been tipped off that today might be a big day.

"Good morning, everyone," Cate said as she seated herself on the dais and arranged her robes around her. The jury box remained empty, and the black bucket chairs left swiveled in their positions. The jurors wouldn't be present for the oral argument.

"Good morning, Your Honor," replied the chorus, more or less on cue, and Cate managed a stage smile.

"Mr. Hartford, you have a motion to make?"

"Yes, Your Honor." Hartford crossed to the lectern and squared his shoulders. "At this juncture, defendant moves for judgment as a matter of law under Rule 50. As Your Honor knows, the standard is well-established, and for these purposes only, the defendant Mr. Simone must accept as true the facts as alleged by plaintiff. We therefore assume that the facts are as Mr. Marz testified, that is, that Mr. Simone agreed to produce Mr. Marz's story idea and treatment for television, and also that he said, verbatim, 'When I make money, you'll make money.'"

Back at counsel table, Temin made notes and Marz sat flushed, his fingers linked on the glistening walnut surface. His wife looked miserable, sitting in the row behind him. Cate could only imagine the pressure Marz was under. His job and his dream, gone.

"Defendant's argument is simple, Your Honor. Mr. Marz's testimony is undisputed that he and Mr. Simone did not write down the terms of their contract. Therefore, we're dealing with an express oral contract. It is also undisputed that Mr. Marz and Mr. Simone didn't discuss a price term for the contract, neither a specific number nor dollar amount. It is equally undisputed that they didn't discuss a method of payment, means of payment, or time of payment. In fact, both parties agree that those facts are true."

At defense table, Simone nodded slightly, and Marz glanced over.

"This Court must grant judgment as a matter of law on the grounds that the single statement by Mr. Simone, taken as true for these purposes only, that 'when I make money, you'll make money,' is too indefinite to form an oral contract that is enforceable by this Court. In other words, it doesn't matter whom you believe in this case, Mr. Marz or Mr. Simone. Even if everything Mr. Marz said is true, he still doesn't have a contract, as a matter of law."

Cate made a note on her legal pad. I'M NOT GOING DOWN WITH-OUT A FIGHT, EITHER.

"As Your Honor knows, this matter comes before this Court on diversity jurisdiction, and Pennsylvania law governs the facts, as all meetings regarding the alleged contract took place in Pennsylvania."

Cate had been up most of the night, researching online, and had learned that a different result would probably have applied under California law, a state more experienced with the way entertainment contracts were formed. It told her just how manipulative Simone had been in arranging that the relevant meetings were held in Philadelphia. She generally approved of shopping, but for the perfect shoes, not the perfect law.

Hartford said, "Under Pennsylvania law, it is clear that express oral contracts that are indefinite as to the price term are not enforceable. The seminal case for this proposition is—"

Cate raised a finger, and Hartford fell instantly silent, demonstrating the deference shown only to Article III judges and Saudi royalty. "Mr. Hartford, what do you say to the fact that Mr. Marz quit his job at the district attorney's office in reliance on his oral contract with Mr. Simone?"

"Your Honor, with all due respect, that would be irrelevant."

"I remind you that Pennsylvania recognizes the doctrine of justifiable reliance. Mr. Marz justifiably relied on Mr. Simone's representation, to his detriment."

"Your Honor, Mr. Marz's reliance was not justifiable on these facts. A reasonable man would have questioned the price term long before Mr. Marz did, especially given that he is a lawyer."

"Isn't that a question for the jury?"

"Not on these facts, Your Honor. A Pennsylvania court would not apply the justifiable reliance doctrine in these circumstances, and with respect, this Court is not free to disregard Pennsylvania law."

Temin scribbled while Marz shifted in his seat, his brow knitting in anger. Simone was smiling slightly.

Cate leaned over the dais. "Pennsylvania also recognizes the unjust enrichment doctrine. What do you say to the fact that Mr. Marz worked for eight months on a treatment, which Mr. Simone accepted and then produced, making millions of dollars? Taken as true, these facts make clear that your client was unjustly enriched at the expense of Mr. Marz."

The gallery shifted. Reporters took notes. Spectators whispered. The courtroom deputy smiled.

"Your Honor, Mr. Marz made an imprudent decision in quitting his job, one that a reasonable man wouldn't make. We've all heard the adage 'Don't quit your day job.' Furthermore, Detective Russo, given the same set of facts, did not quit his day job. The law of unjust enrichment does not ensure against bad judgment."

Cate bore down. "Certainly, Mr. Hartford, the equities do not lie in your client's favor."

"With respect, Your Honor, the equities are irrelevant under the law. There is insufficient evidence of an enforceable contract for this matter to be put to the jury, and the law requires you to enter judgment as a matter of law in favor of Mr. Simone and his company. Not to do so, on these facts, I daresay, would be reversible error."

Cate glared at him, unable to say what she wanted and too mad to write in big letters.

Hartford said, "To continue my argument, Your Honor, the seminal case in Pennsylvania is . . ."

Cate eased back in her chair, barely listening as Hartford recited the litany of case law supporting his position. She had read them last night, and Emily had confirmed them this morning. She was hoping Temin could come up with something, and when Hartford finished, she motioned to him. "Mr. Temin, your response?"

"Certainly." Temin scurried to the lectern, and Marz shifted upwards in his seat. "May it please the Court, plaintiff opposes defendant's motion for judgment as a matter of law. This case presents a clear question of credibility, which the jury can, and should, be able to decide. To grant this motion is to deny Mr. Marz his day in court."

Cate's shoulders sank, hidden in the voluminous robes. Temin's argument was absolutely true, but it wasn't a legal argument. It was about justice, not law, and Hartford was arguing law, not justice. The law was clear that even if Simone had said his famous line, it wouldn't be enough to make an enforceable contract in Pennsylvania. And in that case, the law did not permit the question to be decided by the jury, because they would be swayed—by justice.

Temin was saying, "Mr. Marz has an absolute right to his day in court, Your Honor. It is his word against Mr. Simone's, and only the jury is qualified to make that decision about who's lying and who's telling the truth. To take the case away from them would allow Mr. Simone to take ruthless advantage of . . ."

Cate couldn't listen to him, either. Temin was making a persuasive jury speech, but the kind of words that swayed the heart, not the mind. And her heart felt sick. She'd sentenced a young mother to life in prison last week and felt better than she did right now. Then, at least, she had followed the law and done justice. Today she had to follow the law and not do justice. She had known, as a trial lawyer, that this could happen, but she'd never seen it, much less been the one to actually *do* it. The responsibility was all.

Temin finished up. "And for all of the foregoing, Your Honor, we ask the Court to deny the defendant's motion."

"Thank you, Mr. Temin. I have your argument." Cate looked down at Hartford. "Rebuttal, Counsel?"

"Yes, thank you." Hartford took the lectern, standing very erect, as Temin moved aside. "Your Honor, with all due respect, defendant takes issue with the Court's demeanor as well as its characterization of the facts, and I object to—"

What? Cate frowned. "My demeanor is of no legal significance, and I haven't characterized any facts, Mr. Hartford. I asked a few questions. Trust me, I'm allowed."

"I never meant to suggest otherwise," Hartford said, backing down. "In conclusion, defendant moves that the Court enter judgment as a matter of law. Thank you, Your Honor." He made his way to his seat, and Simone acknowledged him with a nod.

Cate eased back in her chair, surveying the scene. Marz and Temin, on tenterhooks, and Simone and Hartford, on a roll. She knew the law and she knew she had sworn to uphold it. It wouldn't make sense to delay the inevitable. There was no other way. Or was there?

Cate straightened up. "Gentlemen, I intend to rule from the bench and file a written opinion later, but before I do, I want to say a few words." She turned to defense table. "Mr. Simone, I'm speaking directly to you now. I cannot imagine a case of such manifest injustice as I see before me today. I think your sense of right and wrong has utterly failed you, if indeed you had any in the first place."

Simone's eyes narrowed behind his hip little glasses, and Hartford's mouth dropped open. Reporters scribbled away, sketch artists flipped the page, and whispering swelled in the gallery. The courtroom deputy looked up from his desk, his eyes shining. Cate didn't reach for the gavel. She felt empowered enough already.

"I haven't been on the bench very long, and I hope I never encounter a case such as this again. You may have made a fortune, Mr. Simone, but as far as I'm concerned, you stole every penny of it. You're no better than a common thief."

Hartford popped up, mortified. "Objection, Your Honor! That's *slander*!"

"Sit down and shut up, Counsel." Cate didn't even look at Hartford, but locked eyes with Simone. "The idea for the show was Mr. Marz's and the storylines were his and his alone. You manipulated and exploited him, and I want my opinion of you and this case to be perfectly clear, regardless of my judicial decision. You may get a judgment today, but you will *not* get my respect, nor will you use my

Court for public relations, or, worse, television ratings. You're getting away with murder, and you know it. Simply put, against my judgment, I grant judgment for defendant." Cate picked up the gavel and slammed it down. *Crak!*

"No!" Marz shouted suddenly, leaping to his feet. "You bastard, I'll kill you!" Suddenly he lunged for Simone and grabbed him by the shoulders. Hartford sprang away, and Simone toppled over in his chair, with Marz on top of him, throwing punches.

"Bailiff!" Cate yelled, shocked. Simone's fancy glasses flew off, and Marz went for his throat. His wife screamed. The courtroom deputy leaped from his chair and rushed to help. The stenographer sprang from the steno machine. Chaos broke out in the gallery. Reporters wrote frantically. Simone's assistant ran to help him. Russo went after Marz, and marshals ran from the back of the courtroom.

"Judge, let's go!" said a voice, and Cate turned. It was Emily, on the dais. "You should get out of here."

"I'm fine," Cate answered. Her mouth had gone dry. Her heart hammered and her knees felt weak. "I caused it, and I'll stay until it's over."

Back in chambers, Cate sat in her crappy desk chair, staring out the window. The doors were closed and her office quiet, except for the almost constant ringing of the phones on her desk and work table. She didn't answer. On the other side of the closed door, her secretary, Val Denton, fended off calls from the media. A religious woman, Val would give them the wrath of God. The law clerks would still be buzzing, though at least they had turned the TV off, on her command. The news at noon had carried sketches of the fistfight, and her lecture from the bench had gotten lost in the melee.

Ring! Cate tried not to hear any of it, watching the pewter clouds inch across the skyline behind the Ben Franklin Bridge. It looked like a storm brewing, but it could have been her state of mind. She didn't know what she had done. Strike that, she didn't know if she was allowed to do what she had done.

Buzz! The white light flashed on her phone, which was Val's signal for Cate to pick up, which she did. "What? Are the townspeople at the gate? With torches?"

Val chuckled. "Chief Judge Sherman on the line. Should I put him through?"

"Do I have a choice?"

"No, but don't let him intimidate you. It's Meriden you gotta watch out for. I hear he's runnin' around whining about what you said in court."

"Thanks." Cate's nickname for Val was Invaluable, because she was.

"Now hold for Sherman." There was a click on the line, then the soft, quavering voice of Chief Judge Sherman.

"Goodness, dear! I just heard what happened. What a calamity! How *are* you?"

"Fine, thanks. It wasn't as bad as it sounded on TV."

"I don't keep a TV in chambers. I heard about it from Jonathan, who said it was quite a to-do."

Meriden. "But I only decked one guy, Chief."

Sherman laughed softly. "What a case! It's a trial by fire for you, isn't it? I thought I'd handed you a plum, but maybe it's a crab apple. Do forgive me."

"Not at all, Chief. I think it's been fascinating, a real lesson in lots of ways. I'm entering judgment today, and the courthouse will go back to normal."

Sherman clucked. "I rather enjoyed the excitement. I heard Steven Bochco was in the hallway last week! Do you remember *Hill Street Blues*?"

"Was I born yet?"

"Ha! By the way, I heard you said some rather intemperate things on the bench."

Cate cringed. *Here it comes.*

"I've gotten a call or two from the others. It's probably my job as chief to let you know. I would have ruled from the bench, too. But, if you don't mind some constructive criticism, I wouldn't have made those comments in open court."

"In my own defense, what I said was completely in order."

"Undoubtedly." Judge Sherman lowered his voice. "But the next time, make all the comments you want, but keep them in chambers. Off the record, like the old man does."

Cate smiled. "Gotcha. Thanks. And sorry."

"That's my girl." Sherman paused. "You know, all of us are moved by cases before us, certain cases, from time to time. That's part of the passion for the law that I have, and I see in you. We don't choose our cases, they choose us. Like our children."

Cate thought of Warren.

"And I *do* like your fire, Cate. You're a new kind of judge, a new model. You energize our stodgy old court. The law needs new life from time to time, or it grows old and stale. Inflexible, brittle. We have to change with the times, and we do. That's what I love about this court. Our court." Sherman chuckled. "Well, now, I am boring you, aren't I? I lean to the rabbinical."

"Nah, thanks for the advice, Rabbi." Cate would have stayed on the line with him forever. He was her New Friend.

"Take care now," Sherman said, hanging up.

Cate hung up, too. She couldn't help wondering about which judges had called Sherman. Meriden, and who else? Why hadn't they called her directly? Why run to Daddy? She fingered her pearls like worry beads and eyed the sky, where storm clouds conspired, though she tried not to take it personally. She felt a familiar pressure, building up inside, needing a release, and her thoughts skipped ahead.

It would be the third date, after all.

CHAPTER 7

The door banged open against the bedroom wall, and Cate found herself being hoisted against its hard wood. She wrapped her legs around Graham, her slim skirt hiking up, and he kissed her breathless, pressing into her. He pushed harder against her, opening her thighs, then slipped both hands under her panties in the back, cupping her in two rough palms. The sensation thrilled her, and she kissed him deeper, her heart hammering. Suddenly he lifted her up and whirled her toward the bed, and Cate squealed, clinging to him.

"You didn't warn me!" She laughed, spinning in his arms.

"You like?"

"Yes!" Cate fell backwards onto the soft white comforter, her pearls against her throat and her arms opening like a snow angel's. Graham stood between her bare knees at the end of the bed, laughing and breathing hard, then he unbuttoned his shirt and let it drop. A hallway light silhouetted the hard caps of his shoulders and a muscular torso that tapered to a trim waist. Cate couldn't wait another minute. She yanked her skirt up rather than waste time taking it off and wriggled out of her panties. Graham's belt buckle jingled, the leather belt flapped to the side, and as soon as she saw him unzipping his jeans, she reached for him.

"Wait." Graham stepped back, laughing in surprise. "You're not even undressed."

"I'm undressed enough!"

"No, you're not. Blouse's still on, and your skirt." Graham leaned over and found the top button of her blouse, and Cate's hands flew to help him.

"But I can do it faster."

"Faster isn't the point." Graham pressed her hands away. "Now be still."

"Argh." Cate gave up and let her arms flop back on the sleigh bed. Up close, she could see the dark flash of his eyes and the glint of his smile. A raggedy fringe of his hair fell forward, and she breathed in the wintry scent of burning smoke from the fireplace. She stroked his arm while he unfastened the button between her breasts, his knuckles grazing her nipple. "You did that on purpose."

"I'm guilty, Judge. Now take off your skirt."

"I'm fine with it on."

"Take it off. I don't want to mess it up."

Cate scoffed. He was teasing her and it was driving her crazy. "You don't give a damn about my skirt."

"Oh, I do. I care very much about your skirt." Graham finished opening the third button and stroked her breast gently, sliding his fingertips along the fine silk. She arched her back, but he only moved to the next button, chuckling softly. He took his time, and when he finally unbuttoned the last button, he moved aside each side of the filmy blouse, one after the other, as if he were unwrapping a very expensive present.

Cate lay breathless on the bed, her heart hammering, her neck vulnerable and her arms resting back. Her breasts lay exposed in a lacy black bra.

"You are beautiful, you know that?" Graham whispered, seeming to stall over her.

"Argh, come here!" Cate squirmed under his gaze, hating the scrutiny, even in the dark. She reached for him again, and he finally lowered himself onto her, kissing her more softly than before, more gently than he had, even downstairs. She kissed him back, excited by the heat of his skin on hers, wanting to feel that groove again, the one they had against the door. She ran her hand up the length of his thigh, feeling the hardness under his jeans.

"Caught me, huh?"

"Yep." Cate giggled, then she felt again, a box shape. "What's this?"

"I was going to give it to you afterwards, but since you busted me . . ." Graham pulled away, propped himself on one elbow, and dug in his front pocket. "I have something for you, Cate."

"I know you do, but you won't shut up."

Graham chuckled, reaching for the bedside lamp. "You look like such a classy lady, but only I know the real you."

Suddenly the light came on, and she shielded her eyes from the brightness. When she moved her hand, Graham was holding a medium-sized box wrapped in robin's-egg blue paper with a satiny white ribbon on top. Tiffany's. Cate's mouth went dry. "What's this?"

"You have to open it to find out." Graham handed her the box, and she shifted up on the bed with it, bracing herself on her free hand.

"But, a present? Why?"

"Stop asking questions and open it." Graham tugged on the ribbon, which slipped off like silk. "Cool, isn't it?"

Cate unfolded the wrapping paper and took it off. It was a medium-sized box of black velvet, and her fingers trembled as she opened its lid. Inside glittered a gold link bracelet with a heart pendant. It was lovely, which only made her want to cry. She didn't know what to do. Graham took it out, unhooked it, and held it up to the light. The heart gleamed expensively, a rich, eighteen-carat gold. Finally Cate found her voice. "I can't take this. It costs too much."

"Please, hush, give me your wrist." Graham lifted her wrist, put the bracelet on it, and held her hand up, with obvious pleasure. The heart dangled prettily, and he turned it toward Cate. "If you want, we can get it engraved. But I like it the way it is. What do you think?"

Cate winced.

"I ordered this for you after our first date." Graham took her hand, and Cate stiffened. She felt a sudden urge to move, but he was holding her hand, sitting only a foot away. "You might think it's too soon to get involved, after my divorce, but I'm forty-two. I know what I want, and it's you. It was right from that first night."

Cate heard the emotion in his words and couldn't meet his eye. She looked away, and her gaze found one of the bedroom windows in this colonial town house, with bubbled mullions and thick wooden sills, two-hands deep. She had measured them last time, with her own spread fingers. Outside, the winter sun had set and its pinkish rays clawed the deepening blue, only reluctantly surrendering its stake on the sky.

"You don't have to feel the same way I do, I understand that. It's still early."

Silence fell between them, and the temperature in the bedroom dropped a tick, chilling Cate in her bra.

"You okay?" Graham squeezed her hand, and the gold heart glinted in the lamplight. "You don't look happy."

"I'm fine, sure," Cate said, though she wasn't. She knew she should stay and she knew she would go.

"Talk to me, would you?"

Cate wished she could, but she couldn't. She released his hand, stood up, and started buttoning up her blouse.

"What are you doing?" Graham rose slowly. "You're *leaving*?"

"I think I should. I'm sorry." Cate tried to get the bracelet off but couldn't undo the clasp, fumbling.

"Don't leave, baby." Graham reached for her arm, but Cate withdrew it. She had to go. She couldn't explain it to him, this wonderful man. She just had to. She hurried to the door, her bare feet cold on the floorboards. Her shoes and stockings were still downstairs by the fireplace.

Graham followed her. "Wait, listen. I shouldn't have sprung it on you. It just came out. I'm sorry."

"I'm sorry, too," Cate said, but she hurried away.

It took Cate less than an hour to find a good corner bar in a working-class neighborhood south of the business district, near the airport. It had stopped raining outside, and an increase in the temperature made the air unseasonably wet. It was after six, so the TV news wasn't showing more reports of her courtroom, and she sipped her smudgy glass of Miller's, leaving behind thoughts of Marz, Sherman, and even Graham. He had called twice on her cell, but she hadn't picked up.

Behind the bar sat the same line of dusty bottles as in the other bar, and junking up the mirror hung the same leftover Christmas decorations. Cate speculated that the bars rotated the items, to save on filth. The men looked the same, too; two Verizon employees in navy blue coats sat at the end of the wooden bar, joking with the bartender and ignoring CNN. They'd had to settle for Larry King on closed captioning, because the Sixers weren't playing tonight. A few seats down from the two men hunched a dark-haired man with mutton-chops, who reminded Cate of Detective Russo.

Odd. The thought caught her up short. It was the first time Cate thought about work on one of these outings. She kept the two worlds separate, or at least her brain did for her. Her head began to ache, and she shifted on her bar stool, uncomfortably. Russo. Marz. She couldn't keep doing this anymore, as a judge. She imagined that if you looked up Appearance of Impropriety in the dictionary, there might well be a photo of her, at this bar. Without her panties.

"Hi," said a masculine voice, and Cate looked over. It was the man with the black muttonchops, standing next to her. He wore a black motorcycle jacket and was reasonably handsome. "You look lonely. Can I buy you a drink?" The man climbed onto the bar stool next to hers, and Cate felt a tingle she couldn't deny.

"If you're Elvis, you can."

"If you're Priscilla, I will," the man said, and they laughed.

It turned out Elvis knew a motel near the airport with a sign that read CABLE TV—AIR CONDITION. It was three stories tall, with concrete stairs and hallways on the outside, in front of numbered doors painted dark pink. The walls were paved with matching stucco, as if the place was in South Beach and not behind Terminal C. Cate parked the Mercedes in the lot and waited in it while Elvis checked them in, and when he left the tiny office with its plastic window, he gave her a wave, and she got out of the car, chirped it locked, and fell into step behind him.

"Done got us the honeymoon suite, Priscilla," he said in a terrible Memphis accent. He reached back for Cate's hand and led her down the concrete walkway, past a busted vending machine, and up the concrete stairs.

"Second floor?"

"Third, sweetie, but I'll make it worth your while." He laughed again, and the sound echoed in the cold night. Airplanes hung suspended in the flight path overhead, their red lights twinkling in a perfect line, like a strand of precious rubies.

They reached the top floor and Cate followed, permitting herself to be led as they took a right at the head of the stairs. Elvis withdrew something from his jeans pocket, an old-fashioned key hanging from a plastic diamond scored with 325, and he had no trouble finding the room.

"You've done this before," she said, her heart starting to race as he opened the door and flicked on the light.

"The hell I have, darlin.' I been savin' myself for you."

Cate laughed, standing on the metal threshold, thrilled and nervous. A long hallway led into a small room, containing only a double bed covered with a brown-patterned quilt and a metal TV cart next to a louvered closet.

"Come on in," he said, and before she had time to think about it, he pulled her gently inside and shut the door behind her, and she found herself suddenly wanting him when he wrapped strong arms around her and kissed her once, tasting of beer.

"Against the door," Cate heard herself say.

"Whatever," he murmured, easing her back against the door in the dark hallway. She was on fire, and his hands grabbed at her skirt, pushing it up. He moaned when he felt bare skin.

"Watch out," Cate said, giggling. He kissed her deeply, and she reached up around his shoulder, feeling his leather jacket under her hands, which was when she saw a flash of gold, darkly. *The bracelet.* Cate still had it on. She couldn't wear it here. She turned her head from the kiss, pressing him back, saying, "Wait, wait."

"What?" he asked, his hair mussed in front, his expression bewildered. He reached for her, but she was trying to undo the bracelet. He reached again. "Come here. Come back here!"

"Wait a minute," Cate said firmly, holding up her hand, and he stopped, then eased down the hall and flopped backward on the bed, waiting.

"Women!" Elvis laughed, throwing up his arms. "What is it? A weddin' band? Wear it or don't, I don't give a damn."

But the bracelet wouldn't come off. Cate couldn't undo the clasp link, and Elvis was too drunk to help. It made her stop. And think. *What am I doing?* Graham. Marz. Sherman. She couldn't keep this up. It was wrong. Inappropriate, not only because she was a judge. Because she was a woman. She wouldn't do this again. Never, ever.

"Hurry!" Elvis hollered, sitting upright, but Cate had already pulled her skirt down and gone partway down the hall.

"Listen, wait, I'm sorry. I'm sorry, but I don't want to do this. I can't."

"*What?*"

"I have to go, I'm sorry."

"Now, you want to leave?" Elvis sat up, his dark eyes wide with disbelief. "You can't do that! You got me up here, bitch!"

"I know, I'm sorry. Here." Cate reached reflexively into her purse, grabbed her wallet, and handed him cash, trying vainly to make it right. "Here, this is for your trouble. I'm sorry."

"You can't pay me!" he shouted, batting her hand away. Cash scattered in the air.

Cate hurried to the door but Elvis launched himself off the bed, rushed down the hall, and reached her just in time to straight-arm the door shut with a loud *bang*.

"No!" Cate cried, but he smashed his mouth against hers and pinned her against the door with his body. She tried to scream but his mouth was covering hers, his beery tongue thrusting inside. She tried to push him off but he shoved his hand crudely up her skirt.

"Hel—," she screamed, but he mashed his hand over her mouth and started to pull up her skirt in front. He wedged her legs open against the door and plunged his hand between them. His fingers probed cruelly, hurting her, and he grunted in satisfaction.

Cate gave way to panic. He was going to rape her. He was enjoying her pain. No one knew she was here. He could even kill her. She must have been crazy to come here. She torqued her head this way and that. Trying to get free. To scream. To think. Cate trounced with all her might on his foot, driving her stiletto into his instep.

"Owwhh!" he shouted, releasing her and bending over, and in that split second Cate opened the door, bolted out, and half-ran, half-stumbled down the stairs to the second floor.

"You bitch! You bitch!" he yelled, running onto the balcony after her. It was raining hard again, but she kept pounding down the stairs, almost slipping on the last flight, streaking to her car, and chirping it unlocked on the run. She jumped inside while he kept screaming at her from the balcony.

Cate wasn't a block away when her cell phone started ringing.

CHAPTER 8

Cate slammed on the gas, ignoring the cell phone. Probably Graham, again. She gripped the wheel and sped away from the motel like a madwoman. Rain pounded the car and bounced off the white hood. Her heart stuck in her throat, every muscle tensed.

She sped past the row houses lining the street, and teenagers crowded into a hoagie shop with a glass storefront. The counter was full at an open Dunkin' Donuts, and the signs of normal life let her breathe easier. Had she gotten away? Was she safe?

The traffic light turned red, and Cate pulled up, checking for Elvis's van in the rearview mirror. No van. Her heartbeat slowed. He wouldn't come after her. She waited, calming, at the traffic light.

Ring ring! She looked over, and her cell phone had slid out of her purse onto the seat. GINA, read the green letters glowing in the dark. *Huh*? Gina never called at this hour. It could be some emergency with Warren. Cate flipped the phone open. "Geen?"

"I saw on the news that—wait, did I wake you?" Gina said, and Cate felt sudden tears come to her eyes at the sound of her friend's voice. Everything was falling apart, and she finally felt safe enough to cry. "Cate? What's the matter?"

"I'm fine." Cate tried to hold it together. "I really am—"

"What happened? Did you see Graham tonight? Where *are* you?"

"God knows, by the airport." Cate looked out the car window, but between the waterworks and the rain, she could barely read the sign. "Ellsworth Avenue? A stupid pink motel? Can you believe this?"

"What are you doing *there*?"

"Screwing up my life." Cate wiped her eyes but they kept welling up. "This man I went with . . . he attacked me at the motel. I was almost raped."

Gina gasped. "Graham?"

Oh, the irony. "No, someone else."

"Oh my God! I'll meet you. I'll get the neighbor to sit. I'll be right there."

"No, don't. I'm going home."

"But you're upset. You can't drive."

"I can, too. This is ridiculous. I'm acting like a baby." Cate didn't know what was happening to her. Nothing was working. She was losing control. "What about Warren? Is he okay?"

"Fine. Go home, and I'll be right there. Drive *carefully*!"

"Love you." Cate flipped the phone closed and accelerated, the windshield wipers working frantically. She drove ahead, but in the next minute heard a loud bobbling sound from the front of the car. A flat tire. *Not my night.* She hit the car's button for Roadside Assistance, and a female operator was piped through her car speakers. "We'll have a truck there as soon as possible," the voice assured her, echoing like the Wizard of Mercedes.

Cate hung up, counting her blessings. She called Gina to tell her she'd be late, but there was no answer. She flipped the phone closed and waited in the driver's seat, wiping her eyes and trying to get over herself.

It's easier to fix a flat than a life.

. . .

An hour and a half later, Cate had reached her town house in Society Hill and pulled into her driveway behind Gina's brown Pathfinder. A plume of smoky exhaust rose from the back of the car. Gina must have been running the engine to stay warm, all this time. Cate grabbed her bag and got out of the car. At least the rain had stopped.

"Cate!" Gina burst out of her car, arms outstretched in her parka, and hurried to the Mercedes. "What took you so long? I forgot my cell, so I couldn't call."

"Sorry, the truck took forever to come."

"What truck?" Gina gave her a huge hug. "I was so worried. I never heard you cry like that." Her expression looked stricken, and loose hair fell from its ponytail. This time, her trademark high drama was in order. "What *happened*?"

"It's a long story," Cate answered, and they went inside the house side by side.

"So that's it, all of it," Cate said, sitting at the round Moser table in her kitchen, behind coffee in her favorite mug. Halogen lights of multi-colored Murano glass hung overhead on a track, making a cozy glow against walls of warm tangerine. She felt so happy to be home, safe in her kitchen and restored to her life. She told Gina everything and watched her friend's expression change from freaked out to extremely freaked out, though she merely listened in silence. But her brown eyes glistened when she heard what had happened at the motel.

"You should call the cops on that bastard, I swear." Gina nodded angrily. "But you know, you can't. It'd be all over the papers."

"I don't know if there's enough for attempted rape, legally." Cate felt raw and ugly. "So, you hate me now?"

"No, not at all." Gina slumped in her chair, lost in her gray PENN sweats. The plaid flannel collar of her pajama top stuck up from her sweatshirt. "But I *am* mad you didn't tell me about these guys you go with. You wouldn't have told me about tonight if I hadn't called you.

How long have you been doing this, you idiot?"

Cate thought back. "About a year, maybe a year and a half."

"From when you were at Beecker? You were a partner in a law firm." Gina shook her head in disbelief, and a dark curl fell from behind her ear. "I don't know why somebody so smart would do something so dumb."

"Honestly? Me, neither."

"That's not good enough, Cate." Gina smoothed her hair back. "You can do better than that. It's self-destructive. So what's it about? You have dates."

"That's not the same thing."

"So, why then? Think about it." Gina looked at her directly, in the frank way that was second nature to her, and Cate knew she was right.

"It happens when I feel stressed. It's like some people reach for a drink, or a drug. I pick somebody up."

"Yuck."

"Thanks."

"Are you a sex addict?"

"No." Cate recoiled. "It's not like I do it all that often."

"How often?"

"Once a month at most, and in my defense, men have been doing it for centuries. Have you seen a Budweiser commercial lately?"

Gina scoffed. "Oh, are you justifying it now? If you're so proud of it, why keep it a secret?"

"Hey, stop being right."

"It's not about gender, it's about you. That behavior, it's not you." Gina shook her head, adamant. "You leave Graham, a normal man, a stockbroker who gave you something from Tiffany's on the *third date*. That breaks *all* the rules. And you leave *him*—to run to a *rapist*?"

Cate fingered the bracelet, still on her wrist. "Never again."

"You're stopping now? Swearing off working-class hunks? How could you let yourself be *used* like that?"

"I didn't see it that way." Cate considered it. "I guess I just feel more comfortable with that kind of man. Like my husband. I knew him from high school, remember?"

"Barely. The construction guy?"

"Yes. It's where I came from. I worked to get where I am, I wasn't born to it. My mother never went to college. I'm not the Ritz, I'm the pink motel."

"You make fun of Dr. Phil. You should watch." Gina scowled. "You loved your mom, right?"

"Yes, she was great. She was devoted to me. After my dad left, she got a job at my school, in the office. It was her and me." Her mother had died right after Cate had graduated from college, and Cate missed her every day. "It was us against the world. She worked at my school, for the principal. People thought we were trying to be better than them because she wanted college for me. She protected me against everything—the mean nun at school, the monster at night, everything."

"She and your dad broke up when you were how old?"

"Three."

"And you didn't see him again? No visitation or anything?"

"No. He was gone. You know all this—"

"So obviously, you have abandonment issues with men."

"So what? Who doesn't?"

Gina didn't laugh. "You're a smart woman, Cate. Let's figure this out. Something must have triggered this behavior. If it started a year and a half ago, what was happening then, in your love life?"

Cate could barely remember. "I was seeing that guy at Schnader. That one you hated. Marc With a C."

"Narcissist Alert. Watch out for French cuffs. I told you but you didn't listen."

Cate smiled. "We broke up about that time, but I wasn't serious about him anyway."

"But wasn't that when they started talking about you for appointment to the bench?"

Cate thought back. "Yes."

"Marc With a C was threatened by that, I remember you saying. He didn't want people calling him Judge Marc With a C."

Cate smiled again. "More or less. You remember my life better than I do."

"Thank you. You were kind of surprised when your name came up for the vacancy. You thought you weren't political. You didn't think you'd get it."

Cate laughed. "Oh, I knew I wasn't political. I didn't leave work early enough to vote, even."

"And they began the background check and evaluated your credentials, before you could be confirmed. Maybe you were sabotaging yourself, in a way. Worried they wouldn't find you qualified."

"You know better than that. The scrutiny for us isn't like for appellate judges. The confirmation hearing is pro forma. We're basically appointed. I knew I had the credentials, and I was a woman, which didn't hurt. It played out in my favor that I wasn't political. They were so polarized, I was the only one they all agreed on for the job."

"Maybe you didn't want the job."

Cate blinked. "Of course I wanted the job."

"What if you didn't? We've talked about how it's kind of lonely, and you can't see your old partners anymore. You loved the action in court. Aren't you a little ambivalent about being on the bench?"

"How could I be? It's the peak of the profession. Every trial lawyer wants to be a trial judge. There's only seven hundred in the country, on the federal level. It's the ultimate promotion."

"That's not my point." Gina cocked her head. "You really wanted the promotion. But did you really want the *job*?"

Oddly, Cate had never really thought about that. Being a judge was the best she could be, and she always wanted to be the best. "I don't know." She shook her head, too tired to think, and shaken, still. "I guess I should get some therapy."

"Uh, hello, ya *think*? And meds, lotsa meds!" Gina smiled, and then so did Cate, rising.

"Okay, enough. Want more coffee?" Cate crossed to the cabinet, retrieved a paper filter, and slotted it into the coffeemaker. "How's the baby?"

"The neighbor's there. He won't even wake up."

"Great. Thanks for coming over." Cate dumped ground coffee into the filter and went to the sink to fill up the glass pot. "Hey, why'd you call me in the first place? Another tantrum?"

"No, it wasn't about him. I heard on TV about the fight in court. I figured you might be upset."

"Oh, that. Between the rape and the flat tire, I almost forgot." Cate flicked on the coffee machine, thinking of Marz.

"Is that what set it off?"

"Set what off?"

"Your little frolic and detour tonight."

"I'll ask my new shrink." Suddenly the phone rang, and they exchanged glances. Cate said, "I'm not getting it. It's Graham, and I haven't had my therapy yet."

Ring! "It could be the sitter. She knows I'm here, and I left my cell at home."

"Sorry." Cate picked up quickly. "Hello?"

"Judge? Did I wake you?"

"Invaluable." Cate smiled with relief at Val's voice. "What are you doing up so late on a school night?"

"Chief Judge Sherman needed to reach you, but he didn't have your number. So he called me."

"What's up?"

"There's bad news."

CHAPTER 9

The next morning, Cate drove up Market Street in heavy traffic, insulated by the car's perfect seal from the media in front of the courthouse. Reporters held microphones at their sides, and cameramen drank coffee by enamel-white vans with cheery station logos. They were waiting for her, but she wouldn't have answered their questions anyway. She couldn't, because she didn't have the answers. Art Simone had been shot to death last night. And the police were looking for Richard Marz, who was nowhere to be found.

Cate felt a wave of regret. She should have foreseen that it could happen. That if Marz couldn't get justice in her courtroom, he'd get it on the street. She took a right onto Sixth Street. She still couldn't believe that Simone had been murdered. She didn't respect him, but she didn't want him dead. She'd prayed her comments hadn't put him there.

Cate aimed the car for the security booth that would admit her to the judges' parking lot, where she'd take the keyed elevator up to her chambers in the secured half of the courthouse. As a federal judge, she could conceivably go through the entire day without meeting a single member of the public she served. She used to think this was unhealthy, but today she was loving the idea.

Upstairs, Cate opened the door to her chambers, and Val looked up from her desk, her brown eyes filled with empathy. Her full mouth tilted unhappily down at the corners and her smooth skin belied her age of sixty-five. She slipped off Dictaphone headphones covering her steely braids. "Judge, I'm so sorry."

"Thanks." Cate set her briefcase and bag on the navy couch in the reception room, a medium-sized square furnished with an inherited couch and matching leather side chairs. She slipped out of her sheepskin coat and hung it up on the rack.

"It's such a shame. I prayed for him, and for you. Did you get any sleep?"

"Some." Cate walked to the desk with her purse and briefcase. "How about you?"

"I'm fine." Val handed Cate her message slips, over an array of graduation photos of her son and daughter. "The *Inquirer* keeps calling and said it's important that you get back to them."

"I'll get right on that. Next year."

"Graham Liss called twice and said it's very important you call him back. The chief judge called and he wants to see you as soon as you get in."

"Oh, great."

Val frowned. "Hold your head up. You didn't do anything wrong."

Cate had tried to convince herself of that, all last night. She gestured at the law clerks' office, which had fallen suspiciously silent. "They're eavesdropping, aren't they?"

"They're worried about mama."

"How's Emily taking this? It's her case, too."

"Fine, I made her tea. I'll take care of your bags, too. Just go."

"Invaluable," Cate said, touched, and took off for Sherman's chambers.

It was a short trip on the private elevator, and Cate used the time to collect her thoughts, square her shoulders, and check her makeup in the brass plate around the elevator buttons. She looked reasonably presentable with her hair loose to her shoulders, her standard pearls with a white silk T-shirt, and a black Escada suit with matching pumps. She stepped off the elevator, hurried down the hall, and entered the chief's chambers.

"Hey, Mo," Cate said, greeting Sherman's secretary, Mavis Tidell. She knew the secretary's nickname because she was also Val's best friend. Mo looked up from her desk with a smile.

"Back at you, Judge. Go on in. They're inside."

"They?" Cate opened the office door, then was taken aback. The chief sat at the head of his mahogany conference table, but to his right sat Judge Meriden and two other men in business suits, one of whom looked familiar.

"Judge Fante, come in." Sherman stood up in his distinguished, if stooped, way, somber behind his gold-framed reading glasses, and the others followed, smiling grimly, all around.

"Hello, Chief. Jonathan." Cate nodded at Meriden and hoped her surprise at his presence didn't show.

Chief Judge Sherman gestured. "Cate, our guests are homicide detectives with the Philadelphia Police Department." As he spoke, a tall, fit detective in a boxy khaki suit and a maroon knit tie stepped forward and extended his hand.

"I'm Steve Nesbitt," he said, his handshake firm. He looked about forty-five years old, with thick graying hair, a brushy brown-and-gray mustache above even teeth, and a proprietary manner that suggested an ease with himself. He said, "Pleased to meet you."

"Thank you, hello." Cate tried to get her bearings.

"I'm Paul Roots," the other detective said. He was attractive and younger, in a dark suit with an expensive cut and a dark silk tie.

"Great to meet you," Cate said, taking a seat at the opposite end of the table, which cued everybody to resettle themselves. She'd been in Sherman's office only once before and it was everything a federal judge's chambers should be. A thin Oriental area rug lay atop the thick navy carpet, and his large desk was very Ethan Allen mahogany, with matching chairs and end tables on either side of a tapestry couch in muted jewel tones. Antique maps of colonial Philadelphia and award certificates covered the paneled walls, and federal reporters, law reviews, and black binders of committee reports lined the bookshelves. Faint cigar smoke wreathed the air, for that quintessential old-boy touch.

Chief Judge Sherman cleared his throat. "Cate, I called you in because of the crime that occurred last night. I know you must feel this weight very heavily, and I'm sorry it had to happen to you. It's a first for us, at our court. Right, Jonathan?"

"Yes, Chief." Meriden nodded, though he'd been on the bench only five years himself, and Cate segued to officially resenting that he was here.

Sherman continued, "The detectives wanted to speak with you about the matter." His eyes darkened behind his glasses, and the lines that bracketed his drawn mouth deepened. "Perhaps I'll let Detective Nesbitt explain."

Nesbitt faced Cate. "Your Honor, as you know, Arthur Simone was murdered last night. He was killed by a single bullet to the forehead, fired point-blank, outside Le Jardin, a restaurant on Delaware Avenue. The crime took place, we believe, at around 8:15 p.m. Someone walked directly up to Mr. Simone, fired, and ran. He used a .22-caliber weapon." Nesbitt withdrew a skinny spiral pad from his breast pocket, flipped it open, and checked it. "Simone had been having dinner with his attorneys, George Hartford and another person, Courtney Flavert, a jury consultant who worked on the case. Simone left the restaurant ahead of them, to catch the red-eye back to L.A."

Cate shuddered, picturing the scene. "Were there any witnesses?"

"No, there's only the two restaurants on the block, and the other one was closed, it being Monday. That stretch can be deserted at night."

"If there were no witnesses, how do you know all this?"

Nesbitt hesitated. "It isn't public knowledge, but we have a video from a security cam in the restaurant's parking lot. Our prime suspect is Richard Marz, who lost his lawsuit before Your Honor yesterday. It appears to be Marz on the videotape, or someone of the same size and stature. We don't have a positive ID yet. It was dark that late and foggy because of the rain."

"Oh God." Cate heard her own voice catch. So awful. So hard to process.

"We're trying to find Mr. Marz, but his whereabouts are unknown."

"Did you talk to his wife?"

"Sure, yes, and his mother. They don't know where he is. They're upset, understandably."

Cate flashed on the melee in court. The wife screaming.

"Anything you can tell us about Marz that might help?" Nesbitt slid a ballpoint from his pocket and clicked it with a flat thumb.

"Not really." Cate tried to think. "I don't have any inside information on him. I met with his lawyer the other day, and I know he wanted to settle the case, but Simone wouldn't."

Sherman asked, "How far apart were they, Cate?"

"Marz had come down to twenty-five grand from two million. Simone wouldn't pay a penny, his lawyer said."

Judge Sherman tsked. "No wonder you couldn't settle it."

Nesbitt scribbled on his pad. "You learned this in negotiations?"

"Yes. Marz's lawyer was there, and Simone's. No principals." Cate was kicking herself. Maybe if she had asked Marz and Simone into her office, this wouldn't have happened.

"Any record, or transcript of something like that?"

"No, not typically," Cate answered, and Chief Judge Sherman met her eye.

"Well, Judge Fante, let's get to the point." Nesbitt unclicked his pen. "The reason we're here is that we have a great concern that Mr. Marz may come after you next."

"You think he'd do that?" Cate asked, shocked.

"He has a clear motive to hurt you. You're the one who made the judgment against him."

"I was on his side, for God's sake." Cate couldn't wrap her mind around it. "My comments on the bench made that clear."

Meriden sniffed, and Nesbitt continued: "Bottom line, you ruled against him, Your Honor. Your judgment cost him a lot of money, millions and millions of dollars. At this point, we don't know where he is and we don't know his mental state. He could be unhinged. He could kill again."

Sherman added, "Cate, I'm taking it seriously enough to send a court-mail to all members of the court and the building employees, advising them to be on alert. Mr. Marz will be apprehended if he attempts to enter the courthouse." Sherman's eyes softened and he looked at Cate. "I won't take any chances with our newest member of the Eastern District."

Cate smiled, and so did the others, except Meriden.

Sherman continued, "Sadly, it's not unprecedented that we judges are threatened for the decisions we make. We can't hide, nor should we. We have a job to do, and our courtroom calendar is public. It can be accessed by any member of the public, by logging on the directory downstairs or the court website. I myself have had my life threatened several times."

"So have I," Meriden chimed in.

"But Marz isn't a rash, impulsive criminal," Cate said, trying to process the information. "He's a lawyer. In fact, a prosecutor. He may go after Simone, but he wouldn't come after me. He doesn't have that kind of rage. He's an intellectual. A computer geek at heart."

Nesbitt frowned. "With all due respect, Your Honor, you wouldn't think that if you saw the videotape. The man fired without a second thought. I've seen gangbangers with more conscience."

"If it's him on the tape."

"I believe it is, and again, I didn't think he was such a geek when I saw him attack Simone."

"You were there that day, in court?"

"Yes, as a spectator. Frank Russo is my former partner."

"I thought you looked familiar." Cate wondered fleetingly how Russo felt about her, after yesterday. "Have you talked to Detective Russo about this?"

"Yes."

"Did Marz tell Russo he was going to kill Simone, or say anything like that? Or that he was going to kill me, for that matter?"

Nesbitt stiffened. "It's not procedure to discuss an ongoing investigation, and this isn't public knowledge, but Marz didn't talk to Russo yesterday. Marz disappeared right after your verdict."

"Entry of judgment," Sherman corrected. "Only juries issue verdicts."

"Sorry. Entry of judgment." Nesbitt nodded. "Now. Judge Fante, did you notice anyone following you last night after work? Or anything unusual at all?"

Yikes. "No one following me, I don't think." Caught off guard, Cate didn't know how much to tell them. "I had a date after work, and we went to dinner, then to my date's house." She noticed that the room got quieter, everybody interested in the life of the resident Single Girl. She swallowed hard. "Then I went home."

"How did you get home?"

"Drove."

"You didn't notice anyone following your car, did you?"

"No."

Nesbitt consulted his pad. "Marz drives a dark blue Subaru, late model. I'll write down his license number for you." He flipped the page, jotted down the information, and ripped it off, handing it to her. "Keep a look out, tonight. If I may ask, do you live alone?"

"Yes. In Society Hill."

"Did you notice anything unusual around your house?"

"No."

Nesbitt made a note. "Tonight, scan your street before you enter your house and make sure that nothing looks suspicious. Check and see if the parked cars look familiar. Do you have a security system?"

"A burglar alarm."

"Use it. Do you own a gun?"

"No." Cate laughed, then noticed Chief Judge Sherman and Meriden looking surprised. "Chief, do *you* have a gun?"

"Of course."

Meriden said, "I collect guns."

"I collect Blahniks," Cate said, but it wasn't a girl crowd.

"Your Honor, you might want to consider purchasing a weapon for your protection and taking lessons, at a firing range. We don't have the personnel to protect you, but we've alerted the marshal service and they're going to put extra marshals on overtime, at least until we apprehend Marz." Nesbitt gestured beside him. "Judge Meriden and you are the only two judges on the eighth floor, correct?"

"Yes."

Meriden said, "Cate and I share a common hallway, and visitors are buzzed in to get past the locked doors. There's a security camera, so each chambers can see whom they're buzzing in."

"Why are we discussing this?" Cate asked, confused.

Meriden answered, "We had a reporter buzz in this morning, posing as a lawyer in a products case. Luckily, my clerk stopped him."

"That's a different issue from Marz, isn't it?" Cate asked, and Nesbitt nodded.

"Again, bottom line, you'll both have to be on alert. Look out for each other. Be careful out there."

Judge Sherman lit up. "That's what they used to say on *Hill Street Blues*! Tell me, Detective, was that show accurate, in your opinion?"

"*Barney Miller* was my favorite." Nesbitt broke into a smile. "Ask my partner here. He's the expert. He wanted to be a technical adviser on *Cold Case*. He tells everybody, 'I coulda been a consultant! I coulda been a contender!'"

Detective Roots came alive. "Well, I could have, and I *almost* was!"

Nesbitt chuckled. "The difference between a consultant and *almost* is a house down in Margate, a boat, and two million bucks."

"All right, enough." Roots rose, flushing, and brushed down his slacks. "Before we go, let's walk around the eighth floor. See how it's laid out."

"I'll take you there, detectives," Meriden offered, beating Cate to the punch.

For now. But she wasn't going to let it lie.

CHAPTER 10

After their tour, Cate walked back to the chambers with Meriden, falling into step down the hallway. "What's your problem with me?" she asked, when she couldn't keep her own counsel a moment longer. "Is it because of Edge Electronics? That securities case, so long ago? Because if it is, let's have it out, here and now."

Meriden blinked, impassive. "Edge is in the past. Win some, lose some. No big deal. I don't have a problem with you."

"Oh, come on. You never miss a chance to undermine me. The next time you have something to say about me, how about you say it *to* me?"

"You're sure?" Meriden's dark eyes flickered with challenge.

"Shoot."

"Okay, if that's the way you want it, Cate. Here goes. You never should have said what you did in open court. Your comments were emotional and inappropriate for a judge."

"I'm a human being, Jonathan. I don't check my conscience at the courtroom door."

"Your conscience isn't the law." Meriden's mouth flattened to a rigid line. "You lack judicial demeanor in everything you do. The way you look, the way you act, even the way you dress. We wear black robes for a reason, to equalize us. But you insist on standing out."

Whoa. "There is no one right way to act, and it's none of your business how I dress off the bench."

"It is my business, because it's my court. You never should have ruled from the bench. You give new meaning to the term 'judicial activism.' Judges aren't 'knights errant,' or haven't you read your Cardozo?"

"I know the quote, and I don't need you to lecture me on the proper role of a federal judge."

"Beg to differ, Cate." Meriden leaned so close she could smell Listerine. "A prudent judge would have issued a written opinion later. You made a mistake that endangers us all."

Ouch. "Oh, go straight to hell." Cate turned on her heel and stalked down the hall to her chambers. She couldn't let him see how she felt. And worst of all, was he right? Should she have ruled from the bench? Sherman said it was okay, but was it? She'd been locked in that question loop all night.

Cate opened the door to her chambers, where Val was busy on the phone. She waved hello, walked by Val's desk, and went back to the law clerks' office. Just outside their door, she could hear them laughing and a TV playing. She popped her head in, with an automatic smile.

Emily jumped up and flicked off the TV. "We were just waiting for the news at noon, Judge." She was sitting at her desk chair facing the tiny TV stuck on the bookshelf among the case files. She shared the small office with co-clerk Sam Herman, a slight and serious young man. He had a feathery brown haircut, pale skin, and a long, bony nose that divided brown eyes set too close together. He wore a gray sweater and khakis, since they weren't in court today.

"Turn the TV back on. I'd like to see the news, too."

"It's only *The View*. It's not time yet."

"Okay, listen up." Cate leaned against the desk. "Obviously, a terrible thing has happened, with Art Simone being killed. The police think Marz did it, and you may have some feelings about that. You in particular, Emily, since it was your case."

Emily bit her lip but said nothing. Evidently, big Goths don't cry.

"You have to understand one thing. The decision to grant the motion was mine, and no one else's. You guys do legal research and write memos, but it's my decision and my responsibility, you hear? I was right on the law and I had to make the decision I did." Cate would believe that in five, maybe ten, years. "What matters is that the police are concerned about our security. They suspect that Marz may come back to chambers to hurt us."

Sam's eyes flared. "That's not cool."

"No, Sam. Not cool." Cate wondered about this kid sometimes. Both clerks had flawless academic records and had served on their law reviews, but their personalities were a different question. She'd been confirmed at such an odd time of year, she'd missed the regular batch of clerk aps. "I want you two to stay together when you leave the building. All comings and goings, stay together."

"But we stagger our lunches," Emily said.

"Don't. Go together. And don't buzz anybody in without clearing it with Val. The media's an issue, too. A reporter tried to get to us by buzzing into Meriden's chambers."

"Retard," Sam said.

"I don't like that word." Cate was thinking of Warren. He'd been called that on the street, more than once.

"Loser, then."

Cate let it go. "Marz drives a navy Subaru, so keep an eye out for that, too. I have the license plate number and—"

"Judge, it's time for the news." Sam jumped up and switched on the old Sony Trinitron. "We were on *ET* and *The Insider* last night, and that was before the murder."

"Excellent," Cate said dryly, but the news was beginning, with its bright blue and red graphics. The banner came on and behind the handsome anchorman floated a large photo of a grinning Art Simone. Cate stifled a wave of sadness and regret.

The anchorman said, "In our top story, police are still searching for Richard Marz, a former assistant district attorney being sought in connection with the shooting murder of Hollywood television producer Arthur . . ."

Cate watched the TV screen as they flashed photos of Marz, barely able to listen. She shouldn't have said anything from the bench. She'd given Marz the validation he needed to kill. The TV screen changed to file footage of the male lead from *Attorneys@Law*, with a voice-over about a great loss and a tragic crime and how the show would go on. Then the picture changed again.

Cate froze when she recognized the photo on the screen.

CHAPTER 11

It's Elvis, from last night.

The anchorman was saying, "And in southwest Philadelphia, a tragic accident claims a man's life. James Partridge was killed when he fell from a balcony at a motel here."

"D'oh, I hate when that happens," Sam joked, and behind him, Cate stood riveted.

The anchorman said, "Police say that Partridge, a frequent guest of the motel, may have lost his footing in the rain and was inebriated at the time of the fall. And in other news, an overturned tractor-trailer . . ."

Emily leaned over and switched off the TV. "Once again, the proverbial tractor-trailer."

Sam laughed. "It gets 'em every time. Dang things can't stay upright."

But Cate was already backing out of the room. "I have work to do, guys," she said, shaken, and retreated to her office.

She closed the door, hustled to her desk, and called Gina's cell phone. She told her about the man's death, hunched over the phone, confused and stricken. Her head began to pound, and she rubbed her forehead. When she finished, she felt vaguely nauseated. "Maybe I should go to the cops," she said.

"Are you nuts? Why?"

"He probably fell down the stairs, trying to come after me."

"Did you see that?"

"No, he was on the balcony when I left." Cate squeezed her eyes shut but couldn't remember for sure. "At least I thought he was—"

"So what, anyway? So *what*?"

"The man is dead, Geen. I was the last person to see him alive."

"It wasn't a murder, it was an *accident*. He fell down trying to *rape* you. You don't owe him anything!" Gina could barely contain herself. "You wanna go to the cops? Tell them you pick up strange guys, in bars?"

Cate flushed, mortified. What was she thinking? For a judge, she had no judgment at all.

"You'd be risking your reputation, for nothing."

Cate put her face in her hands, rattled to her foundation. What would she go to the police with? Even she knew she wasn't making sense. She was screwing up so much lately, and now people were dying.

"Cate, you're just panicking. Between the stuff with Simone and this, you're just a mess."

"Thanks."

"Take a deep breath."

"I left him alive."

"Of course you did, and then he fell off the balcony because he was a falling-down-drunk, no-good-pig *rapist*."

"God, this is so awful. He's dead."

"Yes, and you're not," Gina said, with finality. "Look, I gotta go, the pediatrician just came in. Don't do anything stupid. I'll call you later."

"Thanks." Cate hung up, so preoccupied she barely heard a knock at the door. "Yes?"

Val stuck her head inside, frowning with concern. "You okay?"

"Fine."

"Marz will have to get through me to get to you."

"Aw, don't even think that." Cate willed herself to get it together. Nobody knew about the man last night and nobody ever would. She waved Val inside. "Sherman and the cops think Marz might—"

"I got the court-mail. I'll keep an eye on the clerks, too."

"Thanks, and you be careful. Marz may know what you look like."

"I can take that little white boy." Val lifted an attitudinal eyebrow.

"Not if he has a gun you can't."

"Pssht." Val waved her off. "By the way, those flowers came for you while you were with Sherman." She gestured at the conference table, where a huge bouquet of long-stemmed roses sprayed from a clear glass vase.

"Jeez." *Graham.* Cate felt her chest tighten.

Val chuckled. "How'd you miss those? There's two dozen there, I counted."

Cate got up, crossed to the flowers, and slid the white envelope from its clear plastic trident and opened it. *Judge, I have a major crush on you, but I promise to take it slower. Like—not love, Graham.*

"And Graham Liss called again this morning," Val said. "It's none of my business, but between the phone calls and the two dozen roses, you might give the man a little attention. It's about time you had a date. Now, did you remember you have oral argument at two o'clock?"

"Of course not," Cate answered, turning with card in hand. "In what case?"

"*Tourneau v. General Insurance.* I ordered you a tuna fish salad for lunch."

"Thanks, great idea." Cate had meant to study the briefs and the bench memo last night. Now she'd have to go on the bench cold. "Where's Emily? It's her case, isn't it?"

Val whispered, "She says you saw Simone's picture on TV and got very upset."

Great. "Don't be silly. Open the door, please, Val. And cover your ears." Val complied, and Cate called out, "Emily! Come out, come out, wherever you are!"

And at the appointed hour, Cate was berobed and back in court, presiding atop the dais. From her first moment in the courtroom, she flashed on a freeze-frame of the very last time she'd sat here. Marz was launching himself at Simone. She saw it over and over until she walled off the thought and concentrated on the proceeding at hand, which involved a question of conflicts of laws. Before today, she'd thought of conflicts as an abstract area of the law, but now she knew that no area of the law was truly abstract. She'd seen the intersection of the law and human beings, and it ended in a head-on collision.

Cate collected herself and mustered a smile for plaintiff's counsel. "Good afternoon, Mr. Gill."

"Good afternoon, Your Honor." Herman Gill was a standard-issue big-firm lawyer; tall, middle-aged white guy in a dark suit, horn-rimmed glasses, and brown wingtips, as if he'd been mugged by Brooks Brothers.

"What do we have today, specifically?" Cate asked, glancing at the papers.

"Your Honor, I will review the facts briefly. Plaintiff Jean-Patrice Tourneau is a decedent, a Pennsylvania resident and former CEO of VistaView Communications, Inc., a Pennsylvania corporation with its headquarters in Blue Bell."

Cate listened, coming back down to earth. The defense lawyer, another big-firm squash player, crossed his pinstriped legs. She made notes, though she knew Emily had included it in her bench memo. The law clerk sat off to the side, taking her usual copious notes. She seemed better than she had been this morning, too. Sitting at his desk near her, the courtroom deputy was catching up on the crossword puzzle. The courtroom was back to normal. The pews sat empty, ten vacant rows of honey-hued wood, and Cate could see clear to the back wall, with its oil portraits of past district judges, all of them men with bald heads, horn-rimmed glasses, and somber smiles. *The way you look, the way you act, even the way you dress.* Cate wondered if she would ever feel like this were her courtroom.

Suddenly the door opened in the back, and the movement drew Cate's attention. A man in a dark suit entered and sat down on a back bench. Something familiar about him gave Cate pause, then she realized who it was.

Gill was saying, "We urge the Court that there is a true conflict, because Indiana law, unlike District of Columbia law . . ."

Cate tuned out, her concentration broken. The man in the back was Detective Russo. He sat still, facing front, his arms folded. He couldn't be here for the argument. Was he watching her? She couldn't see his features at this distance. It unnerved her. She couldn't get her bearings today, with so many distractions. Art Simone was dead, and so was the man from last night, Partridge. It was like a one-two punch, and now Russo was watching her, the sole spectator in the empty courtroom, sitting squarely in her line of vision.

In the next minute, Russo folded his arms. He knew she had to see him. Was he trying to intimidate her? Cate tried to catch the eye of the courtroom deputy, but he was doing the crossword, chewing the end of a pencil. Emily sat absorbed in her note-taking, her legal pad balanced on her lap.

Cate tried to focus on the proceeding but couldn't. She would rule later in a written opinion; she wouldn't rule from the bench, though she would have preferred it that way, and so would counsel. She'd always liked the quick answer when she was in practice. Gill finally concluded his argument, then defense counsel rose, took the lectern, and made an endless counterargument, but by then, Cate was dying to get off the bench. She couldn't shake Russo's gaze and felt it like a weight. Did he blame her for what Marz did? Could he blame her more than she blamed herself? As soon as the rebuttal was finished,

Cate banged the gavel, ended the session, and practically fled the courtroom.

Russo was still sitting there when she left.

Keep a look out, tonight. A dark blue Subaru.

Cate shuddered, driving away from the courthouse. It was almost dark, and she'd ended the workday early, having fussed all afternoon with the same opinion, unable to clear her head enough to write. She hadn't heard a word from Russo. He made no attempt to call chambers or contact her. She'd called Nesbitt and left a message for him at the Homicide desk, but he hadn't called back yet. In truth, she didn't know what she'd have said to him. Russo hadn't done anything wrong and he wasn't the threat to her. Marz was.

Do you have a gun?

Marz really could be out there. She couldn't be in denial. She'd been fairly safe in her office, walled behind locks and federal marshals, but now she was on her own. She glanced in her rearview mirror at the car behind her, but it was too dark to tell its make. Its headlights were too high to be a Subaru. It must be an SUV.

She eyed the cars around her as she traveled down Race Street. Plumes of exhaust curled from the car bumpers, chalky in the bitter-cold night. She didn't see a Subaru, but she wouldn't have been able to tell one from a Toyota or Honda. She felt tense the whole time and took a quick right when the light changed, heading east to vary her driving routine, just in case. She drove all the way to her street with an eye in the rearview, and after she saw no Subaru on her street, wasted no time barreling into her garage, closing the door behind her, and hustling into the house, checking all the locks.

It wasn't five minutes later that her doorbell rang.

CHAPTER 12

Cate hurried to the window and pushed the curtain aside an inch. She couldn't see who was at the door. Maybe they'd go away.

Ding dong!

She went for her purse, dug out her cell phone, and flipped it open, her finger on the emergency button. She went to the door and pressed an eye to the peephole.

Russo. Cate froze. She didn't know what to do. What did he want? Why was he here? Had he seen her come in? Was he watching her house, too? On the other hand, what was she afraid of? He was a detective, and she'd liked him when he testified.

Ding dong! She couldn't ignore him, could she? She hated feeling so afraid, for no reason. She was working herself up for nothing. She finally pressed the intercom to speak. "Yes?"

"Judge Fante, it's Detective Russo. I'd like to speak with you for a few minutes, if you don't mind. I tried to see you after court, but your secretary said you'd left early. It's important."

"Hold on," Cate said, relaxing. She was being paranoid. She flipped the phone closed, set it on the entrance table, and opened the front door. "Come in, Detective."

"Thanks." Russo entered the entrance hall, and Cate closed the door behind him. He took up most of the small room, taller in his brown leather coat than he'd looked on the witness stand. His eyes were dark, and his largish nose red from the cold, though his hair remained in glossy place, as if he had just combed it. He said, "Sorry to bother you at home."

"Would you like a drink? A Coke or something?"

"No, thanks. I won't stay long."

"Come on in." Cate walked ahead and gestured him into the living room, taking a quick look around to see if it was in order, a homeowner's impulse. She straightened two magazines on the glass coffee table and sat down on the soft tan couch. "Please, take a chair."

"Thanks." Russo eased heavily into the side chair, looking around. "This is a lovely house. How long have you lived here?"

"About six years."

"Nice." Russo looked around again, and in the light from the Waterford lamp on the end table, Cate could see the pain in his eyes.

"I saw you in the courtroom today. Why were you there?"

"I just wanted to go back, I guess, like it was a crime scene. I'm still trying to figure this whole thing out. Simone, dead. Rich, a fugitive." Russo's voice softened with naked emotion. "I can't believe he would do that. I can't believe it all came to this."

"I know exactly what you mean." Cate paused. "Let me say something that might not be standard procedure."

"Go right ahead." Russo chuckled, his heavy shoulders shifting once in the jacket. "My coming here sure isn't procedure."

"I'm very sorry about the way the case came out. I ruled the way I had to, not the way I wanted to. That's probably all I should say on the subject. It's not more than I said in open court."

"I understand." Russo's full lips went tight. "I guess it's just hard to swallow."

"I know." Cate felt sad for him. Detective Russo had had a dream, too. He would have been an equal partner with Marz, and unlike Marz, he wasn't a young man any longer.

"Sometimes, what gets to me is, you can never get over. You know what I mean? No matter how hard you try, and how much you work, and even how good you are, you can never get over. We played by the rules and we played with honor, and in the end, we didn't win. That's the worst to me. When you work that hard, and you still don't win." Russo fell silent, seeming to examine his hands on his lap.

"I know it must be hard," Cate said, when the silence became almost uncomfortable.

"It's like, when I was a uniform, a beat cop, I'd risk my ass to collar some knucklehead, some lowlife. Then, a judge would come along and let him off, on a technicality." Russo looked down. "That's what this is like. Like they got off on a technicality."

Cate shifted uncomfortably. "I feel for you, and for Rich Marz. I hope he turns himself in soon. Have you spoken with him?"

Russo looked up, shaking his head. "Not since yesterday."

"I know they have him on videotape, but it's so hard to believe he did it."

"I don't know what I believe, Judge." Russo kept shaking his head, his cheeks slack. "I can't figure this out. It stinks to high heaven. I don't know who the hell's on that tape."

"You don't think it's him?" Cate asked, mystified.

"You tell me." Russo got up abruptly and crossed to the entertainment center. "This your VCR?"

"Yes. Why?"

Russo withdrew a black cartridge from his jacket pocket and slid it into the VCR. "I want to know what you think of this, Your Honor. I value your opinion."

"You have the *tape*?" Cate's mouth dropped open. "How did you get that?"

"I'm a detective, remember?" Russo turned on the TV and pressed the button for the video. "Hey, I got the same TV."

"But I thought this was Nesbitt's case, and the other detective's." Cate got up slowly, regretting she had let him in. "I don't want to see that tape. I don't think I should. It's not right. It could compromise the evidence or—"

"No, it won't."

"Detective, I don't want to see it."

"Come on, tell me what you think. I can't figure this out, and you're so much smarter than me. Sorry. Than *I*."

"But a man was killed." Cate recoiled, as the tape started, grainy and fuzzy. "I don't want to see that. Please don't turn it on."

"Look, Judge." Russo pointed at the image on the screen, which wasn't Marz and Simone at all. It was pornography. Amateurish. Grainy. A muscled man lay on top of a woman, making love to her on a bed. The man's buttocks flexed as he thrusted, and the woman's legs were wrapped around his waist, her breasts heaving. The audio was fuzzy, but for moaning.

"What are you *doing*?" Cate said, appalled. "Are you sick?"

"This man has a criminal record, Your Honor. Ag assault, extortion, attempted rape. He's a thug, a knucklehead."

"Stop it!" Disgusted, Cate rushed to the VCR, then froze. On the screen, the man turned to the camera and winked. He had dark hair and dark eyes. It was the man from last night, at the pink motel. The dead man. Jim Partridge. *Elvis.*

Russo started laughing as Cate pounded the POWER button. The TV screen went black.

"What the hell do you think you're doing!" Cate demanded, horrified.

"You might answer that same question, Your Honor. See, yesterday, after you took my future away, I had to go back to work. I was on duty last night. I caught this case. Some poor slob fell offa balcony. They're not sure if it's a homicide. So I go check it out."

Oh my God.

"I found the videocamera in the closet, next to the bed, but I guess you knew that. The motel owner was in business with your young boyfriend, making amateur videos, but I guess you knew that, too. They sold quite a few. Is that your gig? Did you take a cut, Your Honor?" Russo grew angry, and Cate backed away toward the front door.

"Get out of my house!"

"You gonna tell me you didn't know about that, Judge? That you're not in on it? What, do you take a *piece*?" Russo sneered. "Oh, I wish you could see your face right now! Maybe you didn't know. Is that it? Why'd you throw all that money at him? Was he blackmailing you? What'd he have on you? Did he have a tape on you, already?"

"Get out!" Cate shouted, opening the front door and grabbing her cell phone from the table. "Get out or I'll call the cops."

"You saw what—correction, *who*—Mr. Partridge did the night before last, and you know what he did last night. You're next on the tape, but you don't get laid like the other girls. Why not, Your Honor?" Russo headed for the door, grinning. "I'll go, I don't want you callin' the *po*-lice. But answer me this, what's a federal judge like you doing in a place like that? *What?* Paying off a thug, for what? You tell me. You, so high and mighty, who sits in judgment of *me* and my friend!"

"Get *out* or I'll scream!" Cate yelled, and Russo burst into laughter, his dark eyes flashing with a reckless glint she hadn't seen before, or in court.

"Admit it was you. It was *you* on that porn tape." Russo leaned over and drilled a finger between her breasts, and Cate smacked his hand away.

"Don't you dare!"

"Admit it. It's you. You're a crook."

"GET OUT!" Cate shoved him out the door, and Russo let himself be pushed, but stopped on the threshold, so close she could feel his spit on her face.

"I know what a phony you are. What a *hypocrite* you are. I'm gonna find out what he had on you, *Your Honor*. And what you had to do with his *accident*!"

Cate slammed the door, swallowing her scream. Then she closed all the curtains in her living room and rushed back to the TV.

She had to see that tape.

CHAPTER 13

Cate pressed the ON button on the remote, her fingers trembling, and the TV came back on. The naked couple were having sex, and she fast-forwarded through it with disgust, then slowed to a stop. They were still having sex, so she sped it up again, then stopped. The date on the bottom of the screen had changed to yesterday's date. She sank into one of the chairs to watch and pressed PLAY.

The TV screen showed a man whose face was too close to be in focus, but he didn't look like Partridge. He appeared to be fiddling with the louvered slats on a door, permitting the camera lens to peek out.

There had been a closet next to the bed.

Then he passed in front of the lens, a short shadow, and the scene showed an empty bed. Cate pressed REWIND and watched again, confirming what she had seen. The man must have come in to turn on the camera. Maybe while she'd been waiting in her car, the motel owner had run upstairs. *No.* Partridge had called him from his car, alerting him that he was coming ahead, with a girl.

Ugh.

Cate returned to the TV screen. The slats from the louvers on the top and bottom made a black border, giving the impression of peeking through a keyhole, spying on an empty bed. She didn't even want to think about how many women had been on tape without knowing. She could have been one. As Gina would have said, *serves you right*.

Cate checked the bottom of the screen. The time read 10:05, in white numbers. She thought a minute. That would be about when she and Partridge got to the room.

Against the door.

Cate remembered her own words, sickened now by them. He had wanted to have sex on the bed, and now she knew why. In the end he'd given up on the bed and acceded to her request; he wanted the play more than the tape. Or maybe he figured he'd get her there, sooner or later. Next she heard voices on the tape, indistinct but sounding like a man and a woman. Cate played it back with the volume higher, to try to make out the words, but she couldn't.

On TV, the scene showed the empty bed, with talking in the background interspersed with silences. She figured they were kissing at the door in the hallway, out of the shot. Then she heard the word *wait* distinctly. She rewound to make sure. "Wait!" Cate heard herself say it, unclear, but she knew it was her. She must have been struggling with the Tiffany bracelet, trying to get it off at this point.

Then she heard her voice louder, but she couldn't understand what she'd been saying. It must have been when he'd been walking her backwards toward the bed. He'd wanted to get her in camera range, but she'd been fussing with the bracelet. Then Partridge walked backwards into the TV picture, his back to the camera, and fell onto the bed, throwing up his arms. The view was upside down, with the top of Partridge's head to the camera and his legs stretched out on the bed, hanging over it at the knee.

Cate rewound to watch it again and hear what he'd said. He was laughing, and she caught "Damn" and then "Hurry!" Suddenly he sat bolt upright, and Cate knew he must have been listening to her say she wasn't staying.

She watched herself walk into the frame—almost. She recognized her legs and the black Blahniks she'd worn yesterday, and the edge of her trench coat showed. In the next second she stepped closer, and the following frames showed her upper body in her raincoat, a flash of white silk blouse, and then her chin. But no more of her face.

Cate held her breath, then exhaled in relief. She had stopped there in the motel room, just out of camera range. She hadn't walked far enough into the room to get her whole face. *Thank God!* Still her gut tensed, watching. She knew what would happen next. On the TV screen, Partridge was still sitting up with his back to the camera, and Cate could see her hand offer him a wad of bills, which he slapped aside, sending the cash flying. Next came words, indistinct until he shouted, "You can't pay me!"

Cate played it again, and it came through almost understandably. *Had he said that?* She couldn't remember.

On the TV, Partridge leapt off the bed and ran out of frame. He was coming after her. He'd shoved her against the door now. She tried not to think about his rough hand or the raw terror she felt. Then the screen went still, and there was a shot of the empty bed again, the bedcovers wrinkled slightly.

Cate watched the bottom of the screen. 10:13, 10:14, 10:15. Partridge would have been outside on the balcony now.

Cate edged forward in the seat. She didn't know when he'd fallen. The tape could tell her something about his death. She watched, engrossed, the empty bed, and then Partridge came back into the room, staggering slightly. He stopped, faced the camera, then gave it the finger and burst into laughter. Then he fell face forward on the bed.

10:42, 10:43, 10:44.

Partridge didn't move and he appeared to have fallen asleep. She kept watching, then the tape went black. She got up, went to the VCR, and slid out the tape. It was at its end. So either the section that Russo had given her was over or the camera had run out of tape. Maxell, a two-hour tape. They must have used it, filming the different girls, saving on tape by turning the camera on and off after each girl. She could verify by watching the porn, but she wasn't up to that.

Cate looked up at the screen, gray with static snow. At some point, Partridge must have gotten up, groggy and drunk, gone outside in the rain and fallen off the balcony. She sank onto the padded arm of the chair. Partridge: a jerk, a pig. What had Russo said: *Ag assault, extortion, attempted rape.* It was still sad. He was dead.

Cate set the tape on the edge of the entertainment center, wondering how she had gotten herself into such a mess, then knowing exactly how she had gotten herself into this mess. Her sex life on tape, and now a detective believed she was a crooked judge.

She got up and went to the phone.

CHAPTER 14

Cate reached Gina after Warren had gone to bed. She told the story, start to finish, going back from morning until night. Afterwards there was complete silence on the end of the line. "Geen?"

"I'm here, trying to figure out when your life got so exciting. Sex videotapes? What is this world coming to?"

"No good."

Gina sighed. "But you know what I don't get? How did Russo know it was you on the tape?"

"It *is* me."

"You said you couldn't see your whole face, just the lower half. How does he know for sure that it's you?"

"He does. He sounded like he did."

"How was the audio? Could you tell it was your voice?"

"No, not really." Cate thought about it. She'd been too panicked to analyze it before. "What if he remembered my outfit from court that day, or my shoes?"

"Is he gay?"

"He's Italian."

"Mutually exclusive."

Cate laughed, feeling her body relax into the soft chair. But it was a puzzle. How *did* Russo know it was her? Then she realized something. "Wait a minute. He doesn't know it's me. Rather, he does, but he can't prove it."

"To who?"

"Oh no." The answer struck Cate like a blow. "Hear me out. First Russo comes over and softens me up with his sob story. Then he surprises me with the tape and Partridge's criminal record. Then he tells me things that I know are on the tape, like that he saw me throw the money."

"Okay."

"Then he confronts me with the porny part of the tape, knowing I won't watch it with him there. He knew the tape wouldn't show me, so he was tricking me with the *fact* of the tape itself. He wanted to scare me into admitting it was me. It's Cross-Examination 101, isn't it?" Cate straightened up, convinced. "He even said as much to me, at the door. He said, 'Admit it. It was you.'"

"But so what if you admit it? He goes and tells somebody?"

Cate drew the only conclusion possible. "He must have been wearing a wire."

Gina yelped. "Yo, that's evil."

"But smart. I bet he wired himself. He needed me to say it was me, on tape. Why? To prove it to his friend, his old partner, the detective on the Simone murder. Nesbitt."

"I get it! He finds this juicy videotape in the motel, plugs it into the VCR and sees you, then he runs over to his old partner, whatever his name is—"

"Nesbitt. He tells Nesbitt it's me on the tape, but Nesbitt watches it and isn't buying it."

"Inattentive blindness strikes again. His brain won't let him see you because you're not supposed to be there."

"Ta-da!" Cate smiled. "Thank God that supposedly normal people can be in denial."

"So Russo has to prove it to Nesbitt." Gina paused. "But you think Nesbitt would tell him to wear a wire?"

"Hell, no. Nesbitt seemed like a straight arrow to me. I don't think he'd sanction Russo threading a federal judge with a porn tape. To what end? I think Russo is losing it. He's on his own."

"So what are you gonna do? Tell Nesbitt?"

"No. Right now, I have deniability. It's not me on that tape." Cate flushed, embarrassed. "The last thing I want is them knowing about, well, you know. My dates. I started lying and I have to stick with it. And please don't tell me about tangled webs."

"I wouldn't." Gina's tone warmed. "I feel terrible for you."

"My own fault." Cate shook her head. "And you know what? This morning I told Nesbitt that I went home after my date last night. He must have been surprised when his pal came up with the greatest-hits tape."

"You're still in the clear. Maybe he'll think that was your date."

"Or he'll pretend he does for political purposes. There's no margin in knowing dumb secrets about a federal judge."

"Right. I'd let it lie. It's bad enough you have this Russo gunning for you."

"If I were the bitch he thinks I am, I'd get him fired. I'll tell you one thing, he'd better not show up in my courtroom again." Then Cate heard herself. *My* courtroom? She never thought she'd say that. If that was the silver lining to this cloud, it wasn't silver enough.

"Russo can't do anything to you, Cate. You're not crooked, so he can't prove that you are."

"But he can make my life miserable. And it looks like he's about to."

"We won't let him."

"Right!" Cate said, cheering up.

"So meanwhile, did you say *two dozen roses*?"

Cate laughed. "Uh, yeah. Is that important right now?"

"You're damn right it is. You wanna talk about what you're going to do about The Tiffany Guy?"

"I already know," Cate answered, and told her.

CHAPTER 15

Cate checked her watch: 1:32 a.m. *Argh*. She was sitting in front of her computer, working in her home office. She couldn't sleep after Russo's visit and she had work to do. Books on built-in shelves wrapped around the cozy study on two sides, mostly novels she couldn't bring herself to give away, and a low, metal file cabinet sat against the far wall, containing pleadings and forms accumulated during practice. None of those forms would help her tonight.

A porcelain mug of tea grew cold on her left and multicolored M&M's lay scattered to her right. Stacks of printed cases covered her desk, but she'd read them so many times in the past week she'd practically memorized them. She'd felt too paranoid to turn on the lights in the office, so the room was completely dark except for the square of monitor light that shone on the front of her body, illuminating a face scrubbed clean of makeup, a red cashmere bathrobe, and a high ponytail that made her feel too much the rookie for the task at hand.

Cate wrote, Marz premises this argument on his view that Pennsylvania should disregard the well-established precedent of definiteness

She skimmed the line and shook her head. It still wasn't right. It had to be perfect. It felt so strange, issuing an opinion after Simone's murder, but it was the court's obligation. She deleted the sentence and wrote another.

Plaintiff premises this argument on his view that Pennsylvania should disregard the well-established precedent of definiteness

She paused, her hands on the keyboard. She'd been given a rough draft of the opinion by Emily, but it needed work, and in any event, Cate wanted every line of this opinion to be completely her own. She knew the press and her colleagues on the court would parse every sentence. She had to prove herself rock-solid on the law, especially because it had cost a man his life.

The precedent of definiteness of contract is well-established in Pennsylvania law and

It had hurt Cate to read the transcripts and to remember Marz on the stand. And Russo. But it had to get done, and the sooner, the better, so the press could quote from an opinion and get the facts right. Her stomach rumbled, but she hadn't felt like eating, except for the M&M's, which were medicinal.

Pennsylvania courts have always insisted that a contract be definite in its terms, especially where, as here,

Cate fussed with the sentence, trying to keep Russo and Simone in the back of her mind, in their proper compartment. But nobody was staying put in her head tonight, least of all Graham. She had called him after she hung up with Gina, but he wasn't home, so she'd left him a message thanking him for the flowers and asking him to call her, no matter how late he got in.

It's easier to avoid commitment than to sit around and wait for a man to call back.

Cate was kicking herself. She checked the clock again: 1:35. Graham must be in by now, right? Unless he had a date. And if he had a date, he should be home by now. Unless he was sleeping with someone. How many frigging bracelets did the man give out?

I hate Graham Liss. Unless he e-mailed me, which counts.

Cate brightened. She hadn't thought of e-mail. It was late, and maybe he didn't want to call and wake her. She moved the mouse to minimize the draft opinion and clicked onto Outlook Express for her e-mail, skimming the list of senders: The New York Times Direct, the Ritz-Carlton Reservations, Astrologers, USA-Today.com, and the Benjamin Franklin Society. No e-mail from Graham.

Cate didn't get it. He was the one with the full-court press. He was the one who called all day and sent the stupid flowers. He'd better have a good excuse for not calling, like a car accident. If he didn't have an accident, she could run him over. She clicked to minimize Outlook, then thought better of it. She didn't want to keep checking the little white envelope like an obsessive-compulsive, so she went into Options and checked the box that said, "Play sound when new messages arrive." Then she minimized Outlook and got back to work.

It is axiomatic in Pennsylvania law that contracts must be

Cate kept going, finally producing a reasonably respectable discussion of contract law, writing and rewriting as she went, fueled by M&M's and her drive to perfect the opinion. At some point, she realized that the process of writing was proving cathartic, and as it got later and later, and the world grew ever more still, she forgot about Graham, Simone, and even Russo, and worked efficiently and well, realizing that her truest reader wasn't the press or even her colleagues on the court. She was writing for Marz, wherever he was, in order to explain to him, somehow, some way, as best as she could, that there was a good reason that he lost his dream in her courtroom. That there was a principle, which applied to him and all of us, and abided for all time. The principle embodied the law.

Cate typed the last line. For all of the foregoing reasons, the Court grants defendant's motion for Judgment as a Matter of Law Under Rule 50 and Judgment in favor of defendant and defendant company is hereby entered. SO ORDERED.

Ping! Cate jumped, startled. It took her a minute to identify the sound. Outlook Express. She had gotten an e-mail. Graham! She checked the clock. 3:12 a.m. About time he got home. She minimized the final opinion and opened Outlook, where a single name sat at the bottom of the sender list, in boldface.

Not Graham Liss. PhillyNewsDirect. Another news service. She was about to click away when the subject line of the e-mail caught her eye.

TODAY'S HEADLINES:
LAWYER FOUND DEAD, A SUICIDE

Cate clicked on the e-mail. It opened instantly, and she read with horror:

Former Assistant District Attorney Richard Marz, of Philadelphia, was found dead in a car at approximately 2:01 a.m. this morning, the victim of an apparent suicide, by gunshot. The car, a blue Subaru sedan, was found in a remote section of Fairmount Park by students from Temple University, during a late-night hazing ceremony. Police had been seeking Marz in connection with the shooting death on Tuesday night of Hollywood television producer Arthur Simone, creator of the hit show *Attorneys@Law*. Marz had unsuccessfully sued Simone for breach of contract in connection with the show, and lost his claim for damages in federal court.

At the time of his death, Marz was found in possession of a .22-caliber pistol, also reportedly the type of weapon used in Simone's murder. Police had no comment, though a press conference will be held today at 10:00 a.m.

Cate's mouth went dry. She leaned back in her chair, stunned. She read the story over and over, until she could finally make herself believe it was true.

Then she put her head down on her keyboard and cried.

CHAPTER 16

"Sorry, Judge," Val said, rising at her desk as Cate entered chambers.

"Me, too, thanks." Cate came in, set down her briefcase and purse, and shed her coat. It was a bright winter morning, and the rising sun beamed through the window opposite the reception area, belying her mood. She couldn't remember the last time she'd had a good night's sleep. After she'd gotten the e-mail alert, she'd taken calls from Chief Judge Sherman and Val, both telling her what she already knew. She hung her coat on the rack by the door while the law clerks filtered in and collected around Val's desk.

Cate turned to the clerks, their faces unusually somber. "Hey, guys. Guess you heard the news."

"This is so awful, Judge." Emily's black top and long black skirt seemed appropriate. Beside her, Sam had dressed in his casual sweater and khakis, which somehow bugged Cate.

"Not cool," Sam said, and Cate turned on him.

"Sam, honestly. A man killed himself. Another man is murdered. That's more than 'not cool.' 'Not cool' doesn't even begin to cover what that is." Cate felt her nerves unraveling like a suspension cable. "*Horrible* works. *Tragic* will do just fine. But 'not cool'? 'Not cool' ain't even close!"

Sam flushed with embarrassment, plain on his pale skin. "Sorry."

"I am, too." Cate felt blood pounding in her temples. "I'm sorry you have so little empathy for another human being. He had a wife, whom you saw in court. He had a mother, too. Can't you feel that loss, Sam? Don't you have any respect?"

Sam looked down.

"Damn it!" Cate added for emphasis, which was when she realized the only way she could get control was to leave. She turned to go back into her office just as the intercom buzzer sounded, and they all looked at the security monitor, on the file cabinets next to Val's desk. Its gray screen showed a man in a dark suit standing at the intercom in the common hallway, and Cate recognized him, surprised.

"Detective Nesbitt, here to see Judge Fante," he said over the intercom, and Val looked over.

"Judge, okay to buzz him in?"

"Of course," Cate answered, ignoring the silent law clerks.

"Come in, Detective," Val said into the intercom, hitting the button to open the door to the secured half of the floor. She turned to hand Cate her messages. "All the usual suspects, the *Inquirer* again and a bunch of other reporters."

"No comment," Cate said, and took the messages.

Five minutes later, she was sitting catty-corner to Nesbitt at her worktable, both of them behind hot coffee in Styrofoam cups. "Where's your partner, Roots?" she asked.

"He's back at base, getting ready for the press conference." Nesbitt sipped his coffee, one hand against his tie, so as not to spill coffee on his camera-ready blue print tie and dark navy wool suit. His thick hair stood up at attention, and he smelled pleasantly of spicy after-shave. "This is an unofficial visit, Judge."

"Oh, really?" Cate tried not to think of the last time she'd heard words like that, only last night, from a different detective. *My coming here sure isn't procedure.* She shooed the words away. She wasn't going to tell Nesbitt about Russo unless he already knew about it. It was a dicey game, and she sipped her coffee, hot and sweet, gathering the strength to play.

"I spoke with Chief Judge Sherman about the Marz suicide. I presumed he called you at home."

"Yes."

"Obviously, you won't have to worry about Marz anymore."

"I guess not." Cate thought of the opinion she'd finished last night, too late. Would it have changed Marz's mind? If only she'd gotten to it sooner. "It's a terrible shame."

"Sure is. Anyway, we'll be clearing the Simone case. We're going to announce it at the press conference. Marz shot himself with the same gun he used on Simone. The ballistics tests verified it. So, bottom line, he killed Simone and then killed himself. It fits with some information we got from his wife, too. Depression and all."

"How's his wife?" Cate took another sip of coffee, then set her cup down on the conference table.

"As well as can be expected." Nesbitt shifted in his seat. "But there's something else I wanted to discuss with you, Judge. I'd like to keep this confidential. I'm here as a professional courtesy to you, now that the Simone case will be officially cleared."

Russo. "I understand."

"Let me begin at the beginning. You got the Simone case when you first became a judge, right?"

"Yes, a little over six months ago."

"Jury selection started, what, about a month ago?"

"Right, about then, yes. It took a long time to pick this jury because everyone had seen the TV show." Cate didn't get it. "Why do you ask?"

"When we caught the Simone murder, we went to his hotel suite that night, as part of the investigation. He was staying at the Four Seasons during the trial. He had a huge suite. We liked Marz for the doer, that is, we suspected him because of what had happened in court and because of the videotape. Also he'd taken off. But I thought it wouldn't hurt to look around Simone's hotel room and see what we could find out."

Cate nodded, unsure where Russo fit in.

"I guess I was being a little nosy, because Simone was a Hollywood guy and all. I mean if you had a chance to peek in Steven Spielberg's medicine chest, wouldn't you?"

"No doubt." Cate found herself liking Nesbitt. He wasn't exactly handsome, but he had a nice, straightforward way about him.

"So I looked around on Simone's desk and there were the usual items, a laptop, a PalmPilot, a coupla cell phones—he had five of 'em." Nesbitt paused, pursing his lips. "He didn't have a lot of business papers around except files from the lawsuit. We confiscated them, which is procedure, and I logged them in at the evidence room."

"Okay."

"I did see some loose papers in a fancy folder. The folder was leather and it had a yellow pad inside and a clipboard. Well, inside the folder was a record of your personal whereabouts, starting from about six months ago."

"My personal whereabouts?" Cate didn't understand.

"I found a record, a chronological record of everything you did, for about six months, up to now. From the looks of it, Simone was having you followed for some reason. Everywhere you went. To court, home, or well, out."

Cate's mouth went dry. "That's impossible."

"I thought you might say that, so I made a copy of the papers." Nesbitt reached inside his jacket pocket, withdrew a packet of papers that had been folded in two, and handed them to Cate, who opened them up and read the first page:

September 7—Judge leaves work at 5:15 p.m. Drives to 263 Meadowbrook Lane, at 6:34 p.m. Leaves at 10:16 p.m. Drives home at 11:30 p.m.

Meadowbrook Lane? That's Gina's house! Cate read on.

September 8—Judge leaves work at 7:06 p.m. Goes to Warwick Hotel, 1822 Locust Street at 8:09 p.m. Keynote Speaker at Reception for Trial Lawyers of Philadelphia. Leaves hotel at 11:02 p.m. Arrives Mike's Bar, 1003 Locust Street at 11:37 p.m. Leaves bar with unidentified man at 11:57 p.m. Goes to Holiday Inn with same man at 12:10 a.m. Leaves Holiday Inn at 1:35 a.m., alone. Goes home at 2:05 a.m.

Cate remembered that night. That speech. That man.

September 29—Judge leaves work at 6:23 p.m. Drives to Roosevelt Blvd Conference Center and receives award from woman lawyers association. Leaves Conference Center, 9:07 p.m. Arrives Mack's Shack, 1030 Cottman Avenue at 10:02 p.m. Leaves with unidentified man at 10:32. Drives to . . .

Cate skimmed the record. Oct 30 . . . Unidentified man; Nov 24 . . . Unidentified man; Jan 10 . . . Unidentified man . . .

Cate felt sickened. Her private life, exposed. There were ten pages in the packet, and she couldn't bring herself to read the rest in front of Nesbitt. She was so ashamed she could barely look up and meet his eye. Somehow seeing her behavior in black and white made it look so much worse. Or maybe she'd just been in denial for too long.

"Why would he do this?" Cate asked, stunned, and if Nesbitt thought less of her, he didn't let it show.

"Did you ever receive any unusual calls from him?"

"I've never spoken with him on the phone. That would be an ex parte communication, that is, a communication with one party in a lawsuit, which isn't done." Cate heard the huffiness in her voice and almost laughed at the irony. *I'd whore around but I'd never take an ex parte call.*

"Did you ever receive a note from him, or a letter?"

"No."

"Do you have any reason to think he had an interest in you, romantically?"

"No."

"Did you have any encounter with him at all? An intimate encounter?"

"No, of course not," Cate answered, though she couldn't blame him for asking. "I never met the man until the trial."

"Then I can't explain what he did. It's like he surveilled you, or had you surveilled. I've seen that in divorce cases, mostly. Like *Cheaters*, on TV."

Cate let it go. She was getting sick of TV. "You think he hired a private detective?"

"No, these papers don't look professional enough. Private detectives, their reports tend to follow the same format. This is an amateur's work."

"He wouldn't do it himself. He couldn't. He doesn't have the time and I doubt he was even in the city. I thought he worked in L.A."

"Maybe someone who works for him did it."

"He has an assistant," Cate said, thinking aloud. She thought of Micah Gilbert, the young woman from the front row of the gallery, with the long hair. Simone was never without her during trial. "What kind of man has someone else do his stalking?"

Nesbitt smiled briefly. "That's not all, Judge. There were pictures, too. Look on the last page. I photocopied a few."

"*Pictures?*"

"Not like that. I mean, not of *that*." Nesbitt cleared his throat, and Cate was already tearing to the back of the packet. "They were color but they came out in black-and-white on the Xerox."

Cate squinted at the first photo, taken at night. It was a picture of the Chestnut Grill, a bar in Fort Washington. A black curve at the top of the picture frame suggested the edge of a car windshield. The second photo was a candid photo of a good-looking man with a mustache, also taken at night on a city street. *Oh boy.* Cate recognized the mustache. She flipped the page. *Oh no.* The last photo pictured Cate herself going into another bar, her face clearly visible as she waited at the door for someone else to leave.

My God in heaven. She couldn't pretend anymore. She set the papers down and buried her face in her hands, smearing lots of expensive makeup.

"Don't take it so hard, Judge. I'm divorced three years now because I ran around. I don't judge anybody, not anymore. Besides, you're a single woman."

Cate stayed hidden in her hands. Her cheeks felt like they were spontaneously combusting.

"The way I look at it is, now you know about it, Judge. You can protect yourself in the future."

Cate knew what he meant. "I'm never doing this again," she said, still behind her hands.

"As far as I'm concerned, your business is your business. It's not my business, and I don't want to know about it."

"But now you do," Cate said, finally lowering her hands and looking at him, and they both understood what she meant.

"Judge, my lips are sealed. I'm a by-the-book kind of guy. Always was." Nesbitt made a hand chop. "It stops here."

"But you came to me with these papers. That's not by the book."

"Beg to differ." Nesbitt held up a warning finger. "I don't like people spying, and I'm not violating procedure by being here. I'm giving you a heads-up, and that's something the department does all the time for important people like yourself. A city councilman, or a CEO-type-a guy. We do it more than you think."

"Does Russo know about this?" Cate asked, when it occurred to her.

"No. Just me."

"You didn't tell him?"

"No. This investigation's on the Simone case, so it stays with the Simone case. The Roundhouse can be a friggin' sieve, so I always keep my investigations close to the vest. No leaks." Nesbitt shook his head.

"I didn't even tell Roots about those papers on you. He doesn't need to know. That's why I came alone this morning."

Cate felt grateful. "But you and Russo are friends."

"No, we're not. We used to be partners, is all."

"On the cop shows, the partners are always best friends."

Nesbitt smiled. "This is no buddy movie. Fact is, Russo's okay, but there's a reason we're not partners anymore. We're like Nick Nolte and Eddie Murphy. Opposites. Russo's not a by-the-book kinda guy."

No, he certainly isn't. "He came to my house last night," Cate ventured, since she was feeling safer about confiding in him, and Nesbitt stiffened, his mouth tightening.

"He shouldn't have. What happened?"

"He's angry that he lost the case. He showed me a videotape of amateur porn and a man in a hotel room."

Nesbitt's features darkened. "He shouldn't have done that, either."

"So you saw it? With the man in the hotel room?"

"Yes. He showed it to me. He thinks the woman with the man, Partridge, is you."

Cate's heart hiccupped. "And what did you think?"

"I wasn't sure. I thought it could be you, Judge, but I didn't tell him that. I figured if it was you, with some guy you picked up—" Nesbitt caught himself. "I mean, *dated.*"

Cate flushed, mortified.

"I don't know why you threw money at the guy, but it doesn't mean you're crooked. Or being blackmailed. Knowing what I know"—Nesbitt gestured at the papers lying between them on the worktable—"I figured it was a lovers' quarrel."

Cate winced.

"Hey, whatever. If there's no murder, it's not my job. Partridge wasn't a homicide, so it's just another weird coincidence. Philly's a small town in lots of ways, and given what you were up to, it's not unlikely you'd run into a guy like Partridge. In fact, it was just a matter of time." Nesbitt pursed his lips under his brushy mustache. "Look at it this way. Russo doesn't know about you, what you're up to, so he figures it is what it looks like—a crooked judge. Or a judge being blackmailed. Not that I'm making excuses for him."

"Did you know he was going to my house with the tape?"

"Of course not. You think I'd let him get away with that? Makes the squad look bush league."

Cate believed him, because he looked so offended.

"Don't worry about Russo. I've seen him like this before, and he gets over it. He had his hopes up about the TV thing. Me and him used to talk about it, and he took the verdict bad. He'd started spending the money before he even had it. Picturing himself at one of those infinity pools, or on the golf course. He's a hothead, an emotional guy, but then it goes away."

Cate wasn't so sure. "I thought about reporting him, but I'm not, for obvious reasons."

"Please, don't." Nesbitt looked worried again. "You don't need that kind of blowback, and there's no reason to. Trust me, I've known the guy twenty-some years. He's all talk, no action."

"Have you seen him since the news about Marz?"

"No, and he's off today. I'll catch him soon as I can." Nesbitt rose to go, brushing down his dress pants. "Anyway, I got to get moving. The conference."

"Right." Cate rose, too. "Thanks for coming by. I do appreciate your judgment, and your discretion."

"You're welcome, Judge." Nesbitt smiled. "I'm sure this has been a rough coupla weeks for you, but it's all over now."

"Case closed, as you guys say." Cate walked him to the door, and Nesbitt smiled.

"You mean, 'case cleared.'"

Cate laughed as he turned to go, and she shut the door behind him. She leaned against the door for a minute, then looked out the window without seeing anything, and wondered why Simone would have someone follow her. Was something going on between him and his assistant? Was Gilbert jealous, and that's why she followed her? That didn't make sense. If that were the reason, why do it for so long? And why be so precise? 9:33. 10:23. From these papers, it looked like work, or research. She felt confounded.

Until a suspicion snuck up on her.

CHAPTER 17

Cate had come across it last night, drafting her opinion. She went over to her briefcase, opened it up, and unpacked it on the couch, taking out the three transcripts from the most important days of trial. She shuffled the thick green-bound transcripts and found the day Simone had taken the stand. She opened the transcript and flipped through. Where had she seen that reference? She'd thought it was just a throwaway at the time, but now it was looming large. She turned the pages, searching. 146. 147. 148.

There. Simone on direct examination:

A: For example, I could make this lawsuit into a TV series. Write a spin-off from *Attorneys@Law*. Call it *Judges@Court*. And it could star a blond female judge who looked a lot like you, Judge Fante. Charismatic, attention-getting. The most alive person in the room. What do you think?

THE COURT: Great idea, I'd love it. Get Charlize Theron, for me.

A: Done.

Cate closed the transcript, angered. What if Simone hadn't been kidding? What if he really was making a new TV show, with a woman judge as its lead? What if he'd been having her followed for research? It fit the photos, too. The questions led to more questions. Did he start having her followed, then found out what she did at night, or vice versa? Could he really have turned her sex life into a TV show? Could he still, through his production company?

Cate shuddered at the thought. If he did, every judge on the court would know it was really her, and so would every litigant, witness, and juror who came before her. Her old partners at Beecker, and her clients, CEOs and VPs of Fortune 500 companies. They'd all speculate. Gossip. Whisper.

No. Cate wouldn't have it, she couldn't. She went back to the table, picked up the phone, and called information for the Four Seasons, then punched the number in and got through to the front desk. "May I speak to Micah Gilbert, please? I believe she was with the Arthur Simone group."

"Please hold while I check the number," the operator said, then came back on. "I'm sorry, Ms. Gilbert was never a guest."

Damn. "Thank you." Cate hung up, on fire. Gilbert hadn't testified at the trial, but she had undoubtedly been deposed during discovery. But deps weren't required to be filed with the court. She knew nothing about the Simone organization. She went back to her desk and logged onto her computer, clicked through to google.com and plugged in "Micah Gilbert" and "Arthur Simone." Three zillion entries came up in a list, dominated by *Attorneys@Law*. She clicked the URL and the screen changed to a simple white page with a black border, which read: WE MOURN THE PASSING OF OUR CREATOR, MENTOR, AND DEAR FRIEND, ARTHUR G. SIMONE.

Before Cate's disappointment had a chance to set in, the tribute dissolved, revealing the slick home page for *Attorneys@Law*, with gritty photos of the fictional lawyers and a lineup of standard web-page buttons. Cate clicked ABOUT US and two addresses appeared on the screen, one in the coveted 90210 zip code listing. After CREATOR,

Arthur Simone, came EXECUTIVE PRODUCERS, CO-EXECUTIVE PRO-DUCERS, SUPERVISING PRODUCERS and the like. After that there was one name next to an address in the less-than-coveted 19006 zip code. Philadelphia. *Attorneys@Law* evidently had offices in town, and the PRODUCTION ASSISTANT, PHILLY was Micah Gilbert.

Bingo! Cate passed the mouse over Gilbert's name, and another page popped up, with a large photo of the lovely Micah in a tight black pantsuit, next to a short biography, which Cate read:

Micah joined the posse two years ago and before Micah joined us, she worked forever—okay, only five years but that's like twenty in publicist years—as a liaison slash consultant for the Philadelphia Film Office. Micah is all about Philly and her city savvy helps make *Attorneys@Law* rock on Sunday nights! Micah works way too hard, so she can be reached anytime at our Philly office.

Cate picked up the phone and pressed in the number.

After two rings, a woman picked up. "*Attorneys@Law.*"

"Micah?"

"Yes?"

"Sorry, wrong number." Cate pressed the hook to hang up, feeling her juices start to flow. She hit the intercom button, and Emily answered. "Can you please come in?" Cate hung up, then went back to the table, grabbed Simone's chronology, and stuffed it in her purse. Then she called out, "Come in, Emily!"

The door opened. "Hi, Judge."

"Hey, girl. Close the door and come back here, if you don't mind."

"Sure." Emily swished into the room in her flowing black skirt and black Doc Marten boots and took a seat in the chair opposite the desk, looking nervous.

Cate began, "First off, I'm sorry I was so rude to you and Sam this morning. I lost control and I shouldn't have. I'm sorry."

"That's okay. I think it's nice that you care so much about Marz and Simone. It shows you have a good heart." Emily smiled shyly, a dark maroon slash of lip gloss, and Cate felt touched.

"Thanks. Did you get my final opinion in *Simone*? I e-mailed it to you last night."

"Yes, I just finished checking the cites."

"Great, thanks. Please print me a copy and leave it on my desk. You did a great job on your draft, and I really appreciate it."

"Thanks."

"Now I have to ask you to do some extra research for me, on a different issue, and I need you to keep it to yourself. Don't tell Sam."

"I don't really talk to Sam, anyway."

"Or your clerk friends in the other chambers."

Emily nodded gravely. "I don't have any clerk friends in other chambers."

Ouch. "Okay. As a hypothetical, let's say that someone is being followed, without their knowledge, for a period of six months or so, in Philadelphia. Every movement followed, like surveillance. You need to plug into the harassment cases."

Emily began taking notes.

"I think that's legally actionable. I think the person being followed can get a restraining order. I also think it might be actionable criminally, under the new stalking laws, and I think there is some kind of tortious breach-of-privacy action that can be brought." Cate was thinking out loud. "Something with major damages. Punitive damages."

Emily kept writing.

"Also, if you have time, check into the false-light cases. I want to know if the whereabouts of a public official can be made into, let's say, a movie. Or a TV show."

Emily's head snapped up, her lined eyes wide. "Are they making a TV show about you?"

So much for secrecy. "I don't know, but I want to be ready. One last thing. Don't do the research or the writing in chambers. Go to the library."

"How about the downstairs library?" Emily meant the courthouse library that all the clerks used, and occasionally a judge or two.

"No. Get off the reservation. Go to Jenkins Law Library. Take your laptop. Got it?"

"Sure," Emily said, her young face worried. She finally rested her ballpoint. "Are you okay, Judge?"

"Of course." Cate flashed a convincing smile and stood up. "Now, let's go!" She got up and Emily followed, and they walked together to the clerks' office, where Sam was bent over his computer keyboard, his back to the door.

"Sam?" Cate said. He turned in his swivel chair, his expression cowed, still. "I'm sorry I snapped at you. It was uncalled for, and I'm sorry."

"That's all right, Judge." Sam's lower lip trembled, and for a minute he looked like he might cry. "I know I've been kind of a . . . disappointment to you."

"No, you haven't, Sam. Not at all." Cate felt a twinge for the kid, but she didn't have time for this now. "You and I, we'll have to talk about this when I get back. I have an errand to run. Okay, pal?"

"Okay." Sam managed a shaky smile, and Cate ducked out of the clerks' office and headed for Val's desk.

"Hey, lady," Cate called out on the fly. "Please tell me my calendar's clear this morning."

"Let me see, Judge." Val turned to her computer, which set her long amber earrings swinging. A beige pashmina draped around her shoulders, on top of a brown patterned dress. She hit a key on her keyboard and slid her eyes upward while she typed. "You didn't have to say you were sorry, you know. You gotta teach 'em."

"Nah, it was right." Cate grabbed her trench coat from the rack and slid into it as Val frowned at her monitor screen.

"You have a pretrial motion at eleven-thirty. *Schrader v. Ickles Industries.*"

"Damn." Cate had meant to read those papers, too. She'd never been so behind on her work. "Please call and cancel it. Tell the courtroom deputy and stenographer, too. I won't be back until after lunch." She leaned over the top of Val's cubicle and lowered her voice. "Marz killed himself with the murder weapon."

"So it's over."

"Yes."

"Hallelujah. Where're you going?"

"You don't want to know." Cate hurried for the door.

CHAPTER 18

Cate hustled down the sidewalk under the cold sun, holding her coat at her neck against a biting wind. Bundled-up people hurried this way and that, their breaths making cotton puffs in the frigid air. Morning traffic clogged the narrow street, stop-and-go, mostly business deliveries at this hour, and a white Liberty Fish van honked, stalled by a UPS truck making a delivery. Cate lived only six blocks east of this neighborhood, and if Society Hill were the residential side of colonial Philadelphia, Old City had been the commercial, characterized by large industrial spaces that later proved perfect for restaurants, art galleries, lofts, photography studios, and furniture-design showrooms. And evidently, the Philadelphia production offices of *Attorneys@Law*.

Cate stopped when she reached the address, only a black-stenciled number 388 on a dented metal door wedged between a closed restaurant and a wholesale restaurant-supply outlet. She stepped back and looked up at the brick building, two stories above the restaurant-supply outlet. Fluorescent lights paneled the ceiling on the second floor; the storefront window bore no sign. The sign on the window of the third floor read TATE & SON, INDUSTRIAL DRAWING. The *Attorneys@Law* office had to be the second floor, and in this brick sliver of a building, it couldn't be more than one room wide.

Cate eyed the door frame, dirty and peeling gray paint, home to two black buzzers recessed in grimy brass, unlabeled. She hit the top button, assuming it was the third floor, and the door buzzed loudly. She slipped inside, into a tiny entrance room, then went upstairs and stopped at the second floor, at a security door that read ATTORNEYS@ LAW. Cate knocked.

No answer. But she knew Micah was inside, from the phone call. She knocked again, then again, and was about to kick the door down when it flew open.

"The office is closed!" Micah said, flinging open the door. Then her expression changed to bewilderment. "Judge Fante?"

"Yes," Cate answered, equally surprised. Micah had clearly been crying, her eyes wet and her nose swollen. The sight touched Cate, until she reminded herself that this girl had been following her every move. Or at least she knew who had.

"Whoa, this is so random." Micah quickly wiped a tear away. Her hair fell loosely to her shoulders and she wore a black ribbed sweater, tight jeans, and red Converse sneakers. "You caught me at a bad time. I was just watching the press conference."

"I'm sorry," Cate said, pushing inside. "I was in the neighborhood and I wanted to talk to you about Mr. Simone, to tell you personally how very sorry I am."

"Why . . . thanks."

"It's just so awful." Cate scanned the cramped reception area, furnished with a funky black leather couch, a black coffee table, a one-cup coffee machine, and a dorm-size refrigerator. Slick posters of the cast of *Attorneys@Law*, in the trademark black and red, blanketed the walls. The reception room led to a room in the back, from which came the sound of a television. "Is the press conference still on?"

"I don't think so," Micah answered, her voice thick.

"I heard some on the car radio. TV in there?" Cate darted for the office, sizing it up in a glance; a huge plasma flat-screen TV, a black contemporary desk, a black Aeron chair, and a white iBook surrounded by stacks of papers labeled PRODUCTION SCHEDULES, TRAVEL & EXPENSES, and HEAD SHOTS. Cate turned to Micah, who stood at the threshold, wiping her nose. "I was hoping to catch the end of the conference. What did they say, anything new?"

"I guess you heard that Marz committed suicide."

"Yes. Poor man."

"I don't feel sorry for him. He brought it on himself. The police say he used the same gun that was the murder weapon. So that means he killed Art, which I could have told them." Micah blew her nose loudly, and her pretty cheeks turned red from the pressure. "Maybe I'm not supposed to say this, but I really wish you hadn't said what you said that day in court. I think Art would be alive today, if you hadn't."

Cate felt a stab of guilt. "I'm sorry."

"He was a great man, a genius." Micah dabbed at her eye with the Kleenex. "I know they say that about everyone in Hollywood, but he really was."

"I'm so sorry. It's upsetting."

"It really is and it . . ." Micah's sentence trailed off as she watched the TV, and Cate turned to the life-size screen. A woman with a model's lovely features, long blond hair, and a tight-fitting black pantsuit stood behind a lectern topped with a bouquet of microphones. The panel caption under the picture read MRS. ERIKA SIMONE.

"Is that his wife?" Cate asked needlessly, eyeing Micah for a reaction.

"Yes. She's Swedish." Micah kept her gaze riveted to the screen, her eyes glistening. If she were jealous of Simone's wife, it didn't show, so either she wasn't having an affair with her boss or she was a really good actress.

On the screen, Erika Simone was saying, in a sexy Nordic accent,

"I wish to thank the Philadelphia Police department, and particularly Detectives Nesbitt and Roots, for their great work and the kindness they showed us. The City of Brotherly Love has truly been very good to my family, and I would like to donate one hundred thousand dollars, the reward money we had originally offered, to the Widow and Orphans Fund. Thank you very much."

"That was nice," Cate said, and Micah nodded, her lips tight. "Was that your idea?"

"I didn't even know about it." Micah switched off the TV with a black remote, and the room fell abruptly silent.

"When's the funeral?" Cate asked, breaking the spell, and Micah dropped her Kleenex into the wastebasket beside the desk.

"Saturday, in L.A."

"You get to go on the company jet?" Cate was guessing they had one.

"Uh, no, I'm not going. Erika wants to keep it small, I heard, so it's only immediate family. I can understand her not wanting to turn it into a big Hollywood funeral. That's so lame when people do that."

"Now what happens, for you?"

"It's a one-woman office, and the show must go on, of course." Micah nodded sadly. "It won't run as well as before, but there's a guy in L.A. who's going to executive-produce."

"What is it you do exactly, for the show?" Cate tried to sound friendly.

"Everything and anything, really. There's lots of little things that have to be done here, even though most of the show is filmed in L.A. Like one time, Art called me in a total panic." Micah smiled sadly. "I had to FedEx ten cheesesteaks to him from Pat's and Geno's, so the characters could talk about whether they liked Pat's or Geno's better."

Cate faked a laugh. "So you're the Philly expert, huh?"

"Yes. I went to Girls' High, in the city, and then Drexel. I'm not one of those suburban posers."

"So anything he needs in Philly, you make sure he gets. If he needs somebody followed, do you do that, too?"

Micah's smile faded.

"Like me, for example? Are you the one who followed me? Or should I sue someone else?"

Micah blinked, her long eyelashes still wet. "I don't know what you mean."

"Yes, you do." Cate shoved a hand into her purse, pulled out the folded chronology, and held it up high. "Recognize this? A professional detective didn't do it, and you're the only employee here." Cate slipped the paper back into her purse. "Was Simone making a new TV show, called *Judges@Court*? Like he testified on the stand?"

"I'm just a production assistant, Judge."

"But you know what I'm talking about."

Micah didn't reply, suddenly looking out the window, at the view of brick nothing.

"You followed me, right? You took notes on me. Dates. Times. Men. You even took pictures from a car."

Micah puckered her pretty lips. "How do you know this?"

"Just answer me. Did you do it?"

"I don't have to answer you. I have rights. You have to go." Micah strode to the door, but Cate stood rooted.

"You gonna throw yourself out? Because I'm not leaving."

"You're trespassing. You have to. I'm asking you to leave."

"Make me. Call the cops. Right now." Cate gestured at the tiny cell phone on the desk. "Let's ask them if it's okay to stalk a federal judge."

"The legal department said it was legal."

"Hence the name, but don't argue with a judge. Am I right or am I wrong on you? Listen, I'll make you a deal. Tell me what I need to know, and I won't sue you. How's that?"

"You can't sue. Legal said." Micah frowned like a small child, and Cate almost laughed.

"I can always sue. Didn't your lawsuit with Marz teach you that? Didn't he make your life miserable? Taking your time, costing Simone a fortune?"

Micah began listening, her eyes widening.

"Can you afford to be sued? What do you have, at your age? What are you, thirty?"

"Twenty-nine."

"So what, an apartment in Center City? A white Saturn with two years of payments? What do you have? Because legal fees will take it all from you. And that's if you *win*."

Micah paused, walked back into the office, and sank into the Aeron chair opposite the desk.

"Good call," Cate said, crossing her arms.

CHAPTER 19

"So, how did it come about, you following me?" Cate asked. "How did Simone even know about me? I didn't meet him until trial."

"How do I know you'll keep the deal? Will you put it in writing?"

"I give you my word." Cate ignored the irony. The girl had learned her lessons from Simone. "Now, how did Simone know about me?"

"You have to promise not to tell anyone you heard it from me, too. I need this job."

"I promise. By the way, you're not telling me anything I won't find out in discovery."

"Okay," Micah said reluctantly. "When you first got the case, you held a meeting or something with our lawyer, George Hartford. Some kind of meeting in your office."

"I had a pretrial conference with both counsel, it's standard."

"Whatever." Micah brushed a dark tendril from her eye, recovering her composure. "After the meeting, George told Art about you. He said you had star quality, which is like a nineteen-fifties term for 'hot,' I think. Art had been thinking about expanding the franchise, so he asked me to see if George was right. I went and watched you in court, and we took it from there."

Cate felt her teeth clench. "You began to follow me."

"I had to. He told me to. It was my job."

"You invaded my privacy."

"I didn't . . . think of it that way."

"How could you not?"

"You were in public, it wasn't hidden."

"Just because something happens in public doesn't mean it's not private. You remember when the *Challenger* blew up in midair? Did you wanna see those poor people watch their daughter *explode*?"

Micah looked blank, and Cate realized she must have been in diapers at the time.

"How about the moment of someone's death? You wanna see that, even if it happens on a street? Or when you weep, at Simone's funeral? Is that public or private? Or when you get married? Or hear someone say I love you, for the first time?" Cate heard herself getting worked up. "The location doesn't make something public or private. Your heart does."

"It was research."

"No, it was my life," Cate shot back. "And you found out stuff you didn't need to know, which is now going to be in a TV show. All over TV screens, a new franchise for the @*Law* cult. My life. Me."

"The show isn't about you. It's fictional."

"Me, fictionalized." Cate raked her fingers through her hair, loose to her shoulders today. "And they're going to make this show, even though Simone is gone?"

"Yes. Matt Gaone was hired to exec-produce, from L.A."

Cate made a mental note. "When does production start?"

"It's in production already. It started two months ago. December."

Cate didn't get something. "Then why did you keep following me? You were following me up to last week."

"I didn't know they'd started."

"Will you be the production assistant on the new show?"

"Yes, I'm the Philly girl. More job, same pay." Resentment edged her tone, but Cate had her own problems.

"Where is it being produced? L.A.?"

"Yes. It's too expensive to shoot here. We shoot exteriors in Philly next month."

"Is it called *Judges@Court*?"

"Yes, just like the *Law & Order* franchise."

"When will it air?"

"September, next."

Cate had plenty of time for an injunction, if she could get one. "What's the show about?"

Micah hesitated. "A woman judge."

"Federal?"

"Yes, and three other judges on the court."

"In Philly?"

"Yes."

"Are the characters based on the other judges, on my court?" Cate asked, appalled. She'd been so self-centered she hadn't even thought of that. "Have you been following my colleagues, too?"

"No. Art thought they were boring."

They are, God bless them. "Okay, let's talk about the woman judge. Is she married?"

"Single."

"Describe her." Cate folded her arms in the thick sheepskin coat. "Or should I just look in a mirror?"

"Well, yes." Micah smiled weakly. "Only taller. Hollywood doesn't like shorter women, like us."

"Okay, and don't tell me, let me guess—she sleeps around, and no one knows."

"She has a secret sex life."

Oh, God.

"But she's good," Micah rushed to say. "She's a good person. She's fun and cool, like you. She's a strong heroine. She's empowered."

Cate mock-shuddered. "Make me anything but empowered. I hate empowered."

Micah smiled, for the first time. "They haven't cast her yet. Did you really want Charlize Theron?"

Cate groaned. "I was kidding."

"She sleeps with another judge on the court, who's crazy about her. In the first episode, they have a threesome."

Cate's eyes flew open. "*Three judges*?"

"No, two and a male law clerk."

Cate burst into laughter. *Way to miss the point.* "Oh, God. I thought what I did was bad, but this'll make it look worse. I didn't think that was even possible!"

"It's entertainment, Judge."

Argh. Cate had a terrible thought and sobered immediately. *Meadowbrook Lane.* "Wait a minute. This judge doesn't have a best friend, does she?"

"Well, yes. I mean, she has to, to show that—"

"Tell me about her friend." Cate felt new anger in her chest, and Micah must have seen it, because she edged back in the chair.

"Well, to be honest, she's a lot like your friend."

"No!" Cate thought quickly ahead. *Warren.* "She doesn't have a kid, does she?"

"He's mildly retarded, but in the end—"

"No, you can't do that!" Cate shot up, her body rigid as a stake in the ground. "You *cannot* do that. His mother didn't ask for this. He's a little boy. He didn't ask for this."

"It's not them, it's just characters—"

"It *is* them, and all their friends will know. All the people on their street, and all the kids in his preschool, when he goes next year. You think he doesn't have it hard enough?"

"Judge, maybe it'll help—"

"It won't help! You didn't do it to help! You did it to make money!"

"I didn't do it." Even Micah looked upset. "I'm sorry, I'm just the—"

"That boy doesn't deserve this, to be exploited! To be put in the spotlight! His mother doesn't deserve this! They're just people, living their lives!"

"It's out of my hands, Judge." Micah was shaking her glossy head. "Art really loved the little boy, as a subplot."

"He's not a subplot, he's a *child*!" Cate couldn't stand still anymore. She'd learned all she needed to know. It was going to be worse than she thought. Never mind the threesome. *Gina and Warren.* The people she loved most in the world. She felt stunned, stricken. She couldn't even speak. She went to the door.

"Judge, there's nothing you can do—"

Cate hurried for the door of the office, her stomach churning. What had she done? What had she caused? She ran out of the office and down the stairs and made it to the curb, panicky and sickened. She looked right and left, found an alley, and bolted for it.

And inside the alley, with one hand on the dirty brick wall, Cate got sick to her stomach.

CHAPTER 20

Cate drove down Fifth Street in light traffic, heading back toward the courthouse, her emotions in tumult. A pack of Trident gum couldn't overcome the taste in her mouth. She would never have dreamed that she could have caused so much harm, or set into motion a series of events that would hurt Gina and Warren. Their vulnerability upped the ante. She steered onto Market Street and, preoccupied, almost ran a red light. She had to keep that show off the air, and down-and-dirty legal research from a law clerk was only the beginning. She'd hire the best litigator in town, if not alive, and she'd wage the biggest, baddest court battle she could afford, which was plenty. Cate reached on the passenger seat for her purse and dug around for her cell phone.

Ring! Suddenly, the cell rang in her bag. She fished the phone from her purse and checked the number on the lighted display. It was a number she didn't know, in the 215 area code. Funny. Almost nobody had her cell number. She pressed SEND to answer the call. "Hello?"

"Judge Fante?" It was a man on the line. "This is Vector Security."

"Yes?" Cate said, surprised.

And by the end of the next sentence, she had swung the car completely around and hit the gas.

· · ·

Cate pulled up to the unwelcome sight of a police cruiser in her driveway. She parked behind it, turned off the ignition, and jumped out of
her car, then hurried up her front steps in the cold, readying her keys
to unlock the front door, but it swung wide, having been opened by a
uniformed cop standing on the threshold of her house. His blue eyes
peered businesslike from under the black patent bill of his cap.

"You the judge?" he asked, his tone surprised. His build was short
and stocky in a dark blue jacket, his gleaming badge worn under a
black nameplate that read OFFICER THEODORE GILKENNY.

"Yes." Cate stepped into the entrance hall, introduced herself and
extended a hand, and they shook, his hand in a thick black leather
glove. "How did you get in?"

"Through the gate in the back fence, then in through the back
door. The way they tried to."

Cate groaned. Vector was her burglar alarm company. They had
said the alarm on the back door had gone off. "What did they take?"

"Nothing. You lucked out." Officer Gilkenny closed the door
behind them. "We figure they ran when the alarm went off."

"Did anybody see them? Or him?"

"Don't know. We just got here. We don't usually canvass for a burglary, but if we have time, we'll check it out before we leave."

"Thanks." Cate glanced around, relieved to see the entrance hall
and living room looking untouched. "It just seems strange. Society
Hill is such a safe neighborhood."

"Come with me." Gilkenny turned and walked Cate down the
hall as if she were a guest in her own home. "It's safe now, Judge. We
walked through the entire house. No one's here."

Cate shuddered at the thought, as what had happened began to
sink in. Someone had tried to break into her house.

"Dispatch told us you were a VIP. Said you have that case down
the courthouse, with the cop show, right? My wife watches that show.
Law & Order, SVU."

"It's *Attorneys@Law*."

"My wife always calls it SUV. Like the car."

"Yes." Cate had no idea why she was having this conversation, much less correcting him. They reached the kitchen, where everything was in place. The granite counters glistened, the cherrywood table shone, and the coffeepot sat drying upside-down on a dishcloth, the way she'd left it this morning.

"The kitchen looks okay," Cate said, vaguely aware that she was comforting herself. She'd never been burglarized before, if you didn't count her divorce.

"I can't believe how many times a week they got that show on," Gilkenny continued, chatty. She walked ahead of the cop, through the mud room to the French doors in the back of the house. Gilkenny was saying, "And my mother, she lives in Tampa, she watches the reruns on cable, too. She misses that Orbach guy. Did she love him! And Kojak, too. She loved Kojak."

"Oh, no," Cate said, when she saw the back door. The round knob hung loosely from its stem, and she reached automatically to shove it back in, then stopped. "I guess if I touch it, I'll leave a fingerprint."

"Yeah, but we won't be dusting for prints. Not for a burglary. It's not like on *Law & Order*. Besides, if we dusted for every burglary, this would be one dirty city." Gilkenny managed a tight smile, but Cate barely listened, looking out the mullioned window and catching the eye of another uniformed cop, a woman, who was standing on her patio, making notes on a white paper pad. She reached for the knob, which fell off into her hand.

"Oops."

"Shoulda warned you."

Cate slid the doorknob uselessly back into the hole, pulled the door open by the wood frame, and stepped outside onto the patio. "Hello, Officer," Cate said, squinting to read the nameplate on the cop's puffy navy jacket while her eyes adjusted.

"I'm Jill Wiederseim." The woman cop grinned and extended a gloved hand. "Morning, Judge. Pleasure to meet you. Nice house."

"Thanks." Cate looked past her, appraising the patio. Nothing had been disturbed. A gas barbecue was on the left, next to a table and four chairs, protected from winter with green plastic covers. Flower beds lined the sunny back of the patio, now patches of frozen dirt and ice-encased impatiens. A wooden privacy fence surrounded the backyard, and looked intact. The gate was even closed, probably by the cops themselves. "Everything looks in order. How did they get in?"

"Through the gate in the fence." Wiederseim slid her notepad into her back pocket and gestured to the fence. "That's about six feet high, correct?"

"Yes. Should I put a lock on it?"

"You can, but those coconuts will just jump it." Wiederseim turned to the fence bordering the back of the patio. "There's no alley back there, and all the backyards on the street are connected. You share that with the back-door neighbor, right?"

"Yes. The Marcotts. They work during the day, but maybe somebody's home. Maybe they saw something."

"We'll check it out, Judge." Wiederseim shrugged. "Good thing you had your alarm on. You'd be surprised, the number of people that have 'em and don't use 'em."

"I bet." Cate still felt troubled, but kept it to herself. "How often does something like this happen in this neighborhood?"

"All the time, you just don't hear about it. We had a burglary on Delancey Street last week. They got in through the back door, there, too."

"Really?" Cate was thinking about Russo, but she wasn't about to broach the subject with a member of the Philadelphia Police Department. "I wonder if we could keep this with the Philly cops. We don't need to extend the jurisdiction, if you know what I mean."

Officer Wiederseim smiled. "I'm not calling in the feds, if that's what you mean. They'd turn this thing into a federal case."

"Yes. I don't want this blown out of proportion." Cate nodded. Then the visit from Russo would come out, and the videotape with Partridge. "Come on, let's go in. Too cold to stand out here." Cate opened the door, and Wiederseim followed her inside, jiggling the broken knob. "I have to go back to court and I can't leave the house open, like this. I guess I better get a locksmith, right away."

Wiederseim cocked her head. "We can board it up for you for the time being. Then reset the alarm and you'll be good to go. It'll take about twenty minutes, tops. We'll have you back in court in no time."

Gilkenny nodded. "You got any lumber? A couple two-by-fours?"

Cate brightened, getting the hang of the VIP thing. "In the basement, I think. This way." She led them to the basement stairs, off the kitchen.

Officer Gilkenny said, "Judge, what's Mariska Hargitay really like?"

"She's great," Cate called back.

But that wasn't the detective she was thinking of.

CHAPTER 21

An hour later, Cate was back in the car, driving up Market Street to the courthouse. It was the noon rush hour, and buses, cabs, and cars clogged Market Street. An immense brown-and-white draft horse trotted past, pulling a white-painted cart that held two tourists crazy enough to visit this time of year.

Cate pulled out her cell phone, called information, and waited while the call connected. "Homicide Division," a man answered.

"Detective Nesbitt, please."

"He's not in. Can I take a message?"

Cate wasn't taking no for an answer. "Can you give me his cell phone?"

"Sorry, I can't do that."

"This is Judge Cate Fante. He's been working with me on the Simone case. It's very important that I speak with him."

"Hold on, Judge," the detective said, his voice warming. "I think he's still with the brass, after the press conference."

The line went dead, and Cate drummed her fingers on the smooth wooden steering wheel, idly watching the horse blow steamy breath from nostrils big as quarters, then shake his massive head, almost throwing off a straw hat that read DAVE. Cate had ridden when she was little, mucking stalls at a local barn to pay for lessons. It wasn't a fancy barn, not where she lived. Barbed wire marked the grazing pasture, and the horses drank from an abandoned bathtub. She had loved riding. Her mother watching, clapping.

"Judge, here's his cell number," the detective came back on, interrupting her thoughts. He rattled off a number, and Cate thanked him before she hung up and pressed it in. After a few rings, Nesbitt's mechanical message started, and Cate left him a message with her cell number.

Now where was I? Cate's head was spinning. The burglary. Russo. Gina and Warren. It was triage, and she didn't know which wound to treat first. Suddenly, the phone rang and she picked it up, checking the number on the lighted display.

Graham. Cate flipped open the phone and put on a happy face, or at least voice. "Hey, how're you?"

"Fine, sorry I didn't get back to you. I just got in, actually. I was in Minneapolis visiting a client and my plane got rerouted. I spent the night in Denver."

"Sounds cold." Cate cruised forward when the light changed, approaching the glitzy new Constitution Center, shining metallic in the bright sunlight. Tourists in blaze-orange jackets thronged on the sidewalk, collecting like a mob of hunters. Businesspeople hurried to and from lunch.

Graham was saying, "I see from the newspapers that all hell's broken loose with you. Murders? Suicides? What's going on?"

"You don't know the half of it." Cate considered telling him about the break-in, then decided against it. "Thanks again for the flowers."

"Glad you liked them. Have dinner with me tonight, so we can stop with the phone tag."

"I can't."

"Not another date, I hope?"

"A younger man, like three years old. I babysit tonight." Cate drove forward, finally passing the courthouse, noting that there were only a few reporters.

"Funny way to earn a few bucks. Aren't the taxpayers paying you enough?"

"It's my godchild."

"Oh. Can you do it another night? I'm not free Friday. Got a late meeting."

"It's a long-standing gig. How about Saturday?" Cate asked, her heart curiously leaping into her throat. She had taken strangers to bed with less trepidation. "I think I'm asking you on a date."

"Prime time? You've never given me a Saturday night before."

"You've arrived, pal." Cate laughed, and so did Graham.

"What did I do right? Was it the bling? Tell me, so I'll do it again."

"Calm yourself." Cate approached the security kiosk outside the parking garage and waved at the guard in the booth.

"Saturday at eight, then," Graham said, a new warmth in his voice. "I have a party to go to that night, given by one of my best clients. Would you mind going as my date?"

"I'd love it."

"I'll show you off. How about I pick you up, at your house?"

"Okay." Cate felt a twinge. She'd feel funny, going home tonight. She gave him the address, hoping Nesbitt would call back soon. "Got that?"

"See you then. And wear that bracelet I gave you."

"I will." Cate drove down the ramp to the parking garage underneath the courthouse, then aimed her remote at the sensor and waited while the brown corrugated door lifted.

"You're not wearing it, I know."

"I am, too." Cate smiled to herself. The gold bracelet was peeking out from under the thick sleeve of her coat, but he didn't have to know that.

"See you Saturday," she said, and hung up. She pulled into the garage, checking the car's clock. 1:15. She was late. The parking lot was quiet and still, and she found her space and parked. She grabbed her phone and purse, and juggled both to lock the car and call Matt on the cell. She couldn't remember his direct dial offhand, so she pressed in the main office number, hustling toward the locked door that led to the secured half of the courthouse.

"Beecker & Hartigan," said a woman's dignified voice, when the call picked up, and Cate felt herself stiffen. It was Mrs. Pershing, the prim switchboard diva who'd been with Beecker since the Jurassic. Cate didn't even want to think about Mrs. Pershing knowing her business.

"Mrs. Pershing? It's Cate Fante."

"Judge! My goodness, how have you been? I keep hearing so much about that case before you, with all those movie stars. And that poor man, who killed himself. And so young."

"Yes, it's very sad." Cate fished for her keys in her purse, resting her hot cell phone in the crook of her neck. "I hate to cut you off, but I'm kind of in a hurry, so could you—"

"Judge, we're so proud of you, here at Beecker. Tell me, did you meet Clint Eastwood, at your trial? He's a favorite of mine."

"Clint Eastwood didn't have anything to do with this case, Mrs. Pershing." Cate finally found her key, shoved it into the lock, and twisted until she heard the telltale click. "Would you connect me to Matt Sorian's office?" she asked, just as she burst into the small lobby for the judge's elevator.

Where Jonathan Meriden was waiting for an elevator. In a dark topcoat over his suit and rep tie, carrying a boxy briefcase.

Damn. Cate never would have called Sorian if she'd known Meriden would overhear. She could feel him making a mental hatch mark in the WHY CATE IS A BAD JUDGE column, for fraternizing with the bar.

Mrs. Pershing was saying, "Mr. Sorian is at lunch, Judge. He should be back soon."

"Please mention that I called. Thanks."

"What is this in reference to?" Mrs. Pershing asked.

"Bye now," Cate answered, and hung up rather than go with *It's about my secret sex life.* The elevator arrived, and she stepped inside the cab behind Meriden. They went to opposite corners of the cab, like boxers. She didn't want to speak to him, but she decided to be civil. "Hi, Jonathan."

"Hello." Meriden nodded as he hit the button for their floor. They both watched the orange elevator numbers change, with Cate thinking that lifetime tenure might be a long time not to speak to a person.

"Can this marriage be saved?" she asked, managing a smile, but Meriden's mouth remained a flat line.

"What do you mean, Cate?"

"It was a joke."

"Oh." They watched the elevator number turn to seven, their eyes heavenward. "How's Sorian doing?" Meriden asked, after a minute.

"Matt? I don't know."

"He and I go way back. He's before me next week." Meriden paused. "Do you see a lot of Matt?"

"No," Cate answered, just as the elevator reached their floor and the stainless steel doors slid apart. She stepped off the elevator to the ringing of her cell phone. *Matt?*

"Aren't you going to get that?"

"Not just yet." Cate opened the door to chambers. Inside, an alarmed Val was standing up at her desk, on the phone.

"Oh my God, I was just calling you, Judge!" Val's forehead was knitted with worry. Sam stood beside her, even paler than usual.

"What's the matter?" Cate asked, entering, and before she could stop him, Meriden slipped in behind her.

CHAPTER 22

Cate walked into her office, stunned at the sight. Debris lay everywhere. Case files had been opened and scattered over her conference table. Papers and bound briefs littered her floor. Casebooks had been pulled from the bookshelves, and cardboard boxes she had yet to unpack had been upended, their contents strewn onto the blue rug. Cate thanked God she had kept the chronology with her, in her purse.

"What happened here?" Meriden asked, aghast. He hovered over Cate's shoulder, but she ignored him. She walked numbly to her desk and found all her drawers hanging open, as if they'd been searched. Even her blue mug had been knocked over, spilling coffee onto her papers. Cate stood by her desk, still in her coat.

"It's my fault, Judge Fante." Val stepped forward, her brown-patterned dress flowing around her. "I shouldn't have gone to lunch."

"You're entitled to eat, Val." Cate remembered that Emily would still be at Jenkins. She turned to Sam. "Were you here? Did you go out for lunch?"

"I'm really sorry, Judge," Sam answered. He was almost hyperventilating, and his forehead had taken on an unhappy sheen. "I mean, I'm really, really sorry. I didn't think this would happen. I've been trying so hard to do better and I'm so sorry—"

Meriden interrupted, "This is a major security breach."

"Jonathan, I can handle it," Cate said, stepping closer to Sam, but Meriden shook his head.

"We need to call the FBI, right now. This is an attack on a federal judge, on federal property."

"Let me find out what happened first." Cate turned to Sam, feeling Meriden's stare boring into her back. "Sam, slow down, take a breath, and explain to me what happened."

"No matter what I do I screw up!"

"Breathe, Sam," Cate said, and the law clerk inhaled on command, his skinny chest heaving under his gray crewneck sweater.

"Okay, well. Everybody else was out and I was working in my office. I heard the buzzer, so I came out to see who it was, and there was a man there, on the monitor." Sam breathed again, visibly. "He pressed the intercom and identified himself as Detective Russo, and I knew it was really him, because I recognized him from the trial. So I thought I could let him in. I was sure it was okay to let him in. I mean, he's a detective."

Russo. It had to have been him, breaking into the house.

Meriden scoffed. "Did Detective Russo have an appointment?"

"I don't think so."

"Never buzz anybody into chambers without an appointment, no matter who they are! That's a hard and fast rule in my—"

Cate put a hand on the sleeve of Meriden's cashmere coat. "I said, I can handle my clerks."

"Then when will you start?" Meriden exploded. "They buzz anybody in. My chambers are on this floor, too. That detective could as easily have ransacked my office as yours!"

"How do you know he didn't? Better go and check. I'll try to handle this without your guidance."

"This is absurd!" Meriden turned and stalked to the door, then stopped when he reached Sam. "If you worked for me, you'd be on the street, son."

Sam shook in his penny loafers, Val gasped, and Cate's emotions finally broke loose. "How dare you!" she shouted. "Get out of my chambers!"

Meriden spun around, his split coattails flying, one chasing the other. "*What* did you say?"

"I said, get out of my chambers. Now."

"How distinctly uncollegial of you, Judge Fante."

"You manage your clerks, I'll manage mine." Cate strode past him to her office door and held it open, even though it already was. "Good-bye."

Meriden stormed out of the office, and Cate slammed the door behind him.

"That was fun," she said, brightening. She felt better, even standing amid the debris. It was the same feeling as when she'd said "my courtroom" to Gina. She found herself grinning.

Val said, "You shouldn't have done that. But, way to go!" She broke into a smile.

"Thanks, Judge." Sam's bassett-hound eyes looked wet, and Cate felt for him.

"Don't worry, Sam. Now, let's get back to the story. Russo was in the hallway."

"You're not gonna fire me?"

"No. Now tell me about letting Russo in. What did he say on the intercom?"

"Just who he was." Sam wet his lips with a dry tongue, starting his story over. "Also, I let him in because the chief judge had sent around a court-mail this morning, saying that the security threat had been lifted, now that Marz was dead, and, thirdly, I remembered that this morning, when that other detective came here, Nesbitt I think his name was, that Val asked you if she could buzz him in, and you said, 'Of course.'"

"You're right, I said that." Cate slid out of her coat and placed it on her desk chair.

"So I thought, of course, *of course*, Detective Russo can come in, too. I didn't know he'd do anything like *this*. He's law enforcement." Sam threw up his matchstick arms, bewildered. "I mean, *quis custodiet ipsos custodes*?"

"What?" Cate asked.

"He's hysterical," Val said.

"It's Latin," Sam answered, evidently feeling more himself. "The translation is, Who guards the guards? The Roman poet Juvenal famously posed the question in the first century."

"But why did you let him wait in my office, Sam?" Cate asked, mystified. *After all, Juvenal wouldn't have.*

"I didn't. He said that he needed to see you, about your security. He said he'd only come back to chambers because you weren't on the bench. That you were supposed to be in court at eleven-thirty."

"Okay," Cate said slowly. *So Russo had checked the schedule downstairs.*

"He said the security threat was from a man, an ex-convict, and he asked me if I'd ever seen the man in chambers or in your courtroom. He showed me a photo."

"Of what?"

"Of the man." Sam pumped his head, his movement jerky. "It was of the guy who fell off the balcony the other day. I remembered that story, from the news."

Partridge, with the videotape. "He showed you a photo of *him*?"

Val asked, "Sam, if the man was dead, how could he be a threat to the judge?"

Sam turned to her. "The detective said the man worked with a gang and they were trying to kill her."

Val's mouth dropped open. "How could you believe that, Sam? That sounds crazy. And he shows up, all by himself, without the marshals?"

Cate raised a hand. "Wait, please, Val. We need to get the story. Sam, how did Russo get into my office from yours?"

"He said he had to search chambers for wiretaps. 'Sweep for wiretaps,' he called it. He said that the man and his gang used wiretaps to find out about judges they were going to kill."

Oh, man. "Where did you go, while he searched?" Cate asked, trying to keep him on track.

"He said he had to search the clerks' office, too, so he told me that I had to go out and come back in about half an hour. So I went down to the cafeteria and got lunch."

Val's brown eyes flared. "How could you leave him alone in chambers?"

"He was a detective!" Sam wailed, getting upset again. "I thought he was okay!"

"Okay, relax, Sam. Val, relax."

"Judge, I'm really sorry," Sam repeated. "Please don't say anything, Judge. Word gets around, and I still don't have an offer yet, for next year."

"Don't worry." Cate walked to him, put a hand on his knobby shoulder, and looked at Val. "Did you call the marshals?"

"Not yet. I was about to, when you came in."

Cate's gaze traveled back to the law clerk. "Sam, don't speak to anyone about this, please. Don't tell any of your friends in the other chambers."

"I don't have any friends in the other—"

"Okay." Cate couldn't bear to hear it from him, too. "Don't tell anyone."

"What about Emily, when she comes back?"

"Val will tell her. You can talk to her, of course. But don't either of you discuss it outside chambers." Cate ran a hand through her hair. "Now, go back to your office and leave Mommy and Daddy alone, okay?"

"What?"

"Go." Cate pointed at the door. "Out."

"Sure, Judge." Sam turned and left the office, closing the door behind him.

Cate said, "Somebody tried to break into my house this morning. I think it was Russo."

Val's hand flew to her mouth. "Are you for real?"

"He's angry that I ruled against him, best I can figure." It was partly true, and Cate would die if Val knew about the videotape. "I already have a call in to Detective Nesbitt."

"I can't believe it. Your house, down Society Hill? He take anything?"

"No. He didn't get in."

"Praise God. Wait, that where you went this morning? How'd you know your house was gonna be broken into?"

Micah. "No, I had something else to do, then they called me in the car."

"I see." Val mulled it over. "Well. So, a detective did this? Trying to make your life miserable? Seems like he's after you, or looking for something in here. He didn't mess up my office, or the clerks'."

"I have no idea what he's looking for. I think he's just plain mad."

"Off his rocker?"

"Yep. He can't want to be a detective anymore. He just killed his career." Cate eyed the wreckage of her office. Russo had just broken the last barrier, and she didn't know if he could ever get back. "He must have reacted strongly to Marz's suicide. He must blame me for it."

"I'm glad he didn't kill you. Or me."

"Or Sam."

"Hmph! Save me the trouble of killin' him my *own* self!" An unlikely grin spread slowly across Val's face, and Cate burst into laughter, which felt unexpectedly good. Val said, "I tell you, I've seen clerks come and go, every year new ones. I've watched them get married, have babies, get divorced. But in all my years, I've never seen as strange a two as these. Each one's crazier than the other. Sam, he takes the cake."

"Nah, he just got scared."

"*He* got scared? Now *I'm* scared. *You* scared?"

Cate felt it too, then. "Honest? Yes."

"It's not safe around here, all of a sudden." Val pursed her lips. "I better tell the marshals and they'll tell the FBI. And the chief should send out another court-mail, about Russo this time."

"Oh, here we go." Cate didn't know how long she could keep a lid on that videotape. This was about to get public. There would be questions from the FBI. "I bet Meriden's on the phone to the chief as we speak."

"Probably on the cell on the way down the hall." Val clucked. "That man is a jerk, and he does *not* like you at all."

"All of a sudden, nobody does."

"Can't understand why. I like you." Val smiled warmly, and Cate smiled back.

"I like you, too."

Val turned on her heel, her dress swirling, then turned back. "Judge, I almost forgot. You have a plea hearing at two-thirty this afternoon and a sentencing at four-thirty. I should cancel both."

Cate groaned. "No, I can't keep canceling these court dates. It backs up my docket and I'm on trial next week, in that products case. Keep the four-thirty."

Ring! went a phone, and Cate sprinted for her purse, which she'd left in the reception area.

That better be Nesbitt. Or Sorian. Or the cavalry.

CHAPTER 23

Cate froze, standing in her ruined office, her phone at her ear. When Nesbitt told her, she was facing the window, so she remained facing the window, though she suddenly saw none of the view.

Nesbitt had said: "*Judge, Russo stole my case file, on Simone. He has the record, about you.*"

"Judge? You there?"

"He really has the record?"

"Yes. I gave you a copy. I kept the original in the file."

"The record of my"—*what had Nesbitt called it, only hours ago*— "personal whereabouts?"

"Yes, I'm sorry."

"What about the pictures?"

"Those too. Copies, not the originals."

Cate tried to process it and couldn't. "How did this happen?"

"Come down to the Roundhouse, Judge. We need to talk about it."

"Be there in fifteen minutes." Cate let the phone snap closed.

Cate had never been at the Roundhouse before and couldn't ignore its seaminess. The lobby downstairs was a dark, empty space, reeking of cigarette smoke that blew in from the smokers in front of the building. Nesbitt met her there, clamping a strong arm on hers, and whisking her up a funny, podlike elevator to the Homicide Division. They passed a cramped waiting area with two black couches, arranged facing each other against a wall that read WANTED and was covered by rows of eight-by-ten glossies of scary, affectless faces. Then Cate was pressed through a swinging half-door she'd seen in only the cheapest bars.

"This way, Judge," Nesbitt said, and led her through a large, dim squad room that contained about twenty institutional-gray desks, stacked with files and arranged in no apparent order. Water-stained curtains hung unevenly, and on the right side of the room sat a row of file cabinets of different colors and sizes, in grimy gray, black, tan, and even olive green, lined up like rotten teeth. Detectives in shirt-sleeves talked on the phone at the desks, and one read the *Daily News*, his shiny loafers crossed on his desk. All of them pointedly ignored Cate and Nesbitt.

"Come on in, Judge," Nesbitt said, gesturing her into an office off the squad room, and at Cate's entrance, a tall, thin detective in a houndstooth suit stood up, with a professional smile. Nesbitt stepped in behind her. "Judge, this is my sergeant, Marvin Shiller."

"Hello, Sergeant." Cate extended a hand across the desk, trying to act as dignified as possible. Both men knew her secret, and it felt lousy. She could only imagine the jokes they'd made before she got here, and she wondered how many of the other detectives in the squad room knew, too. She forced herself to meet Shiller's eye as he shook her hand, and he almost crushed it in a large, rough palm. She said, "Quite a handshake."

"It impresses the chicks." Shiller grinned, showing unusually small teeth in a broad, fleshy face.

"And nobody else," Nesbitt added, and both men laughed.

"Thanks for coming, Judge. Sorry about the inconvenience." Shiller was about fifty-five years old, with wide-set blue eyes and bushy gray eyebrows that looked dyed to match his wavy gray hair, expensively layered. He had a large, doughy fighter's nose, and redness tinged his flat cheeks, as if he'd just come in from outside. "Oh, yeah, of course, call me Mitty."

"That's the nicest thing he's been called recently," Nesbitt said, and they laughed again. "Can I get you some coffee, Judge? Ours is the worst."

"No, thanks, and I already make the worst."

"Please, sit down." Shiller waved a large hand at the stiff chair across from his desk, and Cate took one seat while Nesbitt took the other. A synthetic American flag stood in the corner of the room, slightly askew in its gold stand, next to a three-drawer set of file cabinets. Degrees and framed certificates hung on the scuffed walls. Shiller eased into his chair, which squeaked. "Judge, I'll get right to the point. We have a problem with Frank Russo."

"Clearly." Cate told them what Russo had done to her house and office. "So at this point I'm afraid for my safety, and that of my staff."

"Before we begin, you didn't call the FBI, did you?"

"The marshals will, if they haven't already." Cate had known it would be the first thing Shiller asked. Everything was jurisdiction with the locals, and nobody wanted the FBI involved, least of all Cate. "I'm not that happy about it either, for obvious reasons."

"It makes our job harder."

"Understood, and I would like to keep this as confined as possible. I assume everything we say in here is confidential."

"Goes without saying."

Cate shifted forward on her uncomfortable chair. "Now, I understand that Russo stole the Simone file from Detective Nesbitt, and I want to know how that happened and what we can do about it."

Nesbitt raised a hand, his good mood gone. "I can explain, Judge. Most of the detectives keep the files in unlocked drawers, and it's nothing to go in and look through somebody else's cases. It happens all the time. I don't do that, not for my high-profile cases, because I don't want any leaks to the press. Your case file was under lock and key in my desk drawer. I keep the key on my key ring."

"Then how did Russo get it?"

"At some point, he must have gotten a copy of the key or made one, and he took the file and walked out with it. The up man saw him go this morning."

" 'Up man'?"

"The detective who answers the phones at the front desk. We rotate, and he's up."

"And the up man didn't stop him?"

"Why would he? He didn't know he had it and he didn't know it wasn't Russo's file. All the files look the same."

"Didn't anyone see him get it from your drawer?"

"No, and if they did, they wouldn't have thought it was all that strange. We used to be partners. That's how he knew where I kept sensitive cases."

Cate felt her cheeks flush with anger. "Why did you keep it there, if you knew Russo was interested and the case was so sensitive? I mean, he was a key witness. He had a stake in winning."

"Judge, I'm sorry." Nesbitt met her eye, with regret. "I made a mistake. I never thought Russo would go into that drawer without my permission, much less break in and take a file."

"It's unprecedented," Shiller added, leaning forward. "Unheard of, for one detective to do that to another. For all our joking around, I respect Nesbitt more than I can say. He's the best on the squad and the most discreet. To tell you the truth, he's next in line for my job." Shiller nodded at Nesbitt, and Cate could see he felt bad enough.

"But why did Russo do that? Why did he want that file so badly?"

Nesbitt and Shiller exchanged glances. Then Nesbitt said, "Our best guess is that he's been checking on the Simone file all along, without my knowing. After hours. It would be a way to keep tabs on the investigation because he knew I wouldn't tell him what was going on. Then when the case was cleared and we were all out at the press conference, he took the file."

Cate was confused. "So then he's known about the record, and me, for a few days."

"No." Nesbitt shook his head. "Those records about you weren't in the file until today. I kept them at home because they weren't a part of the investigation, like I told you. I knew I wanted to show them to you. I even used my home copier to make the copies. This morning, after I left your office, I put the originals back in the file. Then I went to the press conference and when I came back, it was gone."

Shiller cleared his throat, authoritatively. "Judge, you can rest assured that I'm having Internal Affairs investigate the matter completely. Russo will be put on immediate suspension, and he will be discharged, I can promise you that."

Cate almost laughed. "What good will that do? He's off the reservation, isn't he? Breaking into my house, my chambers? Violating state and federal laws. He's a Rottweiler off the leash."

"We do have procedure—"

"Fire him if you want to, Sergeant, but I think he quit. I'm right, aren't I?" Cate turned to Nesbitt because she knew he'd give her a straight answer, and his mustache tilted down at the corners.

"Frankly, yes." Nesbitt looked at Shiller, then back at Cate.

"Did you talk to Russo about Marz's suicide?"

"Yes, he called me after I left your chambers. He'd heard it on the news and he took it badly. He was upset. He really liked Marz."

"Does he blame me for the death?"

"Yes." Nesbitt checked with Shiller again. "I tried to reach him after I saw the file was gone, but he wasn't answering his home or cell. I went to his apartment and he wasn't there. His neighbor said he hasn't been home for days. My guess it's since the verdict."

"What about Marz's wife? Did you try her?"

"She hasn't seen him. I went over. That's where I was when you called this morning. I had turned the phone off because she's in mourning. Shiva, and all."

"Would she tell you, if she knew?"

"I think so."

"Is Russo married?"

"They broke up, years ago."

"Does he have a girlfriend?"

"Not that I know of. A kid at Penn State, and he hasn't heard from him in months. They were never that close. He lived with the mother."

Cate felt her gut tense, still raw from this morning. "So where is he?"

"We're looking for him. We put out an APB. He's a fugitive."

"We'll find him," Shiller added firmly. "We'll have him by the end of business today, if I have to go out and drag him in myself."

Nesbitt shifted forward on his seat. "I did hear from him one other time, which is what I wanted to talk to you about. At about one o'clock today. I assume that was after he had been to your office."

Cate did a rough calculation. "Yes. Why? What did he say?"

"He was angry. He had read the file and he was claiming he found mistakes in my investigation. My assumptions, even the lab results, et cetera."

"Your investigation of what?"

"Of Simone's murder."

"Isn't that over?"

"Not for him. Russo doesn't think Marz killed Simone."

Cate blinked. "Marz shot himself with the murder weapon."

"Russo thinks the gun was planted. He's got some crazy new theory." Nesbitt glanced at Shiller again, and Cate saw their expressions tense, right before her eyes.

"What?" she asked, after a minute. "Why do you keep looking at each other? What's going on here?"

Shiller answered, "Russo's new theory is that you killed Simone."

"*What*?" Cate almost fell off the chair. "Me? What? Why?"

"Don't get upset, Judge," Shiller said, but it was too late.

"Are you crazy? This mad dog thinks I killed his friend?" Cate turned wildly to Nesbitt. "What *is* going on? What did he say?"

"Judge." Nesbitt put up his palm. "Don't worry. We'll get this under control. Russo's a hothead and he had a big shock, with Marz's suicide. He'll calm down."

Cate thought ahead, trying not to panic. "Tell me what he said. Where is he getting these ideas?"

"He saw the record, of what you do. At night."

"Okay, my personal whereabouts." Cate almost wasn't embarrassed anymore. Nothing like a true emergency to put things into perspective. "And so what?"

"He figured out that Simone was having you followed."

"He was. I checked. So?"

"He remembered that Simone had said something on the witness stand about making a TV series of your life, and that you didn't look too happy about it, even though you made a joke. Did that happen?"

"Yes, but how does that make me a killer?"

"Russo thinks that you had Simone killed to prevent him from making a TV show about you. A TV series that exposed your, uh, personal life."

Cate gasped, but it came out like a hiccup. "But I didn't kill Simone. Marz did."

"Russo doesn't think Marz had it in him. He thinks you do."

"He doesn't even know me! This is crazy!"

"I agree. It's not rational, Judge."

"How can he think I shot Simone? Didn't you say there was a videotape from the parking lot, and it shows Marz pulling the trigger?"

"The figure on the tape isn't clear. It's a short person in a baseball cap. We thought it was Marz, and the suicide confirms it. But Russo doesn't agree."

"I want to see it," Cate said.

"We can't. The only copy was in the file that Russo took."

"But if it's not Marz on the tape, who does Russo think it is?"

"He thinks it's Partridge."

"*Partridge?*"

"The man on the porn videotape."

"I know who Partridge is, but—" Cate cut her sentence short. *Oh my God.* "He showed Partridge's photo to my law clerk."

"Because he thinks you hired Partridge to kill Simone, and that's why you were paying him that night, on the tape. To shut him up because he was blackmailing you. And on the tape, he threw the money back at you. It looked like you were paying him and it wasn't enough. He said, 'You can't pay me,' remember?"

Cate found herself rising from the chair, as it dawned on her. She could see how Russo would think that. It made sense, but it was all wrong. "This is a nightmare. This whole day, this week. It's a nightmare."

"Judge, please, sit down."

"No, I can't." Cate felt suddenly restless, as if she had to move. "Russo thinks I got away with the murder of his friend. That's why he's after me. He's trying to see what he can find out. He's investigating me for proof I was behind Simone's murder."

"He *will* calm down," Nesbitt said, and Shiller stood up slowly.

"Obviously he's having a hard time getting a grip on things, but he will, in a day or two. I remember when he got divorced, he was a mess for a week, then he was good as new."

"I need protection, don't I?"

"Not yet, Judge." Shiller rocked back and forth on his feet. "Russo's a little nuts right now, but he'll come to his senses."

"He tried to break into my house. I have two-by-fours for a back door."

"That's different from aggressing on you, physically. He won't take it to that level."

"Can you guarantee that, Sergeant?"

Shiller nodded. "One hundred percent."

Oh, please. Cate turned instead to Nesbitt. "What do you think, by the book?"

"You need protection," he answered, his eyes frank.

And Cate felt a tingle of true fear.

CHAPTER 24

Cate opened the door to her chambers, immediately taken aback. Men in dark suits, FBI windbreakers, and even bulletproof vests clogged her reception room, spilling into her office along with personnel from the clerk's office, the circuit executive's office, and an array of federal marshals. They milled around, talking to each other and into walkie-talkies so loudly that they didn't hear Cate enter.

"Val?" she called out, and the secretary waved over their heads. Their faces turned toward Cate, one by one, and everyone greeted her while she threaded her way to Val's desk. She thanked them and leaned over the divider. "Full house, huh?"

Val gestured her closer. "You ever see so many cops? They're playing *CSI Philadelphia*, you ask me."

"When they leaving?"

"Soon, I hope. I don't know when I'm gonna clean your office up. They don't want us to touch it while they're lookin' around, but I can't stay late tonight. I have choir." Val held up a business card with a tiny gold FBI seal. "Special Agent Mike Brady is the one in charge. You'll know him right away. He's the tallest one. And Chief Judge Sherman says, call your rabbi when you can. That mean anything to you?"

"Yes." Cate smiled.

"By the way, Mo said Meriden called Sherman five minutes before we did."

"So grade school."

"But the funny thing is, Mo keeps losing his phone messages." Val's eyes glittered with ersatz evil, and Cate laughed.

"Did the FBI talk to Sam?"

"Yes, and so did the marshals, and Mike from the clerk's office and Brad from the court executive's office."

"Oh boy. Is he okay?"

"For a bowl of Jell-O, yes."

"Poor thing." Cate checked her watch. 4:10. "I gotta be on the bench in five minutes. Proceeding's at four-fifteen."

"Four-thirty."

"Sam here? It's his case."

"No, it's Emily's, and she's in her office. I'll buzz her." Val hit the intercom button on the telephone and picked up the receiver. "The judge's here, Emily. Bring the case file and her robe."

"My robe! Good thinking." Cate rubbed her forehead. She hadn't eaten since last night, running on bile and caffeine. She tried to collect herself as Val hung up the phone.

"You sure you don't want to cancel this proceeding?"

"Nah, it's just a guilty plea."

"No, it isn't." Val frowned. "Judge, we canceled the guilty plea, that was the one at two-thirty."

Yikes. "What's this one?"

"A sentencing."

"Uh-oh." Cate worried. Guilty pleas were easy, involving her asking a series of rote questions, but a sentencing was something else entirely. She hoped that Emily had written a good bench memo, the summary for judges who are too busy with murder-suicides. "Okay, we'll just have to see how it goes. Maybe it's an easy one."

Val held out her hand. "Gimme your coat, Judge."

"Thanks." Cate slid out of her coat and passed it to Val.

"And your purse."

"Thanks again." Cate plopped her purse on top of the coat.

"Need a pad?" Val handed Cate a fresh legal pad and a pen, which she accepted. "How was the meeting with the police?"

"I'll fill you in later. Expect a phone call from SpectaSafe, a security company." Cate had called them from the car on the way in. "I'm hiring us a bodyguard until they pick Russo up."

"For real?" Val lifted an eyebrow.

"Yep. He's gonna sit on that couch and keep you safe. He should be here first thing tomorrow morning. They're going to call you back with the details. Give them my personal American Express for the bill." Cate turned to her left as louder talking came from her office, and a basketball player in a suit made his way through the crowd toward her. She tried not to let her nerves show.

"Judge Fante?" The agent extended a huge hand, and Cate felt hers squashed for the second time that day.

"Special Agent Brady, I know you need to speak with me, but I'm due on the bench."

"Judge, where are you?" It was Emily, on the right, over the din. She emerged from the crowd with a file and a black robe.

Yay! "Right here!" Cate hollered, way too eagerly.

On Cate's left, Special Agent Brady was saying, "Judge, if you have a minute before you go on the bench, we can chat now."

Simultaneously, on her right, Emily was saying, "Judge, we're good to go."

"Thanks, Em." Cate accepted the documents and robe, then turned to Special Agent Brady. "You left a card with my secretary, and I'll call you when I get off the bench, first thing."

"Hey, girl, let's go!" Cate said to Emily, juggling the papers to escape through the front door. *A judge, running from the law. What's wrong with this picture?*

LISA SCOTTOLINE

Once they were safely outside, Cate slipped into her robe and they ducked inside the anteroom to the courtroom, where they could be alone. Cate asked, "Okay, what did you find out at Jenkins, on the stalking issue?"

"Judge, there's no case on point, so it's arguable either way."

"How so?" Cate checked her frustration. Clerks always said things like this until they became lawyers and read the law the right way—their client's.

"Your actions occurred in public, so they're entitled to follow you. It shades into harassment and stalking at some point, but the issue is your knowledge. The argument would go that you didn't know that you were being followed, so you weren't harassed by it."

"What about the TV-show issue?"

"If it's fiction and properly disclaimed, there's no liability."

Damn. "What about for private people, like friends of mine or their families?"

"You didn't ask me about that."

I never dreamed they'd stoop so low. "Well, from your reading, does it turn on the fact that I'm a public figure?"

Emily frowned, stumped. "That, I'd have to check."

"Okay, good work." Cate would have to get Matt Sorian on the phone. She checked her watch. 4:25. "We'll talk later. Let's go," she said, pushing open the courtroom door.

"All rise for the Honorable Cate Fante!" the courtroom deputy boomed.

Cate entered the courtroom, whisked up the few stairs to the dais, and took her seat behind her desk. She skimmed the pleadings index while the courtroom settled down. After a minute, she raised her head and caught the courtroom deputy's secret wink, this time with a sympathetic smile.

"Good afternoon, ladies," Cate said at the sight of two female lawyers before her in identical dark suits, like girl bookends. "My, things are changing, aren't they?" The lawyers laughed, only because they had to, and she checked the pleadings for the attorneys' names before she faced the assistant United States attorney on her right. "And you are Jessica Connell?"

"Jessica Conley," the AUSA corrected, with an easy smile. She was a slim brunette with bright eyes.

"Sorry, Ms. Conley. What brings the government here today?" Cate asked, though usually when she said that, she already knew the answer.

"May it please the Court, the government comes before you to fix a sentence for defendant Louis D'Alma, who was convicted by a jury almost a year ago of conspiracy to distribute cocaine, in violation of 21 U.S.C. Section 846, and use of a communication facility in furtherance of the conspiracy offense, in violation of 21 U.S.C. Section 843(b)."

Cate groaned inwardly. A sentencing in a drug case had become a morass since the Supreme Court's decision overturning the federal guidelines. Every district court in the country struggled with the new law, and now, so would she, completely unprepared. She reached for her bench memo, but it wasn't on top. She shuffled through the pleadings and the other papers, but it wasn't there. She felt herself sweating under her robes.

"The delay in sentencing Mr. D'Alma was due to his cooperation with the government in connection with the Danton Bonat matter, in a series of cases being tried these past few months before Judge Dalzell, with a jury."

Oh boy. Cate knew none of this background and was hoping it didn't matter. She looked through her desk as casually as possible, but she couldn't find the bench memo. She started to signal to Emily, but was surprised to find her talking to a blond male clerk sitting next to her. It was the law clerk that Sam had nicknamed Todhunter Preppington; one of Meriden's law clerks. What was he doing here, in her courtroom?

AUSA Conley continued, "The sentencing issue in this matter,

which was tried before Your Honor ascended the bench, is compli-
cated by the fact that the jury did not find the amount of narcotics
attributable to defendant. They convicted him of conspiracy to distribute an unspecified amount of cocaine, a Schedule II controlled
substance. The Government urges that it is permissible for the Court
to make a finding as to drug weight for sentencing purposes."

Cate couldn't stop watching Meriden's law clerk. He was talking to
Emily, nonstop. Meriden couldn't come himself, so he'd sent his kid
to spy. She hated that Meriden had seen what Russo had done to her
office. He must have called the chief right after.

The AUSA was saying, "The Government urges that the Court
can, and should, apply a base-offense level of thirty-two, which is the
level applicable under the guidelines when five to fifteen kilograms of
cocaine are involved."

The gallery was empty except for the defendant's side, where an
older woman sat in the front row, dabbing her eyes with a Kleenex.
She wore a torn black North Face jacket and blue stretch pants, and
was flanked by younger women who could have been girlfriends or
sisters, because they'd been crying, too. Around them, teenage boys,
girls, and two children clustered like a forlorn collection of hollow
street gold, sideways baseball caps, and Sean Jean sweatshirts. The
sight brought Cate to her senses. This was the most important day of
their lives, and she wasn't even paying attention.

Conley said, "The maximum statutory sentence for the Section
846 conviction would be twenty years or two hundred forty months
incarceration."

Twenty years? Cate felt the blood drain from her face. She looked
at the defendant, D'Alma. He couldn't have *been* twenty years old.
He sat slumped in his olive green jumpsuit at counsel table, his face
all dark eyes above a flat nose and small mouth, his hair shaved to a
fade on a head shaped like a Mason jar with a fuzzy lid. A black script
tattoo marred his neck.

"In addition, Section 841(b)(1)(C) provides that if any person commits such violation after a prior condition for a felony drug offense has become final, such persons shall be sentenced to a term of imprisonment of not more than thirty years."

Thirty years? "But he's just a kid!" Cate blurted out from the bench. The courtroom deputy looked up, Emily stopped talking, and Meriden's clerk sat riveted to the dais. Cate didn't care anymore. "Did you say he had a prior conviction? He doesn't look old enough to have a prior conviction."

The AUSA nodded, professionally hiding her surprise. "It's in the record, Your Honor, and in our brief. Also in the presentencing report. Mr. D'Alma does have a prior conviction, and the jury so found, as matter of fact."

Cate didn't know what to say. She was completely unprepared. She didn't know the facts. She was shaky on the law. She'd never felt more the imposter than she did at this very moment. Her gaze strayed to D'Alma's mother, wet-eyed, looking up at her with a naked hope.

The AUSA was saying, "Your Honor, may I continue?"

"No," Cate answered finally.

"Do you have another question, Your Honor?"

"No, but thanks for asking." Cate found herself on her feet in the next moment, with all the faces in the courtroom turned up to her. Both lawyers, AUSA and defense. Emily, with her eyebrow pierces, and the preppie. D'Alma's dark, lost gaze. And his mother's eyes, begging. Cate had never done this before, so she didn't know how it was done. She knew only that it had to be. D'Alma deserved more than she was giving him today, and so did the government. Cate grabbed her gavel and banged it hard. *Crak!* The sound reverberated in the stunned and silent courtroom.

The courtroom deputy rose, looking at her funny. "Judge?" he asked, but Cate waved him off.

"Ladies and gentlemen, please accept my apologies. With your kind permission, I'll have to adjourn Court for the day." Cate faced AUSA Connell. Conley. Whatever. "I'm very sorry, I know you worked hard to prepare for today, but we'll have to reschedule for as soon as possible." She turned to the defense lawyer, whose name she hadn't gotten in the first place. "Please excuse me, and I'll see you again soon. Thank you."

As if on cue, the courtroom deputy boomed, "Court is adjourned!"

CHAPTER 25

The sun was setting over the Schuylkill Expressway, its remaining red rays reflecting on the cars stopped in front of the Mercedes, their hoods lined up like the humpy shells of box turtles, moving just as slowly. Cate pressed the cell phone to her ear, noticing that all of the drivers around her were yapping away on their phones, too. When did everybody start driving on the cell phone? She never used to, but now she had a better excuse than most. If a cop stopped her, she hoped it wasn't Russo.

"I'm honored that you would consider calling me, Judge," Matt was saying, unusually respectful for an old friend. Cate hadn't kept in touch with many of her former partners, and this was why.

"Of course, Matt. You're the best."

"It's very kind of you to say that, Judge. I'm so sorry I didn't get back to you until now. I was actually in court in Wilmington, a jury trial, or I would have called—"

"Matt, do you have to keep calling me 'Judge'?" Cate hated the new deference in his tone, too. "We're old partners. Pals. We were even associates together, back in the day."

"And you became a judge, and all of your former partners like me are thrilled for you, at Beecker."

"But, Matt, you can still talk to me like it's me. I'm still me."

"Sorry, but I'm required to kiss your ass." Matt chuckled, but Cate didn't.

"I order you not to."

"Maybe you should tell me how I can help you. You're driving and I don't want you to get hurt."

Cate gave in and told him a sanitized version of the story, leaving out the unidentified-men part. It didn't help that Matt had her on a pedestal, and he didn't need to know everything to give her an answer. She wasn't telling the whole story unless and until she had to, come hell or client confidentiality.

"Judge, you want my opinion, down and dirty?"

"Yes."

"They're not liable to you, for their TV show. It's fictional. If they run the disclaimer, if they change the names and some of the facts, like the way you look and such, it's not actionable. Like a roman à clef. That's what we're talking about, you see? A Jackie Collins book, only not as good."

Cate fed the car some gas as traffic inched around the bend of the expressway, overlooking Boathouse Row. The decorative white lights that dotted the boathouses began to glow against a blueberry sky, but she avoided the prettiness of the scene and eyed the cars around her for Russo. She didn't know what kind of car he drove; she'd been too upset to see when he'd left her house. Her bodyguard wasn't reporting for duty until tomorrow morning, and she had driven with one eye on the rearview all the way from the courthouse, raising multitasking to an art form.

Cate asked, "But what if they show everything about my life, incorporated into the storyline?"

"Like what, Judge?"

Gulp. "Like private things?"

"Private things you do in public? Like what?"

"Where I go, for example. That part's in public."

"Then it's kosher, and why do you care? You don't go anywhere you're ashamed of."

Cate cringed. "Assume I do, Matt. Then what?"

"*You?*"

"Just assume I do." Traffic broke up a little, and she cruised forward. The car in back of her was dark, but a woman was driving. And on the cell phone.

"Okay, let me think of a hypo. It's an interesting legal question, in a way." Matt's tone gained a newly serious timbre. "Let's say, for argument's sake, that you're having an affair with a married man. You go to his house to meet. Is that a good hypo?"

"Yes," Cate said, though she'd never slept with a married man, as far as she knew. Her husband had cheated on her, so she wouldn't even consider it. *Even a slut has principles.*

"Let's say the TV series shows you doing that, right? A judge having an affair with a married man. Something public, but something you wouldn't necessarily be proud of."

"Exactly."

"Lawful."

Cate winced. She switched lanes to get to open road, feeling safer with fewer cars around her. It was getting darker by the minute.

"Sorry, Judge."

"Listen, Matt, change the hypo. Forget about me. What about my friend? I have a best friend who has a kid with autism. What if they put her and her son in the TV show?"

"Fair game."

"Why?" Cate accelerated, trying not to crash into anything as she glanced behind her for Russo.

"It's not them, it's characters like them. Women have friends. Kids have autism. As long as it's not your actual friends, who are private figures, and not a public figure like you, it's fictional and they can go with it."

"I'm suing anyway." Cate hit the gas decisively. "I want a TRO to enjoin production of the show. I want a complaint for defamation, false light, invasion of privacy. The whole nine yards. Right away."

"I wouldn't advise that, Judge. You'll lose."

"In the end, maybe. In the meantime, I'll tie them up so badly they'll wish they were never born."

"They'll do the show anyway. There's money to be made, I'm sure."

"Maybe they won't end up making the show, if I sue. If I make it expensive enough, or get them bad enough press, then maybe they'll go away."

"Then your affair will become public."

Cate didn't disabuse him. "If they do a TV show, it becomes public anyway."

"It'll cost you a fortune."

"I used to make what you do. I'm rich."

Matt chuckled. "Judge. Look, you're angry."

"Very."

"I understand why you don't want this to happen, now that you're on the bench, especially if it's harming people you love. But did you ever think that filing suit makes a bigger deal of it? Throws oil on the fire?"

Cate had thought about that. She checked the road behind her, which was full of trucks.

"If people didn't know it was you before, then they will after you file suit. We couldn't get a seal on those papers. That might make it harder on you, and your friends."

Cate considered it. She was trying to keep an open mind.

"You still there?"

"I hear you."

"Do me a favor and sleep on it. If you still want to do it, call me. I'm out in the morning, and in the afternoon." Matt paused, and she could hear him flipping day-planner pages. "I'm on trial next week, before Judge Meriden."

I heard. "Obviously, don't say we spoke."

"Of course not."

"He heard me leaving a message for you. He may ask you." Cate thought of that preppy brat who'd been in the courtroom today. Emily had said she had no idea why he was there.

"I'll say nothing, of course. So if you still want to do it, then we'll do it, and again, I'm honored that you called me, Judge. Above all, don't worry. All of us have something we'd rather not broadcast. Suing over it may not be the best course."

"Thanks." Cate pressed END and hit the gas again.

CHAPTER 26

It was dark by the time Cate reached the development, and she drove around Gina's block a few times, just to make sure Russo wasn't following her. The town houses, all painted light blue, stood three stories tall and were unusually narrow, stretching from the ground like fingers from a hand. Each town house had a short driveway and a uniformly fake colonial light beside every front door, illuminating a Ford, Dodge, or Honda minivan.

She took a right turn onto Meadowbrook and drove down the street, satisfied she wasn't being followed. Russo wouldn't have to trail her to find her here anyway; the record he'd stolen would show that she'd spent every Monday and Thursday here since the surveillance had begun. Still she scanned the parked cars as she drove past, out of an abundance of caution, and she didn't see anything amiss. She had hesitated about coming here tonight, but she knew Gina needed the break and wanted to talk to her anyway.

Cate turned the car into Gina's driveway, parked behind her Pathfinder, then cut the ignition, grabbed her purse and the bag of Chinese takeout. She hoped that between her car and the front door, she would think of a way to tell her best friend in the world that she and her beloved son were about to be fictionalized and beamed into three million homes every Sunday night.

They sat in the warm, cozy kitchen across from each other, two old girlfriends nursing fresh-brewed hazelnut coffee in tall glass mugs. White containers of chicken curry sat open on the tiny table, along with empty plastic tubs of egg drop soup and a bright red foil bag covered with a snaky dragon, which held leftover spare ribs. Warren sat quietly in his high chair, ignoring his cooling pasta and tapping his felt-rimmed mirror on his plastic tray, but his mood was calm enough to permit Cate to tell Gina the whole story, uninterrupted and chronologically, from the break-in of her house to the dismal prospects for the restraining order.

"I am so sorry," Cate said, after she had finally finished. She eyed her friend for a reaction. Gina sat slumped in the chair, almost sinking into her oversized sweatshirt, a soft old white one that read FT. LAUDERDALE above an embroidered pink-and-yellow sailboat. Her large, round eyes looked a weary brown, their eyeliner smudged off, but her lips curved into her characteristic smile, which made Cate feel even worse. "Gina, I feel awful about this."

"You shouldn't. It wasn't your fault."

"Yes, it was."

"You didn't know they were following you." Gina's voice was soft.

"If I didn't run around at night, they wouldn't have followed me in the first place. I would have been just another judge on the court, too boring to write about."

"No, they liked you from the pretrial conference, remember? You're hot, you're sexy, you're camera-ready."

"But I gave them something juicy when they started digging. And now you're caught up in it, and the baby." Cate felt her throat thicken, but she didn't want to cry. "I would be furious if I were you."

"No, never. Not at you." Gina managed another smile, but Cate could see wetness come to her eyes, a sad sheen.

"I'm so sorry. You can yell at me, go ahead."

"No. I admit, I'm not thrilled about it, but I'm not mad at you." Gina bit her lower lip. "I mean, what'll they do to me? My character,

I mean. Will they make me do dumb things? Or make me look like a bad mother?" Gina's voice went hoarse, and Cate almost cried.

"Nobody could make you a bad mother. You're absolutely devoted to Warren, and everybody knows that. You changed your whole life to be with him. You're a *great* mother."

"Not always." Gina tucked a strand of dark bangs into her paint-brush ponytail. "It's hard sometimes. I hear moms staying home with normal kids, and I think, they have no idea how easy they have it. It's a long day with him, a really long day."

"I know, and that's why they can't make you look bad. Besides, you have to remember, it's not you. People will know that. We'll *tell* people that. Your friends, his teachers, everybody."

"What if they make me into some sort of saint, because the baby has autism? I'd hate that, too. That's just another way of putting him down." Gina checked on Warren, her gaze shifting to the high chair and back again. "Because he's not so hard, really, and you know, I mean, I love him. And he's a gift, a *gift*. I know that now. You know that, too, Cate."

"Of course, I do, I know that—"

"I just don't want them to make the baby look bad." Gina kept biting her lip. "I'd hate it if they, you know, made him look really . . . *severe*. Because he's not."

"Gina—"

"I mean, I know that it's politically incorrect to say, but he isn't so bad and he never arm-flaps and I think he'd be one of the higher functioning kids next year . . ." Gina's sentence trailed off. "It's just that he already gets teased so much, you know. I don't want it to get worse."

Cate understood. *Retard. Tard. Dummy. Stupid.* She'd witnessed it.

"Like today, we went to the pool at the Y and there was another kid, about four, and he wanted to play with him, and he kept yelling at him, but Warren wouldn't look at him, and the kid yelled, 'What are you, deaf?' " Gina tossed her head, as if to shake it off. "I remember when that was his diagnosis, don't you? When I *hoped* that he was deaf. That would have been easy."

"Yes." Cate reached across the table and covered her friend's hand, the physical connection making palpable the pain. "I am so very sorry."

"Did you ever think that this was meant to happen?"

"No, absolutely not."

"But maybe it was. Like Dr. Phil says."

"Gina, now with the Dr. Phil?" Cate managed a weak smile.

"But it's true. You had a secret. You were running around, and nobody knew it, not even me. Now it's about to come out." Gina shifted forward. "The running around isn't the secret, Cate. It's just the behavior. What's your secret?"

"I don't know, it's a secret." Cate chuckled, but Gina didn't.

"Think about it. Maybe you're supposed to figure it out, maybe this is how. Everybody has a secret."

"You don't."

"I do, too."

"What?" Cate shot back, and the kitchen grew so quiet she thought Gina had stopped breathing. "You never told me any secret."

"I know." Gina swallowed visibly. "It's not the kind of secret you ever tell."

"What?" Cate asked, though she wasn't sure she wanted to know.

"Sometimes, when I got stressed out, before he was diagnosed, I hit the baby."

Cate blinked, shocked.

"I did that. Not often, but sometimes. I hit his butt. I don't know if he felt it through the diaper—" Gina stopped her sentence, then sat straighter. "That's a lie, I know he did. He felt it, because he cried." Gina's dark eyes filled. "But that wasn't even the secret I figured out."

Cate officially didn't want to know the secret.

"The secret was that I wished he had never been born."

Cate's eyes widened. She felt it herself. Her eyes literally opened.

"See? I taught myself that. I used to dream about that, if he had never been born. That was my dream. I would still be married to Mike, I'd still be a successful lawyer. I'd have nice clothes and a place to wear them. I'd have a normal kid and he'd play lacrosse and go to Harvard, which would bankrupt me, and I *still* wouldn't mind. I'd live my dream."

Cate thought about it. Gina. Russo had a dream, and Marz.

"I hear all those people bitch about their college bills, and I want to say, do you know how lucky you are? Do you have any *idea*?" Gina leaned forward in her chair, her tone turning angry. "And then they do a show like *Desperate Housewives,* and I watch every week and think, you should come to my house, pal. You should come *here*."

Cate didn't know what to say, and Gina eased back in her chair.

"And after a while, my dream changed," she said, her tone calmer. "I was happy he was born. I understood why."

"What's your dream now?"

Gina thought a minute, and smiled. "My dream is that someday, he'll say, 'I love you, Mommy.' "

"He will." Cate squeezed her hand, but Gina withdrew it and reached for her napkin.

"Wow, I never said that out loud."

"Friggin' Dr. Phil."

Gina laughed.

"I'm confiscating your TV."

Gina wiped her eyes, recovering. "So. Maybe you're meant to do the same thing, Cate. To know the secret."

"The secret I keep from myself?" Cate made woo-woo fingers in the air.

"Go ahead. Make fun."

"I have a better idea. Instead of figuring out my secret, I'll sue the bastards. I don't want a TV show about me, you, *or* Warren. We don't need that, and I have the dough to fight it. I'll send Sorian to wage World War III. Beecker has the firepower to do it."

"Cate, I don't know if you should sue."

"Why? I want to. I have the money. I'm not sure I'll lose because I don't think it'll get to the merits. I'll make them give it up. I want to take a shot."

"But you have to think about it, don't just react."

"When somebody hits you, you gotta hit back." Cate heard her mother in her own voice.

"But then all you have is a fistfight," Gina said, frowning like she used to when she practiced law, and Cate could see she was her old self, analyzing a legal problem. "You'll never get the TRO, and they could counterclaim, so there's that risk. They have tons of dough, way more than you. As a practical matter, it could make things worse for me and Warren."

"Why?"

"Right now, nobody knows me or the baby. If you sue, making a big deal out of it, then they will." Gina nodded, thinking aloud. "You'll get the heat. I mean, I can imagine there'll be newspaper articles once the series comes out, linking you as the judge in the case. But I don't think the press will be as interested in us, unless you sue."

"You think?" Cate recalled that Matt had said roughly the same thing, but she remained unconvinced.

"I mean, I know why you don't want a show about your life, and I know why you'd sue to stop it. But what's right for you might be wrong for Warren and me. You can take the heat, but can he?" Gina's expression was stricken, and they both knew the answer. "I mean, I guess I'd be asking you to sacrifice your interests to his."

Cate felt torn, but knew how that would have to come out.

"I'm sorry. You don't have to decide now, do you? Sorian said to sleep on it, so maybe you should."

"You telling me to listen to my lawyer?"

"The phone call probably cost you a grand." Gina leaned forward again, shifting conversational gears. "You know, the show's not what I'm worrying about. I'm worrying about that crazy detective. I wish you had your bodyguard tonight."

"I know. I almost didn't come."

"Please, not for us. For you. It's you that Russo's after, and he's experienced enough to know how to strike when you're on your own. You should stay here tonight, so you don't have to drive home in the dark."

"No, I'll be fine." Cate checked behind her, automatically. She'd left the living room light off, so she could peek through the curtains to the street without being seen. She'd checked three times until Gina yelled at her to stop.

"If you think you'll be fine, why do you keep checking the street?"

"Just to be sure." Then Cate got an idea. "Hey, it's trash night, right?"

"Yes, why?"

"Nothing." Cate was already on her feet, going to the sink and opening the base cabinet.

"Why are you stealing my trash?"

"I want to scope things out. See if the coast is clear before I go. You get Warren ready for bed."

"Is this the babysitting part?" Gina rose, going over to the baby, who was tapping his mirror, in the high chair. "I didn't even get to go food shopping."

"I'll come back tomorrow night if you want. Better yet, I'll make my bodyguard do it."

"Maybe he'll be cute. All the celebrities date their bodyguards."

"Not happening." Cate yanked the white kitchen bag out of the plastic trash can and tied the red plastic drawstring, catching a whiff of discarded salmon skin. "Guess where I'm going on Saturday night? Out with Graham the Stockbroker Man."

"Really? That's great!" Gina kissed Warren on the top of his head as she unlatched the fabric belt that held him in the high chair, and he had no reaction. "See, most kids with autism don't want to be touched at all, but Warren's not like that. He never was. He likes when I kiss his head."

Cate felt a twinge. *I should sue those jerks, for sport.*

"Don't you, buddy?" Gina kissed Warren again, and he blinked, clutching his mirror. "You like when I kiss your head, don't you? You're a great kid, you know that?" She hoisted the child to her hip as Cate went to the threshold with the trash.

"Call the cops if I'm not back in five minutes."

Gina frowned. "That's not funny."

"I'm not kidding."

CHAPTER 27

Cate stepped out into the bitter cold, and on contact, her breath became a chain smoker's fog, wreathing her face. She held her coat close to her neck and carried the trash bag in her free hand. She walked down the front steps, head down as if she were watching her footing, but she kept sneaking looks at the cars parked along Meadowbrook. There were more now than when she had first come; people had arrived home from work and parked their second cars on the street, so it was bumper-to-bumper along the curb. Many of the cars were dark, but after a few looks to the left of Gina's house, Cate could see as far as eight cars down, in the bright, purplish light cast by the streetlight. She scanned the far and near sides of the street. One each side, all six driver's seats were empty.

Good.

She walked down the driveway, alongside the Pathfinder and the Mercedes, making an apparent beeline for the dented steel trash can at the curb. When she reached it, she made a show of grabbing the metal handle, freezing in her bare hand, pulling off the lid, and moving the white trash bags that were already inside, as if she were making room. The street looked quiet. Many of the cars were dark, but it was nighttime and there was no streetlight in that direction, so it was dimmer than the other side.

If I were a bad guy, I'd park on the dark side.

Cate stole a glance to the right side and dropped the trash bag in the can. She could only see four cars down on either side of the street, because the streetlight faded at the perimeter. She was squinting past the fourth, making a fuss over closing the trash can lid, when she saw a sudden movement. In one of the cars. On the far side of the street.

There.

Cate tried not to panic. Had she seen it? Was it her imagination? It looked like a shadow in the car across the way. About six cars down, on the edge of the light, in shadow. The front-door lights from the houses only generally illuminated the area. She faked a big deal of clanging the trash can lid around and fitting it on tightly, as if she were afraid of marauding raccoons, not scary detectives. She snuck another look at the sixth car. A shadow. It was there, in the driver's seat. The car was dark. She tried to read the license plate but it was too dark. It could be him.

I'm outta here.

Cate forced herself to walk slowly up the driveway to the front walk, then up the steps, and inside the house. Her heart began to hammer, and she didn't take a breath until she got inside and locked the door behind her. The living-room light was back on, and Gina was coming downstairs.

"He went down like a dream," she said happily, then stopped when she read Cate's expression. "He's *there*?"

"I swear, I saw something." Cate tried not to panic her. Or herself. "Don't get all Lucy and Ethel about it."

"What did you see? Where?"

"In one of the cars." Cate pointed to the right. "On the far side of the street."

Gina's eyes flared. "You're kidding."

"Quick." Cate crossed to the table lamp and switched it off, plunging them both into darkness.

"You really think you saw something?"

"I want to make sure." Cate went over to the window and moved aside the curtain, peering at the dark street. It was harder to see at a distance and in the parallax view, and she inched so close to the window she could feel the frost on her nose.

"What do you see?" Gina came to her side, trying to look out, too.

"I knew this would turn into Lucy and Ethel."

"It's inevitable."

"Shhh, I'm counting." Cate counted the cars to the one where she thought she saw the shadow. Three, four, five, six. There was a distinct shadow in the driver's seat, low in the seat, as if he were slouching down. She drew back, closed the curtain, and looked at Gina in the dark. "Why would he park there, ahead of the house? How can he watch the house with his back to it?"

"Meadowbrook's one-way. If he parks past the house, he can follow you out when you go."

"Right." Cate thought ahead. He must have come when they were having dinner. Or earlier and planted himself. He could have been there all afternoon, a crazy cop sitting in front of Gina's house. "I shouldn't have come. I jeopardized you and the baby."

"I'm calling 911." Gina went for the phone on the end table, but Cate was getting another idea.

"Go, do it. Tell them who I am, that's working well lately. And say his name is Russo, because the cops are looking for him. Dark blue car, looks like a Ford. We can't see the plate." Cate dashed out of the living room and into the kitchen, where the lights were still on. She hustled to the knife rack on the counter and pulled out the biggest, scariest knife she could find and ran back to the living room, hiding it behind her back, even in the dark.

"Two-sixty-three Meadowbrook Road," Gina was saying into the phone. "He's parked in the dark blue Ford, six cars up from my house. On the even-numbered side of the street. Yes, that's right. Fante. F-A-N-T-E. No, F-A-N—"

Maybe I don't have the clout I thought. "Be right back." Cate opened the front door a crack and slipped outside.

"No, wait! Where are you going?"

Cate shut the door and was already outside in the cold. She instantly dropped behind a shrub, so he couldn't see her, and bent over more, kicking off her pumps so they didn't make any noise. Crouching low, she scurried in bare feet around the front of the Mercedes to its far side, traveled low along the Pathfinder, then darted across the sidewalk and stopped behind the parked car. She prayed nobody would start walking their dogs as she crouched lower and dashed across the street, ripping the toes of her pantyhose on the street grime, her feet turning to ice. In two seconds, she was on the other side of the street, hiding behind the back of an SUV, breathing hard.

Yikes. Cate covered her mouth so the breath fog wouldn't show. Then she waited. Breathing as shallowly as possible, as low as possible. Forcing herself to wait. It wouldn't take long for the cops to get here. They'd used the magical Fante name, so famous it had to be spelled. Twice.

Cate waited and waited in the cold for the right moment. She couldn't be early, but she couldn't be late, either.

Now.

She braced herself, holding the knife at her side, then took off, sneaking around the filthy bumper of the SUV to the curb and climbing up, alongside the parked cars. In the distance she heard sirens, too far away.

Wait.

After another minute, she inched forward, making a hump of her back, trying to ignore her freezing feet. The sirens sounded closer, and Cate moved along the car. She hoped Russo wouldn't drive away. He wouldn't know the sirens were for him, because she'd been so clever with her trash-can show.

The sirens got closer, and she moved forward to the fifth car, then waited. She moved along the length of the fifth car, creeping to the fourth. The sirens sounded only blocks away, and she could see curtains being pulled aside in the town houses. Lights went on, here and there.

She inched to the third car, her heart almost leaping from her chest. Her knees aching. Her feet freezing.

Hurry. Hurry.

The twin sirens sounded as if they were right at the development. The entrance was only three blocks from Meadowbrook. Cate prayed they wouldn't get lost.

Suddenly she heard a noise closer, only a car away, coming from the sixth car. Exhaust burst from its tailpipe, a chalky explosion, almost in her face. Sirens blared in the next block. Russo was turning on the ignition.

He was going to get away.

Neighbors started coming out of their houses, curious. Sirens screamed louder than ever. White reverse lights on the sixth car blinked on, momentarily blinding.

Now!

Cate rushed the car from behind, coming out of her full crouch just as the lights blinked to red and the car started to go forward. She raised the big knife like a psycho killer, plunged it with all her might between the treads of the car's back tire, and yanked it out, in one desperate motion. *Pssssst!* Smelly air sprayed from the tire hole.

"You can't get away now, you bastard!" Cate shouted, springing up. The dark car moved forward, only slowly, sinking in the back where she'd slashed the tire.

Two police cars sped onto Meadowbrook, tearing down the street, converging on the moving car from opposite directions. The cruisers slammed to a halt, blocking the hobbled car, then all the cruiser doors popped open and patrol officers poured out on all sides, drawing their guns instantly on the dark car.

"Freeze! Police!" they all shouted at once, adrenalized, their bodies jittery shadows in the high beams of the idling cruisers.

"That's him! Get him! Careful!" Cate almost cheered. Neighbors flowed from the town houses, and Gina ran toward her.

"Come on out, you won't get hurt!" the cops kept shouting. "Take it easy! Hands in the air!" They aimed their revolvers, two-handed grips, on the dark car, which was sinking in the middle of the street. Cate held her breath while the driver's-side door opened and she saw the backs of two hands rising in the night air.

"Don't shoot! I'm a cop!" came a shout from the dark car.

"He's a *crooked* cop!" Cate shouted back. "Watch out! He broke into my house! My office!"

Gina ran up to her side, panting. "He followed her here! He's crazy!"

"Get out of the car, sir! Get out of the car!" the cops shouted, their weapons trained.

In the next second, Cate saw the back of a black watch cap emerge from the driver's seat, and two cops lowered their weapons and rushed him as a team, flipping him facedown against the car, disarming him, wrenching his hands behind his back, then handcuffing him.

"Stay calm! Nice and easy!" the other two cops shouted, their weapons still aimed on target.

Against the car, the watch cap moved up to reveal a man looking at Cate. "Judge?" he asked, in disbelief.

Cate blinked, astounded. The driver wasn't Russo at all.

CHAPTER 28

It was Nesbitt. Cuffed and in custody, against the car.

Cate gasped. "What are *you* doing here?" she shouted.

"What do you think?" Nesbitt shouted back, as the cops tugged him toward the cruiser.

Suddenly Cate heard a sound of a car engine starting. Her head snapped around and she spotted reverse lights on another dark car, farther up the row. *Russo!* Who else would drive away, in the middle of a scene like this?

Nesbitt saw it, too. "No, wait, stop! You got the wrong guy!" he called out, right before the cops shoved him into the back seat of the cruiser.

"Officers, look up there, you got the wrong cop!" Cate cried, pointing and hurrying off the curb, but the two cops in the nearer cruiser were slamming the door on Nesbitt and jumping back inside. The two other cops were trying to get the neighbors to stay on the sidewalk, away from the scene. Down the street, the car squealed out of the space and zoomed down Meadowbrook, almost hitting a group of residents.

"Stop that car!" Cate cried and took off running. "Help! I have to catch that car!" She kept running with the knife, a sight that sent neighbors fleeing in fear. She sprinted past them, her heavy coat flying, her bare feet killing her as she tore down the street.

"I'm behind you!" Gina called out, but Cate didn't look back. If she couldn't catch the car, she had to see the license plate. The car was dark and sleek. What kind was it? It was pulling away so fast, she couldn't even read the plate.

She picked up the pace to the end of the street, panting frantically, and kept running even after it was futile. The car barreled through a stop sign, then swerved onto the main road, passed a minivan at speed, and accelerated. Cate wished she had a gun, like on TV, but all she could do was watch helplessly as the car became two red lights in the distance, then disappeared.

She threw the knife in frustration, as it clattered on the cold asphalt. She bent over, trying to catch her breath. She couldn't feel her feet anymore but they looked like hell, red-pink and cut up. She straightened when Gina caught up with her, and they both stood panting in the middle of the street, like the out-of-shape gals they were.

Cate said, between breaths, "I think I just made a big mistake."

"You sure as hell did." Gina nodded, panting. "Go get my knife."

Back in Center City Philly, at the Criminal Justice Center, it took two hours, four phone calls from top police brass, and a signed statement from Cate to convince the uniformed cops not to arraign Detective Nesbitt. By that time, stringers listening to the police scanners had gotten wind of what had happened, and the press thronged outside the CJC. Cate and Nesbitt found themselves in one of the all-white attorney interview rooms, waiting for a go-ahead from uniformed cops before they could leave the building without being hassled. It was her first chance to apologize.

"I really am sorry. I didn't realize it was you." She shifted in her heels. Her feet were killing her.

"Don't worry about it." Nesbitt shoved his hands into the pockets of a brown bomber jacket, which he wore with jeans and old Nikes. "I wasn't taking any chances. I'd follow you home but some wacky blonde gave me a flat."

Ouch. "Sorry, I forgot."

"No sweat, it was my kid's car. Russo knows my car. He woulda made me if I took my own."

"So now your kid's mad at you?"

"She's at college. If you don't tell, I won't."

Cate smiled. "So. Wacky blonde, huh?"

"Yes, Your Honor. You should've seen yourself with that knife." Nesbitt took a hand out of his pocket and raised it in a bad imitation. "Nigella on 'roids."

"Nigella? What kind of reference is that, for a detective?"

"Hey, I cook."

"Well, I stab. Gimme some credit. I *killed* that tire."

"*After* the uniforms came down the street! What was that about, rookie?" Nesbitt smiled, and Cate gave him a shove, forgetting that federal judges weren't supposed to have fun. He laughed. "What were you thinking? Were you gonna get Russo by yourself?"

"I called for backup."

Nesbitt's eyes flared. "Where'd you get 'called for backup'? TV? I hate to tell you this, but you're no David Caruso. You're not even the *Cold Case* girl, whatever her name is. I'm a professional. Leave it to me."

"Then how come you didn't see me sneak up on you? Huh?" Cate laughed. "Busted!"

"Never mind that. You took a risk."

"So did you. You're supposed to be by the book."

"I was by the book. I got you into the mess and I'll get you out of it. That's number one in the book." Nesbitt faced her fully, no longer laughing, and brushed graying bangs from his forehead, revealing eyes that were a very steady blue, Cate saw for the first time.

"If I hadn't taken the record about you from Simone's hotel room, it wouldn't have been in the file and Russo wouldn't have known about it."

In the next second, the door opened suddenly, and Special Agent Brady came in, his expression animated when he saw Cate.

"Judge! Here you are!" Brady was followed by three other special-agent types. "Sorry I'm late, I was meeting with Sergeant Lester and Inspector Dennis at the Roundhouse." Brady shook Cate's hand with vigor, then introduced her to the agents filling the tiny room. She shook their hands, and Brady said, "What a scare you had! I under-stand Detective Russo was following you?" The question must have been rhetorical, because Brady turned immediately to Nesbitt. "You Steve Nesbitt?"

"Yes." Nesbitt extended a hand, and Brady shook it quickly.

"I met with your inspector and sergeant, just now. They're not very happy with you tonight. Neither of them was aware that you were surveilling Judge Fante."

"That's right. I'm off duty. All blame goes to me."

Cate blinked, surprised.

Brady said, "There'll be plenty of it to go around."

"He was trying to help," Cate interjected, feeling defensive for Nesbitt.

"You can use me, Brady," Nesbitt said, his tone firm. "Jurisdiction or no, I can help. Russo was my partner. I know the most about him. I knew he'd be there tonight and he was."

"I'm not going to stand here and argue with you, Detective. You're out, and we're in." Brady turned to Cate. "Your Honor, any threat to your health and well-being is within the bureau's jurisdiction, not that of the Philadelphia police. With the recent attacks on the federal judiciary and their families, we're taking your case very seriously."

"Why can't jurisdiction be concurrent?" Cate asked, annoyed. "Two heads are better than one, and Detective Nesbitt's point about knowing Russo makes sense."

"With due respect, Judge, it doesn't work that way. The bureau has more resources at its disposal and more experience with attacks on federal judges and officials. We're better able to protect you."

"Then where were you tonight?" Cate shot back, and Nesbitt hid a smile.

Brady answered, "We would have been there, Judge, if you'd have given us the chance. I tried to speak with you before you went on the bench, but you declined. You said you'd call tonight, but you didn't. You'll find a message from me on your home and cell phones. Your secretary gave me both numbers."

Oops. Cate had turned the phone off at Gina's, out of habit. The sudden noise always bothered Warren.

"We can't protect you if you don't cooperate with us, Judge." Brady turned to Nesbitt. "I think we can take it from here, Detective."

"She needs protection tonight." Nesbitt gestured at Cate. "He's not gonna let her go."

"We'll protect her. We'll be outside her house in cars, all night. End of discussion. I think it's time for you to go."

Nesbitt pursed his lips and touched Cate's coat. "Judge, no matter what these guys say, call me if you need anything." He brushed his bangs back, revealing another flash of blue. "I'll check in with you tomorrow."

"Thanks. Sorry about the tire."

"No sweat." Nesbitt turned and walked out of the room, and Cate had an attack of separation anxiety. He'd put himself and his job in jeopardy to make sure she was safe. He wasn't a by-the-book guy, he was an above-the-call guy.

An hour later, Cate had shed her coat, bag, shoes, suit, and underwear on the way to the bathroom, where she'd taken an endless bubble bath, washing the grime out of the cuts on her feet, then dried off and crawled into bed, feeling clean, exhausted, and reasonably safe. Before they'd let her enter the house, the FBI agents had scoured the place, checking her phone messages to make sure Russo hadn't called, and even reinforcing the back door with more plywood. They sat staked outside the house in cars, forgoing her offers of the warm house and vying with the press for the few parking spaces on the street. Cate put it all out of her mind and buried her face in the pillow, her last waking thought of Nesbitt.

Hey, I cook.

Nesbitt was also Cate's first waking thought, and she lay in her soft, warm bed, trying to understand why. A detective with graying sideburns, deep crow's-feet around his eyes, and a brown bomber jacket that fit too snugly around the waist. Hardly the kind of man she usually went for, much less woke up thinking about. She flopped over and became aware that the soles of her feet hurt, which made her remember last night. In the next instant, the phone was ringing. It must have been ringing before, too, waking her.

She opened her eyes, her head muzzy. The room was still dark. It sounded like it was raining outside. She lifted her head and glanced at the clock. 5:45. She double-checked the clock, but she hadn't read it wrong. Who could be calling at this hour? It had to be the press. They'd left messages last night.

She let it ring until voice mail picked up, but in the next instant, her cell phone started ringing beside the bed, the blue numbers springing to life in the dark room. She checked the display.

It was Gina. Cate's brain came alive. *Russo. Warren.*

"What's the matter?" Cate said, opening the phone.

"Did you see the newspaper?"

"No. I was asleep. I know, it has the story about Russo, last night."

"That's not all. Go and get it."

CHAPTER 29

Cate put on a coat to grab the newspaper from her front step, then slammed the front door, ignoring the press collecting on the sidewalk outside her house. She didn't see any of the FBI agents, and she didn't care. It didn't matter now. Nothing did. She slid the newspaper from its clear plastic sleeve dotted with raindrops, and unfolded it, separating its soaked pinked edges.

FEDERAL JUDGE WIELDS KNIFE, screamed the headline on the front page, and Cate read the story with dismay. It was all about last night, including eyewitness accounts of her running down Meadowbrook Drive, brandishing a knife "on the apparent belief that she was being stalked." It made her sound ridiculous, but it was true, and at the bottom of the page was the related story: FEDERAL JUDGE STARS IN NEW SERIES: *Fact or Fiction—You Be the Judge.*

Cate held her breath as the story reported that the offices of *Attorneys@Law* in Old City had confirmed that a new TV series titled *Judges@Court* was presently in production, starring an "empowered-type" female judge with a secret sex life. A representative of *Attorneys@Law* confirmed that the series would be "completely fictional," despite the fact that the show's creator was recently sued in a case before Judge Cate Marie Fante. The representative gave no further details, except to say that the new show would "bring approximately 1,568 new jobs to the city."

As bad as the stories were, they weren't even close to the one that sent Gina into orbit. Cate turned to the metro section, and her mouth went dry. The photo showing her going into the Fort Washington bar was plastered on the top half. She sank to the entrance-hall floor, barely able to read the column.

> Judge Cate Marie Fante, of the Eastern District of Pennsylvania, has been very busy after hours, and she's not working overtime. She's dating. You may think this is none of our business—or yours—until you understand that several of her "dates" are men convicted of assault, battery, check forgery, and even violations of federal weapons laws. Now ask yourself, is this any way to run our legal system? We should note that our many calls to Judge Fante's chambers went unanswered.

Cate could only skim the sentences, as if to read the text thoroughly would be to absorb the full brunt of its impact, like standing still in front of a speeding car. The piece contained every detail about the bars, all culled from the record in the stolen file. Russo must have found another way to hurt her, the best way. He had leaked the entire record to the newspaper, and its reporters had taken it from there; putting two and two together and calling Micah, just as Cate had, then digging deeper. The newspaper even identified four of the men she'd "dated," with their photos. Jeff Rader. Mark Boulez. Mike Holliman. Mustafa Raheed.

Cate closed her eyes, mortified. She remembered the men, though she hadn't known their last names. Or that they had criminal records. She'd gone to the sleaziest bars and picked up the sleaziest men. Why hadn't she thought of that? What else did she expect? Of course, some would be ex-cons, even felons. She turned back to one of the articles, an interview with one of the men, who had served time for fraud and drug offenses.

She picked me up at the bar. There wasn't a lotta conversation, if you follow.

Cate felt as if her heart would break. She thought instantly of Graham. What would he say? How would he feel to know he was one of so many? How would he understand, when Cate herself didn't?

What did I do right? Was it the bling? Tell me, so I'll do it again.

Cate thought of everyone she cared about, reading the articles. Chief Judge Sherman. Val. Emily. Sam. The courtroom deputy. The stenographer. The other judges at her celebration dinner, last summer. Matt Sorian. All of her old partners. Mrs. Pershing, switchboard diva.

We're so proud of you.

Cate thought of her enemies, too. Meriden. How much would he love this? How could she hold her head up, on the court? How had this gone so wrong? She couldn't shake the ominous feeling that her world was about to end. She felt herself sink to her knees and doubled over on her costly Heriz rug, feeling so much pain that not even a single tear would come. Her only overriding thought was to thank God that her mother did not live to see this day.

In time, Cate got dressed in a black Prada suit, ready for work earlier than usual because she had to put her office back together after Hurricane Russo. She slipped on a pair of huge sunglasses and felt as if she were running a modern-day gauntlet, from the press snapping her picture as she drove out of her garage, to Special Agent Brady at the end of the street in an unmarked car, to the security guard in the white kiosk at the judges' parking lot, to Judge Tom McGinn of the Third Circuit, with his characteristic Santa Claus beard, who was getting out of his car at the same time as she was. The appellate court had its chambers on the penthouse floors of the courthouse, and Cate didn't even want to think about the talk up there today. She really liked Judge McGinn and had even met his wife, Sue, who was as kind as Mrs. Claus.

She slowed her step so Judge McGinn would reach the judges' elevator lobby first, and ended up riding the elevator alone. It gave her eight floors to screw up the courage to walk into her chambers, and even so, it wasn't nearly enough. She reached the door, braced herself, and opened it.

The two clerks, clustered at Val's desk, sprang apart, their heads snapping up, surprised at her early arrival. They had obviously been talking about her, she could smell it in the air, and Val, at her desk, looked stiff and miserable, her expression grim. The chambers fell stone-silent except for the rain lashing the window, and nobody said a word as Cate walked in, shed her coat and hung it up, slid off her sunglasses, and walked to Val's desk.

"Good morning, everyone." Cate kept her face a professional mask and avoided their eyes, as they all said their good-morning-judges. "The bodyguard isn't due in until eight-thirty."

Val handed her her mail and phone messages over the low divider, her tone cool. "Chief Judge Sherman wants to see you when he gets off the bench. He thinks that will be around one o'clock. The press has been calling, but I said we have no comment. You're in court at eleven, for the plea agreement we rescheduled."

"Thanks." Cate flipped through the messages for Graham's name, but he hadn't called. It was early anyway. She looked up at the clerks. "Who has the plea today? Remind me."

"It's my case." Sam raised his hand. "The bench memo's on your chair."

"Thanks. Come in at ten-fifteen and we'll talk about it."

"It's only a guilty plea, Judge. It won't take that long."

"I want to be fully prepared today. Things didn't go so well yesterday, as you know." Cate turned toward her office, then stopped in surprise at the sight. The room had been completely put back together, even neater than before it had been ransacked. Case files stood up in order on the conference table; legal pads sat stacked next to a lineup of blue and red briefs. Books had been restored to the bookshelves, and her desktop straightened up, with Graham's bouquet of red roses given a place of honor. It must have been so much work. Cate felt a wrench inside at the kindness of the gesture.

"The clerks stayed late last night and cleaned up, all by themselves," Val said, and Cate turned to the clerks with a smile, dropping her mask. She was getting tired of so many masks, all the time. They never fit right and you couldn't breathe, like a kid at Halloween.

"Thank you so much, both of you." Cate smiled. "That was a lovely thing to do, and I really appreciate it."

"We organized it, too," Emily said, beaming.

Sam nodded. "It was Emily's idea and she did most of the work. She thought it might cheer you up, after you screwed up in court."

"Sam!" Val said, frowning. "Mind your manners!"

"Sam!" Emily snapped. "What are you, an idiot?"

"She said it first," Sam shot back, and Cate held up a hand, laughing.

"It's okay, everybody, I did screw up in court. It's still very nice that you two cleaned and organized my office." Cate turned to go, then turned back. "Listen, I know you saw the newspaper, and I know it's awful. I wish I could tell you that it's not true, the part about my private life, but it is." All three listened with somber expressions, with Val at the desk and the two law clerks behind her, like a frieze of federal employees. "I have nothing to say for myself, except that I'm very sorry for my behavior. I know you thought better of me."

"I don't think what you did is so terrible," Emily rushed to say, her voice thin with anxiety. "You're not married, and they would never be making this fuss if you were a man."

"Yeah, it's cool," Sam added, then he caught himself. "I mean, what you do out of court is nobody's business, and it doesn't belong in the newspaper. They should be writing about the war in Iraq or global warming. Not your personal life."

"Thank you," Cate said, meaning it, and they all pretended not to notice that Val hadn't chimed in. The secretary looked down, showing her graying strands of hair at her temple. She wore a blue-patterned dress and her gold crucifix peeked from her neckline.

Cate asked, "Val, would you come into my nice, clean office?"

"Yes, Judge." Val picked up a pad, and Cate went inside with her mail, messages, and purse, and set all of it down. By the time she'd turned around, Val had taken her customary seat across from the desk, with her pen poised over her paper.

"This isn't business, Val."

Val set the pen on the pad stiffly.

Cate sighed. "I know what I did was wrong, and I know what you must think."

"I don't think you do, Judge."

"You're surprised."

"That I am, yes. I am surprised."

"And you're disgusted with me, and you should be."

"No, that's not it." Val shook her head sadly. "I feel sorry for you. I feel sorry that you think so little of yourself."

Cate felt the words like a slap to the face, though she knew they weren't intended that way.

"I feel sorry that you *respected* yourself so little, and respected your body and your heart so little, as to do . . . the things you did. When I saw that story this morning, I prayed for you."

Cate didn't know what to say, and Val rose slowly and looked at her with newly shining eyes.

"It'll be a struggle around here, with the other judges, for you. There'll be jokes, and people will talk. Especially if they do that TV show." Val stood up and stepped close to Cate, placing a soft hand on her shoulder. "When that happens, tell yourself that none of it matters. None of it. That's all outside, and nothing that's outside matters. Not the other judges or the TV or the gossips. Nothing matters but what's in your heart. Don't think on what they say, because you don't have to get yourself right with them. You have to get yourself right with *you*."

Cate felt moved by her words and the emotions that gave them life. The only person who had ever made so much sense to her was her mother.

"When you get yourself right with you, then you can hold your head high. Now gimme a hug." Val threw her arms open and embraced Cate, who hugged her back, taking surprising comfort in her powdery smells, despite the fact that she was supposed to be a grown-up, a judge, and a boss besides. The phone started ringing, and Val released her. "I'll get it," she said. "You get back to work and don't think on it."

"Thanks," Cate said, returning to her desk as Val picked up the phone.

"Judge Fante's chambers," she said, and after a minute, "Please hold and I'll see if she's available." She pressed the HOLD button, and Cate looked up. "Judge Menking, for you. Will you pick up?"

"Sure."

Val pointed a warning finger at her. "Remember what I said. Inside, outside."

"Inside, outside," Cate repeated, like a little mantra, accepted the receiver, and pressed the button to take the call. "Bonner?"

"Cate! My God in heaven, have you seen this trash? The *Inquirer* is out to get you. Where are they getting this? This is defamatory. You have to sue them, Cate."

Val hustled out of the office, diplomatically closing the door behind her.

"Truth is an absolute defense, Bonner."

"You did all this? You? You?"

"Yes. I take full responsibility. I did it."

"*What?*"

Cate felt her cheeks get hot. "I did it."

"You couldn't have!"

Actually, I can't believe it, either. "But I did. I'm not proud of it, but I did it, and it's over."

"My God, Cate. What were you thinking? It's so . . . common."

"It's over, Bonner, that's all I can say. That, and I'm sorry."

Ring ring! Cate's other phone line started ringing, but she let Val get it.

"But, Cate, this is an insult to the court. We can't have this, a judge of our court. They're saying on the Internet that another man came forward! He's blogging about you right this moment. My clerks found the webpage."

Oh God. "There's nothing I can do, Bonner."

"I'm dumbfounded, Cate! I'm simply dumbfounded! I thought so well of you, and how you represent women on our court. And now, well, it's just shameful!"

"I'm very sorry."

"I am, too. Now they're going to portray you on TV? Our court on TV? How did this happen, Cate? How did you let this happen to us?"

"I don't know, Bonner—" *Click.* Cate sat shaken, looking out the window, watching rain drench the city. The intercom buzzed, and Cate picked up. "Who's on the phone?"

"Judge Kingston. Will you take it?"

"Yes."

"And the bodyguard is here, Judge."

"Good." Cate pressed the button to pick up. Andrew Kingston was a senior judge and a real sweetheart. She remembered trying cases before him as a young associate, and he never made fun of her beginner cross-examinations. "Good morning, Andrew."

"Cate, I've just seen the newspaper, and you must get a copy. Not the *Times*, the *Inquirer*. My secretary says it's in the *Daily News*, too. They're writing the most terrible things about you, and they're trying to make it about our wonderful court. Spinning the story, I know it's called. Maligning us all, when it's in fact the most tawdry piece of pulp. *Pulp!*"

"I know, Andrew. I heard."

Ring ring! The other phone rang again, but Cate let Val pick up. If it was Graham, he'd have to wait.

"What's this world coming to when people write such scandalous stories? To publish such things about a member of the court, our court, it's a travesty! Of course, it's scurrilous!"

"Andrew, I'm sorry but it's true." There was complete silence on the end of the line. After a minute, Cate worried he'd had a heart attack. "Andrew?"

"I'm sorry, I must have misheard you. My battery, on my hearing aid. It must be running out. I thought you said it was true."

"No, I'm sorry, Andrew. I've made some mistakes, I admit it."

"My, Cate. It's true?"

"Yes."

"All of it?"

"Yes, I know, I'm sorry."

"It seems I've made a mistake, too. I'll leave you to it, then. Goodbye, Cate. Good-bye."

Cate let him hang up, then set the receiver down. The phone began ringing again, almost instantly. The intercom buzzed, and she picked up for Val. "Who is it?"

"Judge Mee."

Oh boy. "How many judges are on this court, again?"

"Eighteen, I think."

"Okay, I'll pick up," Cate said, and hit the button.

"Cate, did you see the paper? It's revolting, what they're saying. And on TV?"

"I know." Cate cringed.

"How can they make a TV show about you without your permission? Did you give permission for this, Cate?"

"No, of course not."

Only fifteen more to go.

Cate took the next fifteen calls, from each of her colleagues who had toasted her when they thought she was all the things she appeared to be. Most were upset about the "dating," but many also cared about her safety and their own. They had called about the articles in the newspaper, or online, heard accounts on local TV, on KYW radio, had gotten an e-mail about it, or heard from one of their law clerks about a new website, www.IscrewedJudgeFante.com.

Cate was so busy taking the calls from her colleagues that she didn't get a chance to reach Graham, or take calls from Matt Sorian, CNN, the *Philadelphia Inquirer*, Matt Lauer, MSNBC, ABC, Court-TV, *The View*, NOW, the *Wall Street Journal*, Henry Schleiff, *Time* magazine, *Entertainment Tonight*, *Celebrity Justice*, the *New York Times*, Steven Brill, the *National Law Journal*, David E. Kelley, *American Lawyer*, Judges Amy Nislow, Adrienne Drost, and Fiona McCann of the National Association of Women Judges, the William Morris Agency, and Detective Steve Nesbitt.

By ten-thirty, only two of her colleagues hadn't called, and Cate was due to see one of them, Chief Judge Sherman, at one o'clock.

The other one was Judge Meriden.

Cate tried not to think about it, as a timid knock came at her door. "Come in, Sam," she called out, taking the bench memo from her in-box. She had to get ready for court.

Not that she was looking forward to it.

And what about Graham?

CHAPTER 30

"Good job, Sam," Cate said after they were finished. She got up from the desk and stretched her arms, trying to shake off the dreads. Rain poured outside the window, making the office gray and gloomy, which she factored into her penance. She didn't know what to expect from court today. She'd been in the judge cocoon all morning, and even though it was a lot less friendly than it used to be, at least it wasn't the public. She wondered if she'd ever leave the courthouse. *Maybe Neiman Marcus delivers?*

"Thanks, Judge." Sam gathered the papers and pleadings into a stack. "Be right back. I need to get my tie and jacket for court."

"Fine." Cate crossed to her closet, took her judicial robe from a hanger, and slid into it on the fly, as Sam opened her office door into a crowd of men in suits. She wasn't completely surprised and was getting used to a police presence in chambers.

"Good morning, gentlemen," she called out, entering the reception area, and saw Brady pushing his way to the front of the pack. His eyes looked tired, and he had on the same dark suit, though his white oxford shirt must have been fresh, because it puffed at the chest in a telltale way. A black-patterned tie color-coordinated with the black wire coiling from his ear to his collar.

"Good morning, Judge," Brady said, shaking her hand, too professional to let show that he'd read the newspaper.

"Don't you sleep, you poor thing?" Cate fastened her robe at its gathered yoke.

"I'm fine." Brady gestured behind him. "I understand you hired a bodyguard."

"Yes, and he has concurrent jurisdiction." Cate stood on tiptoe, eyeing the crowd, which smiled at her, to a man. She didn't have to ask how many had newspaper subscriptions. "I haven't had a chance to meet him yet. Is he scary? Bodyguard, where are you?"

"He's coming!" Val called back, and a man shaped like a tractor-trailer drove through the crowd. He looked to be about thirty years old and stood five foot ten. His massive shoulders strained the seams of a dark brown suit tailored for mere mortals, and a dark tie choked his oversized neck like a tourniquet. He had blue eyes, a sandy brush cut, and a smile too sweet to be truly scary.

"I'm Justin Stein, Judge," he said, shaking her hand lightly, to permit blood flow to the heart.

"Hey, if your last name were Case, you'd be Justin Case. A good name for a bodyguard." Cate laughed at her own dumb joke, and so did everybody else. She wondered when she became a motel-lounge comedian. *Answer: When I got scared, embarrassed, and completely self-conscious.* "Well, I'm glad you're here. What do we do next?"

"You do your job, and I make sure you're safe. I called the Philly cops and they sent me a photo of Detective Russo."

"When did they do that?" Cate asked, surprised.

"Early this morning. They turned me down at first, but Detective Nesbitt gave the okay and faxed it over."

"Good. Are you armed?" Cate asked, and Justin nodded. *That makes up for your smile.* She turned to Brady. "Okay, what happens now?"

"The courtroom is clear. We have agents in plainclothes in the gallery, and Special Agent Donnelly and I will be in the room. We'll visually inspect the members of the general public. They won't be admitted until they go through the metal detector, outside your courtroom."

"You got me an extra one, like in the gang trials?"

Brady nodded. "In addition, two marshals will be stationed at the metal detector and one of our agents, as well."

"Yikes." Cate felt overwhelmed. "I doubt Russo will get anywhere near the courtroom, but maybe we'll keep out a reporter or two." Everybody laughed on cue, and Cate smiled, beginning to sweat under her robes. She moved her long sleeves aside and checked her watch: 10:55. Time to go. She called out, "Bye, Val!"

"See you, Judge!" Val called back as Sam wended his way through the crowd, and they all left chambers and traveled down the hallway as a well-armed moblet. When they reached the anteroom, the FBI agents piled in first, leaving Cate and the others to be waved ahead on a silent hand signal, which was when she understood that "making a federal case" was more than a cliché. She walked through the anteroom, braced herself, and entered the courtroom when she heard the courtroom deputy sound off.

"All rise for the Honorable Catherine Marie Fante!"

Cate strode through the door into the courtroom, instantly concealing her shock at the size of the gallery. Sketch artists, reporters, TV anchor people, Court-TV personalities, and reporters packed the pews, shoulder to shoulder, wall-to-wall. They buzzed among themselves, more than usual because so many were civilians, and Cate didn't see if Russo had made it in; she didn't want to make eye contact. With her peripheral vision, she could see heads craning for a better view, mascaraed eyes widening, and moussed heads leaning together in whispered jokes, then parting with sly smiles. The crowd was even bigger than it had been for Simone's trial, but this time they were there for her. Wanting to see the judge who slept around.

Inside, outside. Cate barreled up the stairs and onto the dais, feeling three hundred pairs of eyes travel her body, even in her loose robes, taking in every detail of her hair, face, breasts, and legs. And breasts. *Maybe they're looking for the scarlet A.*

Cate took her seat at the dais, as if it were perfectly normal to host the entire population of Luxembourg at a routine guilty plea hearing. The AUSA straightened his tie, the female public defender sat a little taller in her chair, and even the defendant patted his hair into place, despite his handcuffs. The courtroom deputy shot her their wink.

"Good morning, ladies and gentlemen." Cate turned to the AUSA. "Mr. Crystal, we have a plea agreement in this case, correct?"

"Correct, Your Honor. The government has a deal with Mr. Dow, and I believe Your Honor has a copy of the agreement."

"I do." Cate glanced at the papers, though she had memorized them. It was easier than looking at the crowd, and they were still buzzing. "Let's begin." Cate turned to the pretty blond defender at defense table, whose name she'd recalled from the pleadings, Abby Linderman. "Good morning, Ms. Linderman."

"Good morning, Your Honor. This is Mr. Dow." Linderman reached down and helped her client to his feet, and Dow rose with difficulty, in his ankle shackles. He was tall and thin, with a short brown cut and prison pallor, and Cate addressed him directly.

"Good morning, Mr. Dow."

"Good morning, Judge," he said softly, but Cate could barely hear him over the buzzing. She eyed the gallery with evident displeasure, but they didn't know her glare was judgespeak for "shut up." The courtroom deputy scowled, too, turning watchfully to them.

"Order in the court, please. Order," Cate called out, trying to keep a lid on the proceedings. She reflected that in six months on the bench, she had yet to say that, but she couldn't let this be about her. A man's rights were at stake, and she'd had her focus clarified by yesterday's debacle.

Cate looked down at the defendant. "Mr. Dow, I understand that you have pled guilty to nineteen counts of making false statements to a firearms dealer, in violation of Title 18, United States Code, Section 924(a)(1)(A). This is a hearing to ascertain that you understand the nature and consequences of your decision, because by entering a guilty plea, you are waiving a number of very important constitutional rights. Do you understand?"

"Yes, Your Honor."

"Even though you have come here today to plead guilty, you can change your mind." Cate heard some leftover buzzing coming from the back, but let it go rather than make a big deal. She didn't relish courtroom sketches of her screaming at the gallery. "If at any time during this hearing, you decide you don't want to plead guilty, just tell me, and I will adjourn the hearing and schedule your case for trial. Do you understand?"

"Yes."

"I now have to ask you some personal questions, to make sure you don't have any mental or physical problems that would make it hard for you to understand what we're going to talk about today. Would you state your full name?"

"William Peter Dow."

Buzz, buzz, buzz, went the back, like a wasp.

"Mr. Dow, how old are you?" Cate heard the buzzing again and looked up in annoyance, pointedly scanning the back of the gallery, but she couldn't see the source. Every face looked back at her. The courtroom deputy left his desk, on the trail of the noise. She glanced over at Sam, and sitting next to him was Todhunter Preppington, taking notes this time. Cate put it out of her mind.

"I'm twenty-eight."

Buzz, buzz, buzz.

"Are you a U.S. citizen?"

"Yes."

"How far did you go in school?"

"HOW FAR DID *YOU* GO IN HIGH SCHOOL, JUDGE?" yelled a man's voice, in the back, and the gallery broke into laughter, hiding their smiles behind their hands and looking down.

Oh my God. "Order!" Cate stiffened, horrified, scanning the crowd. She had no idea who said it but it didn't sound like Russo. It had to be the buzzing from the back. The courtroom deputy was already in motion. Brady, standing near there, walked toward the pews, and Justin Case edged protectively close to the dais. Heads in the pews turned and craned, giggling and laughing, wheeling to face the back of the courtroom. Amused reporters scribbled in their steno pads, and delighted sketch artists changed pastels at speed, focusing on the bench.

"I KNOW ALL ABOUT YOU, JUDGE! I GOT YOUR NUMBER! WE ALL DO!"

The gallery burst into its naughty laughter again, and talking and whispering erupted. The courtroom deputy and Brady were pointing at the middle of the back row, and three federal marshals closed in on a tall, wild-haired man in a shabby green parka and stained gray sweatpants. He looked crazy to Cate, but he had obviously read the newspaper.

Crak! "I'll have order! Order in this court!" she called out, shaken, her face flushing red.

"SHE'S A GODDAMN WHORE!" the man screamed at the top of his lungs. The gallery gasped almost collectively. A commotion erupted in the back row. The courtroom deputy and the marshals yanked the man from his seat and dragged him struggling out of the pew. On the way out, his arms and elbows flailed, hitting spectators in the row. "A WHORE! THEY'RE ALL WHORES AND BITCHES!"

"I graduated high school," Dow answered, oblivious, and the gallery broke into new laughter.

"Order! Order!" Mortified, Cate banged the gavel.

The marshal grabbed the wild-haired man, but suddenly he wrenched himself free and all hell broke loose.

Cate dropped the gavel in shock and jumped to her feet.

"WHORES AND BITCHES!" the man shouted, his hair and parka flying, running crazily around the courtroom. The courtroom deputy and the marshals gave chase.

"Judge, let's go!" Justin Case shouted, materializing at Cate's side and clamping two powerful hands on her arms, but she resisted.

"No, wait, this is my courtroom." She watched, riveted.

Men in suits lunged for the running man, who kept bolting randomly away. Marshals and FBI agents poured into the courtroom. AUSA Crystal gave chase. The gallery fled the packed pews, climbing over the backs of the seats. Linderman got knocked over in the melee, and Dow ducked for cover under counsel table.

"YOU'RE A WHORE!" the man screamed, suddenly changing direction and bolting toward the dais, just out of reach of the marshals and the courtroom deputy. "A NASTY, DIRTY WHORE!"

"Gotcha!" a marshal shouted, and two new marshals grabbed the man by the hood of his parka but it came off in their hands.

"SHE'S A WHORE UNDER THEM ROBES!" The man flung himself headlong into the gallery, as if it were a humongous mosh pit. "A WHORE! SHE'S NOT FOOLIN' ME!"

People screamed. Reporters sprang aside. Sketch artists dropped their big pads. The gallery cleared except for the screaming man and men in suits, converging from everywhere.

"We're leaving, Judge!" Justin Case shouted and hurried her down the stairs and out of the courtroom.

Cate took one last look back, and standing amid the chaos was one man she hadn't seen before.

And he was watching her go.

CHAPTER 31

"What happened?" Val asked, from her computer. "You're back early."

"You don't wanna know," Cate answered, coming into chambers with Justin Case, Sam, Special Agent Brady, and assorted FBI agents and federal marshals. They talked excitedly among themselves, hopped up on adrenaline and testosterone. At the disruption, Emily came out of the law clerk's office and over to Val's desk.

"It was so *random*!" Sam exploded, rushing to Val in his excitement. "This man went crazy and ran around the courtroom. He made a mess of everything. It was unbelievable."

"Oh, no." Val's eyes flared in alarm, and she rose from her desk.

"Oh, yes." Cate managed a smile. "And we'll leave out the 'tis a pity she's a whore' part, or the fact that one William Dow entered a courtroom to plead guilty today and his rights were trampled upon." Cate thought of the poor man being knocked over in his shackles. "In fact, he was trampled upon, too."

"That's awful!" Emily said, her mouth a dark-lipsticked O. "Did he try to hurt you, Judge?"

"No, he just wanted to heckle me."

"He was a psycho!" Sam interjected. "A total psycho!"

"Indelicate perhaps, but true," Cate said, but beside her, Justin Case was frowning.

"He could have hurt you, Judge. We still don't know if he was armed or—"

"That's right, Judge," Brady interrupted. "I'll find out all the details after he's taken into custody and let you know."

"How could he be armed?" Cate asked. "He couldn't get a gun or a knife through the metal detector."

"A ceramic knife goes through a metal detector," Justin answered. "I trained with the Mossad, and they routinely use ceramic knives. Those suckers cut a throat cleaner than a metal blade."

Yikes. "Well, our visitor today didn't look like the Mossad. They dress better." Cate patted Justin's shoulder, solid as an oak bookshelf. "Thank you, my hero, for spiriting me away to safety."

"You're welcome." Justin flashed his sweet, ceramic-knife smile. "But next time I say go, you have to go, Judge."

"Right. Sure." Cate saluted. "Brady and the cavalry were all over it, too. Thanks to you all, too. You're last but not least."

Brady nodded, acknowledging the recognition, but his expression remained stoic. "Thanks, Judge, but I'm afraid the apprehension took longer than expected. Too many cooks."

Give it a rest. "All's well that ends well," Cate turned to Val. "Will you call the parties, apologize for me, and reschedule for as soon as possible? Now that we know what this heckler looks like, we won't let him in again."

"Sure, Judge." Val handed her a phone message and met her eye meaningfully. "This call came in while you were in court."

"Thanks." Cate didn't have to look at the message to know the caller.

"Why don't I order you a salad, so you can eat something before you go see the Chief Judge?"

"That's okay, I'm not hungry." Cate nodded to the assembled army.

"Thanks again, all of you. If you will excuse me, I'll go do my job. Are you all set for lunch?"

"Yes, thanks," Brady answered. "When are you in court again, Judge?"

"Not until Monday, right, Val?" Cate couldn't believe how much had happened in one week. Was it just last Monday that she had presided over a trial? And Simone had been alive, and Marz? And her scummy private life had been her own? "TGIF," she said, and they all laughed.

"Right. Monday at nine, Judge. *U.S. v. Blendheim.* Cocaine trafficking."

"Yay! Crime that doesn't involve *me!*" Cate laughed, and they all laughed again. She got funnier the more stressed she got. *Danger agrees with me.* She pointed at Emily. "*Blendheim* your case, girl?"

"Yes, Judge."

"Bench memo ready?"

"Just finished it, and the final draft of the Simone opinion is on your chair."

"We'll talk about both after I get back from Chief Judge Sherman's chambers. Please make me a package to work over the weekend on *Blendheim.* And now, I depart. Thanks again, gentlemen."

"Welcome, Judge," they answered, and Cate slipped into her office, closed the door behind her, and crossed to the phone. She set down the message on her desk and sank into her chair, still in her robes. After two rings, the phone was answered.

"Graham?"

"Cate?"

"Yes. Hi. Sorry I missed your call. I just had a crazy guy loose in my courtroom. Film at eleven."

YOU'RE A WHORE

"Cate, you're so famous." Graham sounded so cold that his voice had its own wind-chill factor. "The news is all you, all the time."

"I know. This was really something. The FBI thinks he tried to kill me, but the Mossad disagrees, as do all sensible people."

"So, is any of it true, in the newspaper?"

I'm fine, thanks. Cate found her thoughts straying to the man in the middle of the chaos in the courtroom, watching her go. Nesbitt. He had been there, evidently looking out for her. And he had faxed the photo of Russo to SpectaSafe.

"Cate? Are you there?"

"Yes."

"I asked you, is it true?"

"About me being stalked or the dating or the TV series?" Cate asked, as if she didn't know. She watched the rain hit the window and run down it in sooty rivulets, like tiny, polluted rivers. She was sure someone had ordered this ecological disaster just for her.

"I meant the dating," Graham answered. "Is it true?"

You are beautiful, you know that?

"In a word? Yes."

"Impossible!"

A NASTY, DIRTY WHORE

"It *happened*? It's *true*? You go into those bars?"

"Yes, but it's over."

"I can't believe it."

"I know, I'm sorry."

"*You're* sorry? I'm going to say this straight. I don't think we should see each other anymore."

Cate eyed his roses, which weren't even drooping yet. *Can the flowers last longer than the relationship?* "Graham, why don't you give me a chance to explain it to you?"

"There's nothing you can say. This party I was going to take you to on Saturday night, it's with all my best clients and their wives. They read the paper." Graham raised his voice, getting angrier. "I've already gotten calls from two of them who knew I was seeing you. You don't want to know what they said."

No, I don't. Cate closed her eyes.

SHE'S A WHORE UNDER THEM ROBES

"You've made me a laughingstock."

"We went out three times. It's not about you."

"Am I going to be in the TV show, too?"

"No, of course not."

"And you gave me that crap about babysitting, and I *fell* for it!"

"I *was* babysitting—"

"I'm sorry. It's over."

"What if we had dinner and talked—"

"I don't think so, Cate. This doesn't work for me."

Cate nodded, suddenly maxed out. "Okay, fine, I understand."

"Take care of yourself."

"You, too," Cate said, and hung up. She couldn't blame him, and she refused to feel sorry for herself. This wasn't the time or the place. She had to move on. She got up, slid out of her robe, crossed to the closet, and hung it back up. Then she returned to her desk, lifted the bouquet of roses from their glass vase, and dropped them, dripping, into the wastebasket. The cloudy water in the vase left a funky odor.

"Eau de stockbroker," Cate said, to nobody in particular. She shook down her wrist, so the gold bracelet slid out from under her black suit sleeve. She unfastened the clasp, and the bracelet fell into her cupped hand.

Give me your wrist.

Cate opened her drawer, pulled out an envelope, and slid the bracelet inside, to be sent back to Graham. She had more important things to worry about.

Like Chief Judge Sherman.

CHAPTER 32

"Come in, Cate." Chief Judge Sherman rose from behind his desk and motioned to her with a smile. "Please close the door behind you, dear."

"Got it." Cate closed the door. Cigar smoke lingered in the air.

"I'm having tea. Shall I ask Mo to get you some?"

"No, thanks." Cate entered his lovely office, crossing the Oriental rug and passing the jewel-toned tapestry couch. Rain beat outside his window, too, because all of the chambers shared the eastern exposure, but it seemed less gloomy here. Warm incandescent light glowed from Waterford crystal lamps on the end tables, and Cate made a mental note to finally move into her office.

"Please, sit down." Sherman picked up his black reading glasses, and Cate seated herself in a club chair in front of his desk. "Did you have some lunch?"

"No, I'm not hungry." Cate had been trying to ignore the jumpy sensation in her stomach. She'd already thrown up this year.

"Our cafeteria served delicious chicken today. Chicken marsala, imagine!" Sherman chuckled, easing back into his chair. "Aren't we fancy?"

"Chief, let me say how sorry I am, about all of this."

Sherman raised a hand, still chuckling. "I must say, when I was growing up, you know what I ate every day for lunch?"

"No, what?" Cate asked, playing along. If he was trying to put her at ease, it wasn't working. She could hardly meet his eye, and she'd been doing so well with the eye-meeting thing this morning.

"Every day, I went home for lunch. The school was only three blocks from my house. I went to Merion Elementary, in the suburbs. Do you know it?"

"No."

"Merion's only twenty minutes outside the city. The golf club is there."

Cate sensed she should know it, but she didn't.

"In any event, every day, I'd go home for hot dogs with baked beans. Every day, my brother and I ate the same thing. The only difference was that sometimes we put the hot dogs *in* the beans, and other days we ate the hot dog on white bread. You know, that soft white bread?"

"Wonder Bread."

"Of course. *Wonder* Bread!"

Cate smiled. "It is a funny name."

" 'Builds strong bodies twelve ways!' "

"What twelve ways?" Cate said, and they both laughed. "They used to *spray* it with vitamins."

"Ha! Imagine if you tried that today. Think of it. At home, Ellen buys that artisanal bread, from Whole Foods. Dark brown, with what, tree bark sticking out, for God's sake."

Cate laughed.

"You can hardly tear it apart with your teeth. I lose my bridge-work, every time. Fifty-five grains, or some such silliness."

"Builds strong bodies fifty-five ways."

"Right! Perfect, Cate." Sherman laughed heartily, holding his chest, his reading glasses still in hand, their stems like crossed legs. "Everything old is new again, isn't it?"

"It sure is." Cate felt her stomach relax a little and eased back in the chair. "Your master plan is working, Chief. I'm starting to feel better."

"Excellent, excellent," Sherman said, doing a passable Montgomery Burns, and they both laughed again. Then he cleared his throat. "Tell me, Cate. How are you holding up through this travail?"

"Not terrible, not great."

"I understand you had quite a morning." Sherman nodded sympathetically. "Tell me about the man in your courtroom today."

"It was bad, but it's fine now."

"Your attacker was unarmed, I understand from the marshal service."

"I figured. He wasn't really an attacker. He was more like a heckler. He began yelling during the colloquy and running wild. It disrupted the entire proceeding and I got off the bench."

"Safely, I trust."

"Yes."

Sherman nodded. "The only problem with public service is the public, it seems. And yesterday, what happened?"

Cate had to think. "Yesterday was the longest day of my life."

"I'm referring to the sentencing, for conspiracy to distribute. D'Alma."

"Oh right." Cate remembered. How had he heard about that? Meriden? "I had to end the proceeding."

"Tell me what happened."

"I was unprepared, frankly. My house and chambers had just been broken into, and I was distracted."

"Understandable. Russo is targeting you, it seems."

"Yes, definitely. He blames me for the ruling and for Marz's suicide."

"Terrible, just terrible." Sherman tsk-tsked. "The risks we take, as judges. The responsibility we carry."

"I hired a bodyguard. He's sitting in your reception area with the FBI agent, as we speak. Between them and the marshals, I feel safe." Cate thought again of Nesbitt, in the courtroom.

"Good." Sherman sipped tea from a white porcelain mug with the tea bag hanging out. The little square of white paper fluttered on its string as the mug moved back to the desk. "Why did you end the proceeding, then?"

"You mean D'Alma? I wanted to hold it when I was fully prepared. It's scheduled for this coming week, I believe." Cate made a mental note to check with Val.

"But you're on trial this coming week, *U.S. v. Blendheim.* How will you do both?"

"I'll squeeze it in somewhere," Cate answered, surprised. Sherman, as chief judge, had access to their dockets and schedules, but she hadn't realized he followed them that closely.

"There was another matter, I understand, that you canceled."

"There was?" Cate had to think a minute. She hadn't expected to be talking about this, after what had happened in the courtroom today. Where was this coming from?

"A pretrial motion. *Schrader v. Ickles Industries.*"

"Oh, yes, right." Cate thought back, nervously. That was what she'd canceled to go see Micah. "I had to run out. I was following up on something about Russo."

"Did you reschedule that?"

"The motion hearing? I'm not sure, but I will." Cate's stomach tensed, its vacation over. "Why do you ask, Chief?"

"I got a call this morning from the parties. They needed a ruling on a question about an out-of-town deposition."

Cate flushed. "Oh, sorry. I guess I didn't call them back yet."

"It was a simple discovery matter, so I ruled during a break in my trial. Mo will send Val a copy of the order."

"Thank you."

"I also got a number of calls this morning, from your colleagues. Bonner, Andrew, Gloria, Bill." Sherman paused. "I couldn't field all of them because I was on the bench. I forget who else called."

"And Jonathan, he must have called."

"Yes, he did, of course. Almost all of them weighed in about this newspaper coverage today, and about your . . . proclivities." Sherman smacked his lips, as if the word had an aftertaste. "Your colleagues tell me that you said the reports are true, about these things."

"Yes, they are." Cate felt her stomach and face on fire, which might be a biological first.

"I see. They were unanimous in their judgment, and I must say, as a personal matter, I'm very disappointed in you. I had such hopes for you." Sherman frowned behind his glasses. "I knew you were young but I was certain you'd mature into the position. I liked your . . . style, I guess I should say. True, you're different, but refreshingly so. I saw you as the future of this court, or used to."

Cate felt like dying.

"We think, as a court, that it's conduct unbecoming. It hurts me to tell you this." Sherman slid off his glasses and examined his reading glasses as if he'd never seen them before. "I normally wouldn't consider your personal life a matter for public discussion, but you hold public office, Cate. You're a public official. The duties you perform serve the public, and the cause of civil and criminal justice."

"I know, Chief, and I'm sorry. It will never ever happen again."

"I'm sure of that. I know you, at least I felt as if I did."

"You do," Cate rushed to say.

"All of us are married, as you know. We have families. Except for the one messy divorce every year, which is our annual allotment—" at this, Sherman smiled slightly—"we lead exemplary lives, on and off the bench. We have to. The first canon of judicial ethics is that a judge must uphold the integrity of the bench. The comments require us to 'personally observe high standards of conduct.'"

"I know, Your Honor."

"Canon Two instructs us to avoid impropriety and the appearance of impropriety in all activities, not merely those on the bench."

"I know, and I'm sorry. I was wrong." Cate felt like it was the quietest, longest and most excruciating dressing-down she'd ever had. "I didn't think."

"The prospect of this TV series about judges, of course, is completely unacceptable."

"I hate the idea, too."

"They're saying it's fictional, but no one will believe that. I don't want *anyone* making a TV show about my court." Sherman stiffened. "It's anathema to me. I assume you will file suit, with your resources. I had heard that you've been in touch with Matt Sorian. He's exactly whom I'd hire, Cate. A lawyer with *teeth*."

Meriden. "I did call Matt, but he advises me that I wouldn't win, and I agree. I've been thinking that suing would do more harm than good. I've decided not to sue."

"How so? Why?" Sherman's lips parted in surprise. "You can't be seen as *acquiescing*. This is a question of appearances. You *must* sue."

"No, I won't. I think it would bring more attention to the show." Cate had decided last night, after talking to Gina. She wouldn't compound the damage she'd already done. "It's protesting too much, giving it publicity. Making it bigger than it is."

"You couldn't make it bigger than it is." Sherman frowned deeply, and his tone took on a new urgency. "*Attorneys@Law* is a hugely popular show. Everyone watches it, even me. Ellen's book group switched their night to Monday, because of it."

"I'm going to weather it, Chief."

Sherman set his reading glasses down quietly. "What are you saying? The relevant question is, can our court weather it? Are you saying you'll stand by and do nothing to stop this? To stop them from hurting our court?"

"I have no choice, Chief."

Sherman eyed her for a moment, over his folded reading glasses. "Then I'll have no choice. You'll be leaving me no choice. If you don't sue, I'll have to ask you to resign."

Cate almost fell off the chair. "Resign? From being a *judge*?"

"Yes. Of course. I'll have to ask for your resignation if you won't sue. At least that." Sherman shook his head, as if the explanation were simple. "I have to protect our court. Our judges, our staff. We all work too hard to get dragged through the mud on television. Or in the press. You have to sue, Cate. Then you'd at least be doing something to remedy this terrible situation you created. Then at least I could defend you."

"Chief, this will die down, it has to, and—"

"Not if they make a TV show about it. Not the way the press massages TV, and vice versa." Sherman scoffed. "It's a twenty-four-hour news cycle, as they say, and I cannot have the entire Eastern District on TV, as news or entertainment. You tell me which is which, nowadays. Cate, won't you sue? Please, rethink your position." Sherman hunched over, in appeal. "Give it a day. Confer with Matt. You're not thinking clearly. You'll be an excellent judge someday, Cate. Don't throw it away. Don't make me ask you to step down."

"You don't have to—"

"Yes, I do, and I will. If you don't sue." Sherman edged away in his chair, watching her as if from a distance, and Cate flash-forwarded on what it would be like to be frozen out of his friendship, much less off the bench.

"But I just got on the court. I'm not giving it up. I earned this job." Cate thought about what Gina had said. *You wanted the promotion, but did you want the job?* And then she knew, just as she was about to lose it. Maybe, finally, because she was about to lose it. "Chief, I want this job."

"Then you should have taken better care of it." Sherman faced-off with her over his desk. "We can do this easy or we can do this hard. Resign or sue."

Cate reconsidered it, her resolve wavering. It would be so easy to sue. Just file the papers. Then she remembered. *But what's right for you might be wrong for Warren and me.* "I can't."

"Then step down."

"I won't."

"Then that's that, I tried." Sherman's tone hardened, and he shrugged as if shedding her. "Effective immediately, your cases are reassigned. *Blendheim, D'Alma*, all of them. You're off the bench. I'll reassign Val to another judge. Nobody wants those law clerks. They're on their own."

"You can't do that, Chief. You don't have the power."

"I most certainly do. I manage the dockets, and your docket just got cleared. You left me no choice. Federal judges hold their office only during good behavior."

Cate rose. "The Constitution doesn't speak to this, Chief, and you don't have the power to execute, even if it did."

But Sherman had stopped listening. He rose, too, then pulled a sheaf of papers from his desk and handed them across the desk. "This is a complaint of judicial misconduct against you. It will be filed by the end of today."

"A *misconduct* complaint!" Cate snatched the papers but she was too emotional to read them. "The misconduct statute wasn't meant for an overactive sex life. The statute is aimed at conduct on the bench, within the scope of office. Bias, conflict of interest. It doesn't cover me! Who drafted this? Jonathan?"

"He feels very strongly that the court is being harmed, and now that we've spoken, I agree."

"Chief, this is insane!"

"No, it's insane to sacrifice an entire court for one individual, no matter who it is. I won't have my court turned into a television spectacle."

"They'll still do the show!"

"If you aren't on the court, it won't be about a sitting judge. It won't involve us any longer." Sherman bore down, leaning across the desk. "Cate, last chance. Don't make me file against you. The complaint goes to the chief judge of the Third Circuit, and he can hold hearings, take testimony. Is that want you want? *You*, on trial? A judge, as the *defendant*?"

Oh no.

"Your misconduct is clear. It's all over the press, and it affected the performance of your official duties. You just admitted as much."

"Admitted?" Cate blinked. Where had she heard that before? *Russo, at her door.*

"You canceled important court appearances. You dismissed an ongoing proceeding because you were unprepared. I had to leave the bench to rule in a motion you hadn't rescheduled."

"*Are you taping me*?" Cate looked around in disbelief, and Chief Judge Sherman flushed red.

"I have a court to protect, and so do you. Now, will you resign?"

"Hell, no." Cate turned on her heel and ran from the office.

CHAPTER 33

Cate stormed into the unfamiliar chambers, ahead of a bewildered Justin Case and Special Agent Brady. Meriden's secretary looked up from her computer keyboard. "Judge Fante?"

"Hi, Denise," Cate called over her shoulder, flinging open the door to Meriden's office and gesturing Justin and Brady inside. "Follow me, gentlemen. Judge Meriden's going to need protection."

"Judge?" Justin said, but Cate was already striding to Meriden's desk, where he sat on the phone, in his shirtsleeves, his rep tie flopped over his shoulder and his feet crossed on the desk.

"Say good-bye, Jonathan." Cate reached over and pressed down the hook. "What do you think you're doing?"

"What do you think *you're* doing?" Meriden hung up the phone and whirled around in his chair, facing her. "I was on a very important phone call."

"Listen, you little bastard." Cate leaned over the desk. "I was just with Sherman and I saw the complaint you wrote. I know what you're trying to do and I know why you're trying to do it. And you won't win."

"You should look at yourself in the mirror."

"No, you jerk. You had it in for me from the beginning. You were never a colleague." Cate glared into his baby blues and realized that not all monsters had scary red eyes. Some even wore starchy white collars and boring ties. "You don't like me. You're jealous and you're mean, small, and petty."

"I don't have to take this." Meriden stood up. "You threw me out of your office, and I'll throw you out of mine."

"Don't bother, I'm going. I was dumb enough to hand you a card, and you played it to the hilt. But this isn't over, because I know how to fight for my life and you don't. You never had to, and so you're afraid."

"Oh please."

"That's why you kept hatch marks on me, why you send your law clerks to spy, and why you run to Daddy all the time. You're not man enough to confront me and you never will be. I'll win because you're afraid. You'll see."

"I'll hold my breath."

"Please do." Cate turned, shaking with anger, and stormed out of the office with Justin and Brady falling in place behind her. She stalked out to the reception area and threw open the chambers door, then stormed down the hall to her own chambers.

"You all right, Judge?" Justin asked, while Brady kept his own counsel.

"Never better," Cate said, fuming. "Bet the Mossad never taught you about a pissed-off Italian."

"No."

"Watch and learn, pal." Cate was at her own door in the next few steps and opened it just as Val was hanging up the phone. She knew from the secretary's shocked expression that she'd just been called by Sherman's office.

"Lord, Cate," Val said, her tone hushed as a prayer.

"He doesn't waste any time, does he?"

"He's *suspending* you?"

"Looks that way."

Val's hand flew to her mouth. "I am so sorry."

"Me, too." Cate walked over to her desk, and the clerks came out of their office and gathered around the way they always did, except that this might be the last time they did it.

"What's going on?" Emily asked worriedly. "What do you mean, you're suspended?"

"Can they do that?" Sam went pale. "Just because you screw around?"

Cate was beyond wincing. "Evidently, yes. At least until I figure out what to do about it."

"What does that mean, for us?" Sam asked. "Are we suspended, too?"

"Of course not, silly," Emily said, rolling her lined eyes, and Cate didn't have the heart to tell them what Sherman had said.

"Gimme a minute, folks. Everybody go to their desks, please. I'll be right back." Cate hurried into her office, closed the door behind her, and made a beeline for the phone on her desk, pressing in the main number.

"Beecker & Hartigan," said the quavering voice, when the call connected. Mrs. Pershing.

"Matt Sorian, please."

"Judge Fante? Is that you?"

"No."

"Oh, I'm sorry, please hold," Mrs. Pershing said, and the next voice was Matt's.

"Matt, it's Cate."

"My God, Cate! I saw the papers—"

"We both did. Listen I have some hard questions. Law-review type issues. One, is it within the power of a chief judge to suspend a district court judge for off-the-bench sexual conduct? Obviously, the issue is what you read about in the paper."

"Well, Cate—"

"Wait, hold on, there's more. Two, does sexual misconduct rise to the level of judicial misconduct within the meaning of the statute? And third, what is meant by 'good behavior' in Article III of the Constitution?"

"Cate, I can't undertake that research for you. Chief Judge Sherman just called."

"He called *you*?"

"We just hung up. He's angry with me, and with Beecker, for advising you not to sue."

"What? What are you talking about? He has no right to do or say that."

"I'll tell you what I told him—that I did not so advise you. I merely suggested that your chance of prevailing would be low, and that the decision to sue or not to sue was a personal decision, which you should make."

"*What?*" Cate thought she'd entered a parallel universe, where your boss taped your conversation and your partners betrayed you. "That's not what you advised me at all, Matt. You advised me not to sue."

"That's not what I said."

"And where do you get off talking with Sherman or anyone else about my legal business? What about client confidentiality?"

"You waived it, Cate. You spoke to him about my advice, and I thought it only fair to clarify what I told you."

"Clarify? You lied! My speaking to him waives nothing, and you know it."

"I can't afford to have my legal advice misconstrued to the chief judge of our district court. Beecker can't afford that, either, Cate. You, of all people, should understand."

"Screw you, too, Matt." Cate slammed down the phone, just as there was a knock on the door. "Come in," she called out, flustered, and the door opened onto two federal marshals, a bodyguard, and an

FBI agent. Cate tried to recover. "Yes, gentlemen?"

"Judge Fante?" The marshals entered her office in their dark blue jackets, looking so somber that Cate felt a bolt of alarm.

"What is it? Is Russo back?"

"Judge, we've been asked to escort you out of the building."

"But I'm not going anywhere," Cate said, then came up to speed, incredulous. "Am I being *thrown* out of the courthouse?"

"The clerk's office asked us to take care of it, Judge. We don't know any more about it. We're just doing what we're told."

"I'm with you, wherever you go," Justin said, his lips pursed.

"So am I," Brady added, and Cate wondered fleetingly whether Justin and Brady could take the marshals.

"Okay, I'm going." Cate rose and looked around her desk, trying to think clearly. She hadn't seen this coming. She didn't think any of this could happen. What should she take? What should she leave? Would she ever come back? She hadn't even got the chance to unpack. She picked up her purse and went to the door, smiling at the marshal. It was one she recognized. "Please don't cuff me, Mel. I'd like to avoid the obvious handcuff joke."

"No cuffs, Judge." He smiled sadly, and Cate led her entourage out and into the reception area, where Val and the clerks were standing, stricken. The clerks looked at her, blinking like baby chicks, and even Val looked worried as a mother hen.

Cate said, "Nobody freak. I'll get us out of this. Here's what matters—Val, they're going to reassign you."

"To who?"

"I don't know yet. I'll assume they'll give you some time to organize my files."

"I'll need time. I mean, I just won't leave you. I can't just walk out of here. I don't want to."

Cate raised a hand. "Do what they say, so you don't get in trouble. And remember, you're Invaluable." Val threw her arms open and gave

her a big hug, which still smelled like powder. Cate willed herself
not to get choked up and turned to the law clerks. "Guys, listen. Did
either of you get job offers?"

"Not yet," Emily answered, and Sam shook his head.

"Morgan just rejected me, yesterday."

Cate patted his tiny shoulder. "Okay, don't worry. Take the weekend to put your life in order. Sleep in. Enjoy yourselves."

"Are we out of a job?" Emily asked, upset.

"No, you work for me now, and I'm giving you both a vacation.
Take some time off. I'll match your pay. In fact, I'll give you a raise,
okay?"

"You don't have to do that, Judge." Emily's eyes glistened, but Sam
nodded.

"Yes, she does."

"I'll be in touch with you next week. Just don't worry." Cate gave
them each a quick hug, went to the coat rack, and slid into her coat.
"See you later. Say good-bye to the courtroom deputy for me," she
said, as she left her chambers. She held her chin up as they crowded
silently into the tiny judges' elevator and rode it down to the judges'
lobby, where Cate turned to Brady. "You must be exhausted. Don't
you have a shift change or something?"

"At two, we'll switch."

"Good." Cate turned to Justin. "I'd like you to go over to a house
on Meadowbrook Road and stay there until the end of the day." She
gave him Gina's address. "Then go back next week and the one after
that. Stay there, just in case Russo gets in somehow."

"You sure?"

"Yes, thanks for everything." Cate shook his hand and nodded to
Brady. "We outta here?" she asked, and she went through the door to
the parking lot, got into her car, and drove it out, picking up Brady's
black Crown Vic on her tail by the time she reached the security
kiosk. She took a right onto Seventh Street, then another onto Race,
around the back entrance of the courthouse.

Traffic was light but the rain was heavy, and she cruised down the street, the windshield wipers thumping back and forth, and she stopped at the red light, numbly watching them beat, trying not to think about the fact that she'd lost everything she had in one stormy afternoon. She reached her street and took a left, stopped by the traffic and commotion she'd never seen before on her quiet street. A mob of reporters carrying umbrellas crowded the sidewalk in front of her house, and at least eight boxy white newsvans, each with its cheery multicolored logo, clogged traffic by parking on the curb, their microwave poles soaring into the storm like modern-day church spires.

Oh no. Cate kicked herself. She should have realized that at least some media would be staked out in case she came home. She'd been too preoccupied to think ahead. She hit the gas, then braked. A WCAU-TV newsvan stuck out into the street, preventing her from going forward. Cate threw the car into reverse just as one of the reporters spotted her, pointing with a surprised shout that was muffled by her car windows. Suddenly photographers aimed still cameras at the car, their automatic flashes firing like tiny explosions. TV cameramen raised their videocameras to their shoulders, pointing long lenses at her. Reporters started running toward her.

Cate had to get out of there. She checked the rear view. The Crown Vic idled behind her. "Brady! Move!" Cate yelled, signaling frantically for him to back up, but it was too late. Reporters banged on the window, shouting questions.

"Judge, are you fit to serve on the bench?" "What do you have to say about reports on your personal life?" Klieg lights sprang to life, aimed at Cate in the car. "Judge Fante, give us a comment! Come on, any comment, Judge!" "Look, this way, Judge!" "Put down the window, Judge!"

Cate slammed on the horn. She couldn't go back. Reporters swarmed the car. Brady stopped. She looked around for an escape. She couldn't get out of the car. She'd be imprisoned in the house. *There.* The sidewalk.

"Judge, why are you dating the criminal element? Judge!" "Judge, where's your ex-husband?" "Judge, are you getting a cut from the TV series?" "Judge, are you gonna sue?"

Cate edged forward as if they weren't there, and the reporters parted when she didn't stop, springing out of the way, hollering after her car, filming and snapping away. Reporters ran after the car, but Cate drove up on the curb, then accelerated, avoiding a cameraman near the front bumper.

She hit the gas and sped to the end of the street, then turned around the corner, driving away. Newsvans gave chase, but they were no match for the Mercedes's eight-cylinder. Cate barreled through the city streets, hit the expressway at speed, and lost them all, including Brady. By the third exit, her cell phone started ringing. She flipped open the phone, tense and upset. "Yes, Brady?"

"Where are you, Judge?"

"Listen, I think I won't be needing you for a while."

"What?" Brady was shouting. "You on 95? I'm on 95, looking for you."

"Brady, relax." Cate drove under the I-76 sign at the Art Museum exit. "I'm going out of town, and where I'm going, nobody will find me. Not the press, not Russo, not anyone."

"Judge, tell me exactly where you are. Where you're going."

"Thanks, Brady, for everything," Cate said, and closed the phone. She didn't want him following her. She didn't want anybody following her. She'd had enough invasions into her privacy for a lifetime. She hit the gas, reaching seventy, then eighty, soaring away. She didn't exhale until she left the city limits, and two exits after that, she realized where she was going. The only place where no one could find her.

Because it didn't exist anymore.

CHAPTER 34

Cate drove with the radio off, insulating herself from the news and leaving Philadelphia far behind. In time, the only sounds were the regular thumping of the rain on the car and the pounding of the big windshield wipers; she switched onto the Pennsylvania Turnpike and drove north for an hour, finally beginning to relax only when she steered off the turnpike. She slowed the car and felt a calming inside, her heartbeat returning to normal at the familiarity of the sights. The FirstEnergy Stadium, the truck accessories outlets, and the plywood gazebos for sale interspersed with the onion domes of Ukrainian Catholic churches, their golden minarets and hatched crucifixes oddly exotic in the rural American landscape.

The elevation changed at Pricetown, and Cate felt the slightest pressure in her ear, like the whisper of an old friend. The rain became sleet, and the car climbed over the wet bridge and into the snowy, tree-covered mountains that embraced the road. The traffic grew sparser on the zigzag route through the Appalachians, and Cate drove over steep hills and down deep valleys, the motion making her aware of her own fatigue, as if she were being rocked to sleep.

Snow began to fall, and she spotted a billboard for a Holiday Inn Express, got off Route 61 in Frackville, and pulled into an almost empty parking lot, where she grabbed her purse and got out of the car. The frigid air took her by surprise, and icy snowflakes bit her cheeks like tiny shards of glass, as if heaven itself was shattering and falling in pieces around her.

When Cate woke up, she wasn't sure where she was. The room was pitch-black, disorienting her, and she sat up, uncomfortably hot. She still had her coat on and shrugged her way out of it, then rubbed her eyes. A window was in front of her, the curtains open, and the hillside glowed a ghostly white from the new-fallen snow. She turned around and found a clock by its green digital numerals, glowing in the dark. 9:30.

At night? Cate got up, walked around the bed, and found a switch, which immediately cast a harsh light around the room, reminding her. Holiday Inn. *Resign or sue.* Russo, after her. Marz dead. Simone, murdered. Gina and Warren.

She searched around for her cell phone and saw that the display had gone black. Her battery was dead; she hadn't plugged it in, of course. She set it down and reached to the end table for the telephone, and her call connected after two rings, when she said, "Gina?"

"Cate! I've been calling your cell. Are you okay? I heard there was a crazy guy in court."

YOU'RE A WHORE. "Oh, that. I'm fine, really."

"Where are you?"

"A Holiday Inn in Frackville."

"You're kidding. Is Frackville near Frickville? What are you doing in Frick-and-Frackville?"

"I got out of Dodge. I was over the press." Cate considered telling her she was suspended, then let it go.

"Don't turn on the TV then. You'll freak."

Cate sighed. "How's the baby?"

"Fine. We still hate the new speech therapist. Hey, why didn't you just come here?"

"After last night, I think you guys are better off if I stay away. By the way, did you get the bodyguard I sent you?"

"Justin? He's parked out front. You didn't have to do that."

"Yes, I did."

"So why don't you come over here, now that we're all safe?"

"No, thanks. I feel better, away from it all."

"When are you coming back?"

God knows. "After the weekend."

"What about work? Don't you have court?"

"I'm not on the bench until later." *Much later.*

"Nesbitt was here today. He came and got his car. Nice guy. He was asking about you. Hubba hubba."

Cate flashed on Nesbitt, watching her from the middle of the courtroom. "Calm yourself. I'm never having sex again."

"Who's talking about sex, I'm talking marriage. Oh wait, the baby's about to knock over a glass."

"I'll let you go. I'm fine, and I'll call you later."

"Okay, stay in touch. Love you."

"Me, too." Cate hung up, suddenly aware that she was hungry and thirsty. She grabbed her bag, found her card key, and left, walking across the parking lot to a Cracker Barrel. The air was black, the night starless, and her Blahniks were wet by the time she reached the restaurant, warming instantly at the sight of its ersatz coziness. Antique ladles and strainers hung from the ceiling, and its fake-country store sold cast-iron skillets, Goo-Goo pies, and souvenir sweatshirts that reminded Cate she had no clothes.

She bought a tourist sweatsuit, a stash of Trident gum, and a take-out meat loaf called Comfort By the Slice, then carried her booty back to her Holiday Inn, where she ate, showered, and slept her way through to Sunday morning, ignoring all media until she picked up the free newspaper in the hotel lobby, *Schuylkill Sunday*. Cate guessed that it wouldn't mention her secret sex life.

She got upstairs and skimmed the newspaper at her desk, over Cracker Barrel's Country Morning Breakfast. Soft indirect light filled the room, reflecting off the pristine snow outside the window, and Cate felt rejuvenated for the first time in days until her gaze fell on the date on the newspaper. February 23. The anniversary of her mother's death. She felt a familiar tightening in her chest. Her mother had died seventeen years ago, of an aneurysm. Today.

Ring! The phone jarred Cate from her thoughts. Gina was the only person who knew she was here. She crossed to the end table and picked up.

A man's voice said, "Judge?"

Cate went silent, the fear rushing instantly back.

"It's Nesbitt. Steve Nesbitt."

"Oh, jeez." Cate sat down on the bed, relieved. "How did you know I was here?"

"Your friend Gina. She called me at the Roundhouse and said you were going home. She's worried about you."

"I'm fine. It feels good to be alone, me and my Cracker Barrel. I'm developing a taste for Velveeta wedges on iceberg."

"You called off the feds, and your bodyguard is eating pancakes at Gina's. You think that was a good idea?"

"Yes."

"When are you coming back?"

"I don't know." Cate hesitated to tell him she'd been fired, but he already knew much worse about her, so she did.

"I figured Sherman for a better man than that."

"Thanks," Cate said, touched.

"I don't know if you're safe up there. We still don't have Russo, and Frackville's not that far from the city."

"But how would he know I'm here?"

"He could dig a little. He knows there's a state prison in Frackville, all of us do. Does your bio show your hometown?"

"No, and Frackville isn't my hometown anyway." Cate had made sure to keep that to herself, in the snotty Philly bar. "Up here, I feel safer than I have in a long time."

"I won't take that personally."

Cate caught herself. "I didn't mean it that way."

"I could call the local police. Ask them to check in on you."

"No, that's okay. I doubt they can spare the car, and I like that no one up here knows my story, or cares."

"Look, it's Sunday, and I'm off duty. I could come up, keep an eye on things. We could have dinner." Nesbitt added quickly, "Obviously, I don't mean anything by it. I mean, well, you know what I mean. Not like a date."

Hubba hubba. "More above-the-call, like in the courtroom?"

"I got you in, I'll get you out. I told you that. So what do you say? Should I come up tonight?"

February 23. "Probably not. It's the anniversary of my mother's death. I might go visit the grave."

"I could sit in the parking lot, keep an eye out."

"That's okay, thanks."

"Well, I'll give a call and check in on you. Take care, Judge." Nesbitt hung up.

Cate set the receiver down on the hook, feeling a warmth that evaporated when she eyed the snow-covered scene outside the window.

Bracing herself for what was to come.

CHAPTER THIRTY-FIVE

Cate's was one of the few cars on Route 61, which had been plowed and salted, its shoulders triangles of clumped snow. She felt fortified by a fresh cup of Mobil-station coffee, her windshield newly cleared by a cheap scraper. The route snaked around tree-covered hillsides into the town of Ashland, and she traveled the main drive, which ended in an immense bronze statue of Whistler's *Mother*, sitting atop the peak of the hill. She looked away as she passed its pedestal, which read: A MOTHER IS THE HOLIEST THING ALIVE.

The road was a single lane each way, and the modest houses were built close to the street. She drove through the entire town in about ten blocks, then traveled straight up a steep grade and reached the mountain that signaled she had arrived home. A tall, white sign marked the spot, but it didn't bear the town's name. Instead, this sign read: WARNING—DANGER.

Cate felt an angry twinge inside her chest as she passed the sign, following Route 61 as it had been rerouted to the right, and traveled to the summit, where the school and church used to be, sitting across the street from each other like family at a holiday table. St. Ignatius Cemetery was off the road on the left; her mother was buried there, but Cate wasn't ready for that yet. She drove ahead, down the valley, passing the abandoned landfill, where it had all begun. Locust Avenue, as this stretch had been called, used to be lined with two-story row houses, but the houses were gone. Cate descended into the valley and encountered a sight that looked like hell on earth.

The trees were dead, their tops stumps and their branches reaching brittle into the gray sky. Green street signs remained, jutting point-lessly from the new-fallen snow. Billowing smoke burned from vari-ous holes and wafted in white drifts that rolled across Locust Street. The smoke looked as innocent as the homey white curls from a chim-ney, but it contained carbon monoxide, carbon dioxide, and toxic steam. Its stench, acrid and sulfurous, seeped into Cate's car; the odor defined her childhood, along with baking apple pie and Play-Doh. It used to make her light-headed, and her mother had been among the first to realize that it wasn't her child who was sick. It was the town.

A fire had been raging underground for decades, fueled by a seam of anthracite coal that lay under Centralia and the surround-ing towns. The fire started back in 1962, in the dump behind Cate's school, and state and federal governments botched chances to put out the fire when it was still possible. As a result, row houses that had housed fourteen hundred people had been demolished, and the town had ceased to exist. Whoever said you can't go home again must have been from Centralia.

Cate took a left, then another, driving up the street, the toxic smoke momentarily engulfing the Mercedes. She held her breath and pulled up at the top of the street, where her house used to be. Under the snow, only a rim of black asphalt remained of their sidewalk, and a sinewy trail of poison smoke snaked from where her living room had been. The gases had seeped in through their basement, causing her mother to fall asleep in her recliner at night. The Fantes were told that the gas levels were safe, but they still kept the windows open on the coldest winter nights and shared a gas monitor with neighbors, placing it in the basement, so that its alarm would wake them before the poison gas sent them to a more permanent slumber. Cate eyed the snake of poison smoke in the middle of the ghost town that was her hometown.

Time to go. She turned around and drove to St. Ignatius Cemetery, set among the bare trees. Steam rose everywhere around the graves. Local lore always held that the mine fire never reached underneath St. Ignatius, but Cate doubted it. Her mother had still wanted to be buried here. Cate drove through the gates, left open, but the asphalt road up the center hadn't been plowed. She cut the ignition, got out of the car, and steeled herself. The cold air hit her fully in the face, along with the awful sulfur odor, and she flipped up the collar of her coat. She approached her mother's grave, her jaw set and her chest constricted. She stood almost immobile at the corner, her feet in warm slush, reading a monument she had never seen before, because she could never bring herself to visit.

DEIRDRE FANTE, it read. APRIL 10, 1937—FEBRUARY 23, 1989. Underneath was BELOVED MOTHER, because that said it all.

Cate bowed her head, and her gaze fell upon the rounded monument next to her mother's, a tiny, white angel, its cherubic cheeks pitted from the natural and unnatural elements in the air.

WILLIAM FANTE. JANUARY 11, 1970—JANUARY 11, 1970.

Cate's baby brother, stillborn. He had been born severely underweight, his brain underdeveloped. Her mother didn't have the heart for the autopsy, she would tell Cate much later. The cause of death was filling their nose, and making their eyes water, anyway.

Cate felt suddenly stiff as she looked at the miniature tombstone. Her brother's birth and death marked the Before and After of her mother's life. Before, her mother had been a vital woman, a natural force, a blonde of the flashiest magnitude, her star brightly set in relief against this dark, grimy mining town. Cate remembered her as laughing, dancing, and making jokes—before the baby was born, and died. Her mother never recovered, blaming herself, the gases, the mine fire, and the borough council. Her father left them just after.

Cate bit her lip, realizing she hadn't brought any flowers for either of them. *This cannot be* was still all she could think, and then tears came to her eyes, too persistent to deny. She was sniffling, getting a snootful of sulfur dioxide, when she heard the sound of a car door slam. A red Toyota was parking in front of the cemetery, and an older man in a gray cabbie hat had gotten out. She wiped her eyes with her hand and heard crunching behind her as the old man made his way up the road, stooped and with difficulty. He seemed to be heading in her direction, and she moved aside to give him room to pass.

"Hello," the old man said, giving her a friendly little wave, a pass of gray wool gloves with brown leather palms.

"Hello." Cate wiped her eyes again, remembering that people in small towns always said hello. She had been in Philly too long. When he drew closer, she asked, "Am I in your way?"

"No, not at all." The old man smiled pleasantly, his teeth even, and brushed back a sparse, flyaway white thatch that had fallen over his lined forehead. His light blue eyes flashed with liveliness behind his bifocals, and he had a bony nose, pink at the tip. "Pardon me, but aren't you . . . Deirdre's daughter, Cate?"

Cate's felt her lips part. "Yes."

"My, my. You have your mother's good looks." The man smiled again, offering his handshake. He was tall, almost six feet one, and too thin, even in a navy blue down jacket. He wore tan Timberlands with his brown slacks. "How nice to meet you, finally. My name is Ed Pell."

"Hello, Ed," Cate said, though she didn't recognize the name.

"Deirdre was very proud of you. My condolences on this very sad day."

"Yes, thank you." Cate felt mystified. "How did you know my mother?"

"Deirdre was an old friend of mine, a very dear friend. We knew each other after you left for college."

Cate thought back. "I didn't see you at the funeral."

"You were too upset to see anything that day."

Mr. Pell's eyes strayed to the grave, and Cate watched them move across the headstone, reading it. After a moment, he said, "It's funny, all the fussing and the fighting, the things that matter so much in life, all come to nothing, in death." He grew suddenly sad, the crease from his nose to his chin deepening. "Excuse me, would you?"

"Of course."

He shuffled to the head of the grave in the snow, and Cate reached out to support his elbow as he leaned slowly over and placed a bouquet of pink carnations at the foot of the monument. "All my love, dear," he said softly.

What? Cate had no idea who this man was, so she asked him.

And she almost didn't believe the answer.

CHAPTER 36

Cate found herself sitting on a worn brown plaid couch in the small, cozy living room of Mr. Pell's apartment, waiting for him to return with the tea. Handmade bookshelves filled with plastic-covered biographies, history books, and mystery novels bought at library sales lined the room, many still bearing the yellow stickers of Sherlock Holmes. Amateur photographs of local landscapes, enlarged and mounted on foamcore, covered the paneled walls. The rug was a shaggy brown, and lamps on the end tables had heavy wooden bases. Across from the couch sat an old TV and a matching plaid chair, on which an overweight gray tabby slept in an oblivious ball.

"Here we are." Ed entered the room with a tumbler of ice and a can of generic cola. He'd taken off his coat and, with his brown slacks, had on a maroon sweater vest over a white shirt, well-worn but spotless. "I'm out of tea. Is Coke okay? It's a classic bait and switch, I'm afraid."

"Thanks." Cate rose, accepted the glass, and set it down on a cork coaster on the table.

"Do you mind if we share the couch?" Ed came around the coffee table and gestured at the cat. "I can't disrupt Mr. Puggy. He looks asleep but he's on the job, you know. He's a paperweight, for chairs."

Cate smiled. "How old is he?"

"He's seventy-five. I'm fifteen."

Cate laughed, and so did Ed.

"Well, this is nice to have you here," he said, patting his leg and leaning back, regarding her through the bottom half of his bifocals. "You do look so much like Deirdre. Yes, you're almost a carbon copy." Ed searched her face in a way that managed not to be creepy. "You have her blue eyes and the exact same color of her hair. You're both lovely women."

"Thank you."

"She was so proud of you, as I said. Of your record as a student. And she was so thrilled that you were going to law school."

"So you knew her just before she died."

"Yes."

Cate felt a twinge. Her mother's life insurance had paid for her tuition at Penn Law. She never could have afforded it otherwise.

"How she would have loved to see you become a judge, even with your troubles of late. I've been following them in the newspaper." Ed shook his head. "Up here, Philadelphia seems like a different world, with its murders and such."

"Oh," Cate said, surprised. She hadn't realized that he knew she was a judge. Bait and switch indeed.

"Oh now, I can see I've gone and upset you. My apologies." Ed frowned. "I can be too blunt. My wife always says that."

"Your wife?" Cate glanced around. It was clearly a man's apartment, everything set up for one.

"I'm a widower. My wife, Melinda, died three years ago. I met her at a photography class I was teaching. Did you come up for the day, today, to visit Deirdre?"

"Uh, no. I've been up—" Cate started to explain, then stopped herself. "How did you meet my mother?"

"I used to be an investigator. Here, I brought this out to show you.

It's my favorite snap of us." Ed pulled a curled photograph from his sweater vest. "Don't judge my photographic abilities by it, please. We took it with the self-timer on the camera. Set it on a ledge at a custard stand, on the boardwalk."

"The boardwalk?" Cate took the photo. It was of her mother and Ed, both grinning broadly, their cheeks pressed together. The sun shone high in a cloudless blue sky and shimmered on the sea behind them. They were giggling, their arms around each other, their love palpable. Cate couldn't get over it. Her mother, with this man. And happy, even After.

"I have many, many pictures of your mother."

"You do?" Cate asked, gazing at the photo. She held it under the low lamplight, with wonderment.

"Boxes and boxes. She was my favorite subject." Ed nodded, his mood lifting. "That one was taken on a trip to the Jersey Shore. Atlantic City."

"My mother went to Atlantic City? I didn't think she went anywhere."

Ed frowned behind his bifocals. "Don't be so hard on her. It was very hard for her to be happy. You must know that."

"I do," Cate said, oddly chastened.

"I believe it was what did us in, ultimately. She just couldn't permit herself to be happy again after her baby died, that way. She thought the fire had something to do with it. The fumes. I think she was right."

"It may have. If the government had paid them sooner, she would have moved in a minute. So how long did you see her for?"

Ed squinted, thinking. "We met the spring of '87 and saw each other for the next year and a half. I asked her to marry me on my birthday. I told her the best gift she could give me was her heart, for the rest of my life. So I blocked her in. She had to say yes." Ed laughed.

"And she did?"

Ed nodded, unmistakably proudly and Cate tried to process the information.

"So you saw each other for a year and a half and even got engaged, and she didn't tell me? I talked to my mother every other day, at least."

"She didn't want us to tell you. I think that was part of her guilt, over her own happiness. It was as if by telling you, she was afraid of being judged."

"But I wouldn't judge her, I'd be happy for her." Cate felt confounded. "I used to tell her to go out and date."

"No, she was judging herself." Ed swallowed visibly. "So about a month after that, she told me that she couldn't see me anymore, that we weren't getting married. Even gave me back the ring, though I didn't want it. She was punishing herself, the rest of her life, for the baby's dying."

Cate knew he was right. She had even suggested her mother get therapy, but she'd refused.

"And a month after that, she died. I read it in the obits. It was so sudden." Ed sighed, falling silent for a somber moment, and so did Cate. "She was in such good health. It took me by surprise. I kept thinking, she'll come to her senses someday. We could have had a wonderful life together."

"I'm sure," Cate said, eyeing the room. She would have wanted just this for her mother, this warm, comfy place with this caring man. In the next minute, she told him as much, and he looked up with a sad little smile.

"Thank you."

"I hate that she's buried in Centralia. The fumes, the fire. It's like she consigned herself to hell, forever." Cate heard herself say it, though she had never thought of it that way until this moment. Her gaze fell again on the photo. "How did you meet, again?"

"I went to see her, for my job."

"You said you were an investigator?"

"For a law firm up here. John Bober's firm. You know, call 1-800-WANNA-SUE?" Ed laughed. "John got all the big cases those days, all class actions. Birth defects, stillbirths, cerebral palsy. And all those breathing disorders. COPD, asbestos, black lung, and emphysema, especially in the Centralia area. My job was to keep an eye on the hospitals and the morgues for unreported cases, for potential members of the class."

"So what did my mother have to do with that? Was it because of the stillbirth?"

"No. Your father."

Cate frowned. "What about him?"

"When I saw that he died of black lung, I went to see your mother and see if she wanted to join the class."

"Black lung?" Cate blinked, confused. "My father didn't die of black lung. He had a heart attack."

"No, it was black lung. His death certificate said so. Coal workers' pneumoconiosis. That was my job, to review the death certificates in the region, for black lung or any similar disease. Progressive massive fibrosis or silicosis. Most of those cases were in Kentucky, Virginia, and West Virginia, but plenty were up here. My beat was the mining counties. Schuylkill, Carbon, Luzerne, Northumberland, Lackawanna, Columbia, and Dauphin. Sullivan County, too."

Cate listened, reeling. *Black lung?*

"Usually I heard somebody got sick and went to visit while they were alive or on oxygen, at home or in the hospital. They all got sick, sooner or later. But a few would slip through the cracks, like your father, and I'd pick him up when I reviewed the death certificates. I used to pay a clerk to tip us off, too."

"Do you remember where you found his?"

"Columbia County, I think. He stayed close to Centralia. Your mother told me he didn't see you much."

"Not at all."

"That's too bad," Ed said, with sympathy. "Then I used to go find the family and see if they wanted to sign up. They usually did, they'd be mad as hell about the black lung. They'd authorize the release of the medical records, and I'd review them and see if they qualified for the class, which they always did, if they wanted in. Is this really news to you, about your father?"

"Yes. My mother said he died of a heart attack."

"No, black lung. He died young from it. He was only fifty. Most miners die or at least show symptoms around that age. Shortness of breath, wheezing, coughs that won't quit." Ed wrinkled his bony nose. "I don't buy all that hooey about when coal was king. Coal was hell for miners."

"But my father wasn't a miner."

"Yes, he was. Can't die from black lung and not be a coal miner. It's caused by the coal dust that gets in the lungs."

"I know, but . . ." Cate didn't finish the sentence. She knew what her own father did for a living, at least she had thought she did. "He had a motorcycle shop. I went to it when I was little. I remember." She did remember, the visits stamped on her brain with a child's impressionism. "The shop was dark and smelly and a little cold. He went there every day. I still have a T-shirt with the name of the shop on it. Mike's Bikes."

"Maybe he did that for a time, but Deirdre told me he was a miner."

"You can't be right. We had motorcycles parked out front of the house, all the time. People came to see him." Cate flashed on the engines roaring. The black exhaust smoke. Her father's greasy hands. "Maybe he became a miner after he left?"

"That's not what Deirdre told me. Or what the certificate showed. She told me he mined and she wasn't surprised when I told her what he died of." Ed brightened. "Then she told me they were divorced, so I asked her out."

"But my father wasn't a miner," Cate repeated, then remembered something. The small bathroom wastebasket at their house. Used Kleenex tissues stained with black dirt against the white. *Don't touch that!*

"She told me no. Said she didn't want to date anyone. She had her job, up at the school, and she was busy. I didn't know then about the baby, of course. So I called her about fifty more times, and she finally gave up. Only woman I ever met with a will stronger than my own."

For a second, Cate could almost hear something. An echo. The hack of a cough, first thing in the morning. A racking that wouldn't stop. Was she imagining it? Was it the power of suggestion?

"We didn't go out much in the beginning, but after a while we did, and always out of town. I told her she used to make me feel like we were cheating. I figured out it wasn't your dad she felt like she was cheating on." Ed slapped his leg. "Hold on, I'll go get you those pictures. I keep the boxes in my little office."

Ed shuffled from the room, leaving Cate with her questions. Why had her mother kept Ed a secret? Why had she kept her father's job a secret? Then she realized the answer, with a start. She hung her head, and by the time Ed returned with a cardboard box, she felt overwhelmed by sadness. With one little fact, everything about her family was explained, once and for all. She reached for her cola and took a shaky sip.

"This is only the first box." Ed set the box down and pushed back the strand of white hair that had fallen onto his forehead. "It could take all afternoon to go through them. That's okay with me, if it's okay with you."

Cate looked up at Ed, who was reaching into the box and handing her a first stack of photos. "Well, did you figure out why they didn't tell me about the black lung?"

Ed stopped the photo stack in midair, and his cheer vanished.

"My father had to have been a bootleg miner. That would explain it. He had the bike shop in the day, but he mined at night, right?"

"Probably." Ed set the photos down on the coffee table. "Don't judge too harshly, Judge. A bootleg miner was only a petty thief. A man who poached coal and undersold it, to make extra money on the side. It's a tradition going back to the Molly Maguires."

"But in Centralia, you know what it means to be a bootlegger as well as I do. As well as my mother did. Part of the reason the mine fire couldn't be put out was because of the bootleg mines. Wasn't that right? Bootleg mines didn't show on the mine maps."

Ed nodded, his lower lip buckling. "Yes. Bootleg miners did what's called robbing back, working the mine the wrong way, back to front, chipping away the coal pillars that were left to support the mine roof. They took out the pillars, collapsing the mines. It made it impossible to stop the fire when the government filled the shafts with fly ash in the seventies, and again in the eighties."

Cate felt a wave of shame. "She must have known he was bootlegging."

"Of course, but it was extra money, and times were tough. Nobody liked the bootleggers, it's true, but mostly they looked the other way. They hated the coal company even more. They couldn't foresee the fire. That the bootlegging would jeopardize everyone. The entire town."

"And a little baby," Cate added, dry-mouthed. "No wonder she blamed herself."

Ed fell silent, and she reached over and picked up the photos.

To meet the stranger who was her beloved mother.

CHAPTER 37

It was almost dark by the time Cate was back in the car, driving south toward the Holiday Inn in Frackville. Trees etched crooked black lines against the overcast sky, an odd gray-purple that deepened to ink behind the mountains. The temperature had dropped to twenty-eight degrees, according to the car thermometer, and the tires rumbled where cold tread met salted road. Only a few cars traveled Route 61, and there was an old black Continental behind her.

Don't touch that

Cate had spent the afternoon looking at the photos Ed had taken. Her heart felt full and her head tired. An emotional exhaustion weakened every muscle in her body. Ed had served her a thick cheeseburger and a hot coffee, which revived her for the drive. He'd also given her a full box of photographs, and it sat beside her on the passenger's seat, along with something else, something even more precious, which gave her a purpose.

Don't touch that

Cate kept her foot on the gas as an old Continental switched into the fast lane to pass her. Her thoughts rumbled along. She would never have guessed that her father had been a bootlegger. Her mother had carried that pain to her grave, lying now beside the child whose death she believed she'd caused.

Don't touch that

Cate bit her lip, driving down into the next valley, where it grew darker. She had always sensed the whispers about her and her mother, and thought it was because her mother wanted more for her. But maybe the gossip was about her father. Bootlegging couldn't have been an easy secret to keep in a town of miners. No one would have been fooled by their secret; no one except their three-year-old.

The Continental switched lanes to get in front of her, its red taillights vivid in the darkness, two round red eyes against the black. Cate flashed on a fleeting memory. The red-eyed monster with the black face, her childhood fear. She'd seen it in her house, coming through the front door at night. She'd run screaming to her mother.

Just your eyes, playin' tricks on you

Cate stared into the red taillights of the black car. It wasn't a monster coming through their front door—it was a miner. Coming home from bootlegging, his face black with coal dust. His eyes red and irritated. Her *father*. It all made sense, jibing with what Ed had told her. So many secrets, consuming them all as a family, burning them alive in a town of fire.

A passing truck jolted Cate out of her reverie, and she decreased her speed, approaching Centralia. Steam rose like ghosts from the earth, and it killed her to think that her father had contributed to this calamity, and her mother had been complicit. She steered the car through steam, hot and wet enough to leave momentary condensation on the windshield, and began the drive up the hill to St. Ignatius Cemetery. She parked outside the gates, set her emotions aside, and cut the ignition, then grabbed what she needed, and got out of the car.

The frigid air hit her in the face, more brutally than it had this morning, and she walked up the center aisle of the graveyard, yanking her coat close to her neck and trying not to breathe. It was almost dark, and steam rose everywhere, rolling in eerie drifts across the marble gravestones and shrouding the stone crucifixes. Cate froze at a shadow behind the smoke. Then it was gone.

Just your eyes, playin' tricks on you

Cate steeled herself. She had something important to do. The task wouldn't get easier, and the sky wouldn't get lighter. She made her way to her mother's grave, and its smooth rose marble seemed to glow in the lessening light, as if the memorial had managed to marshal every last particle of luminescence.

Cate blinked back tears, feeling more fully than ever how much she loved her mother, and how sorry she felt for all her suffering, so needless. Even now that she knew her secret, and her sacrifice, too.

"You should have kept this, Mom," Cate whispered, bending over and plunging her fingers into the cold snow, then burrowing deeper, until she hit earth, scratching a tiny hole. Then she took the small black box containing the engagement ring and placed it inside the hole, burying it with snow. "I love you." She wiped her eyes and turned to go. It was getting dark fast, and colder, and she was beginning to feel woozy and nauseated from the gas.

Good-bye, Mom.

Cate made her way down the road, her feet getting colder in the soaked sneakers. She reached the gates and headed toward the car, digging in her pockets for the keys. Smoke rose around her, and she held her nose, accidentally dropping the keys. *Damn.* She squinted at the snowy ground in the dark. A wave of smoke obscured her view, and she got a powerful whiff of toxins. Cate waited for the nausea to pass, but it didn't. She bent over but couldn't see the keys in the snow, even though the black plastic should have been easy to spot. She plunged her hands into the nearest snowdrift as she heard the sound of a car coming up the road.

Two headlights, on high beams, appeared over the crest of the hill, and Cate took advantage of the temporary illumination to search the snow. She kept fishing and heard the sound of the car as it accelerated. She looked up, struck by a vague sense of alarm. The car was going too fast to make the sharp turn down the new part of Route 61. She could get hit if it didn't turn soon.

Cate straightened up, and what happened next went so fast she couldn't do anything but react. The car gunned its engine, accelerating. The dark hood sped toward her with frightening speed.

Cate heard herself scream and sprang out of the way, diving headlong into the plowed snow by the side of the road. She rolled away just as the car zoomed past her, spraying snow and salt into her face, aiming straight for the Mercedes.

Metal crashed into metal with an ear-splitting *bam*! The dark car slammed into the Mercedes's trunk. The impact sent the car sliding into a snowbank. Exhaust filled Cate's face, and she screamed again, scrambling frantically away. She popped bolt upright in time to see the car's red taillights as it sped away, careering crazily down Route 61.

Her heart jumped through her coat. She was too stunned to think. Her stomach roiled in protest. She scrambled to her feet, brushing wet snow from her cheek and digging a clump from her neck. Snow soaked her sweatpants and covered her coat. What was going on? She could have been killed. Hadn't the driver seen her? Was he drunk?

She ran to the Mercedes and saw its back end smashed. The trunk lid had popped up, but the front end of the car looked untouched. She could still drive it if she could find the damn keys. She had to get out of here. Her phone was locked in the car. There were no police in Centralia. She was too far from any of the few remaining houses, even if they were occupied. Her car would signal Roadside Assistance, but it could take forever for a tow truck to get here.

Suddenly she heard a car coming back up the road. Her gut tensed. Two headlights popped over the crest of the hill from the other way. She couldn't tell if it was the same car. If it was the same driver, he already knew she was here. If it wasn't, she'd get the help she needed.

"Help! Help!" Cate hurried around the Mercedes and waved her arms frantically. It was a dark car. She couldn't tell the make. The driver switched his high beams on. She waved, ducking behind her car just in case. "Please! Help!"

Suddenly the dark car charged the Mercedes, its engine roaring.

"No!" Cate screamed at the top of her lungs, jumping backwards as the dark car barreled into the Mercedes. She was almost pulled under her car as it piled her way, but staggered backwards. She caught a glimpse of the driver, his teeth clenched in rage. *Russo.*

"Help!" Cate screamed at the top of her lungs, her desperation echoing through the hills. He must have followed her up here.

She took off in sheer panic. Smoke wafted around her. Muddling her thinking. Intensifying her nausea. The car gunned its engine, and she ran for her life, stumbling in her wet sneakers. She stopped screaming. No help would come. She'd have a better chance if she didn't betray her position. Her breath went ragged as it hit the icy air, mixing with a swirl of toxic fumes.

A phosphorescent sign stood in her path. DANGER! GROUND PRONE TO SUDDEN COLLAPSE! DANGEROUS GASES PRESENT! The sign stood at the north end of the old Route 61, now closed off. Cate knew the old route by heart, and it gave her an idea.

She ran past the sign, her breathing labored in the poisonous air. Russo must have been reading her mind, because in the next second, she saw his car, visible by its headlights, driving over the hump placed as a barrier at the head of the old Route 61. The car's grille bounced as it bounded past the sign, spraying snow from its tires. Russo was going to run her down or get close enough to shoot her. But Cate knew this terrain. She fought to think through her confusion. She could see the stripped tree trunks in front of her, black shadows against the snow. She prayed the ground didn't collapse beneath her.

She bolted behind the cemetery, her hands hitting stray branches. She fell in the snow, then got up. She climbed higher up the hillside she knew was there. It was the only point on the summit higher than the cemetery. She'd played on it all the time as a kid, since it was so near school. She tried to run fast and lightly, so the ground wouldn't give way under her. Darkness descended, the higher she climbed. The only illumination came from below, the headlights of the dark car as it swung around. The high beams swept beneath her, cutting a lethal swath through the smoky air.

Go, go, go. It was pitch black, no streetlights or highway lights. No moon. Nothing to delineate the terrain to anybody who didn't know every inch of it. Her heart hammered. She kept running alongside the hill, not wanting to go too high, because the land fell off behind. She prayed she was remembering right. Fumes filled her nostrils. She couldn't think.

Russo drove below, going straight, approximating the road she knew curved sharply off to the right. He wouldn't see that. The road followed the curve of the mountain. He wouldn't anticipate that. It was her only chance.

Cate watched him slow his speed, looking for her. Smoke surrounded them, obscuring everything. The mine fire raged underneath. Russo stopped at a smoking rent in the road, the asphalt ruptured like an earthquake. Cate prayed he fell in from his car's weight. She covered her nose to keep her wits about her.

Russo careened around the steaming fissure. Cate bolted along the hillside, bracing herself on dead trees, trying not to breathe too deeply. Russo caught up to her on a parallel track. Almost time to put her plan into action. Soon Russo would get out of the car and hunt her down on foot. She ran harder, panting.

Now!

Cate ran down the hill in the dark, wet and bedraggled, kicking up snow all around her. She cut the mountain at a diagonal toward the car, then half-ran, half-stumbled down onto the unplowed road.

The engine gunned. Russo accelerated toward her. Snow pinwheeled from the tires, and Cate took advantage of her brief head start. She gathered all her strength and bolted across the front of the car. The car burst forward but she was past.

Crak! A gunshot exploded over her shoulder. Cate screamed in terror. A bullet seared her cheek. *Now!* She threw herself down onto the hill and dove into the snow, grabbing for a tree trunk. She hugged it with all her might and scrambled for purchase with her feet.

In the next second, Russo followed her at top speed. Old Route 61 curved to the right under the snow, but Cate had led him to the left. It had worked. The dark car sailed right over her head. She buried her face in the snow. Heat, dirt, stones, and pebbles rained down on her like a storm from hell.

The car flew over the side of the hill, into thin air. The next sound she heard was Russo's scream, joining another's. Hers. Then the hideous crash of his car smashing into the highway below. Debris and broken branches roiled down the hill around her head. In the next minute, everything fell quiet. Russo couldn't hurt her anymore.

Cate should have felt horror, or relief, but a terrible sleepiness took over. Smoke curled from the wooded embankment. Fog clogged her nostrils. Tears filled her eyes. She couldn't breathe. She couldn't muster up a single thought.

She felt distanced from herself. She didn't know if Russo had survived the crash or if he had died. Her consciousness dissolved into smoke. She told herself to hold on to the tree but her grip began to loosen. Her sopping sneaker lost its foothold.

Her eyes closed drowsily. She was so very tired. It had been a long, long day. If she could only put her head down and rest. On a pillow. On a shoulder. A man's shoulder. Not Graham's.

Nesbitt's.

Don't touch that

CHAPTER 38

Cate woke up to Nesbitt's face in soft-focus fog. For a minute, she wasn't sure if she was dreaming. He looked worried, so it couldn't be a dream. Nobody worried in dreams. Also, she didn't dream about Nesbitt. Much.

"Good morning, Judge," Nesbitt said, and Cate blinked.

"Is it morning?" she said. Her mouth felt dry.

"I'm joking." Nesbitt checked his watch. "It's nine at night."

"Oh." Cate felt her head begin to clear. The room came into hazy focus. She was lying in a hospital bed with pull-up plastic rails. Light blue walls and a window on the right, its blue-patterned curtains drawn. An oxygen tube was under her nose. A mounted TV played on mute, a basketball game in too-vivid color.

"How do you feel?"

"I feel good." Cate thought a minute. She didn't hurt anywhere. She felt really happy. "Why am I so happy?"

"It's the drugs."

"I feel so calm." Cate smiled, and Nesbitt smiled back.

"It makes a nice change."

"What happened to me? Did I fall off a cliff?"

"No. They found you by the side of the road, passed out from the fumes. You got the full brunt. You were lying near a big crack of steam."

"At least my pores are clean."

Then Cate began remembering it all, albeit hazily. The cemetery. The cliff. The dark car. Russo. "Is he dead? He's not dead, is he?"

"No. He's upstairs, here. I saw him, and he's resting. A bunch of broken bones, but the doctors say he'll be fine."

"Good. I think." Cate felt her emotions revive, though buffered. "Now that he's alive, am I allowed to wish he was dead?"

Nesbitt smiled. "Now that you're alive, I can say I told you so."

"So we're even."

"Exactly."

"Is he in pain, at least?"

"I believe so."

"A lot or a little?"

"Tell you what. As soon as he heals, I'll beat the crap out of him for you." Nesbitt's smile faded. "We got the call almost as soon as it happened. He had his ID on him."

"And his gun."

"He took a shot at you?" Nesbitt asked, alarmed. "I hadn't heard that."

"I almost caught one, but I missed. Sorry." Cate remembered the heat on her cheek. It didn't even bother her. These must be *some* drugs. She resolved to show more empathy on the next drug case before her, then she remembered she wasn't a judge anymore.

"He'll be released into our custody, and we'll charge him."

"How does that work exactly? Will you charge him and then beat him up? Or beat him up and then charge him?"

"Usually we beat them up first. That way we get the confession."

"Don't vary it on my account."

"Passers-by found his car and they called the locals, who were already on their way."

"My genius car called the cops, didn't she?"

"Right. How much you pay for that baby?"

"Not enough."

"By the way, you're gonna need a new one. That thing's an accordion. Russo do that, too?"

"Yes."

"Were you in it at the time?"

"No. It's a Mercedes hate crime." Cate saw Nesbitt frown, despite her excellent joke.

"We'll need a statement. You'll tell me in detail when you feel better."

"I'll never feel better than I do now." *In fact, I may be in orgasm, as we speak.*

"I'm embarrassed to admit that I didn't know about Centralia. It's incredible. Toxic smoke coming right out of the ground like that. I can't believe the feds don't cordon it off."

"It's a theme park for carbon monoxide."

"I don't understand why they can't put it out, after so many years. We can land a man on the moon but we can't put out a fire?"

Bootleg miners didn't help, but that's another story. "So when can I go?"

"They won't let you go until morning. They want to watch your blood gases."

"My blood has gas?"

Nesbitt laughed.

"I feel fine. Time to go." Cate began to lift herself from the bed, then sank back down, dizzy. "Or not."

"Chill. Or as my daughter says, chillax. By the way, I called your friend Gina, telling her you were fine, so she didn't find out from the TV news. I told her that you'd be out tomorrow morning and she didn't need to come up. That okay with you?"

"Good, thanks." Cate nodded, pleased. Putting Gina out would have been the last thing she wanted.

"I'll take you back to the city tomorrow morning, when they discharge you. You'll need the ride. Okay with you, too?"

"Sure, thanks."

"By the way, there is good news. Jenna Whitcomb was found in bed with Mark Melendez."

Cate frowned, confused. "You mean Jenna Whitcomb, the actress?"

"Yes, the new Julia Roberts. She was caught by *Access Hollywood*, cheating on her husband, Ron Torvald, the new Russell Crowe."

Cate smiled. "How could any woman cheat on the new Russell Crowe? I wouldn't even cheat on the old Russell Crowe."

"It's a major scandal. They've released the photos, and he's already said he's filing for divorce tomorrow. Mark Melendez is the new *new* Russell Crowe."

"How do you know these people?"

"I told you, I have a teenage girl. My house gets *Cosmo*. We vote on Hottie of the Month. We even take the quizzes. Don't tell the guys on the squad. Boys can be so dorky." Nesbitt rolled his eyes, and Cate laughed.

"So why does this matter to me?"

"This is the gossip of the decade, which means the heat is off of you, at least temporarily. You're off the map. There's no press for you outside the hospital, and I bet there'll be very few at your house because there's a big local angle to the story. Mark is from Doylestown."

"Mark? You on a first-name basis?"

Nesbitt actually blushed. "Gimme a break. He's Hottie of the Year. We voted for him."

"So the press is gone? I feel so used." Cate felt a residual sleepiness, and Nesbitt, watching, cocked his head.

"You want some water or something?"

"No, thanks."

"I should tell the nurse you're awake."

"I don't feel so awake," Cate said, her eyelids drooping. Suddenly she felt good and drowsy, postcoital without the coital, and in the next second, she drifted into sleep.

The next time she woke up, the room was dark except for various red and blue numbers on her vital-signs monitor. Her heartbeat was a glow-in-the-dark green outline of jagged peaks and valleys that reminded her of the Appalachians. She touched the tube under her nose, and the oxygen was still there. But Nesbitt was gone, his chair empty. She tried not to feel let down. He was above-the-call, but he wasn't crazy.

Cate breathed in and out, taking silent stock of her situation. On the plus side, she was alive, she hadn't gotten Russo killed, and there was a new new Russell Crowe from Doylestown. On the negative side, she had no job, no boyfriend, and no reason to go home. She lay still in the dark watching the Appalachians march across the vital-signs monitor. She had no idea if it was truly nighttime, in the artificial day/night of the hospitals.

She felt oddly suspended in the middle of time and space. She didn't belong here, up north, among the peaks and valleys. Centralia had loosened its hold on her; she had overdosed on its toxins and they'd almost killed her. She felt oddly free of it somehow. The fire that raged had burned from within, and consumed their family like so much fuel. She wouldn't let it consume her, too.

Cate didn't belong here anymore. She needed fresh air. She wanted to go home, and for the first time, home meant Philadelphia. She had to start over. She'd figure out how when she got there. Maybe on the way back, she'd talk it over with Nesbitt. She told herself she wasn't looking forward to it, before her eyes closed again.

"Judge Fante?" It was Brady at the door the next morning, in his dark neat suit, worn with a black topcoat and a fresh shave. "How're you feeling?"

"Fine, thanks." Cate rose from the bed and shook his hand, dressed in her sweats and sneakers, now dry. She was already in her coat, feeling herself again, and had even showered for the trip home with Nesbitt.

"You've had quite an experience, with Russo and all."

"How is he?" Cate's nurse hadn't known.

"He's fine, resting. He'll be in the hospital awhile, unless they transfer him to Philly."

"Good."

"I heard that your car's totaled. I came to take you back to the city."

"No, Nesbitt's taking me." *Another jurisdictional dispute over little old me.*

"He can't make it. He was called on a job, and when we heard you were stranded up here, I came up."

Rats. I mean, thanks. "You didn't have to do that. I could have taken a train or rented a car."

"I'm detailed to you until the end of the week. I took the liberty of getting your personal items from your car. Your purse, your cell phone, and some boxes. I think your secretary called your insurance company. We're good to go."

"Great, thanks," Cate said, then rose with her signed discharge papers. "We should stop by the hotel to get my stuff."

"I did that, too. There wasn't much, but I took it. We're all packed."

"Wow." Cate managed a smile, and they left.

The trip home went quickly, the sun clear and cold outside the car window. Brady opened up about his feelings, the way people tend to do on long car rides, except that his only feelings concerned the Eagles. He was so annoyed by Terrell Owens that he almost drove over the divider and he believed that Donovan McNabb was "too damn happy" to win a Superbowl. Cate listened idly, making the appropriate noises and watching the RV dealers whiz past the window. By the time Brady had established that Andy Reid "totally deserved"

Coach of the Year, they were pulling into her driveway, where not a single member of the press stood watch.

"Amazing," Cate said, at the sight. "What a difference from the other day, remember?" Her house, peaceful and undisturbed. The street, quiet, and the neighbors, evidently all at work. The snow that had fallen so hard upstate was nowhere to be seen here. It was all back to normal, and she was home.

"I know. Even the Philly press is gone." Brady leaned over and shut the ignition. "He's from Doylestown, I hear, that movie star guy. The reporters moved up in there. Stalking his high school principal. Finding his prom date. You know, who went to the prom with Mark Martinez."

"Melendez." *Don't you read* Cosmo? Cate grabbed her bag and got out of the car, in her dumb outfit. She thanked Brady with an awkward hug good-bye and went up her sidewalk, feeling separation anxiety for her federal babysitter.

She climbed the steps to the front door and remembered that she'd lost her house keys in the snow, so she went into the secret lockbox hidden behind a bush out front, pressed in the code, and retrieved the extra key. She unlocked the door with Nesbitt in the back of her mind, with his yin/yang of magazine subscriptions. She wondered if she'd see him again, now that the murders were solved and nobody was trying to kill her.

Not that it mattered.

Cate stood at the granite island in her kitchen, talking to Gina on the phone and sorting her mail. There had been a stack of it, slid through the mail slot in the front door and spilling in a messy heap when she got inside.

"Of course you'll see him again!" Gina said, on the other end of the line. "Only you could find a bad side to the fact that you're finally safe."

"I'm not sure I want to, anyway." Cate had thrown away the newspapers that came in while she was gone. She didn't need to see those headlines. At least she was yesterday's news. "Is he my type?"

"He's your *new* type. Strong, reliable, and out of jail."

Cate smiled. "This is silly, this whole conversation. I mean, nothing's going on. He was a detective assigned to the case, and that's that."

"He's a man, and you're an Italian. Enough said."

"He's not attracted to me. If he liked me, he would have found a way to drive me home."

"He got busy, catching murderers. Give the guy a break. He called here to tell me not to worry about you and *he* sounded worried about you. That reminds me, did you see a shrink yet?"

"I've been a little busy, dodging bullets." Cate set aside for disposal the catalogs for Nordstrom's, Ann Taylor, Strawbridge's, Bloomingdale's, and Neiman Marcus. Then she retrieved the Neiman's.

"Call. Soon. Now tell me what happened in Centralia. What a nut job! Russo tried to run you over?"

"It's a long story. I don't want to tell you while you're driving around. I'll tell you tonight. It's Monday. Our date night."

"I can't tonight. Uh, Justin's bringing over a DVD he wants me to see, *The Godfather*. I never saw it."

"Are you serious?"

"Lots of people have never seen it."

"No, that you're ditching me for Justin!"

Gina giggled. "Yo. Suburban moms need bodyguards."

"Is it a love connection?"

"I just like the guy. His brother has cerebral palsy, and he lives at Elwyn. So Justin understands, at least some things."

"He's thirty!"

"Younger works for me. Nesbitt's older, right?"

"Older works for me." They both laughed, and Cate warmed at

the excitement in her friend's voice. She hadn't heard her that happy in years. "Good. Great. Go for it. I bought him through next week. Consider him a late Christmas present."

Gina laughed. "I'm not above paying for it, especially when you are."

Cate smiled, stacking a PECO bill on top of a Verizon Wireless bill. Then Comcast. "How's the baby?"

"Fine. He likes Justin."

"He does?" Cate came upon a bill for a *Cosmopolitan* subscription and thought of Nesbitt. "I'm jealous. He's not allowed to like anybody except me."

"Way to be possessive of a kid I'm trying to socialize."

"Hey, maybe we can go on an imaginary double-date. You bring your imaginary law-enforcement hunk, and I'll bring mine."

"I have a bone to pick with you. It said in the newspaper that you were stepping down indefinitely. Chief Judge Sherman is quoted. What does that mean? Why didn't you tell me?"

Gulp. "It means I'm fired, unless I sue the bastards. And first I need to find a lawyer willing to bite the hand that feeds him." Cate came upon a yellow envelope forwarded from her chambers, according to the return address. The name on the front was in Val's handwriting, and she felt a twinge of loss.

"I can't believe this. They can't fire you. District judges are appointed for life."

"We'll see what they can do. For now, I'm going to decompress and figure out my next move." Cate opened the envelope and out slid a small white letter and a Sephora catalog bearing a Post-it from Val that read, "Miss you." Cate thought, *Miss you, too.*

"You should get away. Take a vacation. Get some sun."

"Nah." Cate eyed the letter, feeling a draft from her back door, still boarded up from Russo's break-in. The front of the envelope showed feminine handwriting, and it had been marked PERSONAL AND CON-

FIDENTIAL, which was why Val had forwarded it unopened. Cate didn't recognize the letter's return address. "I have to do some things around the house. Things I've been wanting to do, to make it nice."

"Who is this? You? Wanting to putter around the house?"

"Yes." Cate opened the letter with a fingernail and pulled out a few leaves of white notepaper, folded in two. She skimmed the first few lines. "*Dear Judge Fante, Please forgive me for writing to you, but you are my last resort and . . .*"

Gina was saying, "Are you nuts? Miami's perfect this time of year. Go to South Beach. Walk around Lincoln Road and buy shoes you don't need, like we did last year."

"I have enough shoes I don't need." Cate read, "*I could tell by your compassion during our trial . . .*"

"Then how about the Caribbean? Get away before the papers remember who you are."

"*. . . are the only person I could turn to and . . .*" Cate set the letter aside to read later. Since she'd become a judge, she'd gotten so many letters from girlfriends, wives, mothers, and even children of inmates, asking for her help. They all believed their loved ones were innocent, and even if Cate agreed, there was nothing she could do except send a form reply. But something about this letter made her pick it up again. Then she realized who it was from.

"Or go to a spa. That's the new thing. Cate, you there?"

"*I know that you will feel the same way once you . . .*"

"Hello?"

"I have to go, okay?" Cate folded the letter into thirds. "Talk to you later."

"Where you going in such a hurry?"

Uh. "The bathroom? Give the baby a kiss for me."

Cate felt a surge of renewed energy and ran upstairs to change.

CHAPTER 39

Cate left her heavy coat in the rental car, feeling warm enough in the black wool suit, and walked up the front path to a modest gray stone twin house, much like the others on this winding street in Wynnefield, about half an hour outside Center City. Her black pumps clicked on the frozen flagstone, the cadence slowing as she approached the front door.

She was beginning to regret coming here, though she'd been asked. The timing couldn't have been worse. Cate didn't know what she'd face inside. What if people recognized her? At the rent-a-car, the young clerk had made her instantly, his eyes lighting up the moment she'd walked in. He'd offered her a free upgrade from the Acura, which she didn't accept, but she still didn't relish the notoriety. What if she caused a fuss inside? How would everybody react to her after she'd introduced herself? She wouldn't find any friends here and wouldn't expect any.

She reached the front door, noting the silvery bowlful of water beside the doorjamb, and followed the instructions, plunging her fingertips into the water, though the surface had almost frozen over. The thin ice shattered like red syrup on a candied apple, and the frigid water chilled Cate's hands to the bone. She wiped her hands on her coat, whether or not that was permissible, and followed the rest of the directions, opening the front door without knocking and finally slipping off her pumps, revealing her stocking feet. She looked around the room, hoping that reinforced toes were in order at a shiva.

But the living room was completely empty. The house was quiet. Cate had been told the door would be left open, so that mourners wouldn't be disturbed, but there were no mourners. Odd, low benches ringed the small living room in front of a beige sectional couch and chairs, but they were all unoccupied, like empty chairs at a canceled show. A cushioned stool sat at the fireplace, vacant.

"Hello?" Cate called out, wondering if she was in the wrong house.

"Judge Fante?" Mrs. Marz came hurrying in from another room, walking toward Cate with a nervous smile, her hand extended. "Thank you so much for coming," she said in a soft voice.

Cate relaxed and shook her hand. "I'm very sorry about your loss, Mrs. Marz."

"Please, call me Sarah." Richard Marz's young wife looked prettier up close than she had in the front row of the courtroom gallery, though her eyes were a bloodshot blue, ringed by weary gray circles. She wore no eye makeup, and her small mouth was unlipsticked, her lips tilted down, her grief undisguised. Her brown hair had been styled into a bob that seemed overly coiffed until Cate realized it was a wig, and she wore a black knit suit that was too old for her, draping in a way that hid her compact form. "Judge, come, would you like something to eat? It's lunchtime."

"Yes, thank you." Cate realized how hungry she was when she was led into a dining room filled with the aromas of seasoned roast beef, a fresh spinach salad dotted with tomatoes and hard-boiled eggs, and three baked chickens. The delicious feast looked untouched next to a stack of glistening dinner plates and clean silverware. "This is amazing. You must have food for fifty people here, easily."

"I didn't make it, we're not permitted to. My family brought most of it, but they went back last night." Sarah's face fell, and her voice grew soft. "My mother passed away when I was little, and my father is from California and he had to get back to his business. He couldn't sit the entire week. He's not as observant as we are—as I am. Richard was Orthodox, and his family came for the *sedat havra'ah*, the meal of consolation after the funeral, and they'll be here later."

"That'll be nice."

"My friends from temple choir, they came, and some of our friends from the congregation, but they're all so uncomfortable, with the circumstances. I can tell." Sarah shook her head unhappily. "They seem distant. And there are many people I thought were friends who didn't come."

"Why not?"

"I can only guess that I'm the wife of a murderer now. The wife of a suicide."

Cate fell silent, watching hurt etch lines into Sarah's young face, as surely as a drawing pen filled with ink.

"Maybe I'm wrong, but I think there would have been more people here, everyone, if Richard had been killed in a car accident. But a suicide, and a murderer? People don't know how to react. Maybe out of respect for me, or because of their own discomfort, I don't know. I feel like a social pariah, overnight." Sarah picked up a plate and filled it with the choicest slices of medium-rare roast beef, a few florets of broccoli, and a scoop of golden noodle pudding, replacing a heavy silver ladle on a spoon rest so as not to drip on the lace tablecloth. "I know this will sound terrible, but a woman down the street, her husband was killed in a car crash. She had cars around the block, from all the shiva calls. Evidently all widows are not created equal. But enough. Would you like salad?" she asked, which was when Cate realized the food plate was for her.

"Yes, thanks. And I could have done that myself."

"It's the least I can do, for your coming, for your kindness. Have you made a shiva call before?"

"No. I've been to plenty of bar mitzvahs, but not a shiva."

Sarah lifted a pair of silver tongs and plucked some fresh greens from the huge salad bowl, then set a slice of hard-boiled egg on top. "The round food served at shiva reminds us of the circle of life. Dressing?"

"Yes, thanks."

"It's Italian."

"Works out perfect."

"Yes." Sarah laughed, a surprisingly girlish sound, and spooned some oil and balsamic vinegar carefully onto the salad. Between the wig and the heavy, mature pantsuit, she gave the appearance of a little girl playing dress-up in her mother's clothes, which Cate found endearing.

"You're handling all of this very well, in the circumstances. I don't know if I could bear up with such style."

"It's all an act," Sarah shot back, then laughed.

"Tell me about it." Cate nodded, laughing with her.

Sarah shook her head, seeming finally to relax. "This has been so terrible, as I said in the letter. The family, torn apart, in an uproar. Everybody hurting, in pain." Sarah sighed. "As a suicide, Richard couldn't be buried in a Jewish cemetery, but his father was an Orthodox rabbi and he passed away two years ago. It was out of respect to him and my mother-in-law that they admitted Richard and gave him a proper burial."

Cate's heart went out to her.

"Then the reporters came like locusts, but they're finally gone. That's why I'm glad you came. Just for the company, and the honor. Of course." Sarah finished the plate, and Cate grabbed a cloth napkin and silverware.

"Aren't you eating?"

"I've been eating all morning. Please, sit down." Sarah led Cate back to the living room, where she gestured her into a regular chair, and she took the stool in front of the fireplace.

"Thank you." Cate accepted the food plate and balanced it on her lap, on top of her skirt. More Chanel, but it wasn't making her feel as good as it usually did. Nothing could, with the sorrow that pervaded the empty house. Cate stabbed a piece of salad and ate. "Delicious."

"My aunt made most of this. I love to cook, but can't during shiva." Sarah looked up at her from her baby stool.

"Why the stools, may I ask?"

"It symbolizes being struck down by grief. Visitors don't have to sit on them."

"I see." Cate scanned the room discreetly, noting the covered mirror, which she had seen before, at an Orthodox Jewish wedding. The air smelled a little smoky, from a large white candle burning on the mantelpiece among an array of framed photos, undoubtedly the couple in happier times. Cate got on with it. "So, to your letter. I must tell you, I'm skeptical."

"I know, I understand. That's why I'm so thrilled you came today, just to hear me out."

"That's what you said you wanted, so here I am."

"Well, first," Sarah nodded, hugging her knees, oddly high on the low stool, "I felt that I could turn to you because of what you said about my husband at the trial."

Next time I shut up. Cate cut some beef, which oozed warm juices, and ate a pinkish piece, which melted in her mouth.

"You understood my husband, I thought, and you showed a real sense of justice, and injustice."

"Thank you." Cate nodded, chewing so she wouldn't comment further. She had promised herself only to listen, and didn't want to do anything unjudicial, in case she ever got her job back. Or hell froze over.

"Judge, I know my husband didn't kill anybody, and I know that he didn't kill himself. He would never do such things." Sarah's tone rang with love and certainty. "I spoke with his lawyer after the funeral and told him, but he didn't believe me. He thinks I'm in denial."

"Are you?" Cate took another bite.

"No, and I thought you might understand better. First, Richard came from an extremely observant family. As I said, his late father was a rabbi. Richard almost became one, too. He knew a violent crime such as murder, and later suicide, would violate express Jewish law."

Cate listened, dubious. Six months of being a judge had taught her that respect for law was a flexible concept. Correction, one *day* of being a judge.

"He would have known that both crimes would kill his mother, and he loved her very much. She lives with us, and since this happened, she's on round-the-clock tranquilizers. I even had to hire a nurse for her. He would never do that to her, and she knows it. We both do."

Cate ate, listening. She had remembered from trial about the mother upstairs and wondered where the dog was that she walked for them.

"Also, we loved each other. We did. He felt bad enough that the trial was going so terribly, just for the strain it put on us. He never would have left me alone, this way."

Cate ate, though she was losing her appetite. Every bereft wife felt like this. Suicides left so much pain in their wake.

"What do you think? Do you understand what I'm telling you?"

"Yes." Cate rested her fork on the plate. "I'm very sorry for you, for your loss. I was moved by your letter. But you said there was something you had to tell me, something that would convince me that your husband didn't commit murder, or suicide." Cate paused. It was so hard to say to this girl, her young life in ruins. "And to be honest, Sarah, I'm not hearing anything like that. I know you're in pain, but when there's enough despair, even the most reasonable—"

"Judge, I'm pregnant," Sarah blurted out. "I'm two months along. My mother-in-law doesn't know. My father doesn't know. I told Richard's lawyer, the other day, to try to convince him. And of course, Richard knew."

Cate blinked.

"We had been trying for three years, since the day we got married. We both wanted this baby so much. I told Richard the night before he supposedly committed murder, then killed himself. I have never seen him so happy in my life, and I've known him since high school."

Hmm. Cate couldn't help considering it, given the new facts.

"We were waiting until the third month to tell our families. He insisted that he be the one to tell, when the time came." Sarah's eyes glistened, but her voice held firm. "He wanted a child even more than I did. He even picked out the name. Ariel, after his favorite aunt, who died of breast cancer, or Jacob, after his father, of course."

Cate felt touched.

"We both sensed it was a girl, and Richard wanted a girl so badly. Judge, why would a man who just found out the happiest news of his life kill himself? Or kill someone else?"

Cate had no immediate answer. Her head resisted the conclusion, but her heart was listening. And she didn't know what she could do about it, anyway.

"Richard always had a great perspective, and he loved kids. He coached girls and boys basketball at the JCC on City Line."

"When did you tell Temin about your pregnancy?"

"When he came over after the funeral. But I don't think he understood the significance. He's not a woman."

Cate let it go. She didn't think that sympathy had a gender. "But he knew Richard, didn't he? They seemed close at trial."

"Nate didn't know him that well. Not well enough, anyway. He only knew Richard's professional side."

"But what about at the trial, after I ruled? Richard got so upset about my judgment, he attacked Simone."

"He lost his temper, but it wouldn't last. It never did. He would never kill Simone. He would never stay angry enough to kill Simone, or anyone. He would never ever do that, not knowing a baby was on the way. *His baby.*"

"Maybe he felt even worse because he'd lost, with a baby on the way. Now he knew he'd have a family to support."

"No. My family has money, and I have a trust fund, that's why we're not in financial trouble. We've lived on my trust fund for this past year, after Richard quit his job to write screenplays. His lawsuit was never about money, it was about his pride in his writing and the fact that Simone was getting away with stealing his work."

Cate began to feel the tiniest wedge of doubt that Marz had been the killer.

"He told me, more than once, that he wouldn't be that upset if he lost the lawsuit. He *expected* to lose the lawsuit, and Nate told him he would, too. Besides, Richard was a lawyer, he knew the law. He knew his case was a long shot, but he thought if he got to the jury, he had a chance. And he really wanted to hold Simone accountable."

"He wanted his day in court."

"Exactly."

Cate nodded. It was just what she'd thought. She would have done the same thing.

"Richard did not kill Art Simone. And he did not kill himself. I just know it."

"The police are sure of their case, and it's closed. They're good cops. Smart." *Like Nesbitt*, Cate thought but didn't say.

"But other detectives don't agree at all, like Frank Russo. He knew Richard better than any of them."

"*Russo?*" Cate burst into laughter.

"What?"

"He tried to kill me last night, upstate. He thinks *I* killed Art Simone."

"*What*?" Sarah's brown eyes flared in disbelief.

"It's in the newspaper, didn't you see it? A small headline, relatively, and almost no article. Maybe I should have been offended."

"I didn't see it. I haven't seen a newspaper since Richard died. We suspend our normal activities to sit shiva, and it lasts seven days."

Maybe I should convert. Maybe everybody should.

"What happened?" Sarah asked, and Cate told her, making attempted murder as entertaining as possible. This girl didn't need more *tsuris*. "So I'm not sure Russo is your best argument. Did he know Richard well?"

"Well enough to know Richard wasn't the type to commit suicide. Don't you see?" Sarah leaned forward on the tiny stool. "Russo's instincts told him that my husband wasn't the killer, but he was just wrong about who was. I don't know who did it, either. I just know that Richard didn't. And I think that that person killed Richard and made it look like a suicide."

"Let me ask you something," Cate said, against her better judgment. She set the plate of food down on the glass coffee table. "What happened after that day in court, after I ruled from the bench?"

Sarah thought a minute. "You made your ruling, and Richard got into that fight in the courtroom, then you left the bench and they separated Richard and Simone. Simone left with his lawyer, and Richard hugged me and said he wanted to be alone and asked would I please take Mom home, because she was upset, too. So I did."

"And he disappeared after that?" Cate frowned, and Sarah raised a hand, as if to stave off the thought.

"It's not as weird as it sounds. Richard frequently went off alone, to think. He was a scholar, a philosophy major at Swarthmore. He thought about things." Sarah's eyes came alive with love. "He was internal, always pondering. That's why he liked computers so much. He was an intellectual. Not a man of action, or violence."

"He attacked somebody in open court, Sarah."

"Attacking isn't shooting to kill, Judge."

Cate smiled. *True, that.* "Where did he go, to think?"

"To temple, to the library, or sometimes the park. Off by himself. That's where I think he was when whoever it was killed Simone, outside the restaurant." Sarah raised her voice, vehement. "Richard would *never* do that! We didn't own a gun. Where did he get it?"

"Where everybody does. Bought it or got it off the street from somebody."

"We didn't know anybody who could get him a gun 'off the street'."

"But he was an assistant DA. Didn't he meet criminal types there?"

"No, he handled computer crime. He met geeks. And when did he buy this gun, supposedly? He rushed right out after court and bought it?"

"Why not?"

"He wouldn't even know how to fire a gun."

"It can't be hard," Cate said, though she had never fired one, either. "Too many dumb people are good at it."

"Judge, don't you see what I'm saying?" Sarah asked, newly urgent. "Don't you agree with me?"

"I don't know." Cate shook her head. "I see your point, I do. And even if I was agreeing, I don't know what I could do about it."

"Ask the police to reopen the case. I've already written them, and they refused. Maybe they would do it, if you asked. A federal judge, who heard the case."

An ex-federal judge, but you don't read the papers. "Forget the police, they won't do anything officially. They reopen cases for newly discovered evidence, not supposition."

"But Richard didn't do it, and the killer is still out there. Free."

"Tell you what, I've come to know Detective Nesbitt, who worked on the case. I'll bring it up with him and see what he thinks, unofficially. I'm sure I'll be talking with him later." *At least I hope I will be.*

"Thank you! Thank you!" Sarah jumped up and impulsively threw her arms around Cate, giving her a heartfelt hug. "I knew you would help."

"Please don't have any false hopes, though." Cate rose and hugged her back, then held her off, steadying her. "Hear me? You have to be realistic. Nesbitt believed his original theory and he has hard evidence to support it. I'm not sure your pregnancy changes anything for him, or anybody else."

"I know, I know, but I think it will. I pray it will."

"Chillax," Cate said, using as motherly a tone as she could muster, borrowing Nesbitt's expression, and Sarah laughed, her tone lighter than before.

"I can't, I'm so pleased." Sarah clapped her smallish hands with delight, and Cate started to worry she was getting carried away.

"You know, even if we manage to get them to reopen the case, which I swear we won't, it wouldn't bring Richard back."

"I know that," Sarah said, her expression growing suddenly serious. "That's not what I'm hoping for."

"What are you hoping for?"

"That his name is cleared. That the world knows he's not a killer, and that justice is done. I know it will never bring Richard back, but it will bring back my friends. My community. Look around you." Sarah gestured at the empty room. "I don't want to raise a baby like this, apart from community. I don't want people whispering about our family, or her father. Can you imagine what that does to a little girl?"

Uh, as a matter of fact, I can.

"People will whisper about him, about us, and it's unnecessary. Her father was a great man, and I don't want her raised knowing only lies about him, even if it protects her."

"Good girl!" Cate said, her heart speaking for her.

"Thank you. I don't want my baby to grow up thinking that her father was a murderer. Or that he committed suicide. I want her to know the truth about her father, that's the only way to truly know him. If you don't know your own father, how can you know yourself?"

Yikes. "How did you get to be so smart?" Cate asked, swallowing the lump in her throat.

And she couldn't help but think ahead.

CHAPTER 40

Cate turned up the heat on the well-behaved Acura and wound her way back through the neighborhood to City Line Avenue. She didn't want to be persuaded by sympathy for Sarah or by any resonance in her own life, but she had to admit that she was beginning to doubt that Marz had killed Simone, then himself. She opened her cell phone and pressed in the number, warming to the familiar voice, smooth as syrup on the end of the line.

"Judge Fante's chambers," Val said, and Cate wanted to hug her for her loyalty.

"Keeping my name alive. Thank you, Val."

"Judge, that you? I was so worried, after what I heard. We called the hospital up there but they said you were discharged. Aw, you okay? They said you were treated for smoke inhalation or some such."

"I'm fine. It was nothing."

"We're all thinking of you. The clerks are right here, breathin' down my neck, as usual." Val chuckled, and the clerks shouted, "Judge, Judge!" like little kids.

Cate smiled. "Tell them I said hi."

"She says hi, and settle down so I can hear," Val told them. "Judge, if you're so fine, why'd they keep you overnight? Where're you now?"

"Coming back to the city." The traffic light changed to green, and Cate fed the car some gas. "And how are you? How many job offers you get today?" In the background, Cate could hear the clerks yelling, "We miss you, Judge!"

Val laughed. "I don't want to work for another judge. It's so boring here, without you. Judge, one good thing, we only got two calls from the press, one from the *Daily News* and the other from the AP."

"They're forgetting me. Yay! Anything else I need to know?"

"No, I got it all in control."

"What happened to *Ickles v. Schrader*?"

"Sherman reassigned it to Meriden."

"Doesn't he have a trial this week, the case pig?" Cate traveled City Line, four lanes of stop-and-go traffic.

"You got that right, but he's trying to change his image. Today's his birthday, and he's taking everybody on the floor to lunch. Including me and the clerks."

"You?" Cate almost ran a red light. "My clerks? What's up with that?"

"I don't want to go, but I feel like we have to, to keep up appearances."

"You do. Go. Just don't have fun."

In the background, the clerks were shouting, "We're not going!"

Cate smiled. "Tell them to go. And don't embarrass the family."

"Done deal. By the way, you get that mail I sent you?"

"Yes, thanks."

"I got more here. All official, nothing personal. What was that little pink one, another prisoner letter?"

"No, from Richard Marz's wife. She doesn't think her husband killed Art Simone. You know what? Neither do I. I swear, the case against him stinks. Something's very fishy."

Val clucked. "Judge, don't you get involved. You're already in too deep, with that crazy cop trying to run you down like a dog."

"It's because he knows Marz didn't do it."

"Yes, he did. Marz did it. The man killed Simone and then himself. Judge, you listen to me, leave the investigating to the police. They got the right man, and it's over."

"Okay, Mom." Cate heard the clerks chirping, "What? What investigation?"

"Hush, you two!"

"Tell them I said good-bye and to be good at lunch. Call if you need anything."

"You better listen," Val said, and Cate switched lanes into the turn lane.

Heading for the expressway.

Cate introduced herself to the young receptionist, who snapped her moussed head up from her paperback, so wide-eyed that her liquid eyeliner disappeared.

"Judge Fante, well, please have a seat in the waiting area," the receptionist said, too genuine to hide her surprise.

"Thanks." Cate entered the faux-hip reception room. Two businessmen in suits occupied separate chairs, pointedly avoiding her eye. One talked too loudly on a cell phone, and the other read the *Inquirer*. Cate caught a glimpse of her own photo, staring back at her. Her face grew red, but she seated herself as if she weren't the town slut.

Green & Wachtel had undergone an extreme makeover since the old days, when it looked like the law firm where Ralph Lauren went to die. Its old mint-hued maps of colonial Philadelphia and scenes of fox-hunting in Chester County had been replaced by vast canvases of Self-Important Modern Art, abstract washes that made Cate think somebody had too much water in his tin of Crayola watercolors. Also gone were the burgundy-leather wing chairs with the shiny bullet tacks, and in their place stood massive sectional seats of black suede. Their color reminded Cate of coal slag, but she had Centralia on the brain.

"He'll see you now, Judge," the receptionist said, turning from her desk and motioning. "His office is that way, the last door on the hall."

"Thanks." Cate got up, squared her shoulders, and tried not to hear the receptionist pick up the phone as soon as she was out of earshot. She walked down the well-appointed hallway, completely aware that every secretary was staring as she passed. She had a lifetime of people whispering, and at the end of the hall, George Hartford was standing to meet her. His smile looked plastic, but it always did.

"Judge Fante, great to see you again," George said, at the door to his office, and Cate shook his hand. "Come in, come in. Can we get you some coffee?"

"Great. Cream and sugar."

"Easy, peasy." George signaled to one of the secretaries. "Jen, two with everything."

"Say 'please'." Cate paused as she entered the lawyer's immense office. "My mother was a secretary."

"Please?" George called after the secretary, who undoubtedly flipped his preppy ass the finger. "Please, sit down. Please."

"Thanks." Cate took a seat in the leather club chair opposite a supremely uncluttered mahogany desk. Ralph Lauren Home was still alive here; in fact, it was a knock-off compared to this office, which reeked of old Bryn Mawr. Real silver frames gleamed from retro black-and-white photos, and mahogany end tables shone with hand-rubbed finishes. Sunlight filtered through sheer muslin curtains in the windows, and even the dust mites wore penny loafers.

"Here we go!" George said brightly as a young secretary hurried in with china cups and saucers of aromatic coffee, which she placed on the end of the desk, on coasters. "Thanks so much, Jennifer," George said pointedly.

"You're welcome," the secretary said, stealing a glance at Cate before she left.

"See, I'm educable," George said with a stiff smile. "Old dog that I am." He wore a gray pinstriped suit and an Hermès tie of the palest blue. His dark blue shirt, of British birth, sported a white cutaway collar. But something about him was different.

"Don't you wear glasses, George?"

"Not anymore. I had my eyes lasered."

Can you say midlife crisis? Radial keratotomy is the new red Porsche.

"I lost only a few hours of work, and the procedure is remarkable. And I was made managing partner last week, did you hear?"

"Congratulations, and I hadn't heard. I've been too self-involved."

"So we *do* have something in common," George said with a sly smile, and Cate caught a lechy note in his voice.

"Then you are too old."

"Ha! Some would say I'm in my prime."

"You're not." *In other words, back off.*

George laughed, and Cate joined him so she could pretend she was kidding.

"George, I need a lawyer. A very good lawyer. You did a great job before me at trial, and after Beecker, this is the second-best law firm in the city."

"But still the most expensive."

Cate laughed, and George joined her, so they could pretend *he* was kidding. Lawyers were easy to get along with, once you knew how.

Cate said, "You've been following my troubles in the news, I'm sure."

"Yes, and after last night, I'm surprised to see you looking so well." George let his gaze run over her silk blouse. "What happened? Detective Russo tried to run you *over*? Is he a lunatic or what?"

"In short, he doesn't think that Richard Marz killed your client, Art Simone. He thinks I did."

George's new eyes widened. "That's absurd."

"Of course I didn't kill anybody. But what if he's half right, and Richard Marz didn't kill your client?"

"Impossible." George reared back, and his neck wattle chafed his white collar, with its edge stiff enough to cut hard cheese. "The police said they had videotape of Marz shooting him."

"It's not clear that it's Marz on the tape." Cate sipped her coffee and set it back down. "Take a second to tell me what happened that day, at dinner with Simone. You were with Simone at that dinner that night, right?"

"Yes. I told the police, in detail."

"So now tell me, your new favorite client."

George smiled, relaxing. "Well, after you ruled from the bench, we went to an early dinner at Le Jardin, on the riverfront. I knew that Art liked French restaurants and it was the only one we hadn't been to. I told him we were saving it for our victory dinner."

"Sure of yourself, huh?"

"I was right on the law. I know you weren't happy with the equities, but the legal principle was sound. I represented the principle."

"Let's not go there. Who was at the dinner?"

"Art, the jury consultant, and me."

"The jury consultant was the pretty redhead, with my taste in clothes?"

George chuckled. "Courtney Flavert."

"What about your associate, from the trial? She wasn't at dinner?"

"No. Let's put it this way, she has a brilliant legal mind." George laughed.

Nice. "What time did you get there?"

"Around four, as I recall. Early. We went straight from court."

"You took a cab or had a driver?"

"Cab. We couldn't all fit in one, so Courtney and I took one, and Micah and Art took the other."

A double date. "But Micah didn't go to the dinner."

"No, I think Art dropped her off, and took the cab on to the restaurant."

Cate made a mental note. "Do Courtney and Art know each other?"

"Yes, from working together. Art was very interested in the jury-selection process." George pursed his lips but still managed a smile. "Nothing untoward took place, if that's what you're suggesting."

"Of course not. I wonder why Micah didn't go to the dinner celebration. She was in court every day. Why wasn't she included?"

"Art didn't think of her that way. She was a glorified secretary."

Ouch. Cate let it go, but it still didn't square. "By the way, did you know that Simone was going to do a TV series based on me?"

"I had no idea, and I'm sorry about that." George frowned suddenly. "Hold on, Judge. It's not Art's estate or his production company that you want to sue, is it? Because of course, I'd be conflicted out of that. Though one of my partners might not be, if—"

"No, that's not who I want to sue. But back to the dinner, for a minute. Why did Art leave alone?"

"He had to catch an early plane back to the Coast."

"He flew commercial?"

"No, but he wanted to get back early, so he didn't stick around. He said he needed to be out by six, to catch his plane from the airport at seven-fifteen." George thought a minute. "We were having dessert, but he passed. He was on low-carb."

"Did you walk him out?"

"No. He went out alone."

Cate tried to picture the night of the murder. "Why didn't you walk him out, after dinner? He's a client."

"No reason to."

"He was a client. You met me at the door."

"You're a woman." George shrugged. "There was no reason to. He didn't invite that sort of friendship, nor did I. I didn't waste his time, and he didn't waste mine. We shook, we congratulated each other, he said 'Send me a bill,' and I said I would."

Boy intimacy. "You let him get a cab?"

"No, he said he had a car coming. He just excused himself and went out at six, as he'd said he would." George's light eyes clouded, a flicker of regret. "I wish I'd gone with him now, of course. I don't know if he would have been killed if a witness had been there."

"Or you could have been killed with him. After all, if the killer was Marz, presumably he'd have the same grievance against both of you."

"Evidently he didn't, and even the most aggrieved plaintiff distinguishes between lawyer and client."

"Not really." Cate considered it. "In fact, it makes me wonder why, if it were Marz, he didn't go into the restaurant to shoot you, too. He had to know you were there. Either he'd guess it or he followed you."

"I have no idea."

"It couldn't be because it would increase the risk of getting caught. Why worry about getting caught, if you're going to commit suicide, anyway?"

"I'm sure the police asked these questions."

Cate made a mental note. "Did Simone have any enemies besides Marz, that you know of?"

"Art Simone was an enormously successful Hollywood television producer. What do you think?" George smiled, but Cate didn't.

"Did he mention anyone specifically?"

"No."

"Ever hear him in an argument with anyone?"

"No."

"Do you know anything about his marriage?"

"Now wait a minute—"

"This is important. People are trying to run me over. I'm entitled to ask a few questions of my own."

"The police asked me all this."

"It's the police who tried to run me over," Cate shot back, and George paused.

"I think his marriage was fine. We never discussed it."

"Kids?"

"One, in France, studying art."

"Okay, back to that night. Please, finish the story."

"Then almost as soon as Art went outside, we heard a loud shot. The sound was unmistakable, a gunshot." George shuddered visibly. "We got up from the table, and the staff at the restaurant went running for the door, and there he was lying on the pavement." George wrinkled his nose. "It was really quite awful."

"Did somebody call 911?"

"Courtney did. I bent down to do CPR." George couldn't clear the disgust from his expression. "It was obvious he was dead. The bullet was point-blank in the forehead. Even in the dark, I could see that."

"Did you go to the funeral?"

"Yes, I flew in and out. It was very sad. His wife, bereft."

"Who invited you?"

"Erika called me personally. Lovely woman."

"Yes, I saw her on TV. Was Micah invited?"

"I have no idea. I didn't see her there."

"Was your associate invited?"

"Yes, but she had to work. We have another case going to trial next week and she had to draft some pretrial motions."

Cate thought back to her confrontation with Micah. It seemed like so long ago, in the *Attorneys@ Law* office. "*Erika wants to keep it small, so it's only immediate family.*"

"What about the jury consultant with the red hair?"

"Courtney Flavert? What about her?"

"Was she invited?"

"Yes."

So Micah had been excluded. Why? "She went?"

"Yes."

"Did you fly out together?"

"Yes." George looked away and reached for his coffee, taking two long sips and replacing the cup with a tiny *clink*. "Now, can we change the subject? This is so morbid. Why did you call me?"

"Wait, I'm just curious, was it a big funeral? Did you see any celebrities?"

George brightened. "It was huge, I would say three hundred people, and all the actors from the show, plus the cast of *The Sopranos*, and *Law & Order*, too. It was a real treat. I got Dennis Farina's autograph. The man reeks of credibility. He was a real detective, did you know that? Before he became an actor? He was great in *Crime Story*. Remember *Crime Story*?" George seemed to get happier, merely thinking of Dennis Farina. "Now, so, what is the representation you came to see me about?"

Cate had gotten all the information he could give her, so she switched gears. "I need you to go to war for me."

"I'd be honored to represent you." George smiled. "I did run a conflicts check and we're not conflicted out. We represent the *Inquirer*, but we don't represent the *Daily News*. Though they're owned by the same entity, they divide their legal work among all the top-tier firms."

"No, I'm not suing a newspaper. It's not a defamation matter. All of what they printed about me is true."

"Oh." George's eyebrows flew upwards, but at least he didn't point and laugh.

"As you probably read, the chief judge has effectively relieved me of duty, and I don't think he has the power to do that. It's a constitutional question, probably of first impression. Let me frame the issue for you—does the active sex life of an unmarried federal judge qualify as impeachable conduct within the meaning of Article III of the

U.S. Constitution?" Cate reconsidered. "Okay, to be fair, you probably have to include that some of my . . . paramours had criminal records."

"You want me to sue the chief judge of the Eastern District of Pennsylvania?"

"And the circuit executive, and the clerk of court." Cate thought a minute. "And the chief judge of the Third Circuit, on a *respondeat superior* theory, since he's essentially the administrative boss."

George reddened.

"I want my job back."

"I can't do it."

"Why not? Are you man or mouse?"

"Judge." George shifted in his comfy chair. "You have to understand."

"How can I?" Cate asked, angering. "You haven't explained it."

"I've headed this trial group for seven years. My partners are in front of that bench and those judges, all day long. Furthermore, I'm managing partner now. I represent three hundred and twenty-one lawyers, in this office alone."

"Good. I need a big gun, that's why I'm here. It's a cutting-edge legal question. It could go up to the Supremes. Let's make some law."

George shook his head. "I can't afford the retaliation factor. If I litigate against the chief judge, it's career suicide."

"Or it's protecting my right to my job."

"I can't do it." George sighed heavily and smoothed down his tie. "No big firm could, and none would. You can't fault me."

"So you're a mouse." Cate rose to her feet, not completely surprised, and walked the few steps to the door. "You'll beat up on a kid like Marz, but you won't take on a chief judge."

George rose, too, spreading open palms. "That's just reality, Judge."

"I thought you represented the legal principle."

"But this is different."

Cate turned on the threshold. "How?"

George blinked.

"Thought so," Cate said, and left. She was already feeling more herself, thinking of where to go next. Because as much as she missed her job, she had realized something she could never have known before she got fired, however unconstitutionally.

You don't need a robe to do justice.

CHAPTER 41

Odd. Despite the cold, the front door with the stenciled number 388 stood propped wide open with a brick, and Cate slipped through and climbed the stairs, almost banging into Micah as she descended, carrying a huge cardboard box that held papers and files, a chrome gooseneck desk lamp, and her white iBook.

"Judge?" Micah started behind the gooseneck lamp. "What are you doing here? I heard you were in the hospital, out of town somewhere."

"I was, but I'm fine."

"Detective Russo tried to kill you? That's so random!"

"Yeah, ain't it a bitch?" Cate smiled in a way she hoped was casual. "It's a long story. Meanwhile, what's going on here? You moving the office?"

"No, just me. I'm just not sure where yet. I'm out of a job." Micah's face fell, and the box slipped, but Cate grabbed the bottom.

"What happened?"

"Aw, they let me go." Micah's mouth made a flat line, devoid of lipstick, and she wore no eye makeup, either, revealing a clean look to her pretty brown eyes.

"Here, let me help you with the box. I'll back down slowly."

"Thanks." Micah righted the lamp, gathering up its see-through electrical cord, and Cate eased back downstairs. They reached the bottom, waddled through the open door with difficulty, and stutter-stepped onto the cold sidewalk, with the box between them. Micah nodded down the street, from her side of the box. "My car's the blue one, a few down. I got a great space."

"You lead." Cate let her go ahead, holding one side of the heavy box. "So how'd this come about, your being let go?"

"Gaone is cutting costs and he doesn't think the show needs anyone in Philly anymore."

"But *Attorneys@Law* has to be one of the most profitable shows on TV," Cate said as they inched down the street with the stuffed box between them. It wasn't the hard-hitting interrogation she had imagined, but she could make it work to her advantage. "Why do they need to cut costs?"

"Because he's a greedy jerk?"

And maybe this'll be easy. "But what about the Philly details? They give the show its realistic feel."

"He's willing to sacrifice that. He doesn't care about the quality of the production, only the bottom line." Micah's brown ponytail swung left and right as they walked along. She wore a navy down vest over a thick fisherman sweater and jeans, with her red Converse sneakers. "I heard some of the writers are getting fired, too. Isn't that terrible? Between crap like this and the new reality shows, there's no work for writers anymore. It's like all my friends are getting shoved out."

"That's a shame. A new broom sweeps clean, huh?"

"What?"

"It's an expression. It means when a new guy comes in, he brings in his own people and he kicks all the old guys out, even if they're good at what they do. It sounds like what's happening."

"Exactly." Micah nodded. "Here's my car. Can you hold the box while I get the keys?"

"Sure." Cate glanced over at the car, then did a double take, unable to hide her surprise. At the curb glistened a brand-new navy blue Mercedes, the two-door coupe. *Huh?* "This gorgeous creature is your car?"

"Yes."

"Wow! I'm jealous." Cate almost buckled under the weight of the box as Micah dug in her pocket, retrieved the keys, and aimed them at the parked car. The trunk lid sprang open on cue, and the women struggled to dump the box inside and position it on the black-carpeted bottom. Cate was already wondering how the child owned a nicer Mercedes than hers, especially since hers was now an accordion. "I thought you said you had a Saturn."

"No, *you* said I had a Saturn, with two years of payments." Micah managed a laugh, and so did Cate.

"I'm overruled."

"I'll say." Micah closed the lid and brushed off her hands. "Okay, that's everything except the plasma TV."

"That big one on the wall? They're giving you that?"

"They are now." Micah smiled bitterly.

"Will it fit in the car?"

"It'll have to. Can you help me carry it? I'd really appreciate it."

"I will, if you'll have coffee with me after. I'll tell you the story of how I almost got run over."

"Deal," Micah answered, her smile lingering unhappily.

"I guess I'm wondering about the night Art Simone was murdered," Cate said, after they'd both been brought a Niçoise salad that barely fit on the round Tuilleries-type table of greenish tin, at a neighborhood bistro pretending it was located in a chic arrondissement of Paris and not across from an electrical-supplies wholesaler.

"What about it?" Micah asked. She picked up her fork and speared a slice of hard-boiled egg.

Cate flashed on poor Sarah, sitting shiva by herself, at this moment. *We eat round food to symbolize the cycle of life.*

"I'm wondering why you weren't at the celebration dinner that night, after you'd won at trial. You were in court every day, and I saw you taking notes." Cate was treading a careful line between overt flattery and over-the-top flattery. She had no other way to get the information without the proverbial rubber hose. "I figured you were Simone's right hand, at least as important as a jury consultant, Courtney Whatever."

"I am. I mean, I was."

"So why weren't you there? They were, but you weren't."

"I'm not sure, to be honest," Micah answered, looking down as she ate. Her ponytail curled onto her shoulder. "Art said he thought it would be better if I weren't, and I accepted that. He asked me to get the files back in order after the trial, which I did, back at the office."

"All by yourself? Like Cinderella?"

"Exactly." Micah laughed, hurt.

So, no alibi. "But why did he ask you to do that then? It seems like it could have waited."

"Not for Art. He never waited for a thing." Micah looked up, meeting Cate's eye directly. "He wanted the decks cleared right away so we could get back to work, full-throttle. The lawsuit interrupted all of us and slowed the show's production. That's why I caved so fast when you threatened to sue me, that day in the office. Litigation sucks."

"I agree, but the cleanup could have waited a night, couldn't it? Isn't it possible that you were intentionally excluded from the dinner?"

"By Art?"

Yes. "Not necessarily. By anyone else who was there?"

"Why do you ask? Why do you even care?"

Cate felt at a momentary loss. "I'm trying to understand everything about that night. Because I'm not sure Richard Marz was the one who killed Art Simone."

"And you think I did?" Micah's eyes flared with a shock that looked genuine.

Maybe. "No. You worked for Simone, and were loyal to him, I can see that. I'm just trying to understand what really happened that night."

"The police know what really happened. Marz did it. They have him on security video, as if they needed that." Micah scoffed defensively. "He tried to kill Art right in front of you, in court!"

"Marz's wife doesn't think he did it."

"Of course, *she* wouldn't."

"But neither does Russo, who thinks I did it."

"You? That's ridiculous!" Micah said, incredulous. "Why would *you*?"

"Because I supposedly wanted to stop you and Simone from making a TV series about me."

"By *killing* Art? Ha! That wouldn't have stopped a single thing." Micah's eyes remained wide. "Look, Art is dead and they're making it without him, me, or any of our old writers. If there's money to be made, Hollywood makes it happen."

Cate tried not to think of Gina and Warren, on TV, Sunday nights at nine. "But you'd have to be in TV to know that for sure. So, back to this celebration dinner, did someone want you not to be there? Like the jury consultant?" Cate was making it up as she went along, but Micah leaned forward intently.

"How do you mean?"

"Do you think someone, let's say Courtney Flavert, asked Art not to have you there for some reason, when you rightly should have been?"

"Is that what you think?"

No. "Maybe. I'm trying to figure out her role. In my experience, jury consultants don't always stay so involved after the jury is empanelled. But she was there all the time at trial." Cate pressed ahead, putting her cards on the itsy-bitsy table. Sort of. "And, for example, I know that she was invited to Simone's funeral, and so was George Hartford."

Micah set her fork down, her lips parted slightly. "*Courtney* was invited to the funeral? That can't be right."

"It is."

"I can't believe Erika invited her. Are you sure?"

"Yes."

"How do you know?" Micah asked, the question a challenge that Cate was happy to meet.

"George Hartford told me. They flew out together."

"They *did*?" Micah's eyes narrowed to streetwise slits, and her forehead knit unhappily, if not downright angrily.

"Yes. You told me it wasn't supposed to be a big Hollywood funeral, but that's exactly what it was. All sorts of celebrities were there."

"I saw that on the news."

"If there was room for Courtney, there was room for you."

"That bitch!"

"Absolutely." Cate couldn't stop the questions. *What was going on? Was Micah sleeping with Simone? Had he bought her that delicious coupe? Had he dumped her after the trial, when she was no longer useful? Had Erika excluded her from the funeral because she suspected an affair?*

Micah was frowning. "Wait a minute. Why were you talking to George?"

"Confidentially, I was there to discuss my own legal trouble. I don't know if you heard, but I got fired, too. That's why I'm free today, to haul around plasma TVs."

"I did read that. Sorry."

"I thought I would be an episode already. 'Judges Behaving Badly Within the Meaning of Article III.'" Cate made quote marks in the air, and Micah cringed.

"Sorry. I'm off the show. The scripts I helped with are done." Micah looked sympathetic. "But you were a really good judge."

"The winners always think that."

"No, you cared."

"Bet you say that to all the judges." Cate faked a laugh. "Getting back to the point, George told me he stayed at the restaurant while Art went outside to catch his car. Who arranged for the car?"

"I did."

"What was the car service?"

"Alpha. They're good. We used them during the trial."

"It was due to pick him up at six to make it to the airport by seven-fifteen, for a private plane."

"Right."

"But the car got there a little late, in the rain. Simone was waiting out there alone when he was killed."

"Right, the traffic held up the driver."

Cate made a mental note to double check. "Who made the dinner reservations?"

"George did, or probably he had his associate or his secretary do it. He picked the restaurant, too."

Cate considered it. She couldn't see immediately what George Hartford would gain by killing his own client, unless George was messing around with the jury consultant and Simone had found out. Still, would Simone tell George's wife? No. And did it matter anyway, in one of those crusty upper-crust marriages? Cate thought of Prince Charles and Camilla, her only reference point for upper-crust marriages, since there weren't many in Centralia.

"So you actually think Marz didn't kill Art? But then why would Marz kill himself?"

"Maybe he didn't." Cate readied herself to watch Micah's reaction, since she was about to tell her everything. "Maybe somebody did it for him and made it look like a suicide."

Micah gasped. "You're kidding!" she yelped, then covered her mouth.

Ten out of ten on the Shock-O-Meter. "It's possible."

"Who would do that?"

"Whoever killed Simone."

"Why?"

"To set up Marz as the shooter. After all, Marz was easy to frame. He had attacked Simone in open court and lost a lot of money to him. He had motive and opportunity aplenty. Marz makes the perfect killer, except that I'm not sure he did it."

"You're like a real detective! That's incredible!"

"Tell me about it." Cate leaned over. "I'm asking you if you knew if George was having an affair with the jury consultant, Courtney. I mean, I'm not stupid."

"Honestly, yes," Micah answered, her tone ringing true. She leaned forward, only too happy to dish now that she'd been excluded from the funeral. Or perhaps because she could cast suspicion on someone else.

"Really?" Cate tried not to get excited. It only raised more questions. "How do you know?"

"It was obvious, from the day she was hired." Micah's eyes glittered. "Lots of touching, pats on shoulders, like that. And joking around. I think it's been going on a long time."

"Really. Where was she hired from?"

"The Flavert Agency, her own business. Courtney sells common sense for a hundred thousand dollars a pop."

Cate laughed.

"I told Art we shouldn't pay it, that I knew more about Philly than she ever could. But he didn't want to take any chances, and George insisted she was the best."

"Maybe she was," Cate shot back, and they both laughed like girlfriends. Then Cate asked suddenly, "Do you think she was sleeping with them both?"

"What? Who?"

"Courtney. The jury consultant."

"She was sleeping with George," Micah said testily.

"But was she sleeping with Art, too?"

"Of course not! What makes you say that?"

"It's obvious, isn't it? Art Simone was a very attractive man, with a lot of power and money. And Courtney was the one they both wanted at dinner." Cate paused, letting it sink in. "Remember the threesome plotline for the first episode of the new TV series? The one you told me about? The two judges and a law clerk, in a ménage à trois?"

"Right, the pilot," Micah answered, her face reddening in a way that told Cate she'd struck a chord, however accidentally.

"Yes, the pilot. Two men and a woman. Whose idea was it for the threesome plotline? Yours or Art's?"

"Art's."

"So is life imitating Art, or is Art imitating life? No pun intended." Cate managed another fake laugh, but Micah looked stricken.

"But . . . Art would never cheat like that."

On you. "On his wife, you mean."

"Right. On his wife."

Bingo. "We'll never know, will we? And we know Art got his ideas from his life. Isn't that what he testified to, on the stand? Remember?"

Micah reached for her water glass with a hand that trembled. Cate knew that Micah and Simone were having an affair. The girl's reaction to the threesome clinched it—and the incredible Mercedes. Micah had thought she was Simone's mistress; she never figured he'd cheat on his mistress with another mistress. Which left Cate with yet another question.

And a thought about someone who might know the answer.

CHAPTER 42

Cate could hardly wait for Micah to go before she called information on her cell phone, got the number, and waited for the call to connect as she ran to her car in the cold.

"Flavert Associates," said a woman's voice.

"Yes, is Courtney in?"

"She's on vacation this week. May I ask who's calling?"

"No, thanks." Cate flipped her phone closed, in frustration. She would have loved to have cornered Courtney and gotten confirmation of her theory. She had learned so much. She felt like she was getting close to something. She reached her car, dug in her bag for the keys, and got in, eventually finding her way out of the parking lot and onto the street, where she stopped.

Commuters flooded the street in front of her car, moving en masse toward buses, parking lots, and the train station, wrapped in heavy mufflers and ski hats like wool envelopes. Night had fallen, the rush-hour traffic tangled into lanes of red taillights, and plumes of white exhaust rose above the cars, an urban version of the toxic fumes of Centralia. Smoke obscured everything lately, and suddenly nothing was clear. Marz. Marz's wife. Micah. Cate flipped open her phone, pressed in the number, and the call connected.

"Homicide," said a man's deep voice, which Cate recognized with an undeniable thrill.

"Nesbitt?"

"Judge, what're you doing? You didn't return my calls. I've been wondering."

Aww. "Sorry." Cate was kicking herself.

"You're stirring up a hornets' nest about the Simone case. I'm getting calls about you. Where are you?"

Have to do something about that "Judge" part. "Back in the city."

"Listen, a girlfriend of Marz's wife called, from the temple choir. She's asking me to reopen the case. How did the alto section of Beth Hillel get in on this act?"

Oops. "Maybe from Sarah Marz? She was making a lot of sense today."

"You spoke with her?"

"We sat shiva." Cate waited for her turn to leave the lot, but the traffic was unending.

"Judge, I'm not gonna reopen this case."

"Maybe I'll change your mind."

"No, you won't. George Hartford called, too, from whatever law firm. He also called my sergeant, on top of it. He doesn't want you nosing around in Simone's murder, and I don't blame him."

"How's Russo?"

"Out of the woods. They moved him to HUP."

"He's at Penn?" Cate felt a tingle of excitement. Penn's hospital was twenty blocks west. It was too good to be true.

"Wait a minute. Don't even think about going. He's dangerous, and it's not procedure."

"I'd never go see him. He tried to kill me." Cate flicked on the turn signal to make a left turn, then finally saw her opening in traffic and seized it, heading west toward the hospital. "Where are you?"

"I'm in the northeast, on a job. A double homicide."

"Sounds grim." *And an hour away*.

"I should go. Call you later, Cate."

"Great."

Cate.

It took her half an hour in rush-hour traffic to travel the five miles to the Hospital of the University of Pennsylvania in West Philly, and another twenty minutes to find a parking space in one of the clogged-to-capacity lots. Cate hustled from the Acura, her thoughts churning and her emotions racing ahead. Hard to believe she was visiting the man who had tried to kill her only the night before, but he had to have some valuable information on Marz. Cate kept an image of Sarah Marz in mind to motivate her. She prayed that Russo could answer some of her questions.

And also that she was mature enough not to pull his plug.

An impossibly young uniformed cop sat outside the door to Russo's hospital room, reading the sports page, which he lowered when Cate presented herself, apparently not recognizing her. "Can I help you?"

"How's the patient?"

"Fine, sleeps mostly."

"Is Steve Nesbitt here?"

"Detective Nesbitt? He was here earlier but got beeped and left."

"Oh, right, that job in the northeast." Cate kept her tone even, so she could sound in the know and vaguely masculine. "I'm Cate Fante, to see Detective Russo."

"Fante? I know that name, from somewhere," the cop said, thinking aloud. "You're the judge—"

Eek. "Ex-judge. I'm acting as Russo's lawyer now. Nesbitt said he'd put me on the list, in case he didn't get back in time."

"List?" The cop smiled uncertainly, his teeth perfectly white and even, as if his braces had just come off. "I don't have a list."

"You're supposed to." Cate scowled. "Russo has a right to counsel,

Officer. You can't deprive the man of his constitutional rights just because you lost the list Nesbitt gave you."

"He didn't give me a list."

"He told me he did. You calling Nesbitt a liar?"

"No, never, Nesbitt is—"

"Here." Cate fished in her purse for her cell, flipped it open, and pressed DIALED CALLS. "That's his cell number, right there. Don't make me call him. He's on a double homicide and very busy. You don't want to interfere with him, do you?"

"No."

"Quick. Pat me down. Russo pays by the hour." Cate dropped her purse and raised her arms, and after a minute, the cop rose, folded the sports page, and set it down on his hard-plastic bucket chair.

"Well, okay, seeing as how he said it's okay." The cop ran his hands lightly over Cate's coat and in her pockets, then slipped his hands underneath and patted down her body.

"Wanna check my purse?"

"Sure, thanks." The cop turned around and dug inside the bag, then handed it back.

"Thank you," Cate said, slipping inside the wide wooden door.

And letting it close behind her.

CHAPTER 43

Cate eyed Russo as he slept, taking evil satisfaction in the extent of his injuries. An ugly Frankenstein gash ran down his left cheek, which was covered with skin-toned butterfly things, and a large pink-red egg swelled in the middle of his Cro-Magnon forehead, like a third eye. His greasy black hair had been shaved in a reverse Mohawk; a scalp-deep strip improvised to accommodate a white gauze bandage that wound sideways around his head, completely covering his left ear. His left arm lay in a light blue cotton sling, his right hand in a gauze bandage like a ping-pong paddle, and his knee, lying outside the blanket, was held rigid by a steel brace with navy blue padding. All told, Russo formed a bandaged, if brawny, mound in the white cotton sheet, and an overgrown thicket of dark chest hair sprang from the collar of his gown, like the Black Forest come to Philly.

Cate approached the sleeping man and put her face close to his good ear. "FIRE! FIRE! WAKE UP! EMERGENCY!"

"Ah!" Russo's puffy eyes flew open in alarm. He tried to get up, grimacing. "Oww!"

"Just kidding!"

"Wha?" Russo blinked in pain, propped lopsided on his good arm.

"Recognize me, Detective? Or should I run away and scream?"

"Ahh. Owww." Russo blinked a few more times, then sank back into the thin pillow. His voice sounded hoarse, hopefully from a tube they'd stuck down his throat. Dry.

"It's me, Judge Fante."

"The killer judge."

"Once again, you're half right. I must say, you got what you deserved, and I do excellent work." Cate clucked over his ugly wounds. "You're single, right? Better get used to it."

"What're you doin' here?"

"Came to say hi." Cate plunked herself down next to his swaddled form, bumping him roughly aside. "Make room, would you?"

Russo moaned. "Ow, stop it."

"Oops. Sorry. Did I hurt you?" Cate give him another bump. "Yikes! I got crazy hips tonight!"

"Keep it up and I'll call the uniform."

"Do that. Tell on me." Cate flashed on the swing of his car headlights, aimed right at her. "Doesn't it itch like crazy under those casts, or are you in too much pain to feel it? They say, first comes the pain, then comes the itching. Maybe bedsores. Boils, too. Barnacles. Carbuncles. Pestilence. Maybe your nose will fall off."

"Bitch."

"Feeling's mutual." Cate bounced on the bed until he grimaced again. "Get well soon, would you? So we can lock your ass in jail."

"You killed Rich."

"No, I didn't, you idiot, but I don't think it was suicide, either. Look how much we have in common. I'm so glad you asked me out."

"If I could move, I'd kill you with my bare hands."

"If you could move, I wouldn't have done my job."

Suddenly there was a rattling in the hall, and they both looked over. The door was being opened by the uniformed cop, holding it ajar for a short attractive woman in a white uniform with a nameplate that read, JULIE WILLIAMSON. She was pushing a tall metal cart with shelves for dinner trays. She grabbed a tray from the cart and scooted into the room with it. "Hello, you two!" the woman sang out, carrying a green plastic tray on which sat a plate of roasted chicken beside a spreading pool of mashed potatoes and olive green peas, puckering as they cooled.

"It's about time," Russo grumbled, and Cate stood up.

"Here, let me help."

"Thanks a lot," the woman said gratefully, handing off the tray and hurrying back out to her cart. The uniformed cop nodded, then let the door close.

Cate turned to Russo with the tray. "Hungry?"

"Yeah."

"Me, too. Another thing we have in common. We're made for each other. You complete me."

"Gimme my dinner."

"In a minute."

"What the hell is your problem?"

"I need information. Tell me why you think Marz didn't kill himself, and don't give me all the soft stuff, like that he wasn't that kind of guy. Give me hard evidence. Make your best argument. Sell me."

"Who're *you* kidding? This some game you're playing? You hired the scum to kill him and Simone."

"Like I said, I don't think Marz killed himself. I met his wife and she convinced me, but that's not evidence. You oughta help me out, since only one of us is mobile enough to catch the bad guy. Now answer my question and I'll give you your dinner."

"Not enough blowback for a suicide," Russo answered gruffly. "I don't get you, lady."

"What's blowback? I've heard the term, but I don't really know what it means."

"Blowback's the blood and tissue that gets on your hand when you shoot yourself. The explosion blows it back on your hand." Russo shifted in bed, wincing. "Rich shoulda had a lot of blowback. He had some, but not as much as I woulda thought. Or other suicides have."

"So?"

"So that means somebody else got the blowback. It's proof that your man put his hand over Rich's and pulled the trigger. The hand on top blocks the blowback."

Cate visualized the gruesome scene. "Like a stencil. How do you know how much blowback to expect?"

"Judgment call. Rich had stippling, so I would expect more blowback."

"What's stippling?"

Russo sighed theatrically. "Why you playing this game? You're a freak, you know that?"

"What's stippling? Your chicken's getting cold."

"Tattooing from the gunpowder, against the temple. Looks like a starburst. Shows that the gun was fired at close range. Gun fired that close should produce a lot of blowback. This didn't. So your guy tripped up." Russo's injured face twisted. "He fooled them but he can't fool me."

"Right. You're a genius, that's why you drove off a cliff. Now tell me this, Einstein. Why would Marz let somebody put their hand over his and shoot him?"

"He was drunk. Anybody coulda done it."

"He was drunk?" Cate asked, surprised. "I hadn't heard that."

"We smelled it on him. We found booze in the car. The test'll come back with levels, if it's not back already."

Cate considered it. "Still, it's consistent with suicide."

"That's what Nesbitt says, but I know Rich. He drank on the sly. His liver would show it. I guarantee the autopsy shows it." Russo tried to lift his head but couldn't. "Gimme my dinner!"

"He drank?"

"Hid it real well, but I know the signs. I used to be a drunk myself. He popped Altoids and got lost for a stretch now and then."

Cate thought of what Sarah had said. *Richard frequently went off alone, to think.* "Did you ever confirm this with him?"

"Huh?" Russo seemed to grow suddenly tired and almost cooperative.

"Did you ever ask Marz if he drank?"

"No."

"Why not?"

"He's an Orthodox Jew. What do you think he's gonna say? I want my dinner!" Russo raised his head, then gave up and put it back down again. "Why you askin' these questions? Why'd you come anyway? Get outta here." Russo shouted, "Yo, rookie! Rookie!"

The door opened, and the young cop stuck his head inside. "Yes, Detective?"

Russo pointed at Cate. "Get her outta here. She's got my dinner."

"He's delusional, he'll be fine," Cate said, getting up, shooing the cop out, and closing the door behind him. She rolled the tray to Russo and folded her arms. "Here's your dinner, you big baby. *Buon appetito.*"

Russo blinked, or at least his swollen eyes twitched.

"Aw. Can't you feed yourself?"

Russo dropped his bandaged head backwards into the pillow.

"What a pity. Didn't think of that, did you?"

"Please, God," Russo said to the ceiling.

"You're breakin' my heart. Any other evidence?"

"Are you serious?" Russo's eyes slid to Cate. "You know you hired that guy to do it."

"Wrong. What else you got? That delicious meal sits right in front of you and you can't even eat a bite. That's ironic."

"I'll fix you." Russo lifted his head, fumbled for the call button, and pressed it with a thumb. "The nurse'll come. She'll feed me."

"Not gonna happen. They're busy. I know, I was just out there."

"We'll see about that." Russo kept pressing the button.

"Why don't you ask the Boy Wonder at the door? Maybe he'll feed you."

"That's too gay."

So enlightened. "You're going to prison. Think of it as orientation."

Russo stopped chuckling.

"Tell me about the videotape. You've seen it. Why don't you think it's Marz?"

"I could just tell. The guy on the videotape didn't walk like Rich. Rich walks fast. The guy in the cap walked slow."

"He was going to shoot somebody. Maybe he needed to take aim."

"Not point-blank. It wasn't Rich."

"Let me ask you a question. Could it have been a woman?"

Russo paused. "Possible."

Micah.

"But it wasn't. It was the guy you hired." Russo kept pressing the call button.

"Where did Marz go after the verdict?"

"To get loaded."

"How do you know?"

"I watched him, I knew his habits. He had his routines, we all do, especially drunks. When things went bad with the writing, or we got another rejection letter, he'd disappear."

"You know where?"

"No."

"Another woman?"

"No. The bottle."

Cate considered it. "You said they found booze in the car. What else did they find?"

"The gun, and that's another thing."

"Tell me."

"It was a revolver, a Rossi. Looked new, like it was bought in a store."

"Okay, what's wrong with that? Rich wouldn't have been able to buy a gun from the street, even his wife said that."

"I checked the two gun shops in town, the one in Old City and one in South Philly. Neither had sold to Marz."

"Maybe he bought it in the suburbs."

"I checked ten others in the area, none of them had, either. Also, the gun we found in the car had the serial number filed down, so it couldn't be traced. Why would Rich do that, if he was going to shoot himself?"

"Maybe when he shot Simone he didn't know if he'd shoot himself."

"Rich didn't even know enough about guns to scratch off the serial number. I had to tell him those things for the scripts. He didn't know anything about guns. In one of his first drafts, he had a revolver with a safety on."

"So?"

"Revolvers don't have safeties."

"I knew that." *But Micah could have bought the gun and filed the number off. And she'd know about doing that from the TV show.* "So what else did they find on him? A wallet?"

"Yes."

"Cell phone?"

Russo stopped. "I don't remember."

Bet not. Cell phones show who called you last. Cate pulled her chair over to the bed, picked up the fork from the dinner tray, and stabbed a piece of white meat.

"Come on, Judge. Gimme a break." Russo raised his raspy voice. "I'm starvin' here."

"Shut up." Cate found the foot pedal, raised the top half of the bed, and stuck the chicken in Russo's face. "Eat this before I stab you."

"This a trick?" Russo peered down at the chicken, his bruised chin going triple.

"Eat!"

Russo took a bite and chewed, wincing as he swallowed.

And just at that moment, the door to the hospital room burst open.

CHAPTER 44

"You're throwing me out?" Cate asked, astounded, as Nesbitt hurried her down the hospital corridor, gripping her by the elbow. She'd imagined getting physical with him, but this wasn't the fantasy.

"You're damn right I am." Nesbitt's graying bangs blew back off his forehead, his trench coat billowed open, and his wool tie took flight. "I cannot believe you, *Your Honor.*"

"Slow down." Cate was whizzed around the nice lady with the dinner cart, like a Ferrari switching into the fast lane.

"Suck it up." Nesbitt wouldn't even look at her, leading with his chin like the prow of a battleship. "I cannot believe that you did that."

"If you'd stop, I'd explain."

"I want you out of this building as soon as possible."

"I learned a lot in there, and today. Stuff you should know, if you don't already, which you probably do and kept from me." Cate was confusing even herself. It was hard to make sense at this speed.

"What were you thinking?" Nesbitt seemed not to hear, hustling Cate past pastel landscapes, her heels clattering across the glistening floor. He said, "Russo is a danger to you. He thinks you killed his friend and got away with it."

"His instincts are right. Marz didn't do it."

"Did you forget already? The man tried to run you over last night. You were admitted to a hospital."

"Only for observation."

"You were unconscious. You inhaled toxic fumes."

"I've been breathing that stuff since I was little."

"Maybe *that's* why you're crazy." Nesbitt snorted, propelling her onward. "I opened that door and couldn't believe my eyes. You were right there, not a foot from him. Leaning over the bed, talking to him, *feeding him*."

"I took pity."

"You took your life in your hands. The man knows how to fight, to kill. He's trained law enforcement, remember? They teach us those things at the academy. In fact, we don't graduate clue school unless we learn it." Nesbitt's grip tightened as he steered her past a set of wooden chairs. "Get the connection?"

"He was lying in a bed. He's got bandages out the wazoo. He couldn't do anything to me."

"Of course he could. He's got a few broken bones. He's a little medicated. You think that would stop Russo?"

"He can't even feed himself."

"You're a small woman. He was scamming you."

"No, he wasn't, and after all, he didn't hurt me. All's well that ends well."

"I told you not to go see him and you did."

You're not the boss of me, Cate thought but didn't say, because it would make her sound immature. Then she reconsidered. "You're not the boss of me."

Nesbitt rolled his eyes, on the run. "I'm the boss of *him*. Russo. He's my prisoner. It's my case."

Cate caught a blurry glimpse of an older patient, tossing in his bed. "Shhh. This is a hospital. People are trying to sleep."

"Russo is in police custody." Nesbitt lowered his voice to Controlled Fury. "That cop outside the door isn't there to protect Russo from the world. He's there to protect the world from Russo. You lied, and that cop happens to be my nephew."

He's got a lot to learn.

"I told my sister, the kid can't cut it, but does she listen to me? No. Does anybody listen to me? No. That kid is gonna get somebody killed someday."

"Don't blame him. I wasn't in danger."

"You were, too. You're like my daughter. I tell her, close your purse, but she always leaves it open. You know why I say that? Because I'm a cop. And I know that if she keeps leaving her purse open, sooner or later she's gonna get her wallet stolen. But does she listen to me?"

"No?"

"No. But this is worse than purses. This is like driving drunk. You're in danger and you don't even know it. You think you're invincible, that it can't happen to you, when you're just *lucky* it didn't." Nesbitt spotted the elevator bank and made a beeline for it. "You're just *lucky* that Russo didn't wrap his hands around your throat and strangle the ever-livin' life out of you. Or snap your neck. It woulda been quiet and deadly. Over in a split second, nobody the wiser. Before my nephew finished the box scores."

Cate shuddered. "Kind of graphic, Nesbitt."

"You think it doesn't happen? You think nice ladies don't get strangled?" Nesbitt's voice got louder again. "It happens. I just left a murder scene in Tacony. A young wife and a three-year-old, a little girl, strangled to death by the husband. It happens every goddamn day."

Cate heard the anguish in his tone, and suddenly it wasn't funny anymore. Nesbitt punched the DOWN button for the elevator, and they both fell quiet as a woman nurse wearing a loose, patterned uniform passed by, eyeing them curiously. Her shoes squeaked as she walked away, emphasizing the abrupt silence between them. The elevator arrived and the stainless-steel doors slid open, and they stepped into the long rectangular cab without a word. The doors closed, sealing them inside.

"Look, I'm sorry." Cate hit the scratched-up button for the ground floor. "It's just that I felt like I was getting close to something."

"You might've messed up my case against him, too," Nesbitt said, after a minute. He shook his head. "You're the victim, asking questions of a suspect in custody. What a frigging mess."

"It shouldn't affect the case. I didn't interrogate him. We didn't talk about what happened in Centralia. We talked about Marz and Simone."

"That doesn't matter." Nesbitt kept shaking his head. "The issue is what he'll say you asked him. He had no lawyer present. Better yet, you *posed* as his lawyer. This is so against procedure, there *is* no procedure. No precedent. I told you, I'm a by-the-book kinda guy. I gotta tell the ADA, and my case against him might be out the window."

"What happened to me doesn't really matter. What matters is what happened to Marz and Simone. Because somebody killed them and got away with it."

Nesbitt's head snapped up, his brown eyes flared. "No, they didn't. Marz killed Simone and he's dead."

"Don't be so sure. If you'd let me tell you what I—"

"And what do you mean, it doesn't matter what happened to you? Russo's guilty of attempted murder. We have procedures. *Laws.*" Nesbitt looked stricken, his mouth opening, forming a circle like an open wound. "I can't believe I'm saying this to *you*, a *judge.*"

"You are, and for once, I'm using my judgment. Russo wasn't a menace to society, he was a menace only to me, because he thinks I killed his friend. And Russo isn't the point, Marz is. Simone is. For the first time in a long time, I feel like I know what I'm doing. We have to find out who killed Simone and Marz and bring them in."

"We *know* who killed them!" Nesbitt raised his voice again. "That case is cleared because I cleared it. You're not a detective. I am."

The elevator doors opened onto a wide-eyed group of people, who'd evidently been able to hear the argument. Cate flushed and Nesbitt gestured her out without another word. They headed through the crowd for the exit doors, feeling a chilly blast that came only partly from the doors being opened and closed. People streamed out, tugging on knit hats, buttoning up winter coats, and wrapping themselves in overlong mufflers before they hit the sidewalk. A couple of teenagers came in, carrying white bags of McDonald's that trailed the warm scent of fresh French fries.

"Where're you parked?" Nesbitt asked calmly, when they got outside to the sidewalk. She walked next to him, their shoulders distant, their footsteps hitting the cold concrete on the way to the parking lot. "I'll walk you to your car."

"That's nice of you."

"No, it isn't. I want to make sure you leave."

Or not. Cate's mouth went dry. "In the lot across the street, at the hotel."

Nesbitt held a hand up to stop a station wagon and waved Cate across the street.

"If you'd listen, I could tell you what I learned today, from Sarah Marz and George Hartford."

"I don't want to hear it."

"You might be persuaded."

"I won't be. I don't want to hear it."

"Fine."

"Good."

Cate crossed the median slightly behind Nesbitt, feeling hollow inside. The night had fallen a frigid, starless black, the moon hiding. The massive concrete Civic Center sat on her right, an empty edifice looming in the dark, and the University Museum was on her left, with its ornate dome designed by Frank Furness, oddly exotic in this

American cityscape. The Penn Hotel lay straight ahead, a tall column
of bright yellow windows, and the garage was off to its right.

Cate said, "You know Micah Gilbert, Simone's assistant? I think
she did it."

Nesbitt kept walking.

"I think she had an affair with Simone, and he ended it when the
trial was over. In fact, the moment the trial was over. And she was
hurt and angry, and went and shot him. Then she set Marz up for
the murder. He would be the perfect candidate, given what had happened in the courtroom, and he was drunk enough that she could
overpower him."

"How would she know where Marz was?"

"She called him on his cell. Marz had a cell phone and he wasn't
found with it on him. Micah had access to Simone's files, so she would
know Marz's cell number."

Nesbitt didn't respond.

"I think she called Marz and said she had to meet him. That she
had something important to tell him, maybe inside information
that would help in an appeal. Or just good, old-fashioned dirt on
Simone."

"Can you walk a little faster? I want to get back to Russo, Judge."

Judge. I've been demoted. "What do you think of my theory?"

"You don't wanna know."

"Yes, I do."

"I think you're wrong and I'm right."

Hmph. "Well, I think I'm right and you're wrong."

"Great."

"Fine." Cate buttoned her coat against the cold. She must have
been crazy to think anything could happen between them. If he had
been interested in her, he certainly wasn't any longer. Anyway, they
were too different by nature, and now they stood on opposite sides
of the fence. She followed him onto the sidewalk, crossing to the en-

trance to the parking garage. Nesbitt's slowing cadence posed a tacit question.

Cate answered, "I'm on the first floor."

"What're you driving?"

"A rental." Cate walked ahead, and Nesbitt let her pass, his features impassive in the semidarkness. A group of businesspeople came out of the lot, laughing and talking, a fluorescent light flickering like an inner-city strobe on their padded shoulders and cashmere topcoats. Cate led the way to her car, digging in her purse on the fly. She found her keys with less rummaging than usual, stopped at the back fender of the Acura, and looked up at Nesbitt, who eyed her, his mouth tilted down unhappily.

"This you?" he asked.

"Yes. Thanks for the walk."

"Stay outta trouble, Judge." Nesbitt turned on his heel, his trench coat catching a cold blast as he walked away, the soles of his shoes scuffing the gritty concrete of the parking lot.

So be it. Cate didn't watch him go, keeping the melodrama to a minimum. She chirped the car open and got inside. The interior was freezing, the leather seats chilly against the back of her legs. She turned the key in the ignition, backed out of the space, and went up the ramp to find the exit sign, in that counterintuitive way of parking lots, then drove down to the exit. She stopped at the white kiosk, equipped with crappy TV, paid the fee to a young cashier talking on a cell phone, and was about to drive forward when her headlights swung onto the figure of a man.

Nesbitt.

Cate slowed to a stop, and Nesbitt hurried toward her car, yanking open the passenger-side door, folding himself into the seat, and turning to her.

"I'm sorry I treated you that way," Nesbitt said, his tone still louder than usual. "I do want to hear what you think you learned, but not now. I'm too pissed off to hear you now." Nesbitt met her eye in the semidarkness. "If you want, when I calm down, maybe by tomorrow night, I can take you to dinner and we'll talk all about your theory. How's that?"

Whoa. "Are you asking me on a date?"

"What do you think? You think I *like* to follow you all over creation?" Nesbitt threw up his hands. "You think I like driving after you to your friend's? To the hospital? You think I went up to Centralia for my *health*?"

Cate felt a warm rush of emotion. Nesbitt was really sweet. And he knew the whole truth about her, all that awful stuff, and he still wanted to date her. For a minute, Cate didn't know what to say.

"This is more than a job to me, obviously," Nesbitt said, his tone softer. "You know that. *You're* more than a job to me. I care about you. I hate what you're going through, what you've been through." Nesbitt paused, looking at her. "Maybe we can have some dinner?"

Cate felt her throat catch. "Yes."

Nesbitt smiled. "Excellent."

It fell suddenly quiet in the car. They sat together in near darkness. Nesbitt's face was one foot from hers. Cate could feel him breathe. She suddenly realized she knew nothing about romance. He should be kissing her, but he wasn't. "Aren't you gonna kiss me?" she asked, after a minute.

Nesbitt grinned. "Not yet," he answered as he turned away, opened her car door, and climbed out, leaning over and peeking through the open door, letting in a gust of cold air.

Cate laughed, surprised.

"Pick you up tomorrow night at eight. Good night." Nesbitt closed the door and gave it a slap, and Cate laughed again, then gave him a wave as she drove away.

She hit the street and turned left, heading back toward the city, feeling happy and excited. She was definitely on to something, after what she had learned from Russo. She knew the next logical step to take. If she could find out more, then she'd have more of a case to present tomorrow night, to get Nesbitt to reopen. She had a lot to do and she felt oddly adrenalized. Maybe because she was getting closer to the real killer, or because she was proving Nesbitt wrong. Or maybe it was Nesbitt's not-a-kiss.

She hit the gas.

CHAPTER 45

PISTOL RANGE IN REAR, read the blue neon sign, and Cate pulled up in front of the gun shop just as a man was locking the door. She had come straight to the gun shop in Old City and had gotten here just in time. If Micah were going to buy a gun, this had to be the place. The shop was only blocks from her office and apartment.

Cate switched off the ignition and jumped out of the car, shouting, "Excuse me! Please don't close!"

"What?" The man turned from the door, his steel key ring still in the lock. A security spotlight shone above him, showing an immensely beefy six-footer. The man's head was shaved, his bumps in bas-relief under the bright light, and he wore only a red Sixers windbreaker, despite the cold.

"Please! Wait!" Cate dashed around the car to the big man. Traffic rushed behind them on four lanes.

"Lady, you need a gun that bad?"

"Uh, yes, I do." Cate wanted information, not weaponry, but she hadn't had time to get a story in order. His assumption was as good as any. "Yes, I need a gun."

"Wait a minute." The man looked down at her. Up close, he looked about thirty years old, with large dark eyes and thick lips with a scar that vanished when he smiled, like now. "I know you. You're that judge, been in the papers."

Rats. "Yes, that's me." Cate introduced herself and stuck out her hand, and he shook it without crushing it.

"Lou Behrens."

"Pleased to meet you, Lou." Cate had to find a way to use it to her advantage. "So then you know that I've been getting a lot of publicity. My house was broken into, and I need protection. I can't go another night without a gun." She tried to sound like a damsel in distress, which she had seen on TV. "I feel so unsafe. Please, can you stay open a little? I won't take long, I promise."

"Well, okay," Lou answered, his voice softer, and Cate started to think sexism had been getting a bad rap.

"Thanks so much. I appreciate it."

"But you can't buy a gun and start blastin' away, you understand." Lou twisted the key ring in the lock, setting it jingling, and opened the front door. "You have to take lessons. Learn firearm safety. We have classes on Saturdays and some weeknights."

"I will, I will. I just want to have a gun tonight, so I can sleep better. Just in case."

"Come on in, let's see what we can do for you." Lou flicked the switch, turning on old-fashioned fluorescent lights. He ushered Cate inside, then closed the door behind her and headed toward a doorway on the left. "Wait here while I turn off the burglar alarm."

"Sure, thanks." Cate looked around at a rectangular store that seemed almost stop-time. Old glass display cases framed with real wood flanked the room on either side, and ancient red-and-black linoleum tile covered the center aisle. On the right wall hung an array of dusty flags, a faded blue one that read COLT and next to it a sun-bleached yellow for RUGER. Under the flags, at least fifty antique guns had been mounted on cheap pegboard, leading to a rack of modern rifles lined butt down in the back, next to a room closed off with bars and padlocks. The air smelled vaguely of dirt and stale cigarettes, like a hardware store with attitude.

"Step over here, Judge," Lou said, reemerging from the doorway. He set the store keys on the glass top with a clatter and went behind the counter on the left. A grimy cash register sat at the end of the counter, and the wooden shelves behind were filled with stacks of colorful boxes that read American Eagle, in cherry red and white; Winchester, in tomato red; and Remington, in kelly green and chrome yellow. It looked like a cute and cheery display until Cate realized the boxes contained bullets. She shuddered, thinking of the heat that had whizzed past her cheek last night. It reminded her of her purpose.

"So what's a good gun for girls?"

"A girl gun?" Lou smiled, his scar dissolving into sweetness. "You mean pink? Or like these with the mother-of-pearl handle?" He waved a hand at some smaller guns, their whitish handles shining with opalescence.

"I mean a gun you'd sell to a woman, for example." Cate leaned over the counter, which displayed an array of guns on top of their boxes. She skimmed the brands: Beretta, Colt, Rossi. *Rossi.* That was the gun that was the murder weapon. She remembered the name because it sounded like Russo. "What do you think about those Rossi guns?"

"The revolver? Good choice." Lou reached for the keys, unlocked the back of the counter door, and plucked the gun from the top of its blue box. He pocketed the keys, brought out the gun, set it on the counter in front of Cate. "This is a good basic gun. It would be a fine choice for you."

"Revolvers don't have safeties," Cate said, for lack of something better. How could she find out if Micah had bought this gun from him?

"Don't worry about that. You don't need a safety on a revolver. It takes some doing to squeeze off a shot. Check it out for yourself. Pick it up and squeeze."

Cate hefted the heavy gun and pressed the trigger, which made a loud *click*. "I see what you mean. The other judges already have guns. I don't want to be the last judge on my block to get one."

Lou laughed.

"Judge Sherman told me he likes the gun he got, but I don't know if he got his here. Do you know?"

Lou set his scarred lips. "I shouldn't say, to be honest with you. We keep our customers strictly confidential. Nobody will know from me that you got your gun here."

Great.

"But on the QT, I can tell you that the Common Pleas Court judges shop here and most of the Sixers. A few Eagles, too. We sell to police, also. We're responsible. That's why I say you have to have the lessons."

"Cops buy this gun? I thought you said it was a girl gun."

"Men use it, too, of course. It's one of our bestsellers. It's on TV all the time. Gangster gun of choice." Lou ran a thickly ridged fingernail along the glistening silvery chamber, with its perfectly machined indentations. "Leaves no casings behind to identify the gun. Not like a semiauto."

"I don't usually watch the cop shows. Except that now I'm going to be on one, I guess."

"I read that." Lou warmed up immediately. "They use this gun on *Cold Case*, if you saw the episode the other night. It's the same gun as you're holding, only not all black. They like to use the stainless steel on TV, because it shows up better for the camera."

"Really?"

Lou nodded. "They film parts of *Cold Case* in Philly you know, 'cause it's set here. They had a casting call when they first started, and I went down to try and be an extra, but they didn't hire me. Too big. I stand out."

"I bet." Cate smiled. "*Attorneys@Law* is filmed here, too. The exteriors." Cate remembered the lingo from Micah. "I wonder if they use this gun in the show."

"Sure, the Rossi's on all the time. It's the one the main detective carries. They buy from me."

Cate blinked. *Just like that?* "For real?"

"Sure." Lou perked up. "Hey, this is kind of a funny thing. If they make you into a character, you bought your gun here, for real."

Funny. "Who buys the guns for them?"

"One of the assistants. She's a nice girl." Lou leaned over the glass counter. "Hey, they gonna make you a consultant? You could get five Gs an episode, they do that. It's real money. You got an agent or a manager?"

"I'm a judge."

"So what? You need an agent. I know people. I could ask around. Get yourself a good deal. Least they could do, since they based the character on you."

"Good point." *Hmmm.* "So you sell them the guns? This very store?"

"Yep." Lou's immense chest puffed under the red windbreaker.

"Who buys the guns for them? There was one assistant who used to watch the trial."

"Micah Gilbert." Lou grinned, his scar disappearing.

Yikes! "Yes, I think that was her name." Cate squinted as if she were thinking, but her heart almost leaped through her chest.

"Sure, Micah. I know Micah. She works for Art Simone. She comes in here all the time. She buys the guns for the show, for when they shoot in town." Lou chuckled. "I mean, shoot scenes, not guns."

"Sure, right." Cate managed a laugh. "So she buys the guns?"

"Yes. She handles props on the Philly end. They don't want to deal with airport security, flying the guns here from L.A."

Whoa. "So Micah bought these guns for the show? This exact one? I want to buy exactly what she bought."

"That's the exact one. Your gun will be on TV."

Yay! "When did she buy it?"

"She bought a few. That one, she bought from me about six months ago. She bought three, as I remember. Two black Berettas, too, for the other characters. She picked up a few silencers, too."

"You sell silencers?"

"Sure. They're easy to use, you just thread 'em on. Can't put a silencer on a revolver, though." Lou pointed through the case. "Beretta, Walther, Glock, H&K, they take a silencer. A Sig, too, some of the models."

Cate could barely contain her excitement. "Did she have to take the lesson, too?"

"No, but she wanted to. That girl can shoot. I taught her myself, at our range." Lou smiled with a fatherly pride, and Cate reached for her wallet.

"I'll take it," she said, and Lou laughed.

"Don't you wanna know how much it is?"

"Doesn't matter. This is a celebrity gun."

Cate couldn't wait to get to a phone.

CHAPTER 46

"Please pick Micah up!" Cate begged Nesbitt, after she had finished telling him what she had learned at the gun shop. She sat in her car with the engine running in the empty parking lot of a warehouse near the gun shop. Her celebrity gun occupied the passenger seat, in its gift box. The Rossi had cost $495, roughly the price of Manolo Blahniks. The world would be safer if people overpaid for shoes, not firearms.

"That's quite a little theory." Nesbitt sounded intrigued, which was more fun than Contempt and Scorn.

"Please go see her. Just feel her out. Find out if she has an alibi. I think she told me she was at work, but see if she can prove it." Cate gripped the steering wheel, tense. "Please! She's the killer. The gun was the last piece of the puzzle. It all fits."

"I'll talk to my sergeant, then do it tomorrow."

"But it can't wait. She could be a flight risk. She's free and she has money. If she wants, she could just take a little trip."

"Why would she? She doesn't suspect anything."

"Why take a chance if—"

"Don't you even think about going yourself," Nesbitt said, raising his voice. "That would screw up any case against her, on the off chance that you're right."

"I know that." It was true, but Cate hadn't even thought of it. Could Nesbitt be more diabolical than she was? "I don't want anything irregular, I agree, there's too much at stake. Just go, please go tonight. I'm about to burst."

"Okay, calm down. I will."

"Thank you! Thank you!"

"Now go home and I'll call you as soon as I know something. You got that?"

"Got it."

"Go home. Stay home."

"I will. I am. This is me, going home."

"And *stay*!"

"Arf!" Cate felt alive with excitement. Her theory had been right. Her search had ended. She wished there was someone she could tell, Sarah Marz or even Russo, but she couldn't. She'd have to go home and wait it out. "Go get 'em!" she said, in a fit of enthusiasm, but Nesbitt had already hung up.

Cate had just pulled out of the warehouse lot when the cell phone rang again. She took a left and flipped it open. "Nesbitt?"

"No, it's Val," the secretary said, her voice unusually soft.

"Val, what's the matter?" Cate cruised to a traffic light and stopped.

"I'm bone-tired. I've been here all day. Didn't you get my message? I called you around five-thirty."

"I must have missed it." Cate pulled the phone away and checked the lighted display. A telltale tape icon signaled a voice mail. She'd turned off the phone in the hospital and must've missed the message icon when she turned it back on again. "Sorry. What's going on?"

"I have bad news. Chief Judge Sherman told me to pack up your office."

"*What*?"

"He came up here himself, at the end of the day. He said that all your case files had to be boxed up and sent downstairs to him in the morning, and all your books and personal files had to be shipped to your house."

"He can't do that." Cate felt her face heat with anger. "He can't throw me out of my own chambers."

"I feel just terrible for you, Judge. He offered me overtime to do it, but I don't want that money."

Cate tried to get her bearings. She couldn't process it all fast enough. Her thoughts were still on Micah. "He can't do this. He doesn't have the power."

"I know. It makes my heart sick. I'm so sorry, Judge. I had to do it, you know that."

"Of course, I don't blame you, Val. And I'm sorry you had to do such a big job by yourself." Cate hit the gas, accelerating unnecessarily into traffic.

"And Meriden was with him, practically rubbing his hands together."

"Meriden! What's the matter with that guy?"

"God knows. It's his birthday, and all he can think about's makin' trouble for you. The man's a child. A little boy."

"So you're packing my office?"

"Yes. Books, papers, everything. I've been at it all night, and the clerks helped. But I didn't want to go through your desk without talking to you. I know those are your personal items."

"I'm coming in." Cate steered the car toward the courthouse. "I'll be there in fifteen minutes."

"I don't think that's a good idea, Judge. Chief Judge Sherman's on the warpath. I don't think he'd like it."

Cate checked the clock on the dashboard. "It's past eight. He's not there this late, and if he sees me, so be it. He has no right to throw me out, and I'd love to tell him that to his face."

"You sure? Chief Judge Sherman—"

"Yes, I'm sure, and don't worry, I won't say you called me. I'll say I stopped in."

"But Chief Judge Sherman is so determined. Mo said he'd been bothered all day, and now I know why. I don't know if you can fight this one."

"Yes, I can, and I will." Cate's fire returned. "I got blown off by George Hartford, but I don't need a lawyer to talk for me. I *am* a lawyer."

"Is that where you were when I called?"

"No, I got sidetracked. But I think I figured out who killed Art Simone, and it's not Richard Marz."

"For real?" Val asked, hushed. "Who did it?"

"Tell you when I see you. It's a long story." Cate narrowly avoided hitting an all-black Septa bus that advertised a radio station with a scrawled WIRED. It could have been a caption under Cate's photo.

"I'll send the clerks home."

"Good idea. See you in a sec, and I hope he's there." Cate flipped the phone closed and threw it on the seat.

Bastard! If she couldn't find a lawyer with the guts to represent her, she'd file the papers herself. Cate felt absolutely fearless, and it had nothing to do with her new gun. She was armed with the law.

And her aim was very, very good.

Fifteen minutes later, Cate parked on the street, because it was quicker at this hour, then hurried through the frigid night air to the panel of glass doors at the front of the courthouse. She went directly to the door at the far right, used for after-hours entry and late filings. She buzzed the intercom, hoping that Sherman hadn't put out a court-mail denying her entry altogether. Still, she knew most of the marshals, from working late, and they liked her. And her legs.

"Yes?" came the mechanical voice through the black plastic.

"It's Judge Fante, come to clean out my office," Cate said, with a tone that brooked no disagreement, and after a second, the door buzzed loudly and she yanked it open. She climbed the dark marble steps and pressed through the glass doors at the top as if she owned the courthouse. The judges' entrance was to the far right, and the public entrance was fifty feet across the lobby on the far left, manned by two marshals, hanging out by the metal detectors. Cate recognized one and gave him an official wave.

"Hi, Tony," she called out, her voice echoing in the cavernous lobby, her heels clacking across the granite floor as she hustled to the judges' entrance. "I'm moving out tonight."

"Okay, Judge." Tony tipped his neat, dark head, and Cate knew he didn't have the heart to embarrass her by stopping her, and she owed him forever for it. She fished out her white passcard on the fly, passed it over the wall-mounted magnetic sensor, then bustled without breaking stride toward the walnut doors that led to the judges' elevators on the right. She reached the doors without being tackled, then yanked the door open, only to find the elevator doors opening onto a bundled-up Val, her eyes drawn with strain.

"Judge," Val said, startled, stepping off the elevator, and Cate wrapped her arms around her secretary, in her nubby wool coat.

"You okay?"

"I have to go, I'm so sorry. I got a call from my daughter, and the baby has the croup. She said he can't catch his breath, like a spasm. She has to take him to the emergency room and she needs me to stay with Tiffany."

"My God. Go. You have a ride?"

"Jerome's a block away. He just called."

"Give him my love. You need help?"

"No, thanks." Val gave her another, final hug. "You're all packed upstairs, except your desk, and the clerks went home."

"Thanks."

"Sorry, Judge." Val hurried to the doors, buttoning her coat. "See you."

"Good luck," Cate called after her, hitting the UP button. The elevator cab opened again, and she stepped inside, inserted her pass-card, and watched the doors close on her, thinking about what she'd find in her chambers.

There, Cate surveyed the reception room, trying to maintain control of her emotions. Boxes of files covered the rug, wedged between the wing chairs and coffee table. She let the door close behind her, then went over to one of the open boxes and thumbed through the accordion jackets, reading the case captions. *U.S. v. Alvarez, U.S. v. Bustagni, U.S. v. Chollo.* It was her docket, on the way out. Cate felt her anger rising.

She went to the next file box and thumbed through the pleadings. More of the same. There had to be at least twelve boxes blocking the way. She turned, looked over the boxes, and walked to the threshold of her office. The large room sat perfectly quiet and seemed bigger, now that it had been emptied. The expanse of glass windows formed a black mirror, with the glittering lights of the city and the Ben Franklin Bridge ghosted darkly beyond. Her few framed diplomas had been taken down; the law books she'd shelved had vanished. Her long work table had been wiped clean, as had all the chairs she'd used to store her case notes. Boxes lay everywhere, closed and labeled in Val's careful hand, in Magic Marker. CIRCUIT CONFERENCE. SPEECHES. JUDICIAL CODE.

Cate picked her way through the boxes to her desk, and walked around it, sliding out of her heavy coat and setting it on the top, along with her purse and plastic shopping bag. The bag held the celebrity gun; she hadn't risked leaving it in the car. She sat down in her desk chair and scanned her office, assessing it with new eyes. The truth was, except for the sealed boxes, the place didn't look all that much different. She felt her jaw clench in anger, now at herself. *So many things I'd do different. So many ways I went wrong.*

"Gimme a second chance," she said aloud, then realized something. Nobody was going to give her a second chance, least of all

Sherman. If she wanted the second chance, she'd have to take it. She pushed thoughts of Sherman, and even Nesbitt and Micah, to the back of her mind, rose to her pumps, and walked over to the first cardboard box. Brown masking tape sealed the box, and she ripped it off in a sticky curl and opened the top flaps. It was time to start over. Now, she knew she could be a judge. And she would begin by moving into her new chambers.

Cate unpacked the first few books, mostly casebooks from law school, her go-to reference books, with sentimental value. She chose one, noting that Val must have wiped each one down before she packed it. She took the book to the empty bookshelves near the work table and set it on the shelf with a satisfying *thud* that echoed in the silent office, her thoughts skipping ahead with renewed energy. She'd replace all of her rules books and other reference books in the shelves nearest her desk, then rehang her diplomas and awards. She'd haul boxes she had never opened from the closet and unpack them for the first time, making arrangements of treasured photos and certificates from practice. She'd unwrap the office-warming gifts that her partners had given her and decorate the place. She'd finally make the office her own.

She turned back to the box of casebooks, shelving the next two with a happy, determined feeling. She'd just reached the middle of the box when she heard a noise in the reception area. The sound of the door to her chambers, opening.

Cate looked up from the law books in surprise.

CHAPTER 47

Even at the sight of her old enemy, Cate felt unusually calm, like Zen Judge. Maybe it was all this perspective she'd been getting. She hoped she hadn't changed too much. She'd start throwing out Chanel jackets.

"What are you doing here?" Meriden asked, from the threshold to her office, his thin lips pursed. He stood disapproving in his houndstooth topcoat, maroon cashmere scarf, and black leather gloves that would have embarrassed most serial killers.

"Moving in," Cate answered pleasantly. "I'm the new judge. What are you doing here?"

"I was working late and saw the light under the door, on my way to the elevator."

"You mean you were killing time in your office until Val left, then you came in to snoop." Cate smiled, but Meriden frowned.

"You know you're not permitted in this building. Chief Judge Sherman has ordered your belongings shipped out and your docket reassigned."

"He doesn't have the power to do that."

"Chief Judge Sherman runs this courthouse."

"Granted," Cate said, with a shrug, "but might doesn't make right. He's overstepped his power. Sherman may be the court administrator, but the Constitution affords him no greater status than it does me." She remembered, in the beginning, being intimidated that her job description was in the United States Constitution. Now she rather liked the idea.

"He's chief judge of the Eastern District."

"I don't see the words 'chief judge' anywhere in Article III. He has that title because he's the most senior, and that's all." Cate slid another of her old casebooks from the box and shelved it with another great *thud*. It was fun to make noise.

"So you won't go willingly."

"Thank you, no. I earned this job, and I want this job. It's mine and I'm keeping it."

Meriden arched an eyebrow. "Have you been drinking?"

"No, I've been growing up."

"About time."

"I agree."

Meriden snorted. "So you'll fight us? You'll *sue* the court? Your *colleagues*?"

"If you were colleagues, you wouldn't try to throw me out. I don't think of it as a fight. I think of it as asserting the power of the law. No one's above it, not even judges. Especially not judges."

Meriden shook his head. "What lawyer would be crazy enough to sue the Eastern District?"

"I would. Thanks."

"You're going to represent yourself?" Meriden burst into loud laughter. Cate didn't like his noise as much as her noise.

"Looks that way. Nobody else wants the job, and I used to be passable at the trial thing." Cate shelved another casebook. She didn't need to refer to the fact that she'd kicked *his* ass, because she was above that now.

"You're so self-righteous. For a whore."

"Guilty." Cate smiled. Even that slur couldn't trouble her Zen waters. All her secrets having been told, they lacked superpowers.

"This is ridiculous, what's happening here!" Meriden said, raising his voice, and Cate unpacked another casebook. *Thud!*

"On that we agree. My working, you watching. Why don't you help me unpack? Open that box in front of you."

"I'm calling the marshals."

"Go ahead, use my phone. Tell 'em I said hi." Cate gestured at Val's desk, near him. "But after hours, they don't have the manpower to answer phones. It'd be faster to go down and get Tony."

"Is that the way you want it?" Meriden shouted. "You *want* that indignity? Don't you ever get enough of embarrassing yourself? They'll throw you out, bodily!"

"I doubt that. You have no authority to order them to do anything, and my body is way better than yours." Cate unpacked another book, *Prosser on Torts*. She had loved that class.

"We'll see about that." Meriden turned on his heel and stormed through the reception room, out of chambers, letting the door slam behind him.

Cate smiled and stuck Prosser, thick and green, on the shelf. *Thud!* She had maybe ten minutes before they came up. God knew what would happen then. She reached for another book.

But only three minutes later, the door to chambers opened again.

CHAPTER 48

"I'm in here, gentlemen," Cate called from her office, examining her casebooks on the shelves. They made a nice, neat hardback row, and she ran her index fingers along the pebbled spines. She hadn't seen them since law school, which may have been the last time she'd thought that she loved the law—until now. She'd have time to study it now, as an intellectual exercise, and to affect its development as a code of conduct for the governance of a society. She couldn't imagine any job more exciting and important. It would more than make up for not being in court anymore, as a trial lawyer. Now, the action would be on the bench, merely a change of venue.

Cate reached in the box for another casebook. Heavy and red, clothbound with gold stripes on the spine: *Antitrust Law* by Areeda & Turner. She placed it on the shelf and reached in the box for a bookend, a bas-relief of Carpenter Hall, in brass. Then she remembered. Somebody had come in. So where were they? Maybe they hadn't heard her.

"Hello?" Cate called out, holding the bookend. No sound came from the reception area. Her chambers were quiet. She felt a tingle of something. Suddenly, a dark head popped in the doorway, and Cate jumped, startled. "Emily! I thought you went home."

"No. Did I scare you?"

"I thought it might be Meriden."

"He's gone. I saw him go down the judges' elevator." Emily entered the office, and her dark eyes shone with wetness, as if she'd been crying. She wore her dark raincoat and a long black skirt with her Doc Martens, and after a minute, she pulled something from her coat pocket. A black semiautomatic, its barrel lengthened by a silencer.

Cate blinked. "I don't understand. Is this a joke?"

"You figured it out, didn't you?"

"What did I figure out?"

"That I killed Simone."

"*What?*" Cate couldn't believe her ears. She froze, bookend in hand.

"I was standing at Val's desk when she called you. You told her you figured out the real killer."

"I did. Micah Gilbert." Cate's mouth went dry. *Emily holding a gun, with a silencer?*

"I don't believe you. You knew it was me."

"No, I thought it was Micah. It isn't Micah? She had an affair with Simone. I even know where she bought the gun." Cate remembered that her celebrity gun sat uselessly in a shopping bag. Not that she'd bought bullets, anyway.

"You really didn't know? I mean, I never thought it would get this far." Emily's eyes went newly wet, and she raised the gun higher.

"No. Wait. What do you mean?" Cate suppressed the urge to panic. "Explain this to me. You owe me that. I thought we were friends."

"Art Simone called me at home, after the pretrial. He said he'd pay me. All I had to do was call Micah and let her know when you were leaving chambers at night. So that she could follow you." Emily's Goth mascara began to run, her eyelashes turned to spiders. "I need the money really bad, you know that. I have school loans and no offer. He said he'd hook me up with the network's legal department."

Keep her talking. She's already in a state. "So what happened?"

"He wanted more details, like what you wore, or how you looked the next day, after you'd been out. I said no, I wanted to end it but he said he'd tell you."

"How'd you do it?" *Where were Meriden and the marshals?*

"I followed him to dinner and I shot him." Emily's eyes brimmed over, running black tears. "I had to. My family depends on me. You remember that day, when we talked about people and their dreams? This is their dream. *I* am their dream."

"What about Marz?" *What was taking them so long?*

"I had to do it. After what happened in court, I knew it was my chance. His phone numbers were on the pleadings, and I called him on the cell. I told him to meet me, that I had inside info." Emily sniffled. "He was so drunk, it was easy to make it look like a suicide."

"How did you get the gun past the metal detectors?"

"The judges' elevator. I went in and out with everybody for Judge Meriden's birthday. When they went to lunch, I went to the gun store." Emily's eyes brimmed over, and a black tear rolled down her cheek. "I didn't want to, Judge, but I had to. Or thought I had to, because of what you told Val, that you figured it out."

"I would never think it was you," Cate said softly. Her own emotions bubbled to the surface and she used them to her advantage. "Jeez, Em. You would really hurt me? *Kill me?*"

"I have to, to end it." Emily sobbed and raised the gun higher, giving a panicky Cate her answer.

"Wait! No. Please, Em." Cate heard sheer desperation in her voice. She had run out of time. The stalling wasn't working. "You can't do this. It'll only make things worse. They'll know it was you."

"No, they won't. Val thinks I went home. No one knows I'm still in the building. I've been hiding in the bathroom. The cleaning people already went through, and I'm staying the night. Tomorrow morning, I'll be the one who finds you dead."

My God. Cate's fingers tightened around the bookend. She would get one shot.

Emily squinted, taking aim. "Sorry, Judge."

CHAPTER 49

Suddenly Cate threw the brass bookend at Emily, hitting her in the cheek.

"Ahhh!" the clerk yelled, staggering backwards, her hand flying to her left eye. Blood appeared at a cut on her cheekbone. *Pfftt! Pfft!* Bullets flew into the tiled ceiling as she fell, knocking over stacked boxes.

Cate bolted for the door of her office, past the boxes. She flung the door open wide.

Onto an angry Jonathan Meriden. "Cate, the marshals are on rounds, and I—"

"She has a gun!" Cate screamed, barreling into him, plowing him backwards into the opposite wall.

"Stop, Judge!" Emily bellowed from chambers.

Meriden's eyes popped. "*What?*" he asked, shocked.

"Run!" Cate screamed, disentangling them. She thought fast. Meriden still held his passcard for the judges' elevator. He'd be dead if he went with her. She shoved him to the left, setting him in motion. "Take the elevator!" she shouted, tearing down the hallway in the opposite direction.

"Help!" Meriden shrieked, taking off toward the judges' elevator.

Cate ran for her life to the stairwell.

"No!" Emily yelled, the sound coming from the hallway now.

Cate hit the staircase at speed and straight-armed the door, banging into the stairway and grabbing the rail not to fall on the concrete stairs. She flew, grabbed the railing, and whirled around the corner at the landing, half-running and half-stumbling down the tight stairwell as it wound tightly down.

Pttt ptt ptt! Bullets exploded into the concrete wall.

"Help!" Cate screamed. The marshals might hear her. They were on rounds. Her breath came in panicky bursts. She almost caught a heel on the stair. She grabbed the railing, frantic.

Cate tore down the third floor, then the second. Did the fire stairwell go all the way down? She couldn't remember. She couldn't take a chance. She'd be trapped at gunpoint.

Pttt! Bullets flew into the wall.

Cate burst through the stairwell door into the hallway near the clerk's office, skidding across the waxed floor. She ricocheted off the wall, righted herself, and went flat-out for the two-story escalator that led to the courthouse lobby. The escalator was turned off, and Cate ran down the up escalator, her heart thundering. In the next second, she heard Emily's heavy tread behind her. Ahead lay the polished expanse of black granite. The lobby floor. *Almost there!*

But the metal detectors and the security desk were empty. *No one left on guard?* Cate tore down the steps, trying not to fall.

Ping ping ping! Bullets strafed the stainless steel of the escalator.

Cate's shoulder suddenly felt odd. Had she been hit? Emily was right behind her. The clerk had a clear shot to finish her off.

Suddenly Cate's heel caught in the ridge of an escalator step. She fell, hurtling forward and down, banging her head against the metal side of the escalator, scraping her cheek against the sharp stair edge, rolling end over end. She tumbled to the bottom, her bruised cheek smacking into the cold granite.

She heard a man shout, "Help! Help!"

Meriden. He must have reached the lobby.

"Judge Meriden, stop!" Emily shouted, thudding down the escalator stairs in her heavy shoes.

Cate raised her head and saw Meriden streaking for the courthouse exit, his topcoat flying.

"Stop right there!" Emily bellowed. She raised her gun and aimed it at Meriden.

Cate gathered all of her strength and staggered to her feet just in time to throw a surprise block into Emily.

Emily grunted when they made impact, colliding and tumbling together onto the hard lobby floor. The clerk grimaced and doubled over, the wind knocked out of her. Still she hung on to the gun and twisted it around until the muzzle pointed at Cate.

"No!" Cate shouted, feeling a furious surge of adrenaline. She grabbed Emily's wrist with all her might and slammed it down into the hard floor.

Emily shrieked as the gun jarred loose and went skidding across the slippery floor. Both women dove to recover it, struggling and wrestling.

"Hey, freeze! Freeze, you two!" yelled authoritative voices, and Cate saw two marshals charging from the elevator bank, drawing their revolvers.

"Tony, it's me!" Cate yelled with relief. "Get the gun!"

"Gotcha, Judge!" Tony shouted, running forward.

"Freeze!" the other marshal hollered, reaching them and aiming his gun at Emily with a two-handed grip. "Hands up! Get your hands up!"

Emily burst into tears and released her grip, prone on the floor and raising her hands, as the other marshal kept his gun on her. Cate scrambled away, her high heels skidding.

"Let me help you up, Judge," Tony said, taking Cate's right elbow and hoisting her to her feet. She felt her battered body sag in a sort of surrender. Aches appeared all over, and new pain stabbed the back of her upper arm.

"What's up back there? I can't see."

Tony frowned, peering. "We'll get you to the hospital. You'll be good as new."

"How about the jacket?" Cate asked, coming to her senses.

CHAPTER 50

"Go away, people!" Cate and Nesbitt slammed the front door against the noisy media mobbing her driveway and sidewalk. It was after midnight by the time she got home, but the TV klieg lights flooded her street with a noontime brightness and illuminated the drawn curtains in her darkened living room. Cate shivered against the residual chill and switched on the brass candlestick lamp on the hall table as Nesbitt turned the dead bolt and looked at her with concern.

"How's your shoulder?"

"Fine," Cate answered, though she could feel an ache under the bandage they'd put on at the hospital. The bullet had only grazed her arm, but her jacket was DOA.

"Let me help you take that coat off."

"Thanks." Cate turned and let him lift the long topcoat from her shoulders. It was his, because hers was still in chambers. Her car was at the courthouse, too, and Nesbitt had driven her home. Unfortunately, her garage door opener was still in her car, so they'd had to park in the driveway and run the gauntlet of reporters. She could still hear them outside. "You know what bugs me about them?"

"What?" Nesbitt asked, folding the coat and setting it on the back of a chair.

"That they'll camp out there forever and do almost as much harm as that dumb TV show."

"But of course, it would make a better story if you had guessed the real bad guy." Nesbitt smiled, his blue eyes bright and his crow's-feet creased with warmth. His longish hair fell sideways, dark silver in unexpected patches, like weathered cedar shakes on a shed. "Imagine how much fun I had—me, a law enforcement professional—accusing a completely innocent young girl of a double homicide."

Cate cringed. "Be fair. How could I know that Micah would be at her therapist's that night? I said I was sorry."

"I'll never live it down. Roots called my cell twice when you were in with the doc. Even my useless nephew is lording it over me. He's like, 'Love is blind.'"

Love? Cate caught her breath, and Nesbitt's eyes flared a little when he realized he'd let the L-word slip.

"Uh. Well, anyway."

"Whatever," Cate said, and they laughed uncomfortably, which stopped the moment Nesbitt leaned over and kissed her on the cheek. She closed her eyes, enjoying the cold brush of his mustache. When he pulled away, his eyes looked fairly soft for a detective, set in his wonderfully lived-in face.

"I should go."

"I agree," Cate said with a smile. They understood what they meant, and neither needed to spell it out. Because she sensed, in her heart, that Nesbitt was going to be the last man she took to bed.

In her life.

CHAPTER 51

Cate rode the judges' elevator upwards, checking her reflection in the gold-plated panel of elevator buttons. Her makeup looked neutral and classy, her hair was combed into its judicial chignon, and she wore her favorite gold tweed suit. She had been resting at home for two weeks, and during that time, her cheek had almost healed, her shoulder felt better, and she'd ordered the new S 500 sedan, in Glacier White. The Mercedes was pure sublimation, because she was still on her sex diet, though she and Nesbitt had finally segued into light petting, which was officially tenth grade.

Also during that time, Chief Judge Sherman had met with the members of the court, the chief judge of the Third Circuit, and the circuit executive to decide what to do about reinstating her. Cate wasn't betting on it. Taking her back would require a federal judge to admit he was wrong, which was highly unlikely. That was why they had appellate courts.

The elevator cab opened, and Cate stepped out, strode down the hall to Chief Judge Sherman's chambers, and stood before his door, which was when her sense of humor vanished. She wanted this job, and she would fight to keep it. She could do it now, she felt it inside. What had Val said? *When you get yourself right with you, then you can hold your head high.* Well, Cate had gotten herself right with her. She was ready to be a judge in a way she hadn't been before. So she raised her chin, squared her shoulders, and twisted the doorknob.

"Hello, Mo," Cate said, and Judge Sherman's secretary looked up from her computer keyboard.

"Hello, Judge Fante." Mo's gaze was cool, and if she knew the verdict, she didn't let it show. She swiveled in her seat, holding up a finger. "Wait a minute, please. I'll let him know you're here."

"Sure." Cate swallowed hard while Mo picked up the telephone receiver and pressed the intercom button. The door to Sherman's office was closed.

"Judge Fante is here, Chief," Mo said into the receiver. Then, "Of course." She hung up and raised her dark gaze to Cate. "He'll see you now, Judge."

"Thanks." Cate walked forward, opened the door, and almost fell over with surprise. The office was filled to bursting with judges, who broke into polite applause, including Chief Judge Sherman. Judge Bonner Menking clapped next to Bill Sasso and Gloria Sullivan. There were all eighteen judges of the Eastern District, and among them, beaming and applauding, were Val and Sam. And in front of the clapping throng stood Jonathan Meriden.

Huh? Cate felt so shocked, she didn't know what to say.

"Come to order, please." Chief Judge Sherman waved the judges into silence, and his hooded eyes met Cate's, his lips pursed. "Well, Cate. I won't lie to you, you haven't been the easiest judge to manage, and I can't say I agree with you one hundred percent, in all things. But you showed enormous bravery, not only in saving the life of Brother Meriden, but in discovering the true murderer of two citizens who came before us seeking justice. In so doing, you brought honor on all of us, and on our court."

Cate felt astounded and touched.

"We judged you too harshly, which may be an occupational hazard. So, we have discussed the matter, and in view of what has happened, our vote was unanimous. We, each of us, respect your talent, abilities, and commitment, and we welcome you back." Sherman paused, with a sly smile. "And we will weather whatever TV does to us, together, as a court. As long as they get Eli Wallach to play me."

Cate laughed and delivered good news of her own. "Chief, you should know that they're not doing the *Judges@Court* series. They're not interested in judges anymore. Househusbands are the new judges." She'd heard it from Micah, who was quitting show biz and was going to law school, which was basically the same thing.

"Even better!" Sherman grinned, and Meriden raised his hand to speak, his smile genuine, if begrudging.

"And, Cate, may I publicly add my gratitude for saving my life, especially when we all know you hate my guts." Everyone burst into new laughter, and so did Cate, who noticed for the first time that several bottles of merlot sat uncorked on Sherman's polished conference table, behind rows of filled plastic glasses and a silver-foil tray of cheese and pepperoni slices, speared with multicolored toothpicks.

"Speech, Cate!" the other judges called out, clapping. "Speech!" Judge Sasso formed his hand-megaphone and bellowed, "And keep it short!" Judge Gloria Sullivan shouted at him, laughing, "Bill! Hush!"

"Thank you, okay." Cate flashed on the dinner they'd held for her last summer, to welcome her to the bench for the first time. "I am deeply sorry for all the embarrassment I caused the Court. I apologize to each of you, and thank you for welcoming me back to a job I love. You all said a lot of nice things about me just now, and there's one thing you need to know—I don't deserve a word of it, but I'm going to try."

"Brava!" "Way to go!" they shouted, giving her a fresh round of applause.

"And now a toast!" Chief Judge Sherman picked up a glass from the table, walked over, and handed it to Cate, giving her a kiss on the cheek. "Do I need to ask you for a signed release, my dear?"

"Not if you withdraw that misconduct complaint," she answered, and they both laughed as everyone milled around the conference table, picked up glasses of wine, and raised them.

"To Cate!" Chief Judge Sherman called out, hoisting his glass.

"To Cate!" they all repeated, except for Sam, the forgotten law clerk. He stood proudly, basking in the new spotlight that he'd earned merely by not trying to kill his boss, and he called out:

"To Judge Catherine Fante, of the Eastern District of Pennsylvania!"

Judge Catherine Fante. Cate had never heard words so sweet, or seen a sight that made her happier. She raised her glass and couldn't speak for a moment. Her eyes brimmed over, and for once, she didn't try to hide her feelings.

Look, Mom, she thought, unaccountably. *Look.*

CHAPTER 52

The August sun burned hazy and low, dipping by this time of the afternoon behind a leafy maple tree. Cate and Gina sat on the elevated wood deck in gym shorts and tank tops, side by side in plastic beach chairs, soaking their feet in the warm water of an inflatable baby pool. Warren sat in the shady side of the pool, watching the dappled light on the water's surface, turning from baby to boy before their very eyes.

"Happy birthday!" Cate said happily, hoisting a jelly glass of Miller, golden in the sunlight.

"Thank you, girlfriend." Gina grinned, raising her glass, and they clinked in the middle, making a sloshy, satisfyingly low-rent *clunk*.

"I'm younger than you now." Cate took a sip of cold beer, tart and perfect on her tongue.

"By twenty minutes."

"Older is older."

"How can it be my birthday? I feel younger, and happier."

"It's the sex."

"No, it's the beer," Gina said, and they both laughed, while she drained her glass. Cate wiggled her toes in the pool water, which was cloudy with Waterbabies sunblock, hiding Mickey Mouse's black eyes and Gina's red toenails.

"Open your present, kid."

"Yo, I'm woozy." Gina frowned. Her hair was back in its paint-brush ponytail, because she'd cut it too short again. "I forget, did I eat lunch?"

"No. You were doing You and Me with the baby. You didn't even have your birthday cake."

"I will later." Gina set down her empty glass and picked the wrapped gift from her lap, shaking it with vigor. "A present! Yo, did I tell you Justin got us a treadmill?"

"Yo, three times." Cate smiled. "You're so in love."

"You, too."

"True." Cate thought of Nesbitt. "We both have great men. Wonder how long it will last?"

Gina checked her watch. "Ten minutes."

"Five, according to my shrink." They both laughed again, and Cate said, "Open your gift."

"Happy birthday to me!" Gina tore off the flowery wrapping paper, threw it on the grass, then tore off the box lid and threw it on the deck, and unfolded the white tissue paper. She looked inside the box and yelped. "I love it!"

Suddenly there was a splash, and Cate looked up as Warren tried to stand in the pool, reaching out for the deck's wooden railing.

"Warren, no! You'll fall!" Gina shouted, leaping up from her chair, dumping the sweater off her lap and onto the deck, and splashing through the pool to Warren. She scooped him up, and he burst instantly into tears.

"Gina, relax," Cate said, surprised. "He wasn't going to fall."

"How do you know?" Gina turned and snapped, tears in her eyes. She cradled Warren's head against her shoulder as he cried full-bore. "It's all right, it's all right, baby. I have you, it's all right." She rocked him until he finally stopped sobbing, then wiped his pink cheeks with her fingertips. Warren blinked, his eyelashes clumped, and he pointed to the pool with a chubby index finger. "You want to go down, Warren?" Gina asked softly, then set him back down in the water, and he sat peacefully, looking at the leaf shadows on the water's surface, as he had before. Gina returned to her chair, shaken, her T-shirt wet from the baby.

For a minute, Cate didn't know what to say.

"Sorry, I guess . . . sorry I yelled at you," Gina stammered, leaning over to the deck and picking up the new sweater, now wet from the splashing. "It'll dry."

"Sure, no problem."

"It's okay. I guess I drank too much." Gina folded the sweater and put it back into the gift box. Then she moved her bangs from her damp forehead, her eyes still wet.

"Are you okay?" Cate set down her glass and leaned over. "Geen?"

"It's nothing." Gina's eyes glistened. Her lower lip trembled. She seemed to be losing control.

"He's okay now. He wasn't anywhere near the railing, which is five feet high anyway. What were you worried about?"

"The deck was wet."

"He couldn't have slipped off."

Gina wiped her eyes. "I never told you," she said, after a moment.

"What?"

"I thought it would compromise you."

"What would?"

"You're a judge."

Cate didn't get it. "Tell me what? You can tell me anything. I'm your best friend."

"I know I didn't do anything illegal, or criminal, that much I remember from law school. I just feel terrible about it, still. It's awful. Morally, it was wrong. It is wrong. I think of it all the time. I even pray about it."

"What?" Cate asked, bewildered.

"That night, the night you went to that motel. The night you called me. The night you almost got raped. When you didn't get home right away. Remember? I was there waiting for you."

"Okay."

"You called me and told me you were at a pink motel on Ellsworth Avenue, by the airport. Then you got the flat tire and were late. But I didn't know that."

"Right. Because I couldn't reach you. Because you left your cell."

Gina nodded, biting her lower lip not to cry. "Well, something happened."

"What? You're scaring me."

"That night, when you didn't come home, I was worried about you, so I went to the motel. You told me where it was, it wasn't hard to find, and it's not far from here. I went to the office and asked where you were, a classy blonde, and he knew, a really skeevy guy, he told me the room. I think he thought I wanted to join you. So I went to the room looking for you and that man, Partridge, he was in there drinking with the door open, watching TV."

My God. Cate felt her eyes widen. She put a hand on her friend's back.

"I asked what he did to you, I guess I was yelling, and before I knew what he was doing, I mean, he came at me." Gina's eyes welled up again. "He *attacked me!*"

Cate gasped. "Gina, no."

"I tried to fight him, and he covered my mouth, and he started to tear at my jeans and he was angry, really angry." Gina's voice quivered, and she fought to maintain control. "And I thought, he's going *to kill me*, so I broke away and ran outside but when he came after me, I pushed him away and the balcony was wet and all of a sudden, he kept falling backwards and he went right over the railing and off the balcony."

Oh no. Cate froze. A chill numbed her, despite the hot sun.

"And I looked over and his neck was broken and I knew he was dead, so I ran away. I ran to my car and drove to your house and calmed myself down until you got home. And I didn't tell you because I knew you'd feel terrible or maybe even turn me in, even though it was self-defense. I swear it was." Gina was crying now, hoarse, choking sobs, bent over in the plastic chair, her elbows on her bare legs. Her back shuddered under Cate's hand. "I feel awful about it. I have nightmares. It's a sin. *I killed a man.*" Then she looked up, her face tear-stained, her red eyes boring into Cate. "What will you do, Cate? Will you turn me in? Do you have to?"

Before Cate could answer, a splash came suddenly from the baby, and they both looked over. Warren splashed the water with his small, flat hand, then watched the pattern of dark and light. Then he said, "Mommy."

Mommy. Cate felt a chord struck inside her chest. She had heard that sound before, long ago, in that identical little-boy register.

Gina's mouth had dropped open, and her tears stalled. "Did you hear that?" she asked, her voice thick.

"Yes."

"Did he say *'Mommy'*?"

"I heard it, too." Cate couldn't keep the thrill from her voice. "He said, 'Mommy.' Just like he used to."

"That's me! *I'm 'Mommy'!*" Gina rose, set the gift down on the deck, and walked through the pool to the baby. "Warren, Mommy's here. I'm Mommy. You're Warren."

"Mommy," Warren said clearly, without looking up.

"Warren!" Gina scooped him up again, joyfully this time, holding him close as she stood in the baby pool. "Warren, it's Mommy. Warren, it's Mommy! Mommy loves you! I love you, Warren," Gina said over and over, happiness lifting her voice. She rocked him in her arms, and Warren's large blue eyes looked up at the sky.

Cate bit her lip, her emotions in tumult. *What will you do, Cate? Will you turn me in? Do you have to?* The beer soured in her mouth. She could imagine Gina bursting into the motel room, demanding to be told where she was, screaming at Partridge in her fear. Unknowingly walking into a nightmare. All for Cate.

Cate kept her eye on her friend, rocking her baby back and forth, the two of them a solitary silhouette against the leafy maple, the sun peeking through, here and there, in the most unexpected spots. Cate watched the patterns a minute, considering. The leaves were in the way, but the sun was there all along, abiding, giving warmth and light. Sometimes it would be hidden by a tree, or a cloud cover. By winter, or even by pain or hopelessness. But it was always there, and always would be.

Cate felt her heart wrench to look at them, mother and child, wrapped for just a moment around each other, and she knew that no courtroom or law would ever punish Gina more than she herself did now, and would forever. And all of a sudden, Cate understood something that she hadn't before. That at certain times, everything will fall surprisingly into place, even on a humid summer afternoon, with her feet in a baby pool.

And in those times, justice and love will look so much alike that they will become the very same thing.

AUTHOR'S NOTE AND ACKNOWLEDGMENTS

The author of a novel doesn't get a chance to speak directly with the reader, except in the acknowledgments. I hate that. At least I must, because I've noticed that my acknowledgments keep expanding, and are currently longer than anyone else's (in the world). In my defense, I want to take the time to meaningfully thank the people who helped me research this book, and that often necessitates further explanation. So, if you will permit me, here goes.

For the record, Centralia actually exists, or at least, it did. The way it's described in *Dirty Blonde*, as well as how it came to its present state, is real and true. I won't retell the details that find their proper home in the book, but Centralia was a coal-mining town in northeastern Pennsylvania and was barely locally known, despite its horrendous underground mine fire. I didn't know anything about it until fifteen years ago, when I drove through its ruins and found myself engulfed in sulfurous steam. It was an impossibly eerie experience, and I always wanted to write about it, and last year began to do the research.

By way of background, Centralia and the surrounding Appalachian towns were one of the few places in the country that anthracite coal, which is especially hard, could be found. Anthracite began being mined in Centralia in the 1800s, so that by the 1900s, the town sat atop a beehive of mines, exploited by different companies and poachers. The mine fire that would eventually ruin Centralia started in 1962, in the landfill near St. Ignatius church, school, and cemetery. The borough council cleaned up for Memorial Day by burning the trash in the landfill, but unfortunately, a coal mine lay beneath. Flames must have fallen into the mine and set fire to the coal, and over the next several decades, state and federal governments lost chance after chance to put out the fire when it was still possible to do so. It rages out of control, even today, leaving Centralia to be called "the poor man's Dante's Inferno." Those of you who want to read further will find every question answered in the excellent book, *Unseen Danger: A Tragedy of People, Government, and the Centralia Mine Fire* (1986), by David DeKok. The nonfiction account reads like a great detective story, owing to David's skilled reporting and writing. When I found the book, I contacted David, and he was generous enough to read *Dirty Blonde* in manuscript and backstop me on accuracy. I thank him very much for all his help. (Any errors are mine, nevertheless.) David also permitted me to use his photos of old Centralia on my website, which make a fascinating contrast with my own current photos. To see them and to read more about Centralia, you can visit www.scottoline.com.

I visited Centralia to research the scenes in the book, accompanied by the amazing friend to whom this book is dedicated, Laura Leonard. Laura was my first publicist at HarperCollins, almost fifteen years ago, and now she works with me as my assistant and partner in crime. Laura is so dedicated to my books that she would walk through fire—or, at least, stinky steam—with me. I won't enumerate all the other things she and her family do for me and mine. Laura, this book is dedicated to you, with love and deepest thanks.

In other thanks, love and gratitude to Rachel Kull, for her friendship, support, and expertise in the area of children and autism. I

AUTHOR'S NOTE AND ACKNOWLEDGMENTS

also relied greatly in this regard upon the wonderful librarians at the Princeton, New Jersey, public library, who helped me so much (though I never identified myself and look nothing like my author photo, which is complete fiction). I am also indebted to the following authors for their excellent books on the subject: Kathy Labosh, *The Child with Autism at Home* (2004); Lynn McClannahan and Patricia Krantz, *Activity Schedules for Children with Autism* (1999); Richard Simpson, *Autism Spectrum Disorders* (2004); Philip Abrams and Leslie Henriques, *The Autism Spectrum Parents' Daily Helper* (2004).

Deepest thanks to Glenn Gilman, Esq., criminal defense genius, who helps me on each book, and Arthur Mee, retired detective extraordinaire, who put away bad guys and looked way hot doing it. Thanks again to Jerry Hoffman, Esq., and his son, Professor David Hoffman, Esq., of the genius lawyer family of Philadelphia.

In addition, I have a tradition of permitting worthy causes to auction off the names of fictional characters in my books. I always make these people good guys, because their generosity helps so many. So thanks to Adrienne Drost (for Pennsylvania Home of the Sparrow for abused women and children); Julie Williamson (for Kids Love a Mystery, the MWA's program for children's literacy), Marvin "Mitty" Shiller (Thorncroft Therapeutic Riding Center), Bonner Menking (Kids Love a Mystery), Jill Wiederseim (French & Pickering Conservation Trust), Paul Roots (Miami Valley Literacy Council), Gloria Sullivan (Thorncroft Therapeutic Riding Center), Jessica Conley (West Chester University), Abby Linderman (Great Valley Community Education Foundation), William Sasso (Philadelphia Free Library), Andrew Kingston (Sleuthfest), Amy Nislow (Philadelphia Free Library), and Tom and Sue McGinn (Everyone's favorite Santa and Mrs. Claus). And in memory of Fiona McCann, whose name was a gift from Joanne Leone and Sherill Silverman-Posner to the Make-A-Wish Foundation. And in memory of my old friend Bob Rogers, whose kindness and hard work for so many charitable causes was limitless.

AUTHOR'S NOTE AND ACKNOWLEDGMENTS

On the publishing front, love and deepest thanks to my wonderful agent Molly Friedrich, and to Aaron and Arleen Priest and Paul Cirone, too. Thanks to Lou Pitt, for his support and his expertise. Thanks and love to my wonderful and forever editor, Carolyn Marino, and the whole great HarperCollins team: Jane Friedman, Brian Murray, Michael Morrison, Jonathan Burnham, Kathy Schneider, Josh Marwell, Brian Grogan, Nina Olmsted, Christine Boyd, Roberto de Vicq de Cumptich, Will Staehle, Adrienne Di Pietro, Tom Egner, Ana Marie Allessi, and Jennifer Civiletto.

Finally, deepest thanks and love to my friends and family, fur covered and otherwise.